Demimonde

Demimonde

a novel

JAMES E. CRESSLER

WordCrafts Press

Demimonde Story Map

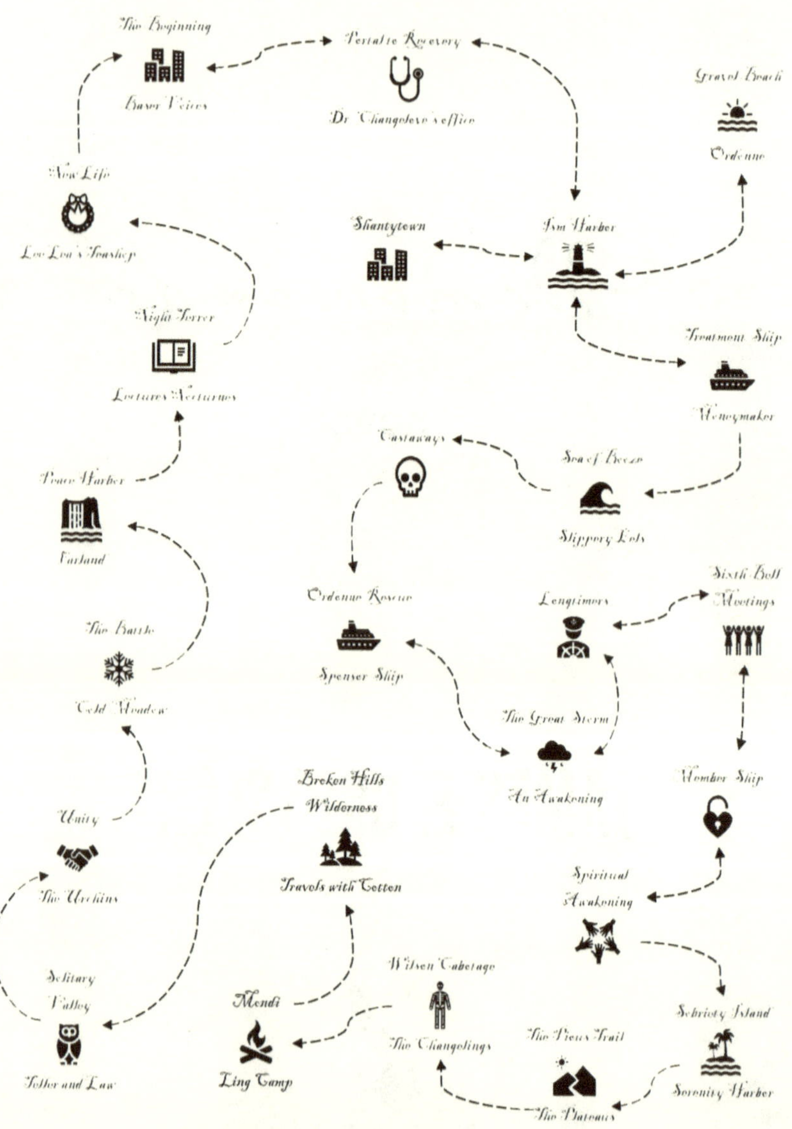

The Conversation

I don't like you, Vonn Thrasher, not one bit.
Why not?
Because you are a mystery.
And you don't like mystery?
No. Judges need order. I like Ordonne.
Then you must hate Demimonde?
No. I respect Demimonde.
A power greater than my court, than time itself.
Your Honor is a poet.
Why do you say that?
Because poets are melancholy.
They love to fear, to explore the shadows.
And you?
I'm a singer.
Singers love to wander in darkness, to drink and make merry.
May we never meet again.

Chapter One

Naked

I lived on borrowed time.

Old voices and angry faces paraded through my mind, nagging and condemning.

Dad criticized. "Vonn Thrasher, when will you grow up?"

My gym coach threatened. "Hey, Knucklehead, when will you tell the truth?"

My pastor pleaded. "Vonn Thrasher, you're ruining your life. You're going to die young and burn in hell."

My surroundings lacked texture, substance. Last night ended like hundreds before—in a drunken blackout. That's how I drank—to oblivion. I attended a Halloween party until the wee hours; did shots of bourbon and then *bingo*—made a ditch my bed at the edge of town. My drinking buddies would give sordid details soon enough. They never failed to report.

I rolled over and rubbed the sleep from my eyes, squinting through a bright sunbeam.

Usually my mornings began with pain and pills, but not today. No hangover. I felt nothing.

What—naked? Where were my pants?

The man lying nearby wore my clothes. "Hey, dude, wake up. What's up with my duds?"

Oh, no. The same dream.

I was guilty.

I was a raging alcoholic. My heavy burden hid under a cloak of fear and remorse. My life presented a dilemma. Bourbon, beer, wine and cocktails, and liquor of any kind were both my problem and my solution. Tormenting secrets taunted me with angry voices. Their accusations strengthened every year, reminding me that I was drinking myself to death.

Bourbon, my Pearl, quieted their charges. She took my sins and bestowed an all-too-brief taste of heaven. I loved her warm glow, sense of ease, and comfort. Had I lost my mind? Regardless, I had to protect my Pearl from all the naysayers who would steal her.

Nags and hecklers indicted me.

"You childish fool."

"You dimwit."

"You are disgusting. Get out and never come back."

Everyone pretended to be a rehab counselor. Each told a cautionary tale about a drunken cousin, complete with a hospital-detox, ghoulish prison stories, and the standard ending: "Dead at thirty from a horrible car wreck." They knew nothing. They didn't understand. They wanted to steal my Pearl.

No way.

They had no right, no idea what they were doing.

I dismissed their irrelevant advice with one powerful conclusion. This will never happen to me. I'm different.

I was lonely.

A lifelong window-shopper, I understood perpetual isolation, being solitary in a crowd. I watched parties from a place called Fringe, on the corner of Loathed and Ignored, consuming a bitter drink called Loneliness.

Bourbon, my Pearl, became my true love and constant companion in middle school where we met at a school dance. I'll never forget our first kiss in the alley behind the gym. Sour and burning hot, yes, her breathtaking embrace and warm glow gave me the solution, the social elixir that I needed—love at first drink.

A few drinks did for me what I couldn't do for myself. They opened social doors, prompted me to dance, granted courage for debates, and convinced me I was Romeo. Together, we escaped the ugly toad in the mirror.

One day, long after our first dance, the rosy path turned bleak. My Pearl became my taskmaster—John Barleycorn—a relentless beast that drove me from obsession to insanity.

Sundowning. I was twenty-two when John Barleycorn called my marker. Inside or out, work or play, when the sun went down, his cravings and obsession gripped me. He snatched my nights and conscience, and replaced them with blackouts—darling misadventures when I time-traveled from one place to another and lost everything in between. Dawn brought pain. Dusk brought intoxication. Hangovers, confusion, drunk-tanks, and hospitals charted the path of my life.

Was I a real-life Doctor Jekyll and Mister Hyde?

Maybe. Sometimes.

I rationalized that good times outweighed the bad, and the bad was the cost of doing business. Besides, I was different. I could walk away from booze anytime I wanted. Overdose? Ha, I wasn't *that* bad. Everyone drank like me, right?

My fiancée disagreed. Last month, we were coming home from a Halloween party across town. She dressed as Cat Woman, and I wore a Batman costume. I thought we had a great evening. She didn't. She killed the radio while I sang and played air guitar. "Vonn, I love you, but this is our last date. I'm breaking up with you."

"What?" There she went again—more nagging.

"I never know which Vonn I'm dating. You have three personalities in your drunken head." She tugged my hair. "I hate two of you."

"Buzz killer." I threw her hand off and slid down in the seat.

Her voice broke with tears. "I love the outgoing, generous

you. But every morning you flip to a sick introvert who isolates and won't answer the phone."

"You know I'm not a morning person."

"Tonight, you played the midnight rogue I truly fear. Constantly drinking. And you stole wallets and hit on my girlfriends."

Before she could attack my Pearl, I went on the offensive.

I leaned over and snarled. "I see what you're doing. Three Vonns? What a line of bull."

She winced and almost hit a curb.

"I saw you mooning over Danny tonight. This's your lame excuse to dump me. Vonn out—Danny in."

The tires barked as we slid to a stop at a red light. I rolled down my window for a breath of fresh air. Music and muffled voices drifted to me from somewhere nearby. A dog started barking. People were still partying.

We stared straight ahead.

"Fine," I said. "You want out, then let me out. I'll walk."

A minute later I stood at the too all-to-familiar corner of Loathed and Ignored, watching her taillights vanish. I was alone again—no fiancée, no ride home. No matter. Pearl was safe and I heard an invitation in the air.

Blackout. Like a thousand times before. John Barleycorn took the rest of the night.

When I woke, hung over and sweating in my own bed the next morning, I swore I'd stop, that I'd ask for help. But the apartment's four bare walls bore witness that I had no truth, no power left. I drank that day like all the others.

I was numb.

I'd never felt this way before—strangely stiff. I needed to waken my friend here. He owed me some answers. "Dude, that must have been one hell of a Halloween party."

Good grief, he was covered with puke and dirt.

"We're wearing the same Batman costume..." No response.

I tapped his leg with my toe. "Buddy, you don't look so good." Was he breathing? I brushed away the leaves stuck to his face. My heart skipped a beat. "Oh, hell no, this can't be."

Trick or friggin' treat—it was me. That's why he wore my clothes—I was dead.

I hated this recurring dream.

A police car sped past my house, siren blasting, slapping me back to reality. My heavy breathing echoed off the dirty white walls. Sunlight burned through the cobwebs that adorned the east window. I threw off the sweaty sheet and stared at two flies dancing on the ceiling. Another day. Another nightmare. Another hangover. I turned away and hid my eyes in my pillow.

Thursday morning. "I won't drink today, solemn oath. Today will be different."

A high-pitched, elderly voice mocked. "Are you kidding? Try, at least try, to tell the truth for once." Mr. Conscience was brain barking again.

His brother, Mr. Consequence spoke in a slow, rumbling voice. "You're twenty-nine going on sixty and the laughingstock of every club in Baser."

Ten years earlier, a texting driver clipped me halfway across the Crosstown Bridge. A fender bump to the curb gave me a minor concussion and an ambulance ride to the hospital. Grim faced cops, unhappy parents, and fresh memories of blinding high-beams and squealing tires scared me into a series of public declarations and solemn oaths. I promised to be a changed man. I was done drinking and drugging.

My intentions worked—for about three weeks. Then, Pearl called me back. Somewhere along the line the Con Brothers arrived and dominated my thoughts ever since. Oh my, where would I be without the Cons?

They beat the same drum, "Sick and hung over again, you're an incurable alcoholic."

"You're a walking trashcan."

"They're going to fire you."

"You're nobody's friend—everyone laughs at you."

"Why don't you get help?"

"Why? Brother, I'll tell you why," Mr. Consequence growled. "He doesn't want to stop."

"No," I argued. "This is not happening, not to me. I'm different."

"Oh? How are you different?"

"Shut up. I'll quit when I want to. Leave me alone."

But they didn't. Their ever-present voices, relentless guilt trips, and never-ending insults crushed me. Every time I heard their nagging voices, I became more convinced they were right. My life was slipping away.

Wednesday night was like hundreds of others. Go to work and come home. Down a couple beers and a shot to prime my pump, then head to my favorite haunt, the Bloody Bucket Tavern. Then *bam*. Another blackout. Money, people, booze, and good times gone. Strange, I remembered finding my own body in that ghastly nightmare, but not the last eighteen hours. I'd never been so sick, so hung over. Was the cause bad whiskey or alcohol poisoning?

The bathroom reeked of beer puke. I smelled my armpit. Nope, all me. I leaned over the rust-stained sink to get a good look at the man in the filthy mirror. Rough. Someone must've kicked him down a couple staircases. I washed my face and held out my hands. They shook like leaves in a stiff wind. I'd keep them in my pockets. Better yet, I'd call in sick, this time for the flu.

"Hey Mr. Con, I'm going to tell a small white lie. After all, I do have brown-bottle flu."

"Not funny."

I shook my empty bottle of oxys. "Darn, no hillbilly heroin today. Hey, Mr. C, two or three aspirin?"

No one answered.

I padded to the kitchen. "Four aspirin morning." The refrigerator cycled with a familiar click and hum. It sat empty, except for seven open bottles of Pepto-Bismol and a pizza box. I took a deep breath and washed down four aspirin with tap water.

"You're disgusting," Conscience said.

"I bet there's a warrant out for your arrest," Consequence added.

"You'd better do something about your drinking today," they chorused. "Jackass, this is your last chance. Next time, you'll wake up in Hell."

"Stop hounding me." I held my hands over my ears and yelled, "Enough."

Flash. Bright spots and ringing ears. My neck twisted and petrified. A wave of electric pain spun me to the floor. I gnashed my teeth. My legs kicked against the crushing weight that pinned me down. The ceiling rocked back and forth and went black. This seizure outdid all the others.

The relentless phone rang and rang. I crawled on my hands and knees and pulled the receiver down on top of me. Bill, my shop foreman, sounded irate. "Thrasher, this's my third call. Don't try to lie. Eleven o'clock and you're still drunk."

"I'm not drunk. Deathly sick," I stammered. "Sorry, boss. I should have called in—"

"Yeah, right."

"I'll go see Doctor Changelove."

Dial tone.

I eased onto a throw rug and slept another hour—and somehow, fell off a cliff. I plummeted past grand mal and death, through a spiritual threshold, and landed at recovery's door a broken man. Although I didn't believe in God, He believed in me and intervened. A few hours later I began the great adventure called sobriety.

I sat on the edge of Dr. Changelove's examination table kicking my feet, staring at an old artsy human anatomy chart. A dusty banker's chair leaned against the wall, stacked full of books and files. An imposing grandfather clock guarded the door, counting each second. Two hanging brass weights shared an open well with a round silver pendulum scarred by dozens of small holes. Why would Changelove put something that imposing in his exam room? I was too numb to care—a bizarre mess of buyer's remorse, boredom, and hope.

Despite the clutter, the room smelled clean, of camphor and witch hazel. An old placard, wrinkled and yellowed with age, was fastened to the closed door. The Wicket, The Way, The Light, The Truth.

Dr. Changelove finished recording his exam notes and eased off a swivel stool. A slight man, scarcely five feet tall, his shock of white hair betrayed his age. His brown woolen suit and Gatsby white collar dated to his younger years. Similar to the clock's pendulum, an old silver dollar clasp rimmed by dozens of small holes dominated his bolo tie. Only his stethoscope indicated his role as a doctor, not a banker.

He removed his reading glasses and gave me a piercing look.

"Vonn Thrasher, how may I help you today?"

My head throbbed. Confusion and fear churned up competing thoughts.

This appointment is a mistake—no, stay and hear him out.

Run. You overreacted—but what about the seizures?

You can't live without Pearl—Pearl is a dangerous lie.

I needed time to think, a diversion.

Ask about the old placard. "What's a Wicket?"

"A small gate within the larger gate across The Way. On the other side, many people find enough light and truth to have a better life."

"Dr. Changelove, I—"

His wintry blue eyes stole my words. For the first time in decades, I was out of lies.

"Yes?" His kind voice empowered me.

"People say I have a drinking problem. And, well..." I cleared my throat. "I think they might be right."

"Might be?" Doc Changelove's smile overpowered my fear long enough to give me a moment of clarity.

"Yes. I can't leave booze alone. I'm drinking myself to death."

Did I say that? Yes. I spoke the unspeakable and outed my darkest secret. The unwashed truth kept coming. "Last night I had a terrible seizure. I need help."

The Wicket, The Way, The Light, The Truth.

A dampening hush shuttered the outside world. The grandfather clock's measured beat overpowered the room. The pendulum timed an unseen drummer's hand, beating an eerie rhythm, louder and louder, stretching time until eternity lived between each swing left to right.

I waited.

Bong, bong, bong, the clock chimed.

I was dizzy.

The bong sounded like a heartbeat, striking the center of my soul.

I counted five more rhythmic measures before stopping at eleven.

How? The clock indicated 2:15.

A haunting feminine voice shouted, "You live in the eleventh hour of the eleventh day."

I could barely breathe. Real or madness?

I gripped the exam table until my knuckles turned white.

"Time to turn before you cannot." Her voiced echoed from everywhere and nowhere.

"What?" I gasped. The clock's rhythmic ticking stopped. Dr. Changelove's smile froze.

"When the past catches the future, the twelfth and final hour begins," she declared. "The ledgers and books are opened, and all are called to account. All are judged in the twelfth hour."

"Judged? No, this is the DTs."

"No, I am Watcher, guardian of reason. I bring your last chance."

"Last! What does that mean?"

"Stop drinking and drugging before the midnight hour.

Tomorrow is too late. Life doesn't exist in the thirteenth hour. Not for you. Not for any creature. The thirteenth ends in death."

"Death? No. Listen, I came by today to talk and refill my prescription—"

"Vonn Thrasher, I see your future. Fate has given you the number thirteen, for the thirteen steps ascending a gallows deck and the thirteen twists in a hangman's knot."

"Gallows? No, that's wrong." I coughed and wheezed. "They use the needle now." What am I saying? "Please… I'm an alcoholic. Guilty as charged, but death? No."

A mortifying static squashed the room. Or was my head buzzing again?

I jumped to my feet. "I'll take that chance. Tell me what to do."

"Vonn Thrasher, behold—The Wicket." The office door swung open. A body wrapped in a sheet lay on the reception room floor. Both feet were exposed, and the left big toe was tagged.

"I'm not going to read that."

Watcher's voice echoed like a trumpet across a canyon. "Follow The Way, accept The Truth, and you will find a new life."

The reception room morphed into a backyard complete with green grass and flowers. A gentle breeze carried a meadowlark's song from a giant elm. Two children sailed back and forth on a bright red swing set, laughing and singing.

"Hey, I know them. That's me and… Annie Johnson. No, that's Ruth. No, Susan, maybe Patty… I don't remember, but we were best friends in grade school." Mom leaned out the door and called them to lunch. "Wow, she's so young and beautiful."

The exam room door slammed shut.

The static hum returned and became a heartbeat. *Ba-dum, ba-dum, ba-dum.* Horrified, I checked my pulse. The heartbeat was mine.

"Watcher, you said that you're a guardian of reason." I beat my chest and shouted. "Hear me. I choose life. I promise that I'll turn. No look, I'm here—I have turned."

Ba-dum, ba-dum, ba-dum increased, like a kettledrum.

"Watcher, come back," I pleaded. "Please, don't leave me like this."

~

"Vonn, look at me," Dr. Changelove said. "Mr. Thrasher, can you hear me?"

I opened my eyes.

"You're hyperventilating." He gave me a cloth. "Wipe your face and breathe through this towel for a minute."

"Thanks." I buried my face in the soft, clean cotton.

"Nasty little spell you had there."

My hands shook, stiff from clenching. "Please, a minute to collect myself."

The clock ticked, but remained on 2:15.

"Doc, was that a seizure?"

"No, you were awake and somewhat in control of your faculties."

"I heard—a voice." I leaned forward and whispered, "A woman's voice. She claimed to be some kind a spirit, a watcher. Did you, you know, hear—"

"You shouted a lot, but you're the one with the bad liver and nerves, not me."

"But she was real—"

"Or delirium?" He put the stethoscope on my chest. "Breathe deeply and exhale slowly."

I didn't smoke, but the familiar rattle and dull ache in my chest told Doc that I'd spent lots of nights in smoky barrooms and bowling allies, and imbibed in other things.

"So, did this voice tell the truth?"

"Maybe. Yes."

"Pull up your shirt so I can listen to your back." The room was chilly. "Could this truth be from God?"

"Wait a minute, Doc. I don't believe in all that churchy stuff."

"Breathe deeply."

My lungs felt like someone had sandpapered them.

"Personal theology aside, you must decide between delirium

tremens and this Watcher spirit. Some might say you heard an angel."

"Why does everyone have to talk about God and church?"

"Maybe others see something you don't. Hmm, worse, never better?"

"What's wrong with me now?"

"Does your drinking worsen each month?"

Thirteen twists in a hangman's knot. "Yes."

I exploded into hacking and coughing dry-heaves. My stomach turned inside out and tried to fly out of my mouth. Doc positioned a trashcan and patted my back. "Hang in there. Almost done, let the bile out.

"Oh man, my gut's in a knot."

He put an oxygen mask on me and adjusted the volume. "What is your body telling you?"

Make a decision. Open the Wicket Gate. I held my hand up and focused on breathing for a couple minutes, then removed the mask. "I need help."

Doc scribbled a note in my medical record. "Your file says you don't smoke, but your heart and lungs tell a different story. That rattle and cough isn't from a cold. I could give you a list of things to do and not to do, but we both know you'll never read the first word."

"I don't read much these days. But you could give me, you know, a pill that can—"

"No. I'm fresh out of lifestyle pills, and I don't treat drug addictions with more drugs." He tapped my chest with the clipboard. "Alcohol is the king of drugs."

"Sorry, I—"

"Young man, here's my prognosis. Your life is a garden overgrown with weeds. You'll never grow old, and what's left of your future is full of insanity and failure. Emphysema will turn cancerous and take every dollar you earn. And one day soon, no one will care. They'll read your obituary and snicker, 'Yessir, Vonn finally did it.'"

"Hmm," I rubbed my temples and glanced at my feet. No toe tag. "The voice, Watcher, or whatever she is, told me that a hanging was in my future."

"Interesting. Maybe someone is reaching out to you from the other side."

Tick-tock-tick-tock. The clock said 2:33. "This isn't the first time I've heard voices. The Conscience and Consequence Brothers are relentless. They torment me every day, and every night, and provide a variety of nightmares about how I'm going to die."

"You have a lot going on inside that noggin of yours. Have you heard of Demimonde?"

"Demi-what?"

"Pronounced like almond, it rhymes with correspond. Demimonde is an old French word meaning *half-world*, used to describe a pleasure-seeking portion of society, unbound by morals, religion, or traditions. They're calloused and cruel, doing whatever, whenever they want. Demimonde is the role you're playing in your party cliques and favorite nightclubs. I suspect you play well enough, but that's not who you are. You're pretending your way into an early grave."

"Demi… *monde*? No, sorry, I have to disagree."

"Demimonde has already caught and cast you into a world between what we know and what we fear, where science and superstition walk hand in hand."

My chest tightened. I wheezed. "Then Watcher and the Con Brothers are real?"

"You decide if they're from heaven or hell or insanity. Regardless, you must stop drinking first, or you'll never escape Demimonde."

"But how? If I could, I would have years ago."

"True. You've given away the power to choose and decide."

"Then what can I do?"

"You need more than I can offer you. Your best chance is on Sobriety Island. The islanders know how to stop drinking."

"Sobriety Island?"

"Yes. You've probably heard rumors and stories. I understand that you reach the island after a challenging voyage across the Sea of Booze. Many alkies book passage on one of the ships operating out of Ism Harbor. Others go it alone and vanish, hence all the mystery and hype."

"I've been to Ism."

"There's a ship called Treatment. Something else called Ordonne has a vessel too."

"Or-what?"

"Ordonne," the doc replied. "Pronounced like ore-dawn."

"Got it."

"Go down to the harbor and choose wisely." He continued. "The Sea of Booze takes several weeks to cross. You'll need a good captain and crew to find the island." He walked me to the door. "I can do a referral for your insurance, but whether you recover is on you."

I peeked into his very normal waiting room. "Doc, I got to ask. The door poster, the grandfather clock—Watcher… is that part of your examination?"

"Answer my question and I'll answer yours. What is the name of your childhood best friend?"

"I don't know. Why should I remember?"

"That's my answer." He shook my hand and smiled. "Go to Ism Harbor. Open your mind. When you find your way, embrace the truth and never let go."

Parking was always bad in the portside of Ism, so I left my car at the edge of town and walked. Tall stacks of gray clouds hid the sun and promised afternoon rain. A familiar sea breeze reminded me of the time Mom and I walked the beach looking for driftwood and shells. Box stores and four-lane roads gave way to cobblestone streets lined with quaint maritime shops. The salt air morphed into the smell of popcorn and hotdogs. Somewhere, an organ played circus music.

A dozen men and women on bicycles pedaled by me laughing

and shouting catcalls. Their backward baseball caps, leggings, and cutoffs didn't cover their wrinkles and faded tattoos. Old gray men and blue-haired women acting like sophomores are hard on the eyes. Stranger yet, I wanted to chase them, to escape this place.

But I didn't. I walked around a blind corner and almost knocked down a couple standing on the sidewalk. Paper, pens, and clipboards tumbled from their hands.

"So sorry. Here, let me help." When I bent down to pick them up, I saw a smiling girl's grainy high school yearbook picture on the missing person flyers.

"Sir, have you seen our Rosa? Is she here somewhere?"

I said nothing.

She persisted. "Do you know her? Have you heard of her?"

"Rosa? Rosa, who?"

"Our granddaughter, Rosa Dodge."

I handed the sad-eyed man a handful of flyers, and we shook hands.

"Louie Amor, and my wife, Maria."

I smiled in sympathy. "Vonn. Sorry, no, I just got here and don't know—"

"If you come across Rosa, tell her we love her." Maria looked behind her at four other people soliciting help and handing out flyers. They waved and quickstepped across the street in our direction. Maria moved closer, grabbed my forearm, and stared into my eyes. She reeked of patchouli and radiated fear and worry. "Tell her to come home. Tell her that we want her back."

Scary. "So… I'm almost late for an appointment," I lied. "Got to go. But good luck with Rosa."

All six urged me to help. "Wait, take a flyer, help us find—"

I jogged down the block and around the corner, stopped, and peeked back down the sidewalk. They called out to every car and pedestrian, "Have you seen Rosa Dodge? Anyone know Jenny Nicks? Our Steve Shirk ran away. Where do runaways go?"

Naive parents wandered around Ism Harbor in the middle of

the day, looking for children who didn't want to be found. What a waste of time. I leaned out toward them. "Hey."

They froze.

"They're probably junked out and hiding. Go home. Dress like you're going to a party and come back at midnight. They'll be out and about then."

They stared. One man threw his flyers in the air.

"Trust me. People here live by different rules."

I hurried across the street and stepped inside the first open door. Lee Lea's Teashop was wallpapered with Chinese dragons. Ornate paper lanterns and drama masks hung over each table. Spicy incense and soft music filled the room with an erotic, old-world feeling. "Nice. They won't follow me in here."

"You sit and rest. Umma take care of you." Mamasan stood in front of me, all smiles and traditional dress. "I bet you go on ship. Better have last beer, ha, ha. No more onboard."

Treatment could wait a few hours. "Well, I—"

"This my friend Moon Lee. She give you best pedicure, shampoo, and haircut." Umma gave me an exaggerated wink. "Then do massage."

That'll fix what ails me. I felt for my wallet—gone. Frantic, I slapped every pocket. "Mamasan—my wallet's gone."

"You a slicky-boy. Lost wallet old story. No pay, no friend here." She pointed to the door.

"Mamasan—"

"Get out." She pushed me through the doorway.

I raced up and down the sidewalk. Nothing.

I swallowed my pride and asked Louie and Maria if they'd found a wallet. They mocked me. "No. Go home and dress like you're going to a party. Come back at midnight and you'll find her."

"Guess I deserved that."

Running and walking, I retraced my way to the car.

"Idiot," I groaned. My wallet lay on the passenger seat.

Breathing easier, I buttoned my wallet into my cargo pocket and followed the music back down the hill. Wanting to avoid

Mamasan, I chose a different route, and walked into the heart of Ism Harbor, a commercial beehive.

Peculiar, broken people sidelined by society crowded dozens of odd shops and kiosks. They filled the streets and spilled onto the docks. Dickens' characters right out of *Oliver Twist* found a home on recovery row.

Outdoor speakers blasted contemporary Christian music on one side, and a piano banged out "Entry of the Gladiators" on the other. Hawkers enticed nervous customers into their stations. Signs advertised recovery from every ailment known to man. Too drunk, too fat, chronic pain, diabetic, hooked on sex, drugs, even rock 'n' roll. Get fixed here—for a price—teen and senior discounts available.

Ism Harbor was a booming vanity fair, a carnival.

I swiveled to look around and wondered, *What's going on? What's the angle? Is this about money or getting help?*

The answers were canned clichés.

Faith-based reps shouted, "Recover here—we have sin-eaters, healing hands, and mental medicine."

Agnostic street hawkers brayed, "Kudzu pills and snake oil tonics, salt rooms, mineral baths, and recovery boot camps."

"What about Ordonne? Where's Ordonne?" I asked.

The faith-based folks admitted, "They aren't here, but believe me, that's the last place you want to go. Ordonne is a secret cult. Only the hard cores go there. You can do better with us."

"They do too much God," the agnostics complained.

Many considered Ordonne too simple; others concluded, too hard.

"Strange. Have you ever been an Ordonne?" I asked.

"No, but—" Everyone was an Ordonne expert. Their opinions went on and on.

My head swam in contradictory information.

A corner sign read: Madam Ism's Tarot Cards and Palm Reading. I already know what you need.

"Wow. I wonder if she'd know about Demimonde."

"Over here, honey," called a buxom middle-aged blonde sitting on a bench across the street. "You look lost." Her crossed legs, her low-cut blouse and mini skirt left little to the imagination.

The store window marquee behind her scrolled:

Treatment Ship

and flashed:

Now Booking

with an arrow pointing to the doorway. A musky fragrance carried all the way across the street. Why not?

"Let me guess, you're from out of town and looking for help." She had a whiskey voice and a cute New Jersey accent. "You need a friend."

"Well, I'm just shopping for the best way to recover from a drinking problem. Not for me—for a friend."

"Out-of-towners always shop for friends, ha, ha."

"Well, I—"

"Honey, I start every conversation with a hug." She grabbed my hand, pulled me into an embrace, and planted a big wet kiss on my cheek.

"I'm Nurse Season," she whispered. "But honey, you can call me Summer. Hmm, you are a wet one. Ready more ways than one I bet—"

"Summer… ya, okay." I wiped my cheek. "Vonn, Vonn Thrasher from Baser."

"Come, sit a while with me." We walked into her small, but stylish office. Motivational posters lined the eggshell, pink, and lavender walls. "You're in luck. Treatment Ship is in port today conducting orientations. They last about an hour. There's no commitment—just paperwork to get started."

"Not for me, for a friend."

"Of course, just some brochures and a walk-thru," she pointed to a stuffed chair. "You're lucky to have found me." She popped her lips on her chewing gum. "I'm in recovery so I understand alkies. But all those crazies out there," she rolled her big green eyes toward the street, "quacks, all of them. They claim to have the real deal, but they don't."

"I planned to find—"

"Vonn, honey, let me tell you what. When I hit Ism all bright-eyed and ignorant, those track hawkers convinced me that voyages to Sobriety Island were a hoax, and sold me a wolf ticket to a program that almost killed me."

"You look great. How long you been, you know, without—"

"Over seven months counting treatment time." She studied her long red nails. "Love sobriety. Now, does your friend have insurance?"

CHAPTER TWO

Treatment Ship

An hour later, I left the Treatment Store smelling like Summer's perfume, with a Treatment Ship visitor's badge hanging from my neck.

Then, I took a wrong turn and got lost in a maze of backstreets and quays. An old sailor stood on one of the countless unnamed corners, holding a cardboard sign:

Hoopy's advice and directions for a dollar.

"Aye, friend, you'll find the Treatment Ship on Money Way." He pointed down the street with a tin cup, empty except for my dollar. "Keep straight until you hit the piers, then walk nine berths east."

"And, Ordonne?"

He shook his cup under my nose until I produced another dollar. "Aye, thank ye. Nah, if ye keeps a'going, sun at yer back, past all da' docks, there's a beach. That's where you'll find your Donnybrook."

"You mean Ordonne. What is that anyway?"

"I think Ordonne is some kind a religious rescue group. Don't know for sure, but I heard they'll ruin a fella's drinking."

The sun burned off the afternoon clouds, bathing a three-deck paddle wheeler in bright light. Painted classic white with red trim, she boasted 200 feet, bow to stern, with dozens of colorful flags standing tall in the sea breeze. A handsome crew dressed in pastel scrubs walked here and there, chorusing the lines from an old folk-rock song. They sang about brothers and sisters and understanding problems. The refrain about all of us needing somebody to lean on pierced my heart.

I heard recovery magic in every verse, and I wanted more.

An inviting banner posted over the gangplank read,

New Life Treatment Ship

Welcome

Traditional and Holistic Permanent Growth and Freedom.

"Whatever that means." Leaving my fear on the dock, I hummed, "We do all need someone to lean on," and walked on board.

"My name is Captain Know-It-All, program director and humble servant. Please, all my shipmates call me Captain Know."

The skipper wore an impeccable white summer uniform, complete with a captain's hat and gold epaulettes on each shoulder. His jet-black handlebar mustache, waxed and curled into a full circle on each end quivered from a facial tic. His right eye strayed to the point of distraction. Was he looking at me or out the starboard window?

"Mr. Thrasher, we have what you need to correct your difficulty with alcohol. Our three-week Sobriety Island voyage will give you time to recover. Together, we'll restart your life and create beautiful, strong sobriety."

"Just three weeks?"

"Yes, I recommend the three-week treatment voyage for first-timers. Our success rate is among the highest in the industry. I can't think of the last time someone failed to leave us sober and ready for a, new life," he over-emphasized the last two words.

"Ah, hah, New Life Treatment Ship and—"

"Hmm, I can smell Nurse Summer's fragrance. She tells me that your insurance will sign off for you without question." He leaned sideways so our shoulders touched and rolled his eyes.

"Just between you and me, this is better than a paid vacation. You'll fall in love with New Life."

"Well, I didn't—"

"Come, come, and let me show you around."

I almost jogged to keep up as we hustled from one deck to another.

"At New Life, we focus on total wellness. That includes exercise activities in our weight room with stationary bikes and table tennis. We even have a sauna to sweat the booze out of you. Ha, ha."

"But how does that get the monkey—"

"Second deck, please," he hurried up the stairs, taking two at a time. "Up here we have daily meditation and goalsetting get-togethers. There's group therapy, yoga, Tai Chi, a juicing body detox, acupuncture, and massage services."

"Wow, that's—"

"Hold that thought, my friend. For depressed guests, there's a weeping bath with crying towels. And for angry alkies, we offer a soundproof chamber with punching bags and breakable furniture."

"Who would've thought of that?"

"Vonn, what makes you happy—makes us happy. That's our goal."

"Sounds good." I laughed.

"You look like a sports bar, dart board kind of guy."

"I can diddle for the middle, beer in one hand, dart in the other."

"Bullseye. On our next voyage to Sobriety Island, we have for the first time ever, a not-my-fault dartboard. Throw off your resentments with a dart."

The captain did an about face. "Follow me. Top deck, here we go." We rushed up the stairs and walked a long deck lined with berthing doors. "Let's look at a couple state rooms so you can test the bunks."

We finished in back of the pilot house, and reclined in two of the many deck chairs scattered around the top deck. My hangover was finally gone. While Know scribbled on my paperwork, the blue tarp that shaded us quarreled with the sea breeze, popping and groaning and pulling against the ropes. An idle slow-moving ceiling fan whirled and wobbled, lulling me almost asleep.

A wonderful fragrance filled the air, and a young lady wearing pink scrubs and a big smile arrived, carrying a tray with three sweating glasses of iced tea. Her slender, tanned body and golden hair braided into a single plait hanging nearly to her waist presented the picture of health and beauty.

New Life was aesthetic. I was impressed, excited about recovery. Who doesn't need to check out once in a while and meet new friends?

"My name's Sister Sweet." She sat the tray down. "Therapy tech." We shook, and she handed me a glass and napkin, then stood over me—her knees touching my forearm. I could've rubbed my head on her hip. The clinking ice invited me to hold the cold glass against my forehead and hide for a second.

"Welcome, Mr. Thrasher. I hope you've decided to join us," she said in a silky voice.

"Just Vonn, please," I craned my head to look past her cleavage. "Thank you." Was that the same musky scent Nurse Season wore? My eyes burned. From her perfume—or lust? For two seconds, morality and lust wrestled for control of my monkey mind. Guess who won. "Maybe." My mouth watered. "Yes, I am."

"Welcome aboard." She ran a polished fingernail down my arm and squeezed my wrist. "A toast." We raised our glasses. "To Vonn, his new life, and a great voyage to Sobriety Island."

"Hear, hear." We clinked our glasses together.

"Sister, is the perfume you're wearing called Reckless Abandon?"

"You're too funny. No, it's called Usher." She winked. "I love Usher. I love this ship. I love you and you." She pointed at us with both hands and did a double pirouette. "Sobriety is amazing. New Life is, well, like Noah's Ark—a lifeboat that keeps everyone safe from out there."

"Out there?" I asked.

"The raging sea." She nodded toward the mouth of the harbor. "You know, the Sea of Booze where all manner of alky eating—"

"That's enough for now." Captain Know glanced at the pilot-house. Both of us watched her stop at the corner, wave and blow a kiss, then skip around the corner.

"Sweet's such a darling. But her imagination does wander enough to come up with some of the oddest stories." Know cleared his throat. "Now, where were we? Ahh yes, paperwork, a necessary evil I'm afraid. Now, Mr. Thrasher, you have good insurance, but can you afford the $300 a week co-pay? We'll need the $900 up front."

Mom's credit card. "Yes, I can."

He held out a clipboard. "Then sign here and here. Initial here and here." He pointed to highlighted signature boxes on the forms. We need a referral from your doctor, and the copayment before departure."

We stood up and shook hands. "Congratulations, you're booked on the next voyage." He handed me my copies and a fat newcomer's packet. "We sail day after tomorrow with the evening tide. Check-in is early, seven to eleven in the morning."

"I'll be here."

"The packing checklist outlines everything you need to bring. Most importantly, bring cash or credit card and your doc's referral. No pay, you stay, and wave bon voyage from the pier."

I wandered around before making my way to the gangplank and off the ship. I had no second thoughts, but before walking into Ism's cluttered streets, I had to look back one last time. Sister Sweet waved from the third deck to catch my eye.

"See you in a few days," I shouted.

She blew me a kiss and a double thumbs up. I patted my heart and bowed.

"Later," she called and skipped inside.

"Hmm, hmm, three weeks on a love boat—sign me up captain, I'm in love with sobriety. Now, just so I can cross Ordonne off my list, let me look into this thing."

Shantytown

What'd Hoopy say? *I think Ordonne is some kind a religious rescue group. Keep the sun at yer back, past all da' docks, there's a beach. That's where you'll find 'em.* Problem was the clouds hid the afternoon sun. But, like a good alcoholic, I cleared the docks and went where east ought to be.

Money was the green bee in my bonnet. An obsession? Maybe, but obsessions aren't all bad. Sports can be a healthy obsession. What about hobbies, or an author's inspiration? A passionate drive to fund three weeks on a treatment ship has to be good.

My monkey-mind grabbed my checkbook and raced like a scared baboon through the jungle, swinging from limb to limb, stopping to scratch and spit, "$900 copay in two days?" And howl, "Ha, you don't have $90 to your name, let alone $900."

Mom? No, she cut that card up after the last go around.

What about rent and utility bills?

Dad? Ha, no, really no.

How can I pay for all that *and* booze? Booze—what am I thinking? This money is for alcohol treatment.

Friends? No way. Too embarrassing.

Then I had a great idea. "Work—I'll go the medical emergency angle and get an advance from payroll." I fist pumped and jogged a step or two. "Maybe skim a little folding money too. The boss won't be happy, but, oh well."

A truck's air horn blasted me back to reality. "Idiot," a gruff voice shouted. "Get outta the road."

I was standing in front of a bar, reading the sign painted on its false front.

Pretty Face Saloon

Shantytown's Finest since 1919

People drifted in and out of batwing doors. Someone laughed and shouted for another round. An out of tune piano banged out an old ballad about Sundays and Mondays, rambling and gambling, and being in jail.

Where had I wandered? I looked up and down the street at the chaotic panorama that was Shantytown, a tangled mass of old weather-beaten houses sitting on dirt roads that served as sewers. No street markers, not even a stop sign.

I didn't have a clue—lost again.

The air was an odd mix of diesel smoke, whiskey, and cigarettes. A waft of hogwash turned my head. Every storefront, walk, and alley teemed with the lost—boys and girls that never grew up—geriatric Peter Pans and Wendy Darlings dressed like they were going to a costume party. I heard a headboard thumping in time with the moanings of unabashed sex. A naked Sister Sweet flashed through my mind. Revolting? No, magnetic—aroused a lust that I couldn't help but entertain. Raunchy? Yes, but was raunchy so bad? Maybe the beach could wait.

"Well, lookee who's here, ha, ha, ha."

I turned around. The sarcastic voice belonged to a scrawny woman in a hiked-up miniskirt and cowboy boots. A half-burnt cigarette hung from the corner of her mouth, and a tattooed breast peeked out of her faded tee-shirt. Heavy makeup, bleached blonde hair, and designer nails couldn't hide her puffy, dark-circled eyes, missing teeth, and jaundiced skin. She was a rough forty-something actor dying for a younger part.

She stepped forward and bumped hips. "Take a good look, cowboy." Her perfume didn't mask the odor of oral infection—or was that the breath of a polluted soul?

No frigging way. "Hi there," I grinned. "Do you know—?"

"I know what I like. You here to party?"

"Ha," I tried to be funny and waved my arms. "I'm just passing through, making my way across the big Milky Way. Can you tell me—?"

"I can tell you anything you want to hear, and surprise you with even more," she purred and ran her hand along my shoulder. "Couple a drinks and I'll look like a red carpet movie star. What say we slip over to the Pretty Face, and you buy us a pitcher and some shots?"

"I would but—"

"Shhh." She glanced at the visitor's badge, pulled me close with the lanyard, and put her index finger on my lips. "We need to quiet those shaky nerves."

Fear. I should've hid the badge. A spasm rippled across my chest and unleashed another fit. Panic attack? Asthma? No, much worse. It was me and her and a hundred faceless men and women cut from the same filthy cloth. Ripped and torn—and there wasn't enough booze in Shantytown to fix us.

She took a long pull on her cigarette. "This is such bullshit."

Finally, my chest relaxed. The rank Shantytown air was pure heaven to my starved lungs. "Sorry, that was a bad one. I don't smoke but—"

"Yeah, yeah, we all have something. You ready to go?"

"To Ordonne. Can you tell me the best way?"

"Not me," her voice had an edge. "Not ever."

"Okay, well, I'll go ask someone else." I held my hand out to shake.

"Where the hell do you think you are—some kind a petting zoo?" She swatted my hand away, eyes hooded, face red with rage. "Mr. High and Mighty a'standing on my corner gawking. Do something. Show me what kind of stud you are." She ground what was left of her cigarette into the dirt with the toe of her red cowboy boot.

"Lady, I ain't looking to hookup." I stepped back and held my hands up. "Just passing through, asking for directions, no more."

"Poor little lost fool," she rasped. "Hey everyone, we got another accidental tourist."

My skin tightened. I wanted to slap her and run.

"Uh-oh, someone's getting mad." She swayed and hiccupped. "Well, pardon me, Mister I'm-going-to-get-sober," she taunted, "welcome to hell—roomie—let me show you to our room."

I stepped off her dirt corner. "Roomie? Ha, we don't even know each other."

She winced and shrieked, "You wouldn't remember if we did," but this time with a different voice. Two, maybe three women harmonized to make a deep, eerie old-world foreign accent. Her eyes darkened, flickered with anger, and her face contorted with contempt. "You not da first hypocrite to stand on my corner."

Passersby stopped and stared. The sun was blinding. Memories flashed and sputtered. Was this woman blackout madness? I wanted to hide, but the best I could do was to bury both shaky hands in my pockets. Sweat stung my eyes, and my stomach turned over. Delirium or not, I was melting in the sweltering street.

"Look, we're done here, and I'm leaving."

"Really? Nobody ever leaves Shantytown, not for long," she mocked in a Slavic accent. "Mister Cutie Vonn, you just like all da others, sick little butterflies playing recovery. But when you think nobody's looking, you stop to smell da hos and cocktails."

She flapped her arms like a bird and did an awkward pirouette. "Flitting and flying and stopping where they may, telling cute little woe-begone stories. Oh Mommy, oh Daddy, I'm going to get sober. Oh please, pretty lady, tell me where I can find Ordonne?"

She stepped forward, nose to nose and poked my chest with a long, painted fingernail. "You're just like all da other sick, vile little butterflies," she hissed. "You can't resist the smell of vomit. You love to suck on dirty sunflowers."

Her putrid breath pushed me back. "I'm done." I walked away.

She followed right on my heels. "Go ahead, Ordonne, beg me. Pray that you get outta here for all the good it'll do you. Deny, deny, fly butterfly fly." She hacked up a goober and spit on my feet. "And don't forget to ask for a quickie on your way to your damned treatment boat."

"Get him, Scrawny," a man yelled. Dozens of Shantytowners were in the street. Others taunted from windows. "Hey, butterfly, sing a little kum ba yah for us."

I stumbled and fell with a splash. A hundred voices thundered in laughter.

I rolled and regained my footing.

She crowded my face. "Vonn wanna play?" She ripped the New Life lanyard off my neck and threw it in the mud. "Saint Vonn, why didn't you didn't ask for my real name?" She stiff-armed me. "Don't you care who I am, how I got here?"

Someone yelled, "Hypocrite." The Shantytowners circled, slapping their legs and stomping in rhythm. "Kick a poser, cut a poser, beat, beat, beat."

Angry shouts from down the street, "Over here. Scrawny got an Ordonne."

From alleys, "Kick 'em down. Break his legs."

From windows, "Beat, beat, beat."

A tall skinny man emerged from the milling crowd. Naked except for tattoos and a stovepipe hat, he came right at me carrying a blood-stained rope. "String him up from the ballroom rafters," he shouted. Hundreds of voices chorused with the same foreign accent, "Hang 'em, hang him high."

A man wearing a white judge's wig announced over a bullhorn. "Fistfight and a hanging at the Pretty Face." I recognized his voice. He was the same Baser judge who said, "I don't like you Vonn Thrasher, not one bit."

Someone jumped on my back. "Gotcha."

Scrawny grabbed my shirt and dug her nails into my arm. "Mine."

I threw a couple of elbows, stomped on someone's toes, and shoved him to the ground.

A dozen police whistles screamed, and the crowd backed off. Before I could run, the Shantytowners swarmed. Three broad-shouldered men anchored a tightening ring of angry faces and fists, some standing, some crawling on hands and knees, all reaching to pull me down.

I dodged a flying whiskey bottle. Someone struck my back with a broomstick. A fist hit my jaw and another rang my ear.

Their blows rained down.

Their faces blurred.

Fight. Death's heavy curtain lifted.

Fight. I heard and saw red madness.

Fury. Go down and they'll kill you. Adrenaline enriched-fear and rage gave me a second wind. Numb, yes, but I would not fall. Every face came into focus—I was indestructible.

Nothing to be proud of, but I've always been good with my fists and can trade punches with the best of them. More than once my barroom brawling skills got me out of a tight spot. That day they saved my life.

Two men reached for me, leading with their chins. A straight left and hard right broke one's jaw and the other's nose. They howled and went down. I kicked the tattooed man's naked groin like a football. Something popped, his eyes rolled back, and he dropped in a writhing mass of rope and mud.

A biker mama in black leathers and chains jumped in front of me swinging a bat. I absorbed a blow to my ribs, drove inside, and laid my right elbow across her nose. Blood splattered everywhere. I grabbed her bat and fanned the rest of them off.

Someone yelled, "Get my shotgun. I'm gonna put this mother down."

The mob surged forward.

Blood boiled into primal rage. The bat rang off heads and crushed hands.

There—an empty alley on the left.

Only one man blocked my escape. Dressed like Roy Rogers and brandishing a bowie knife, he stepped forward with a toothy grin, "Time to gut a hippie."

I crushed his cowboy hat.

My escape lane open, I raced down the alley splashing through rivulets of street sewage, darting left and right, then through an empty lot.

Two explosions rang out—*Boom*—*Boom*. The shotgun. Pellets sprayed near me. A window broke. I ducked around a corner. Ringing ears and shaky hands, but no blood—somehow, they missed.

I peeked across the street and counted six armed vigilantes searching door to door. A chubby guy wearing a shoulder holster over a white shirt strutted my way.

"Watcher," I whispered. "I need a little help—they're about to kill me."

He stiffened and drew, "There!" The street erupted in gunfire. Bullets snapped like bullwhips over my head.

"Damn." I dashed behind a building and charged helter-skelter downhill, ducking behind anything that would hide me from the vigilantes. Finally, I lost them in the maze of firetraps. At the bottom of the hill their shouts and shots trailed off and stopped. Safe. For a moment exhaustion overwhelmed adrenalin, but like the wounded hare that ran inside the wrong rabbit warren, I was still lost and in trouble.

Nearby, feet splashed through mud. Someone was coming quickly.

Her again. Scrawny stopped, blood splattered and soiled, alone in the middle of a mucky street a half block away.

A mirror image of you and your future.

We locked eyes for ten long seconds.

"Hey, Jesse Owens," she barked and pointed to a window on the second floor above me. "You beat me home, ha,ha." Her scathing laugh bounced off buildings and rutted streets.

I turned, slipped, and fell across two trashcans. The bat rattled across the cobblestone street. "Whoops, boogeyman gonna get you, ha, ha."

Rats ran in every direction. I raced a big one down the street until it ducked inside a row house. "Run-a-boy, run." Her voice broke into mixed Yiddish and Cockney.

"You be back."

I dashed around the corner and over a footbridge.

"You's mine. I be waiting."

I stopped on the far side of an old burn.

The fire had consumed several city blocks, leaving dozens of standing walls protruding from a field of rubble. Some structures had unbroken windows and closed doors that opened to piles of ashes. Creeper vines and ragweed covered the area. Vultures and ravens soared overhead, patiently waiting for their next meal.

I leaned against a gnarly elm to watch the footbridge and gray streets that dumped into this hellish courtyard. Few leaves remained on the tree's twisted branches. Like everything else in Shantytown, it was dying.

Rain fell, beating a nearby rusty chunk of tin like a cymbal and dowsing Scrawny's cyclic screams, "I own you. Vonn Thrasher, you's mine."

A ten-story housing project stared across the burn with a hundred glass eyes. Somewhere, a baby cried. A man and woman laughed over a card game. The delicious aroma of fried chicken and potatoes contradicted a sad man's cries, "Ashley, where are you?" His grief echoed off the rubble, "Ashley, please come home. Ashley, I love you."

His words pierced my heart. I thought of lost Rosa and her worried grandmother, Maria crying out, "We want Rosa back. Tell her to come home. Tell her we love her."

Drunk or not, we're all lost.

Chilly in damp clothes, I pulled my collar up and walked down blocks of weathered shacks and streets littered with broken glass. People stared from doorways and windows and burned out cars sitting on blocks. Others may have observed from behind trash piles and waist high weeds. In Shantytown, life always found a way—but only after the bartender and the dope man were paid.

"Shot at. Almost hanged. What had I gotten myself into? Watcher, did you or Demimonde dump me in this mess?"

No answer. But then, I didn't want one.

Minutes later, the air cooled and the sea breeze changed direction, carrying the rain and trash fire smoke away. I turned and walked into the wind, following the fresh smell of saltwater.

Steel bars guarded every window of the busy little store on the corner of Merlot and Concord Way. Over the door a neon sign flickered:

Bottoms Store
Wine & Beer - Bread & Lotto

An enormous red-bearded man sat on a stool by the entrance, inspecting each departing customer. Two men leaned against the side wall, sharing a quart of amber liquid.

Merlot wandered to the left and up the hill. The sea breeze ran straight up Concord, calling my name. I answered and stayed right.

Block after block, I passed young men dressed in dirty wedding tuxedos. Old women in pink hoodies and black leggings preened and stretched in front of sidewalk mirrors. Teenagers in school uniforms clustered in front of bodegas and teahouses. Plumbers in coveralls and roofers with nail aprons encircled burn barrels, warming their hands. A grandmother tied her apron next to three soldiers in blood-soaked camouflage. Nurses dressed in torn hospital scrubs stood among Skid Row bums in trench coats.

Everyone spoke a different language.

They talked and laughed like manic magpies, a hint of Scrawny's strange accent in every voice.

Nobody listened and no one lacked a brown bag. They were winos.

When I greeted them or waved, they clenched their fists and turned away, glaring over their shoulders. They owned Concord; I was trespassing. After the Pretty Face, I was happy to duck my head and keep moving.

A ringing ship's bell told me that the harbor was ahead. I yearned to run through big waves and wash off.

Across the street, a woman in bib overalls and flip-flops swept the packed dirt sidewalk in front of her shoddy little hut. Large painted letters over the building announced:

The Concord Apothecary

Her waist-length, salt-and-pepper hair swung back and forth

with the movement of the broom. Bent and twisted, she must have suffered a terrible back injury.

"Hello, hello," I said in my friendliest voice.

She glanced at me for a second and kept sweeping.

"That's a mighty clean patch of dirt you got there."

No response.

"Question—is The Bottoms where all the winos go?"

She paused long enough to study me. "Not all."

"But, how do they get here?"

"Why are you talking?" She sounded young. No double-voice foreign accent.

"Just curious, I saw lots of brown baggers on my way."

"I doubt you're curious." She studied my shaking hands. "More like terrified. They chased you off the hill, didn't they?"

My sore jaw, ringing ear, and bruised ribs were still talking to me. "Yeah, well—they get pretty mad when you don't drink their whiskey."

"I heard the shots." She straightened and moaned. "Tell me, how you got here?" Her hollow blue eyes and grimaced face erased my story. "You don't know, and the truth scares the hell out of you."

"I know where I'm going," I lied. "Lived here long?"

"Me? Around here we don't count days and weeks." She stopped sweeping. "Boy, I can tell what you're thinking, and it wasn't whoring and booze. I used to be somebody, a tenured college professor, the mother of four fine children. Then I took a tumble down a set of stairs."

"That had to hurt."

She leaned the broom against the wall and rubbed the small of her back. "Never recovered. My life collapsed." She pulled a tin container from her chest pocket, removed two pills, and emptied the contents of a silver flask to wash them down. "The ministers of pain, oxys and arthritis, brought me to Shantytown. And you—how'd you end up all splattered with shit?"

"Shantytowners stare because you look worse than them," Mr. Consequence added.

"Thank you, Mister Brain Barker," I whispered. Watcher and the Con Brothers never failed to impeach. At this rate, I could host a mental ethics committee inside a year.

"What'd you say?" she asked.

"How'd I get here? That's a good question. I left a Treatment Ship on Money Way, and got lost in Shantytown. I'm looking for Ordonne."

"Did you ask the locals for directions?"

"Up there?" I pointed to the hillside slum. "Well, yeah."

She gave a slow nod. "That's why they were shooting at you." She took off her flip-flop and beat the dust off against the wall. "There's a blood feud going on between the Shanties and the Ords. Look, I don't care. Do the best I can to tidy up my own side of the street, but I know a couple dozen local yokels with your story. If you don't take the right path, you'll be another."

I felt the urge to keep going. "Is the Gravel Beach this direction?"

She nodded. "The road wanders a bit. Go neither left nor right, but straight along the way."

"Thanks," I said over my shoulder.

Farther down and around of couple bends, the town shifted to sandy patches with green trees. Like a page out of an allegory, the street ended at pounding surf.

I peeled off my filthy running shoes, knocked the dirt out of the grooves, and leaned back in the sun. The pleasant surrounding had plentiful native trees. The sea grape's green fruit hung like giant mulberries from its round leaf canopy. Tempting, but they needed the rest of summer to turn blue.

A gunshot rang out from the top of the hill. A dozen more volleyed from the west side. Another poor fool like me had just died. "Bloody Shantytown." I looked at my raw knuckles and yelled into the air, "This place is poison, a deadly snare full of bizarre people who hook and horn and kill. Sobriety Island? Ha, I'll be lucky if I survive today. I'm sorry I ever left Baser," I bawled. "Watcher, get me outta here."

"Was that a hint of surrender?"

I blotted my eyes on my sleeve, lowered my arm, and sighed, "Watcher?"

"You'll never leave if you don't go today."

I pulled on my socks and shoes. "Surrender or not, I'm done. Those people really hate me."

"Most of those people will die here. Demimonde warps every shred of love into hate. They live by the feud, and attack everyone who has what they don't—hope and freedom."

"I'm more than ready to stop drinking. But, this…" I stopped, turned, and shouted. "Last night I was in Baser, drunk, yes, but functional. So far today, I've stumbled into a recovery carnival, fell in love with a therapist on a treatment ship I can't afford, got lost in Shantytown, been beat up, shot at, and had to run for my life. Now I'm talking you—and you're invisible. Frankly, I'd bug out, but I don't know how, because I'm in the middle of nowhere."

"So, you're admitting you're powerless. Do I detect a little humility?" Watcher chuckled. "Now, put one foot in front of the other and don't fall. Have faith, Mister Baser Man. Ism, Shantytown, and Gravel Beach have a purpose."

"Pain and suffering."

"Tell me, are you jonesing? When was the last time you had a craving?"

I stopped to think. "Sometime yesterday, before I emptied two bourbon bottles."

"Yesterday. How about that? What would life be like without cravings, blackouts, and seizures?"

"A dream come true."

"A legitimate hope. Vonn, you had quite an exchange with the two Shantytown women. What are their real names?"

I laughed. "Streetsweeper and Scrawny. I don't care. Let's forget them and this place."

"Names aren't merely description." She raised her voice, "Try giving instead of taking, because when we give, we get so much more."

"More what?"

"What money can't buy—friendship, love, kindness, a spiritual way of life."

Mr. Conscience mocked Scrawny's voice. "Saint Vonn, why didn't you didn't ask for my name? Don't you care who I am, how I got here?"

A formation of white pelicans flew over. I took a deep breath and watched their broad black and white wings glide effortlessly on the wind. I pointed. "Their sky world must be uncomplicated and beautiful."

Watcher groaned. "Why do I try? Just start walking, Vonn. Let Mr. Conscience be your guide, and ask yourself; *Why am I selfish?*"

CHAPTER THREE

Gravel Beach

Shantytown gave way to a lonely, unspoiled beach with a rock-strewn shoreline built by storms and tended by high tides. I picked my way through driftwood and boulders smoothed by a million waves. Seagulls soared on a stiff north wind, crying out, "You—you—you are alone."

The breakers challenged me to jump in. Wash away the Shantytown filth. "The Sea is indignant," Mr. Consequence warned. "Churning, reaching to smash the living and dead."

A harbor bell rang six times, calling the waning light far to the west to cast long chilly shadows, silhouettes that scouted the sand and rocky shoreline.

Each step produced a different thought. Ideas became painful cravings. Despair fought hope. Fear pulled down willpower. I yearned for a burning drink, that familiar warm glow.

Demimonde whispered in a seductive voice. "My poor little lovely, go home. Come back to me before you lose your hiding place. A drink will warm your body's chill. A pull on the pipe will lighten your outlook. Go home. Live the easier, softer way."

I longed for my party friends, laughter, football talk, a woman's cleavage. An earworm played a favorite song, calling me back to a barroom dance.

But the distant cliff and jagged ridgeline beckoned me, dared me to stand with them between earth and sky. Tightening my jacket, I put one foot in front of another. Why? A hunch. Maybe something important like sobriety awaited me.

A distant glow flickered against a pile of boulders. An old lifeboat lay on the rocky beach. People huddled around a campfire. Could they be Ordonne?

A towering red rock reached into the gathering cloud bank, dwarfing humans to insignificance. Dozens of menacing sandstone faces beyond them guarded a path that climbed and snaked before disappearing in the wilderness. Ism Harbor held nothing but white capped waves. Even the fishing trawlers had anchored in port. Where was Sponsor Ship?

The wind shifted and brought the smell of food, reminding me I hadn't eaten since noon the day before. I felt well enough to approach. Men and women laughed around the fire, toasting fragrant bread with long-handled pie irons. A camper's blue porcelain coffee pot sat on a flat rock at the edge of the fire. Bushel baskets held food, one rounded with fruit.

They waved me over.

They seemed friendly enough. I'd ask for directions.

"Welcome young man, join us. Coffee's ready," a tall man with glasses said.

"Thanks, but I only need directions. Do you know where I might find Ordonne?"

He held his arms out to his sides. "You've found us. Please, sit." He pointed to a tree stump by the fire. "We like answering questions."

"Well, okay, but just for a minute."

The youngest of the three men asked, "Been walking long?"

"Maybe a couple of hours. I had quite a trek from Money Way."

"Pee-yew. I smell Shantytown." The young woman across the fire nodded at my soiled clothes, stood, and headed for the boat.

"Gravel Beach is a long way," another woman said. "That's why we're the last place most alkies look. Rest assured that the trail is dangerous up there." She pointed with a long-handled pie iron to a well-worn trail next to the cliff.

So, there was a way to keep going.

"Really? Even after Shantytown?" Mr. Conscience hissed.

"Here." The first young woman tossed me a roll of clothes. "Change over yonder and throw those in the fire."

"Thanks, but I—"

"Can't say no," she interrupted. "We give, never take. Past the big rocks you'll find a pool sheltered from waves and currents. Wash up and change."

The rolled bath towel held underclothes and socks, a sailor's jumpsuit, deck shoes, and soap. Everything I needed. I returned to the tree stump and threw my old clothes in the fire. The flames hissed and complained, then devoured them.

A man wearing a sweat shirt announcing *Clean and Sober Tribe* handed me a steaming cup of coffee and a porcelain plate rounded with food. "Best hobo pie in Ism Harbor."

"Hobo Pie?" I said.

"Two slabs of homemade bread, cheese, blueberries, and a slice or two of bacon toasted over a fire in a pie iron. The spices, ha, now that's hush-hush." He put his finger to his lips and whispered with a hint of a Spanish accent. "Secret recipe. Food's too hot right now, so rest your plate a bit and then enjoy."

"Thanks."

The taste of real food, the fire, and their lighthearted conversation assured me that I was safe. I was content to simply listen—until I finished my coffee. Then I'd ask couple questions about Ordonne and get on my way. New Life was still my first choice.

"Welcome home. I'm Captain Bill," the tall man said, extending his hand. "This is Captain Bob." He pointed. "Ordinary Joe and Normal Nancy are next to him. Last but not least, the lovely lady who gave you the clean clothes is Serenity. Welcome to our humble tribe. We are Ordonne."

I shook his hand and nodded to the others. "Home? How's that?

"Home is where the heart is, where you're loved," Bob said. "Like any good family, any noble house, we share what we have with those in need. We come alongside and show you a way out of your dark place. We know ways to quiet the tormenting voices without drinking."

"Voices?" I yearned and feared with equal measure. "Interesting. No one could tell me about Ordonne before."

Bob grinned. "You have to find us to ask us. Your name?"

Mister Mouth. "Vonn Thrasher."

"Welcome Vonn," they said.

"Thanks. My doctor, Changelove, said I have a drinking problem too serious for him to treat, so I'm going to Sobriety Island for the cure. I understand that Ordonne and New Life know the way."

"Sobriety Island is what we do," Ordinary Joe said.

"I just came from the Treatment Ship. They have a nice set up, very helpful. What about Ordonne?"

"You're always welcome at an Ordonne fire," Joe said.

I took a bite of hobo pie and sipped my coffee. "Where's your ship?"

"We have one anchored a quarter of a mile out in the harbor," Captain Bob said. "She's a fine, seaworthy craft we call Sponsor Ship."

"I don't see a rowboat, let alone a ship."

Captain Bill explained. "Don't trust your eyes. Like our common enemy, Demimonde, Sponsor Ship is there. Ordonne ships have a spiritual covering that makes them invisible to normal sight. If you want, we can hop in our lifeboat and row out. Once we get next to her, I promise you'll easily see our vessel."

Oh boy. "Hmm, a ghost ship?"

"Sponsor Ship is no phantom. She's real wood and canvas, and has successfully navigated the Sea of Booze thousands of times."

"And there are others?"

Captain Bob said, "Aye. Fellow Ship is one that comes to mind."

I suspected a fish story—another huma-huma snake charmer cure. "Okay then."

The fire's red, yellow, and blue flames danced along the wood, making light and heat. Like the children's game, he who talked first, lost. Nobody moved until Joe cleared his throat, stood, and poked the coals. The burning wood flared, popped, and crackled, sending sparks into the wind.

"Vonn, Ordonne will work for you," Nancy said softly. Despite her windblown gray hair and weathered face, she looked good. In her twenties, she'd have been the queen of every dancehall. "All you need is a desire to stop drinking. Have a little faith in yourself and Ordonne. Our next sober voyage leaves Ism Harbor the day after tomorrow. You're welcome to stay here or come back later. Bring a willing heart, and we'll be off."

"What does a boarding pass cost? Do I need insurance or a doctor's letter?"

"We require no letters or referrals. You'll be fine with a few dollars," Joe said. "We're all about sobriety and people, not money and insurance."

"Uh-huh." I tipped back my cup. "Good coffee. I'm curious about the high ground. Why aren't you camping up there?"

"The answer's in the name. Calamity Ridge," Joe said.

"And the cliff is aptly called Butcher's Bluff," Bob added. A gust of wind fanned the flames, illuminating the camp. A stethoscope hung around his neck, and a doctor's bag sat at his feet. I wondered if he knew Dr. Changelove.

"Everything beyond Calamity belongs to a half-world sometimes called Demimonde," Serenity said. "I think you know what that is."

I stood. "Yes. I do."

She held up a hand. "Vonn, we're here to offer alcoholics a way to turn back before they venture up Calamity Ridge."

"Or end up in Shantytown," I said. "That's a well-worn trail. Are there any alkies up there now?"

"Yeah, somewhere," Joe said. "Unlike you, most of them look and wave goodbye."

Bill said, "The wilderness on the other side is called Bitter End." His long face and glasses glowed in the firelight. He looked almost angelic. "Few get that far. They slip and fall off a cliff. Sometimes we find them floating face down in the Sea of Booze."

Bob studied my swollen knuckles and ear. "Demimonde is cunning and relentless—"

"And deadly," I added.

My back stiffened and complained about sitting too long. I'd be sore in the morning. The wind rolled a thunderhead over the early evening sun. "Smells like rain."

"Yes," Nancy said.

We stared into the fire. The mood fluctuated between serene and awkward. "Well, you've given me a lot to think about. Truth is I'm a little overwhelmed." I stood and stretched with an exaggerated yawn. "Let me sleep on it. Maybe I'll see you guys in a couple of days."

"I hope you have that long," Serenity said. "You don't look so good."

"Believe me," Bill said, "Sobriety Island is more than a three-week boat ride. A sober life is a spiritual journey. One you can't do on your own."

"I need—"

"Vonn," Nancy raised her voice. "Demimonde is patiently waiting for you. If you remember nothing else, remember that we Ordonnes know how to survive Demimonde's deadly ways."

"We know Sobriety Island," Joe said. "Treacherous waters, where to put in, the Pious Trail, and how to get back. You're better off with us."

Serenity stood at the edge of the firelight, white blouse and chinos billowing in the wind, reaching with willowy arms to the heavens. She turned to me and in the sweetest voice said, "We care about you. We care about the thousands of lost souls that will walk down that Gravel Beach for decades to come."

I left without saying another word.

"You're always welcome in Ordonne," they said to my back.

Rumbling thunderheads filled the horizon with charcoals, blues, and splashes of crimson. Wind gusts chanted a storm warning, twisting and rolling the waves into angry whitecaps, reaching across the rocky beach to drag me into a watery grave.

I watched the distant camp at the base of Calamity Ridge. The five Ordonnes doused the fire and pulled the boat to the edge of the water, defying the wind and waves to leave Butcher's Bluff. But to where? I still couldn't see Sponsor Ship. Everyone in Ism said that Ordonne was strange. They were rich, yet Spartan, otherworldly, yet earthly.

Salty wind and sand slapped my face, turning me away and stinging my wounds. Pain, always more pain. "No," I answered the roaring waves. "I want pretty women, soft beds, and hot showers on my recovery boat."

I picked my way along a tree line at the top of the beach. Ahead of me, the sand and waves went on and on. "Hey, Watcher, I don't remember being this far out of Ism Harbor."

No answer.

Run-Vonn-run, run away, drink again another day, played over and over in my head to the old Del Shannon "Runaway" tune.

"Hey, Captain Hook, you're fading wide-right into romancing a drink again," Mr. Consequence announced.

"I can't control ear worms."

"Guess what happened to Mr. Runaway Del about twenty years ago."

"Ear worm. The song is an ear worm, not me."

"Suicide. He shot himself to death with a rifle. At 55."

I wanted to run, but I'd learned I couldn't run from the Con Brothers. Besides, a slip and fall in the middle of nowhere might've been the death of me. So, Ism was a slow, ear-wormy walk back.

"The Ordonnes must be discouraged," I said. "Another day, another lost opportunity, another book with a bad ending."

"Don't be sad for them," Watcher whispered. "They have faith. They love each other."

"They wanted me to stay with them, but where? They have nothing. Ordonnes are nice, yes, but they're old enough to be my grandparents. And the name thing is too weird. Sponsor Ship, Normal Nancy, and Ordinary Joe? They've been in the sun too long—"

"Vonn, remember what I asked you to do? To think about why you're selfish."

"Yeah, I remember," I lied. "And, I don't agree with you. By the way, I thought this recovery-sobriety thing was a nice, uplifting experience. Today has been a forced march through the edge of hell."

I waited for a reply. Silence.

"So, Watcher, what do you think of New Life? The harbor's a nice part of town. I can see Treatment Ship and the crew. Oh yeah—hot babes in scrubs."

I didn't wait for an answer. I skipped a step and kicked a rock down the beach. "New Life Treatment, here I come."

Light rain hurried me along the rocky beach, past Shantytown to Money Way, an easy track through the deserted carnival to my car. As I pulled away, the drizzle turned into a downpour. The first tropical storm of the summer.

The windshield wipers tapped like a metronome, aiding thought and reflection. What a day. What a long day. Started with a nightmare and ended in a tropical storm. And I picked up another voice—Watcher. Like I needed another brain barker.

"Pray about your day," Watcher whispered.

"Pray?" I chuckled, "To whom? No thanks, not me."

Halfway up Saddle Pass, peals of thunder rumbled, and lightning danced across the dark sky. Sheets of rain shook my car. The wiper blades screeched and bounced. I stared into the rainy whiteout and hoped nothing was in the road.

The radio lost all stations, leaving me with skip and static.

I shut off the noise.

"Where's your wallet?" Watcher said.

I felt my cargo pocket then slapped the others. "Gone. Son-of-a—" I pounded the steering wheel. "Idiot! I threw my old clothes and wallet in the Ordonne fire."

"You're sure?"

"I watched them burn."

"Check the glovebox."

My wallet sat neatly on top of old receipts and registrations, safe and sound. When I reached for it, the car hit deep rainwater and slid sideways. I over-corrected, veered off the road, and bounced along the shoulder. Before I collided with a tree, the tires found traction, and I drove back onto the blacktop. The motor grumbled around a sharp corner and up the mountain pass.

"Okay, that's three times. I know that's you. Thanks."

"Amazing what a lost wallet does to a man," Watcher said. "You'd still be at Lee Lea's if you hadn't lost it the first time. That misplaced moment restarted you in the right direction."

"Yeah, well—"

"Now you're driving in a storm, a literal car wreck waiting to happen. You not only lost your wallet again, but burned the poor thing to a crisp." Her pithy voice continued. "But what's this? Abracadabra, wallet is back in your car again—complete with your dope-man's secret phone number. And, what does Vonn do?"

"Run off the road."

"Another successful reset. Works every time."

"I know you're flexing your muscle to show me things."

"You might think you know—but you're guessing. You know nothing. Do you have an answer to my question?"

"Why am I selfish? Hmm. Hangover? Nope. The hippy-dippy recovery row and Treatment Ship? No and no. Lost and almost killed in Shantytown. No selfishness there. Streetsweeper and I got along. She helped me find the rocky beach. But check this out. I stopped drinking. Nothing selfish about that." I bounced in the seat and fist pumped. "In a few days I'll be on my way to Sobriety Island."

"How about the two people looking for their granddaughter?"

"Maria and Louie? They needed more than I could do."

 No answer.

"Watcher." The thunder rippled, and blinding rain shook my car. I checked my wiper setting and slowed. "I needed to find Treatment Ship and Ordonne, not look for lost junkies."

"Your words are still cruel and selfish. Who are you to judge another man?" Watcher scolded.

"Judge? Well, I—

"What'd the judge say when you stood in front of his bench?"

"That he needed order and—"

"We're back," Mr. Conscience said.

"Like we ever leave," Mr. Consequence added.

"You're interrupting my conversation," I countered. "Why don't you get lost?"

"Listen to the wayward boy," Conscience replied. "He's trying to be funny—"

"He's looking for an easier, softer way," Consequence said.

"Recovery takes courage," Conscience said. "He doesn't have the guts."

"Do too," I said. "I decided to go with the Treatment Ship."

"Dear Mister Decided," they sang. "Time's up. You will walk the talk or reunite with Shantytown Scrawny—till death-do-you part."

"She has a powerful crush on you. Rest assured, my friend, I won't get in your way. A conscience isn't allowed in Shantytown. Demimonde is too strong. You'll be on your own."

Consequence chimed in. "Except for me. I have free reign there. You and I, dear boy, will explore new levels of intimacy."

The eastern window amplified the morning sunbeam, illuminating the dust particles that danced and decorated Doc Changelove's office with a layer of shiny flecks. The grandfather clock's ornate, round face smiled, counting each second with pleasure. *Tick-tocks* competed with Doc's scratching pen for equal time. The room smelled of camphor and courage, of witch hazel and hope.

My world had changed. Sometime between Saddle Pass and waking the next morning, hope sprouted.

Doc pointed to the exam table. "Have a seat. Are you sure you want New Life's Treatment Ship rather than Ordonne's Sponsor Ship?"

"Yes. The insurance money is there, and after considering both yesterday, I'm sure."

The phone rang in the reception room. We paused until the answering machine clicked on. He nodded, "A good place to start."

"Start? I get sober in three weeks—"

"I wish recovery were that easy. Demimonde is patiently waiting in every crack and crevice of society."

"Doc, tell me about Demimonde. The line between good and bad, insanity and reality has blurred. Two people drink from the same bottle—one person is and the other isn't—one recovers and the other dies young?"

"Let me know when you solve that mystery. Demimonde is a place, a half-world, where many people from many ages and lands live in bondage."

"Shantytown?"

"Good example." He perched on a stool, rolled across the floor, and plucked a rubber stamp from a carousel. "Demimonde is also the people—or what's left of them—that lost their roots. Lost souls trapped in a half-world without family and history. They can't return to their origin or go forward. They're twisted into something they were never supposed to be."

My heart skipped a beat. I lived in a world stuck between dreams and drunkenness.

He stamped the paper. "Demimondes are mostly individuals hiding on the fringe of society. But there are whole races of them. You see, when a nation conquers another, the King takes the children from the defeated people and moves them to his kingdom. They're taught a new language, customs, dress, and diet. Captors force children to accept a new religion. One day, the children assimilate and become one of them. They grow up and forget their culture and roots."

"But some don't?"

"Some children hate the King's world. They refuse and escape to their homeland. Others find a way to return as adults, and look for what was stolen to confirm their vague memories. But they find no home. Now they're strangers from the past, an unwanted burden that their people reject. Likewise, they find no place in the King's world. Old or new, they're outcasts and never accepted."

I summarized. "Stuck in the middle and nobody wants them."

He handed me the insurance referral. "Get your boss to sign off and you'll be set."

"Treatment Ship's a good decision." I stood and flicked the referral with my finger. "Anything else before I go?"

"Yes. Remember, Demimonde is here today. Syrian refugees stuck on the Greek Islands, American Indian nations on reservations, exiled Jews and Palestinians. Bigotry, resentment, and greed build monsters that endure for hundreds of years. They roam and drift, looking for something that doesn't exist—a better past. They lose hope. Most find drugs and alcohol their best escape from the world they hate. Many lose their minds. All find Demimonde, and live a miserable existence in a half-world."

"That's not me," I said.

"Oh really? Here in Baser we have Demimonde living in hobo camps and homeless shelters, strip-clubs and backstreet bars."

"My neighborhood bar isn't like that."

"What about the boilermaker gang? Isn't that what you call yourselves? Don't you spend more time with them at the Bloody Bucket than with your own family?"

"Well, I—"

"Oh, that's right; you don't talk to family anymore—"

"Because all they do is heckle and complain."

"Don't kid yourself. You live on the fringe just like the others."

Doc donned his stethoscope. "Sit and strip to the waist. I want to listen to your chest rattle."

"Mom and Dad don't understand me," I said between deep breaths.

"Hmm, where have I heard that before? Nobody understands Demimonde people, and they don't understand the world. So, they drift together into Shantytowns, where they find acceptance from each other."

He checked my eyes and ears with a handheld light scope, and nodded for me to get dressed.

"We like to hang out and do things together."

"That's the hook. Then one year the party becomes an occupation and a favorite waterhole their church. If they live long enough, time twists their minds. They become arrogant and proud of the difference between themselves and society. After all, the Demimonde tells them, 'Better to be touched by the backhand of God, than never at all.'"

"That explains the oddballs in Ism Harbor and Shantytown."

"Yes. By the way, have you answered the question, 'Why am I selfish?'"

I clocked into Honesty Manufacturing early the next day, busting at the seams to share my recovery plans. Scary, yes, and otherworldly, probably, but that morning Ism Harbor and Ordonne, even Shantytown were my good news. My co-workers weren't interested. They refused to listen beyond, good morning, or how are you doing. They came to work to make aluminum doors and windows, not to listen to my problems.

A stack of standing work orders rushed us until late morning. Just before lunch, I knocked and stepped into the boss's office. Mr. Honesty looked up from his laptop, frowned, and waved for me to close the door. I sat and stared at my feet. I waited for him to finish typing, wondered what he'd say about a three-week absence, and the cost of treatment. Will he judge me as a slacker, think this is a scheme to get a free vacation? Well, I had three years of seniority, and everyone knew alcoholism was a medical condition for crying out loud.

Mr. Honesty came unglued.

"Vonn, you don't realize how close you are to the unemployment line. I run a manufacturing company, not a drunk tank. We have high standards, and you don't meet them."

"Sir, alcoholism is a medical condition—"

"No, alcoholism is a Vonn Thrasher condition. Yesterday I decided to fire you because you no-showed again. When you do come to work, you're usually hungover and worthless. Even worse, you're the company's standing drunk-joke and the source of every foolish rumor. You distract others and degrade the work environment."

He studied my face. I kept quiet.

"And today, today you come in with this—this Treatment Ship. I know something about alcoholism, and recovery takes much longer than three weeks on Gilligan's Island."

"Sobriety Island," I countered. "People go there to get sober—"

Honesty held up his hand. His pale blue eyes burned the words on my tongue.

"I'm going to support you on this deal and sign off on the insurance. But this is your last chance. If you don't come back sober with your head screwed on right, don't come back at all. Sobriety Island is your last opportunity to prove you're not incurable."

"Thank you, Mr. Honesty, I—"

"Stop. Here's your authorization." He pointed to the door. "Now do something. Make me believe this isn't a waste of money."

I gave Peggy, the secretary, the file copy of signed referral forms. "How's he today?" she asked with a grin.

"A little brutal, but good." Mr. Honesty left little doubt where I stood in the company.

My one-way conversation with Mr. Honesty set the tone for my talk in the company lunchroom with my old drinking partner Johnny Denial and my significant other Minnie Codependent. They were clearly uncomfortable with me quitting; they took my decision as a personal affront and wanted nothing to do with recovery.

"Come on, you're overreacting," Johnny pleaded. "Everyone drinks like us. All you need to do is ease up for a few weeks to prove Mr. Honesty wrong."

Minnie burst into tears. "Selfish ass, you can't pull out and leave me behind. I party to be with you and now you're going to leave?"

"Minnie, come on, Treatment Ship is only three weeks—"

"What about me? We're a popular couple at the club. Quitting will ruin everything."

Johnny grimaced, crossed his arms, and stared out the window.

I tried to console her. "Baby, wait for me. In three weeks, I'll be back, promise. Hey, we'll do that trip to Spain we've always talked about."

"Yeah, right. I guess I'm not good enough. You don't love me anymore."

"Minnie—"

"Don't blame me if I'm with another man when you get back." She stood, kicked her chair out of the way, and stuck a trembling finger in my face. "I turn down better men than you every night."

"Whoa, whoa, slow down now. Where's this anger coming from? You should be happy for me."

She marched out of the room, with Johnny in tow, yelling, "Just go. Go and pretend with somebody else."

Ida Chinwag and Gabby Grime held their iPhones high and recorded the lunchroom scene.

Johnny paused for a close-up. "That boy doesn't care about anybody."

How embarrassing. Why would me being an alcoholic threaten them? How could going to a treatment ship send them off the deep end? I needed to get out of there.

The air conditioner provided a little white noise, but didn't hide the tension that filled the room. Mom and Dad took my treatment ship news with tight lips. I learned many years ago about weighted conversations with Dad—the first one to speak loses. So, I sat in silence, looking at the picture of a blue-eyed Jesus hanging prominently on the living room wall. He had long, light brown hair and a perfectly trimmed beard—a great looking guy. They say he was perfect.

The plastic cover on the rounded club chair squawked when I shifted my weight to cross my legs. Shoes were always left at the front door at Mom and Dad's house. They stared at my feet. My toes poked through my dingy white socks.

Dad spoke. "Vonn, when will you stop this bulloni? Grow up and quit blaming everyone else for your problems." His voice cracked as he fought tears. "Quitting isn't that hard. Just stop drinking. I did."

"But I—"

"A Treatment Ship? Really?"

"I've tried a hundred times. I can't stay away from booze. Even Doc Changelove can't help me."

"This's another debacle, another bullshit Vonn episode."

"He says I need special help—"

"You love to tell the world that we're horrible parents," Mom wailed. "You blame us for everything wrong with you."

"Mom, therapy isn't about—"

"Vonn, do you realize that those boat people or whatever you call them will record everything you say?" She dabbed her tears with a tissue and blew her nose. "They'll spread our dirty laundry all over Baser. Have you thought about the church? They'll strip your father of his deaconship."

"The Treatment Ship people said that my drinking devolved into a disease. Doc said I've fallen into a Demimonde."

"A what? Oh please, you're so brainwashed," she said between sobs. "Tell me where we went wrong?"

Dad pointed to the door. "You swing from one disaster to another. We don't know you anymore. Just go and leave us alone, and please, don't talk about us with your quacks."

What a day. Despite being kicked from one corner to another, I managed all the treatment arrangements, leaving one more day to say bon voyage to Baser. All I had to do was stay dry tonight. Easy? Not for me. Driving home made me thirsty. Music or commercials or the neon signs, who knows? Alcohol cravings turned every minute into an hour.

My habit of stopping by a favorite watering hole had grown into a demanding ogre. When I turned the ignition key, the beast's long arms tapped my shoulder. I recognized every car in the Bloody Bucket parking lot. They were my people. They were waiting for me inside. Every cell screamed for my dark refuge, the stale barroom smell, and a drink.

I rolled by and around the corner. I passed the first trial. But a mile down the road cravings crushed willpower. The voices, my demons that ruled the long hours of darkness, were back.

You're ugly.

You're disgusting.

You're weak.

You'll never stop drinking.

Quitting isn't that hard. Just stop drinking. I did. Right you are Daddy-O. Thanks for all your love and support.

Stop today? No—tomorrow—tomorrow I'll stop. Tomorrow I'll be safe from myself on Treatment Ship. Tonight, I must escape. Tonight, belongs to bourbon. Tonight, I'll dance and sing with my first love and lament the good times gone by.

I drove into the yard with two bottles sitting beside me, singing Auld Lang Syne. Powerful anticipation triggered a melancholy tear when I opened the refrigerator door.

"You're unbelievable," Mr. Conscience scolded. I recognized his elderly, high voice. "Singing to your bottles? Come on—the cat's out of the bag. You're a confirmed alcoholic going to treatment in hours, and you bought two bottles on the way home?"

"Why are you haunting my refrigerator?"

Mr. Conscience said, "Why do you have your head stuck in here every night. Top shelf is a good place to talk."

Mr. Consequence joined the conversation. "Calling Vonn Thrasher, your hangover is ready."

His sarcastic deep voice always made me feel worse. "Why don't you take the night off?"

"Why don't you answer the question of the month? Why is Vonn Thrasher selfish? Why didn't you care enough to ask the poor Shantytowner's name?"

"Why don't you tell me, Mr. Con?"

"Because, dear Vonn Thrasher, you live in fear," Consequence rumbled. "You are too scared to ask. Too frightened to pull a dead man's coat back far enough to see who's underneath. Because you know that one day you will be the one wearing the dead man's clothes."

"That's disgusting."

They responded together. "You're right. Death is disgusting."

"Shut up. Shuddup," I roared and kicked my trashcan across the kitchen, and then slammed down a pint of bourbon.

The last thing I remember was puking in the kitchen sink and staggering outside to listen to the neighborhood. A man and two women bickered, babies cried nonstop, and dozens of dogs howled and barked. They, like everyone else in Baser, hated me.

CHAPTER FOUR

Sobriety

The next morning, scared and hung over, I sat waiting to check into the New Life Treatment Ship. Red-eyed and gray-skinned, my head pounded through waves of nausea. The newcomer's bench was positioned on the gangway so I could get to the railing in three steps. *At least I won't start this by puking on their deck.*

Delivery men hurried supplies up and down the boarding ramp on dollies. The paddle wheeler was leaving in a few hours. The two people waiting with me had already entered the sign-in room and disappeared. *Maybe there was a private exit if you weren't accepted.*

The plaque on the wall above me read:

I am Courageous.

Right. Courageous about what? I was sick about last night. I'm a coward. Despite Strangelove's diagnosis that I was killing myself, I ended last night like every other night, drunk again.

"Next," a voice called from the intake room.

Maybe I should dive off this deck and never come up—dying seemed so much easier.

"Next," the voice repeated with irritation.

What the hell. "Coming, coming." I struggled through the door loaded with luggage and fat manila envelopes of paperwork.

A forty-something lady in nurse whites sat behind a wooden desk covered with patient files. She looked like a Norman

Rockwell character. Not a button or crease was out of place, like the hairs of her flawless afro. Each perfectly shaped and decorated nail told a unique story. A large white USS Enterprise coffee mug sat on the corner filled with pens and pencils. Her desktop nameplate read, **Marge Reality**. She emoted conviction and skill.

"Name?"

"Vonn Thrasher."

"Paperwork." She held out her hand. "Drop your stuff in the corner. This won't take long." She quickly shuffled through the papers.

Without looking up from the forms, she said, "Seems in order."

"Good, you know I—"

"Drug of choice?"

Come clean; tell the truth for once. "Oh, boy—bourbon."

"How long since your last drink or drug?"

"Last night."

"How long since your last drunk?"

"Last night."

She studied my face. "How long since you were sober, you know, dry time?"

The question caught me off guard. I didn't know. How embarrassing. "Well, I—guess, that—"

"Okay. We understand where you're at, but guessing won't help. When's the last time you went ten days without alcohol or mind-altering drugs?"

"Sorry, I can't remember. Ten years, maybe longer."

She wrote. *Patient intoxicated. Estimate that patient has been using/addicted to alcohol most of his life.*

Would I be the theme of one of her nails next week?

They stood in my cabin doorway, all smiles and cheer. "My name's Betty Stoned." She held her hand out. "And this, this is Jack Pickled. We're here to welcome you to Treatment Ship."

"Vonn Thrasher." I shook her hand. Betty wore pink sweats, was about my age, and carried a nervous grin like a shield. Whatever her addictions, they'd taken some of her previous good looks, because old facial scars had defeated her makeup concealer. Her left eye was damaged, lazy, and off-center.

The ship's horn blasted three times as the paddle wheeler churned the water, pushing Treatment Ship away from the Ism Harbor pier. The movement flipped my stomach over twice. I sat on the end of the bed to steady myself.

We were underway.

"Jack Pickled, and welcome aboard." He leaned forward and took my hand. Jack, a man of retirement age, was tall, white-haired, and wore wireframed glasses. "Get yourself settled in your cabin. We'll be back shortly to show you around, and then we'll eat lunch. We have group afterward, and you'll get to meet everyone else."

"Group?"

"Group therapy, you know, for recovery."

"I've never done recovery or sobriety before. This is all new to me."

"Well, we've all been newcomers before," Betty said. "We're a good bunch of junkies. You'll fit right in. We got here early, so Captain Know gave us a cook's tour of the paddle wheeler and made us the welcome committee. Wait until you meet Moneymaker. He's back and doing treatment with us."

"Money who?"

"Moneymaker. His friends call him Money for short. He's big and adorable and funny and rich." She took a deep breath. "They say he owns this ship and most of Shantytown."

Jack said, "You'll meet him. He holds court with his cronies every day in the ship's galley." He checked his watch. "We gotta welcome two more newbies, and you need to unpack. There won't be time for that later. If you have a weak stomach, close your eyes and breathe in regular deep breaths."

On the way out, Betty said, "We'll be back in a half hour and go to lunch."

When the cabin door closed, I laid back and closed my eyes. Un-frigging-believable. *Look where you got yourself now.*

Captain Know stood next to a big man dressed in blue scrubs sitting alone in the corner. The passenger was easily over 400 pounds. His shaved head and face gave him the appearance of Uncle Fester or Buddha—an angry Buddha. Clearly irritated with the captain, he pressed his back against the wall and stared at his feet. His tattooed forearms folded across a belly so large that his elbows were shoulder high. Obviously, he'd enjoyed a long lunch, because the table was littered with plates and chicken bones.

"That's Moneymaker," Jack said as we moved in line toward the food pass-through window. "And the guy sitting over there, waving at me, is Whit Windbag, one of the recovery team leaders."

Food tray and silverware in hand, Jack and Betty split off to Whit, while I worked my way across the busy dining room to an empty table close to the captain and Moneymaker. I wanted to overhear their argument.

"Control issues? I have control issues?" Moneymaker mocked. "No. *I* control, and *you* have issues. Little skipper, you need to practice some acceptance."

"Money, this is your eleventh treatment voyage to Sobriety Island. You can't come and go, picking and choosing what you want to do. We run a serious program with reasonable goals. Will you give our therapy an honest try this time?"

"Who owns this boat?"

"You do." The captain sighed.

"That's right. And fortunately for you and the staff, I like Treatment Ship well enough to sign a lot of paychecks every month. I like the patients too, and enjoy the food and fellowship. I appreciate the therapy and discussions." He paused and pointed his oversized finger at the captain. "But I do what I want, when I want—understand?"

"Yessir, but there is a spiritual recov—"

"Take your clichés and funny little prayers," he bellowed. "And get the hell away from me."

Dining room conversations shut off like a light switch. Even the clatter of trays, plates, and glasses stopped. The captain made his way across the galley. Trying to downplay the rebuke, he made small talk with several patients standing by the door.

Whit Windbag stood up. "Everything's all right, just a little in-house disagreement."

Marge Reality echoed from across the room. "Yes, yes, normal treatment stuff. Please enjoy your lunch."

"Now that was interesting," a new voice said. I'd been joined by a man and a woman. "I'm Muley Mary and he's Pighead Tom. We've been here since early morning. You?"

"Vonn Thrasher. I just arrived." Muley was homely and plump and brandished a big happy smile. She was crocheting a pair of calico mittens. Pighead wore an El Dorado Carnival muscle shirt, displaying his cut muscles for all to see. But I couldn't stop looking at his face. His lower jaw and cheek bones were too large—possibly distorted from long-term steroid use. Were they carnies?

"Welcome aboard. I go by Muley and you can call him Pig. Where're you from?"

"Baser, on the other side of the pass. Good to meet you both. I see you'd rather crochet than eat. Is the food good around here?"

"Breakfast was good all right," Pig said, "good and fattening. They don't post the nutritional value of the ingredients. How can I maintain my fitness program?"

"What about all the cocaine and scotch you use?" Muley scolded. She leaned over and touched my arm. "Sorry. Pig and I go back years in Shantytown. I can't decide if I have dysentery, DTs, or just a plain old hangover. Anyway, I'll pass on lunch."

Pig put his head down and shoveled in food like a ravenous animal.

She almost yelled. "We're old friends ain't we, Pig?"

He paused, and then stuffed a chicken wing in his mouth.

"I've been to Shantytown," I said.

"Lost or trapped there?" she snorted. "There ain't no in between."

"Lost on the way to Gravel Beach. Not a fun place. I was attacked by a street woman and chased out of town."

"Count yourself lucky. Most never leave." She wheezed and coughed. "Sorry, smoker's cough is a mother."

We ate in silence. More accurately, Pig ate. Muley and I pushed our food around and wished our hangovers would go away. Wings, fries, and split-pea soup mocked us.

Pig tossed the last french-fry in his mouth. "We know Money from Shantytown. They say he owns or controls all the dough in that sorry place. He lives in the Drunken Monkey, the nicest club there." He put his index finger to his head like a pistol and squeezed the trigger. "And drinks every bottle he doesn't sell."

"A rich and powerful man. Dangerous too?" I asked.

"Oh yeah. Don't cross Money. But here's the deal. We—you and me, all of us—have a blight that keeps us crazy, chasing the buzz," he nodded and rolled his eyes to the corner. "He's one of us all right. But that man's a special case."

He leaned back in the chair and wiped his face with a cloth napkin, flexed his triceps, and rolled his head around to admire himself. "They should mount some mirrors on the walls in here."

"You know that's not happening," Muley said.

Moneymaker was joking with Betty Stoned and two other people I hadn't met. I didn't want him to know we were talking about him.

"Pig, would you finish the story?" Muley whined.

I whispered, "Yes, please. How is Money special?"

"In Shantytown he's a brutal drunk, a dangerous user. But he's normal sized—I mean he isn't fat. He has a regular build."

"What?" I said. "But he must weigh 400 pounds."

"Closer to five."

Muley leaned forward, "Money is trapped in a crazy cycle; been there for years. After he goes home, he relapses and tries to drink Shantytown dry. Somehow that makes him lose hundreds of pounds. I wished I knew how. I go on a bender and bloat up like Petunia Pig."

"That doesn't sound strange," I said. "Lots of alkies are skinny."

"That's only half the story. One day the booze turns on him. The more he drinks, the more miserable he becomes. No more happy fat man like today. He's full of pain and deadly as a cottonmouth snake." She set her needlework down and lowered her voice. "Get this. When Money is full of self-loathing, mirrors freak him out—make him suicidal. Last year, in an insane rage he broke every mirror in the Drunken Monkey. He's outlawed them in every place he owns. You can't buy one in his stores."

"Incredible. I thought my three voices were bad," I said. "The Con brothers have been with me for years. And since I decided to quit drinking, I have a new voice—Watcher."

"Oh honey, we all have a few voices rattling around in our heads." Muley chuckled. "I call mine the upstairs committee meeting."

"Life in a blackout. Nobody knows why we overdose and die. Stupidity or suicide? Do we really matter?" Pig asked. "We end our stories in jails, hospitals, and lonely graves. Hopefully, somewhere we reach a point of no return—a precipice—where we jump off and sober up." He belched and smacked his lips. "Or die."

"Moneymaker might be a big dog, but he's no different," Muley added. "He's back to Treatment Ship, eleven times now." She stopped crocheting and leaned close. "He never goes to Sobriety Island. He stays onboard as long as he wants, voyage after voyage. As soon as he weans off the booze, he starts eating and gaining weight again—at a supernatural rate—until he's morbidly obese. Sober and fat, drunk and skinny, his size tells us where he is."

"Are there others like him?"

"Not that I know of. But what do I know?" She and Pig stood at the same time. "Ten minutes until orientation and first group afterward. We'd better go."

I turned to leave with the others.

"Young man," Moneymaker pointed at me. "Over here. I want to meet you."

Did he hear our table talk?

"Vonn Thrasher," I held out my hand. "Glad to meet you."

He ignored my hand and pointed at the chair across the table from him.

Loud voices and dishwasher steam flooded the dining room when a ship's steward pushed his cart through the galley's swinging double doors, hurried to Money's table, picked up the dirty dishes, nodded, and scurried away.

I pulled a chair out from the table at a safe distance and eased into place. I noticed the tattoos that covered most of his forearms: a Hawaiian hula girl next to three deep-blue swallows on one forearm. An Asian dragon coiled around the other.

"Navy tatts?" I inquired as I sat down.

"You're quite observant. I am too. I heard my name being used in vain at your table."

Why do I always put myself in this situation? "Sorry, Muley and Pig were just telling—"

"Boat monkeys. They try to chatter and gossip their way into sobriety."

"Well I—"

"Forget it. Show me your tattoos."

"I haven't got one, but I have several in mind."

Awkward silence. Not impressed.

"But I do like to study body art. They usually tell a story, a biography really. For instance, have you noticed Nurse Reality's nails?" I asked, "I think they tell a story too."

"I have, but she doesn't tell patients anything. She's all business."

"Do you mind," I nodded at his tattoos.

"All right. Try to decipher my story."

"Well, you only have five images so they must be important," I leaned forward to analyze the ink on his outstretched arms. "They're on the top of your forearms for all the world to see, so you're proud of them and what they represent."

"Right on."

"The dragon is for Navy service in the Orient—I'm guessing Southeast Asia. Vietnam?"

Moneymaker cleared his throat. Did I see his eyes water a little?

"The hula girl is easy. You got that in Hawaii. But the birds—"

"Three Swallows," he corrected.

"Yes, the Swallows. They tell me that you're a real deep-water sailor—a swallow for every 5,000 miles."

He leaned back and studied me. "I'm impressed. You're the only guy around here that can interpret tatts. You and me, we could be friends."

Is that good?

He stood and hip bumped his chair across the floor. I waited for him to move and followed. He stooped like people with back and hip problems. Still, Money was scary big. I felt like a ten-year-old boy standing next to my dad.

He moaned through his first two steps, "Walk with me to orientation. You know that I own this boat, so I know where I'm going."

I heard voices ahead, a happy crowd. "Sounds like everyone is up front."

"It's called a bow, with landing stages. And yes, we meet on the main or sun deck. They'll wait for me—they always do."

"There are so many words to learn, so many faces to remember."

"If you're like me, I couldn't remember my telephone number when I got here the first time. My head was full of cobwebs and loose screws. All their treatment slang and spiritual platitudes drive me crazy. I tell them to talk to me in plain English, not in funny poems and clichés. If I hear, *it works if you work it,* one more time I'm going to blow up."

Money shifted his hips to the left and right to make his legs work well enough to walk the two hundred feet of Treatment Ship deck. He needed the full width of the walkway, but we got there.

"The ship's calliope sounds nice today. Chad sure can play a steam-powered organ. I've never regretted spending the extra money to hire him."

I didn't recognize the song. "Sounds like the organs I've heard at county fairs."

"*Achy Breaky Heart*. And yes, that's a dumb song."

"But the calliope makes the song fun."

He stopped and nodded back to the galley. "Nobody on this boat has been where I've been and seen what I've seen. If you want to be my friend, don't judge me. Don't try to figure me out. If you can't do that, then leave me alone."

"Judge? Me? How could I? I'm seriously screwed up, sick, barely hanging on. No sir, my hope and prayer is that someone will show me how to stop drinking myself to death."

"Good. There are already too many outhouse umpires here. You'll be surprised at all the Pharisees running around this boat judging who will and won't survive the voyage." He chuckled. "If they're weighing in on my fat ass, they don't have to look in a mirror and weigh in on themselves."

I laughed—the kind of hard uncontrollable belly laugh that replaces fear and pain with feel-good joy. I'd forgotten how wonderful letting loose was, tears and all. I wiped my eyes with my shirt sleeves. "Where did that come from? Man-o-man, you're too funny."

"Vonn, right now you're as screwed up as Hogan's goat. But mark my words, you're going to do this. One day you'll be sober and living life large."

Money oozes charisma. "Hogan's who?"

"Hogan's goat—old sailor's talk. Means that something's broke and stinks to high heaven, like an old Billy goat."

"Thanks. I need to hear that I can beat this disease."

"Yessir, hope you have better luck than I have."

Just before we reached the others, Money stopped, leaned over the railing, and turned to me. I saw grief in his eyes, heard resignation in his voice. "Vonn, don't follow my brand of sobriety. Chaos. I live on Jacob's ladder, always climbing, never getting anywhere, trapped in the middle of this hellhole since I was a kid." He cleared his throat and put on sunglasses. "My brand of sobriety is controlled madness."

We stared across the vast expanse of the sea, watching Treatment Ship churn a white frothy wake. Ism Harbor had disappeared over the horizon.

"I'm addicted to food and booze. I'm a trashcan. If I see food, I eat food. If I see booze, I drink every drop—but never at the same time. I either binge on food, or binge on alcohol. Even worse, booze changes me, makes me a monster. I can weigh 200 just as easy as 500 pounds. If I stay at either place too long, I'll die. So I try, rather unsuccessfully, to stay in the middle as long as I can. This boat is my middle. I'll never recover. I accept that."

"I don't know what to say."

"Then say nothing. Try to like and understand me." He waved his arm in a broad sweeping motion. "For me, all this is junk—a façade—too late." He exhaled a long deep breath, rubbed his hands together, and gave me a conspiratorial smile. "Such is life. Still worth living most days. Shall we join the others?"

Everybody applauded and sang us into our seats when we entered the orientation area.

A strange first day indeed.

There were twenty-six alcoholics on board the paddle wheeler steaming toward Sobriety Island. As the days rolled by, we learned a lot about addictions, in what we came to know as—*focused recovery experiences*—a big flowery term for rooting in each other's past until we freaked out.

They divided us into two groups, Serenity and Freedom, from the names on the rooms where we met every day.

Whit Windbag led my group of thirteen in Serenity; we called ourselves The Gang. The other was nicknamed The Band, led by the aforementioned Marge Reality.

I remember my gang's names. First, there was Moneymaker.

Then Smokey Sarah, who was either puffing a cigarette or impatiently waiting for a smoke break. Relapse Ralph and Blaming Birdie were married, but not to each other. I think they had a love boat thing going on. I'll never forget the Eeyores: Mora Moaning and Gloomy Gums. They could awfulize winning the lottery. We had two sets of three: Round John, Tall John, and Little John. And the three Kathys, aptly named Crazy, Crying, and Coughing—who came with emphysema and oxygen carts. That was the lot of us: thirteen wayward souls stuck together four hours a day.

Why all the odd names? Anonymity.

We weren't allowed to use our last name or reveal our addresses. So, to differentiate ourselves, our appearance or personal history defined our names. Although odd and uncomplimentary, the nicknames were effective. Round John feared he'd never lose his new moniker, and would have it forever.

Delirium Tremens. Who would have thought that after a couple of days off the sauce some of us would see pink cattle and blue bales of hay in their berthing? Relapse Ralph had a long talk with Satan the second night out to sea. Aside from my persistent shakes and auditory hallucinations of my dad contorting my name in anger, the first week was a good experience.

Many lectures and films on alcoholism explained the disease, its effects, and those affected including many celebrities and politicians, some in recovery and some not. We enjoyed great food, self-reflection time, relaxation, games, and workouts. I loved the steam room and sauna. After all, Sister Sweet handed out the towels. I never grew tired of her Usher perfume.

Most days I didn't think about my easy sobriety. Despite my history of uncontrollable drinking and drugging, two weeks without substances encouraged me. For the first time in my life, I came to believe that life without alcohol was possible. Hope flourished.

On the seventeenth day, four days from Sobriety Island, everything changed. A dark foul cloud reeking of seaweed and dead fish lay heavy on the deck, rendering sight and sound worthless. The Delirium Fog, the great barrier around the island, hid threats to ship and crew.

At first, the murky haze hovered at night and early morning. Like many hangovers, the midday sun burned into a bright, cheery day. The closer we sailed, the worse the fog got—nearly impenetrable.

Captain Know deflected our worries. "Our crew has been here many times. We'll pass through this natural phenomenon before reaching Sobriety Island."

Rampant rumors and galley talk focused on shipwrecks and hideous faith eaters and monstrous slippery eels who plucked alkies from the surface and feasted on them beneath the waves of the Sea of Booze. The staff's attitude shifted from *be kind and gentle* to *sink or swim*. They tried to prepare us for an unexpected ending.

My friend, Moneymaker, grew distant and skipped more meetings and classes than he made. Twice, I thought I smelled booze on his breath, but I kept my suspicions to myself.

Money blew up during his last session that Whit Windbag led. Windbag nominated Pighead Tom to chair the meeting. Alcoholics dislike change. In addition, Money and Pig disliked each other. Even worse, they had an unpopular topic. "Why do I—why do you—drink and drug?" The question churned up issues of obsession and insanity, powerlessness and spiritual bankruptcy. Suffering alky-addicts have no good answers.

The habitual talkers, from the Perpetual Victim Camp, PVC, jumped on the opportunity to speak. They droned on about abusive mommies, drunken daddies, hateful kids, ugly wives, and horrid husbands. PVCs experienced each encounter from bosses, cops, and courts as persecution. Despite discounting God or the church, they blamed both for ruining their lives. No wonder they had to drink—maintaining martyrdom drained energy and distorted thoughts.

Blaming and finger pointing required skill because close

friends and family tended to fire back. Whoever or whatever got scapegoated or slandered had to be big—the bigger the better. Any power or institution offered fair game: God, the president, the army or marines, the church as a whole, and the United Nations made great fall guys. Dead people, genetics, and destiny worked. Anything that kept the alky in the victim camp also fended off the dreaded A and F—amends and forgiveness.

This brilliant ploy worked when people obeyed the rules; and there were therapy rules. Number one was insurance and rich parents who refused to pay unless Treatment Ship delivered a Certificate of Sobriety. Noncompliance meant the attendee paid the balance. So, we obeyed group rules like not speaking out of turn—until Whit gave us a haughty nod.

That day's discussion droned around what we called the circle of blubbering love. Crazy Kathy over-described a work relation-ship. Mora and Gloomy faked attention with a box of tissues and journals on their lap. The rest of us mentally checked out, orbited the moon twice, and returned to earth in time to murmur profound advice when our turn came. We only said what Whit expected, so he'd check another success block on our records.

Pig wanted to push the envelope and flex his ego. He called on Moneymaker to share—out of order—not because he cared, but to wind the big man up.

"My turn? Why?" Money cleared this throat and gave Pig a scowl. We waited in a pregnant period of silence. Money sighed. "Okay, why do I eat and drink like a Yorkshire Hog? Because I'm a professional."

Some laughed; the rest remained in orbit.

"I've been an alky most of my life and probably know more about alcoholism than every John and Jane on this boat."

More laughter. Muley barked like a hyena. Pig and a couple others whispered.

"I drink because soap and water can't wash the blood off my hands. But if I drink enough whiskey, the red stain memories goes away for a few hours."

A collective breath-holding followed.

"I can't believe I just said that."

Whit assured him. "Money, what you say here, stays here. You're safe with us."

"Bloody hands. Been bloody for years. Sometimes at night my past haunts me—red gore—red hands, scalded soul, burning heart. And when I'm really down… all the rotgut whiskey and beer and wine in Shantytown can't wash away the blood."

"We understand." Whit pressed his hands in namaste. "Our group therapy and medication will help remove that."

Money flared at him. "Don't pump sunshine up my ass. This isn't my first rodeo. I don't drink and drug because I'm under-medicated or missed your therapy session. I'm not a glutton because my stomach is too big." He stood and beat his chest.

Muley and Betty ducked.

Money yelled at the room. "I use everything I can get my hands on to escape this wretched, bloody life."

"How's that working out for you?" Whit said.

Please no. Windbag, leave him alone. Quit asking questions.

"Works well enough to find oblivion, thank you very much. After this three-week voyage, I'll probably eat, drink, and drug until oblivion make all assholes and pain goes away." He pointed his finger in Whit's face. "That's why."

Pig took two steps toward Money. "You need to sit down and stop cussing." He looked like a Jack Russell facing down a Saint Bernard.

Pig, don't poke the bear.

Money blasted him. "Pig, don't think your dumbbells and roids will help you. Shut up and sit down—now—before I show you places in this room that nobody's ever seen."

Whit moved between them. "Timeout, timeout, please. Everyone take a deep breath and relax."

Pig turned toward a window.

Whit said, "Money, Pig, please take your seats. Let's restart our session and try to get along."

Silence focused our attention on the clock's quiet beat and the whoosh of the steam engine turning the paddle wheel.

Pig broke the ice. "Moneymaker, I'm sorry. Everyone, I'm sorry."

Betty Stoned said, "We have to love and accept one another, help each other if we're going to recover."

Pig asked, "Do you want to finish sharing?"

"No—but I will." Sweating and shaking, Money seemed ready to break. "Isn't what I did—it's what I didn't do. My poor wife and daughter paid dearly for my sins. If I hadn't been drinking. If they hadn't been in the car with me. They'd here today."

Whit leaned over and touched Money's arm. "Thanks. We'll have to stop now because we're out of time. During our next session, we'll discuss triggers and if there's time, forgiveness."

Money threw his hand off, stood, and glared around the room. "None of you have any idea what you're up against." He stomped out and never came back.

That was the closest we came to finding out how Money ticked, and later, why he turned on us.

When the euphoric ambiance of the first two weeks vanished, I wasn't worried. After all, Sobriety Island was the real deal—right?

On the twenty-first day, the end came. Alcoholism's hard reality crushed our lingering, naïve expectations when we woke up to an anchored New Life Treatment Ship. The night winds brought something worse than Delirium Fog—change.

We couldn't see from port to starboard, let alone Sobriety Island. The tight-lipped crew rushed here and there. Breakfast was a grab-and-go burrito.

"We've completed our voyage to Sobriety Island," Captain Know announced over the loudspeakers. "Hurry and get your luggage and assemble on the portside front deck. You have an exciting day ahead of you."

Muley said that ferry boats were coming for us. Others talked about navigating shallow waters.

Then Captain Know gave another order. "Don your aftercare life preservers."

Some alkies balked. "I'm not ready," they complained to any crew in sight. "I'm scared. You're supposed to take us to Sobriety Island."

But the staff pushed us, moving through the front deck and helping reluctant passengers put on their aftercare life preservers. "Everything will be fine. Just stay calm and follow directions."

Captain Know high-stepped into the milling crowd. "Nobody can see the island in this accursed fog. But trust me, the final leg isn't that far. Have faith, swim hard, and you can reach Sobriety Island."

Several people yelled, "What? What do you mean, *you can?*"

"You can—we can't—Treatment Ship has to stop here. The waters around Sobriety Island are too shallow and treacherous for a vessel this size to come any closer in the fog. We're not chartered to stop in any long-term port. So, thanks for being great patients, but we part company here."

Stunned silence spread.

The ship's rigging creaked and groaned. Seagulls overhead cried as though commenting on our human spectacle.

The Captain reverted to a grandfatherly tone. "Remember what we taught you. Everything you need is within you, so never quit on yourself. Now let's have a moment of silence to think positive thoughts."

Waves slapped the bow almost hiding the sobs of some patients. A laugh pierced the hush from the upper decks.

"May the universal spirit of recovery provide you with a kindhearted sea current to deliver you to Sobriety Island," the captain said.

"Do you have lifeboats or recovery craft we can use?" we questioned.

"Nay, nay, we're only equipped for a twenty-one-day sober experience. Now at this time, everyone proceed down the gang plank and into the sea. I suggest that you swim together."

Remarkably, nearly all of us picked up our meager belongings, walked the gangplank, and jumped in like we were taking a swimming lesson. When holdouts refused, the orderlies tossed them and their bags overboard, pulled in the gangplank, and slammed the gate closed.

The pleasantly warm water brought a hot tub to mind.

"Will you tell someone that we're here, just in case we need help?" I yelled over many indignant voices.

"Hell no," bellowed a familiar voice. I could barely see Moneymaker on a top deck. "You're all delusional. Wake up people. Nobody cares about you—or me—or this ship of fools. Ladies and gentlemen, and you too Vonny-Boy, time is money and guess what, your time's up." He howled a cruel laugh, coughed, and spat.

An empty Jim Beam bottle flew from his hand through the fog and landed next to me.

Money said, "Captain Know, I've seen enough, we've earned our money this trip. Turn this bucket around and let's get the hell back to Ism. I have overdue business in Shantytown."

The ship turned hard starboard and started to move. A face peeking from a portal caught my eye. Hoopy, the old sailor from Ism Harbor, waved for my attention.

I'll be damned, that old sot has been a stowaway all along.

Hoopy's portal glided past as the ship moved beyond the aftercare flotilla. He yelled, "Don't try to swim, you'll never make it to the island. Wait for Sponsor Ship."

Then the ship vanished in the fog, leaving twenty-five castaways bobbing up and down like fish bait at the mercy of the lonely winds and craving currents.

The next couple of hours were a mixture of howling and despair. In time most of us regained enough composure to discuss our next steps. Two declared, "Every man for himself," and swam for the island.

When I relayed Hoopy's suggestion, rebuke followed. "Mind your own business."

Then the two swimmers vanished in the distant waves, never seen again.

With no other option, the rest of us decided to wait together. Some hoped a ferry would show up. Others wished a Sponsor Ship would come. Muley and Pighead Tom said they'd never board a Sponsor Ship because the Ordonnes were "A bunch of superstitious religious fanatics."

Secretly, I'd already decided our chances were slim-to-none, and if any boat happened by, I was getting on board.

Watcher rejoined me. "Have you forgotten, 'The Wicket, The Way, The Light, The Truth?' Have you forgotten me, dear boy?"

I looked at the others. No response.

"Don't worry, they can't hear me. I'm here for you."

"Wonderful. Then please call the Coast Guard."

"That would spoil everything. Now that you've passed through The Wicket, you must find and choose The Way, not your way— *the* way.

"Bobbing around in an aftercare preserver surrounded by chaos and sea monsters?"

"Today is all about faith and unity—faith in a Higher Power and sticking together. Those that persevere, my friend, find eternal life. But those that quit, roll over, and drink from the warm Sea of Booze, neither win, nor lose, they simply die— lost forever."

"I wish you'd stop talking in riddles. What do I do next?"

"Singing is good for the soul."

"Singing?"

"What are you babbling about?" asked Phil.

Watcher was gone.

The kindhearted sea currents that the captain spoke of never came. By midday the Delirium Fog lifted enough for us to see we were drifting away from Sobriety Island. As the sun went down, the once laughable stories of gigantic slippery eels became a reality.

My closest treatment friend, Betty Stoned, floated to the edge of the group and vanished. One minute she was there; the next minute she was gone.

The eels had found us and had begun to feed.

The Delirium Fog thickened with the sun's last rays and covered us in utter darkness that blocked sleep and rest. No stars. No moon. For some of us—no hope.

Terror encircled us with fear of the unknown: monsters of the deep and the alien feel of the eel's caress. Scaly bodies slithered along our legs. Flaccid lips nibbled our knees and tugged our shoes. They hissed and pushed us around like pitiful playthings.

We panicked, and called out each other's names. Some never answered. When the sun finally arose and burned off the fog, five more were gone. Phil Blitzed wept bitterly as he told how he was holding Jack Pickled's hand when a slippery eel ripped him from his grasp.

I murmured. "These booze creatures are merciless. They'll take us one by one until we're all gone."

"What'd ya say?" asked Phil.

Overwhelmed by hunger, angry and exhausted, I yelled, "Positive thoughts? Swim together? Ha! How could New Life Treatment leave us here and steam away? Aye, aye, Moneymaker, mission accomplished. No, I tell you, no."

"Damned right," Pig howled. "There's no chance we'll survive another night."

"A sail," someone shouted from the far side of the group.

"The Way," whispered Watcher.

"Where?" we clamored.

"I see a ship over there," another exclaimed. "We're saved."

A vessel under full sail with dozens of oars churning the water approached our aftercare flotilla.

Seventeen survivors cheered and waved.

Confusion arose. Some of us could see the ship, but others couldn't, even when we reached shouting distance.

Muley fussed in frustration. "All I see are seagulls and you idiots. Where's the rescue ship?"

Pig smacked the water. "More bullshit. I don't want be here. I don't want another boat. I'm a paying customer, and somebody better fix this mess now."

But I saw a beautiful, carved long-ship, with a dragon mounted on its prow. The words *Higher Power* blazed across the main sail. Twelve long oars on either side rowed in perfect unison.

"People in the front are waving at us—we're saved."

As the vessel drew near, they lowered the sail, raised their oars, and coasted into our midst. The ship's moniker read, *Sponsor Ship*. A familiar voice, Captain Bill from the Ism Harbor Ordonne group, called, "We have room for everybody. Up the rope ladder, folks. Come aboard. Everyone's welcome."

I whispered, "Watcher, I know this is you."

Ordinary Joe beamed a smile when he pulled me over the gunwale. "Take that aftercare preserver off and throw it overboard, then move to the quartermaster's window. You've got to get out of those boozy wet clothes and dried off. We have a place for everyone."

I made my way through the excited crowd to an open spot at the front of the ship between two men I'd never met. Unbelievable. My position was actually a sea chest, with *Vonn Thrasher* burned on the lid. "Pyrography—my name—now that's cool. How did this get here?"

"Stranger things than this happen at sea. All of ya have one of your own. Hard drinking and lost opportunities paid the price." The man to my left held out his hand to shake. "Legless Mark here from Viler, and the guy on your right is Well-Oiled Ray from Sordid. What's your name?"

"Vonn Thrasher, from Baser way."

"They call me Oily for short. Are you an alky?"

"Sometimes I lie, but yes."

"Us too. Welcome aboard."

My chest smelled of new oak and linseed oil, and like

everything else aboard, the sea. Knee high with leather tabs for latch and hinges, and just large enough to hold two blue sailor's jumpsuits, fiddler's cap, underclothes, socks, toiletries, and deck shoes. Of course, they all fit.

I'd lost everything but the clothes on my back to the Sea of Booze. The clean dry uniform and friendly crew washed hope over me like a gentle breeze and carried away my fear. And somehow, I knew that this was sobriety, my new family, and it was all I could do to choke back tears.

"Look at you in that jumpsuit, a real sailor," Oily said and laughed.

I pulled my cap on and adjusted the brim. "I always wanted one of these fiddler's caps."

Legless stood and stretched his back. "We call 'em fisherman's hats around here, cause we're fishers o' men, rescuing lost and drowning alkies."

I thumbed overboard. "I'm so glad to be free of that mess. Deadly business out there. We had two swim away, and after sundown the slippery eels took six more."

"We understand," Oily said. "The slippery eels lurk on the bottom of the Sea of Booze. The sun drives them deep most days, but they sure enough love dark nights and Delirium Fog. Every sunset they surface to hunt and feed. They can tell who's weak and who isn't. Their favorite prey is alkies, the newcomers that still like the taste of booze."

"Treatment Ship was full of newbies," I said.

"Not after they tossed you guys." Legless aligned his sea chest with mine and sat. "A slippery can eat an alky every day."

Oily said, "That's why we saw so many early this morning. They'd been over your way. Just before we spotted your bunch, a trio of thirty-footers rolled to the surface, eyed our ship and hissed, then dove deep. But enough of that, you're safe here."

"Well-Oiled, I don't have to ask how you got your name. But, Legless, how'd you come by your moniker?" I asked.

He grinned. "A bottle o' rum made me lose me legs. Back in

the old days, I kept a wheel chair in the trunk of my car. Better than falling and good for free drinks. I don't remember anything because of blackouts, but they say that I bragged to have fought in both world wars and Afghanistan too."

"No problems here?"

"No booze, no rubber legs. My real problems are up here." He tapped his forehead. "Now, be the good newcomer and follow where I'm a pointing. Our ship's captains are Bill and Bob."

"From the Gravel Beach Ordonnes?"

"Aye, that'd be them and several others aboard."

"There are twelve rows of oars we call Steps on the port side, and twelve more rows we call Traditions on the starboard side," Oily said. "There are three stations on each long oar called unity, service, and recovery. Our row is step one, and for now your station is service. Ya saw our center mast with its Higher Power sail. Sponsor Ship is powered by the sweat of our brow and God's grace that fills our sail with fair winds."

A ruckus on the side of the ship interrupted my orientation. Everyone rushed to see what was going on. The last two alkies from the treatment ship, Mary Muley and Pighead Tom were angry, and refused to board. Captains Bill and Bob, and Normal Nancy pleaded for them to reconsider.

I remembered what they said earlier, that they would never board any Sponsor Ship. "They're old atheists and want nothing of any higher power. This ship is superstition to them."

"And we never force anyone to join," Oily said.

"Hoist the sail," the Captain Bill commanded. "There will be more alkies in trouble ahead who are willing to accept help."

The three of us were quiet as the ship responded, and we watched Muley and Pighead vanish in the distance, yelling insults at the ship and crew. "Now that's insane," I whispered.

Watcher added, "No more than their decision to swim to the island on their own."

Chapter Five

Sponsor Ship

A well-muscled, clean-shaven, middle-aged man in loose-fitting cotton whites stood in front of me with hands on his hips. "You'll be the newcomer, Vonn Thrasher?" The only hair on his head was two eyebrows and a thick brown handlebar mustache shaped like the ship—long and curled up on each end.

I started to stand. "Aye sir, good to—"

He put his hand up and motioned for me to sit back down on my sea chest. "Who are you?"

"Vonn Thrasher." What's going on?

"And?"

"Alcoholic," whispered Legless.

"Oh yeah, I'm an alcoholic. I'm Vonn Thrasher, alcoholic, sober over three weeks."

"Welcome to Sponsor Ship. I'm Pilot, recovering alcoholic, and number three on our voyage to Sobriety Island. Question: do you want to be here?"

"Well I—"

"A simple yes or no," he said in a matter-of-fact tone.

"Yes. But—"

"The *yes buts* are where we get in trouble. We've no time for that."

"Yes."

"Good. You may call me Pilot. Now, take the cotton out of your ears and put it in your mouth." He put one foot on my sea chest and leaned forward. "We don't have much time before the fair winds become a treacherous gale. We'll have to lower the sails and put our backs into our oars to escape these boozy waters. No choice."

"What can I do?"

"Good question. I like that. That's why I'm here, to tell you about the oars, about step-rowing."

"After three weeks on the Treatment Ship, I'm ready, strong."

"So I see. In my voyages I've seen the rights and wrongs of Sponsor Ship. Lesson number one: you don't need strength as much as technique, rhythm, and unity between step-rowers."

"Well, I—"

"Lesson number two: stop talking. You don't have to talk because everyone else is. We've learned that the first thing out of a newcomer's mouth is usually wrong. We'll ask if we want your opinion. Vonn, if you are going to survive, you'll have to learn the language of the heart—action. Let your actions be your words."

"I, I—"

Legless bug-eyed me and shook his head. "We don't debate."

Pilot licked and raised his finger into the wind, reading the clouds fore and aft. "Listen well, Vonn Thrasher, I'm not in the habit of repeating myself. Fierce storms are coming, and you must help this ship cross dangerous waters. We cannot be blown into the Delirium Fog."

"Yes, sir." Treatment Ship helped me. Here, I help them.

"Now, do you see how long the oars are and how we've put them through the holes on the hull?"

"Yes, I was admiring how well thought out and—"

"There's one oar shared by the three scullers in every step— unity, service, and recovery," Pilot said. "Well-Oiled Ray's on the outside, you're in the middle, and Legless Mark holds the end of the oar. Everyone sits backwards on the sea chests, close together so you can pull the ship forward. The stroke is short and the gunwale high. You can't see the oars in the water or our heading.

Therefore, everyone must watch each other to take the stroke of the oars at the same time, all the time. Do you follow me?"

"Yes, but isn't there a drumbeat to help us stay together?"

"What'd I say about yes, buts?"

"Drumming is what Demimonde does to its slaves, not what we do on Sponsor Ship," Oily whispered. "We're free—now stop gabbing. You're going to get us all in trouble."

I put my head down and pulled the edge of my hand across my lips like I'd zipped my mouth closed.

Pilot grabbed my shirt collar and pulled me close. "You're not a slave—look at me."

"Yes—yes, sir."

"Here's the rub. If your oar gets stuck in the water because you have the wrong angle, the ship's momentum will cause your oar to throw you backwards—all three of you at once. Sometimes breaking wrists, sometimes even worse things happen. That's why your job is all about good teamwork and tempo. If you can't do that—your strength is worthless."

"Aye," said Legless. "Watch, and do what we do, and ye'll be fine. Step one be easy with practice."

Pilot nodded. "The ship and your shipmates always come first. Remember that." He turned and walked the length of the ship, back to the stern, making sure everyone was ready.

"Good grief, that was rough. I think he hates me."

"Naw," Legless replied. "He loves ya. Pilot loves us all in his own rough sort of way. But his first love be with Sponsor Ship."

Pilot went up a short set of stairs two at a time and stood by the ship's wheel. Captain Bill nodded to Captain Bob. "Number Three, shall we begin?"

"All eyes on me," bellowed Pilot. He paused, checking to see every face looking back. "All—Row!"

Everyone took one stroke and waited, holding our oars at a high and ready position. The massive ship responded ever-so-slightly.

"Look at the inside rower on the twelfth step, way back on

the stern," said Oily. "He's the old-timer wearing the bright red shirt. Name is Mister Way, and all of us hold our pace by watching him. We call it silent rowing."

"And—Row!"

Everyone pulled in unison. Soon, our timing smoothed, and the ship picked up speed, turning into the wind and away from Sobriety Island.

That was Pilot's last command. Except for the sound of murmuring and breathing in time with each pull of the oar, we quietly crewed in unison, propelling Sponsor Ship to deeper waters. There, we'd face the storm away from the island's rocky shallows.

The ship's bell rang three times for the third watch.

It rang in the night of the raging tempest.

It rang in the longest night of my life.

It rang in the night's verdict. A call to vote: life or death.

'Twas a bad one all right—a storm that stretched every minute into an hour. During those long minutes between wave and swell, I learned about real power and real fear. To this day, when a ship's bell sounds three times it prickles the hair on the back of my neck.

Angry clouds hid the western sun, dampening our spirits. The sail down and secured, we rowed hard into the face of the storm. Every soul on board understood why. To sail north or south, to bring Sponsor Ship around and head back would give the watery opponent a deadly grip on ship and crew; spelling a certain death at the bottom of the sea.

The wind roared. Waves rolled out of the dark, invisible, except for their whitecaps they wielded like clubs. They broke over the keel, slapping and pulling at men and women. Unsecured items went overboard. Between each wave, swells as deep as the ship's mast tried to finish what the waves didn't—swallow the ship and crew.

Alkies shrieked. The captains bellowed, "Keep rowing, keep rowing. Keep her faced into the wind or the ship'll turn broadside."

The gale raged harder, louder, muting our cries to a single thought: *God save me.*

Then terror hit.

A rogue wave, a wall of seawater that set Sponsor Ship on its stern, swept the length of the vessel and swallowed us in an unholy baptism. For a half minute I was drowning with both hands on the oar. Violent swells flattened and rolled every sailor into a tangled mess of arms, legs, and oars.

We broke through and surfaced into a relentless sea. I coughed up brine. A lightning flash illuminated the deck. Oily and Legless struggled to get back to step one.

Pilot pulled me up and set me at my station. "The worst is over," he shouted over the howling wind. "Row and we'll live."

The ship and storm embraced in a death dance—eternity in the balance. Every whitecap or swell could break the ship's back. Minutes became hours, and hours brought blood-blistered hands, aching backs, and stiff knees. Bruised and exhausted, we pushed on because our only other choice was to die. Every one of us prayed to God, to a Higher Power, even if we didn't understand or believe.

By sunup the worst lay behind us. The fury had subsided, no longer a deadly force. Sponsor Ship and all but two of the seventy-eight aboard survived. Was that a miracle?

I wonder?

I never knew their real names. One was a careless teenager we called Juice. Athletic and invincible—never been sick a day in his life. The other went by Granny; willful and stubborn, she laughed everything off and claimed sobriety was too little, too late. They considered Sponsor Ship a horrid vacation before a return to their old life. Their grave miscalculation made them careless, unwilling to try. Like a hunting lion culling the weak from the herd, the storm took the foolish young and the stubborn old down to eternity at the bottom of the Sea of Booze.

We stunk.

Raw hands accompanied countless scrapes and bruises from my sea battle. My jumpsuit hung in tatters, and my water-saturated shoes weighed twenty pounds from the seawater. The ship's crew suffered beyond seasickness. Puke rolled back-and-forth across the deck. And still we rowed for mile after mile.

Uncontrollable misery morphed into fresh resentments and self-righteous racing thoughts. What did I get myself into? This ain't right. I looked for help and found obstacles and agony. I cannot do this.

Anger boiled over. "This suuuucks."

Everyone laughed.

At me?

"Oh yeah," a loud voice called from the eleventh row. "Rather take your chances with the eels? They've been following us, waiting for ya, ha, ha."

I bristled. "That's not funny. What's this storm got to do with recovery? Where are we going anyway?"

"Boy-O's got a sore brain," someone snorted.

Another said, "Suffering is good for the soul."

A dozen more laughed. "Embrace the pain little bird. Be aaall yourn."

I shouted back. "Suffering isn't funny. We didn't suffer on Treatment Ship. We were okay."

Pilot roared, "Stop thinking so damned—"

A scream came from the Traditions side. "Shuddup." Crazy Kathy stood, tattered and trembling with tears rolling down her cheeks. "You—we didn't do okay. You and that fat bully, Moneymaker, mocked everything. Everything was funny, until it wasn't. And we were the fools. Left bobbing like fish bait."

Not another one. I started to stand. Oily and Legless sat on either side of me, looked straight ahead without expression, put their hands on my shoulders, and pressed me back down. "I'm no fool," I screamed at the naked mast and rolled up sail. "We said a lot of things in group. All of us did."

"Oh really?" Crazy countered. "Remember Moneymaker's parting words? 'Nobody cares about you—or me—or this ship of fools. Ladies and gentlemen, and you too, Vonny Boy, time is money and guess what? Your time is up.' He laughed with cruelty and threw an empty whiskey bottle at us. He was drunk and played you like a cheap guitar."

"Don't scream at me. Money owned Treatment Ship, not me."

"Vonn Thrasher, don't screw this up for us. I might be Crazy Kathy, but I can see. We have nothing to offer—nothing—and they still love us."

Crazy's friends and mates encouraged her to sit and relax. After a few long grumbles and angry stares from the traditions side, the ship fell quiet.

Captain Bill's loud voice broke the silence. "Suffering tells the truth, and the truth sets you free; sets everyone on Sponsor Ship free. But we have to accept the truth, or live a lie and wait for the bitter end." He leaned over the quarterdeck railing. "Watch out for your shipmates. Row for them even if you don't care about yourself. Row like your alcoholic life depends on every stroke—because we just don't know."

Red sky at night is a sailors' delight. Red sky in morning; sailor takes warning.

Indeed, the ancient rhyme told the truth, for a bright blue sky topped a golden sunrise. The ship was anchored. We rested on a calm Sea of Booze.

I shed my waterlogged shirt and shoes, rolled up my pant legs, and stretched out on the oak deck in the sun. My bare feet loved the salt air. Was it too soon to congratulate myself? I'd survived my first twenty-four hours on Sponsor Ship.

The ship's bell rang four times. "Four means ten o'clock in the morning or ten at night."

"Aye, aye, Mister Thrasher," Pilot said. "All right seadogs, up and at 'em. There's work to be done. Let's bandage our wounds and put the ship back in order."

That afternoon, we pulled anchor and headed out under full sail. The smell of biscuits, fried eggs, and bacon reminded us that we hadn't eaten since yesterday. About fifty of us gathered in the chow line.

"Thrasher." The red-shirted old timer, Mister Way, stood behind me. "Your main malfunction is looking to get your feelings hurt. This isn't about you. Do you actually think the storm was a personal problem?"

"No, sir."

"We're all out here together. Sticks and stones may break our bones—*our* bones. But words will never hurt us—*us*. We live or die together. Now, grow the hell up, or you'll be the death of us all."

He waited for an answer. Wisdom kept my mouth shut. I nodded.

Grow the hell up. No joke—but how?

Watcher said, "Good question, dear boy. First-things-first. You must make a decision to trust—me, Sponsor Ship, and yourself."

I turned to find her.

"You can't see me."

Her voice haunted every corner of my being. "You'll see me if you grow up—if you live that long."

"You're scary, but I trust you. You've been with me from the beginning and a whole lot easier to take than the Con brothers."

Silence.

Was that positive or negative? "The ship—well, I'm here aren't I? But trust *me*? Ha, not a good idea. When I get hungry or angry, lonely or tired, the cravings come. And I get drunk, hell or high-water."

"Thrasher, who's ye talkin' to?" Legless called from the back of the line.

"Tell 'em goodbye and get a tray," Round John said. "Or get out of line so we can eat."

I waved and closed the gap between me and Crazy. She smiled at me.

Nice.

"There's a word for what you just described," Watcher whispered. "Ask around, you'll understand when you hear it. Now listen, I know you trust me. That's why I'm still here, but just because you're on board doesn't mean you trust in Sponsor Ship. You must come to believe that you can do this."

I hummed an affirmation.

"Make this your mantra: 'God grant me the serenity to accept the things I cannot change, the courage to change the things I can, and the wisdom to know the difference.'"

I whined. "No way."

"Yes, I know—you're hung up on the God word. Try to focus on the things you can change, like willingness, open-mindedness, and honesty. Ask your shipmates how they do God."

"Shipmates?" I whispered. "Why me?"

"Remember Demimonde?"

I grunted a yes.

"Have you forgotten the thirteen steps ascending a gallows deck and the thirteen twists in a hangman's knot that await you?"

I almost dropped my breakfast tray.

"Sponsor Ship isn't a three-week fix."

Ship life was taxing. Emotionally tough. Never had I been told to shut up so many times. But, as the days rolled into weeks, step work lost its sting. Instead of whining and bristling about my victimhood—I toughened up—I found my place.

I'll never forget the time I told a small group of alkies, "My parents hate me."

They laughed. Two snorted a hold-my-belly burst.

When I said, "My parents aren't a joke," they laughed even more.

A seventh stepper said, "Welcome to my world. I haven't been invited to Thanksgiving for five years, and I've been sober for two, but I have to remember the last time. I arrived drunk and late, puked all over the bathroom, and passed out at the table. Families tend to remember the smell of vodka puke."

I began to trust others, and my shipmates trusted me. They taught me how to use the serenity mantra to escape the awfulized thoughts that clouded my mind. Their frank conversations taught me how to live in the day and sort my moods out by using acronyms like HALT; hungry, angry, lonely, and tired.

Sponsor Ship gave me a new history, a fertile ground to cultivate my spiritual life. With a fresh and improving story, and something good to believe, my past couldn't bind me. I began to climb out of my dark canyons of failure. A kernel of faith grew into a new freedom. Living in the day, in the here and now, I found what I'd been searching for most of my life—sobriety.

More than a way out. Now I belonged to something real, and began to live, safe from Demimonde.

I was home.

CHAPTER SIX

Spiritual Awakening

The ship's foredeck was an out-of-the-way, mesmerizing, peaceful place to disengage. I whiled away hours watching a fine crew of men and women put their backs to their oars in perfect unison.

I closed my eyes and stretched out on a pile of burlap rice sacks. Salt air caressed me, running invisible hands through my hair like a playful lover. Waves sang a cadence, clapping their rhythm on the ship's hull. The keel and oars cut through, joined in, and hummed their chorus. The pungent smell of burlap, rice, and the sea, lifted my melancholy spirit to neutrality. I opened my eyes, and without contempt or preconception, saw the world anew.

Was I daydreaming? Was this meditation?

I was at peace, content to watch the shape and movement of the delicate white filaments hanging in a stunning blue sky. Each cloud was different, an individual, but at the same time united in a common direction. They came from behind, overtook, and shaded our vessel, then disappeared over the horizon that we sailed toward. The heavens, the sea, and the ship were fused on a single nautical bearing. We traveled with the wind, along the edge of the Delirium Fog—not for Sobriety Island.

The easy weeks on Treatment Ship failed to fix my broken thinker; drifting in after-care preservers didn't soften my heart. But voyaging on a carved long-ship full of hardheads,

I experienced a psychic change and gained spiritual sight and hearing. I began to understand that there is a Higher Power, an ultimate authority. God.

Our destination no longer concerned me. Wherever we went I remained happy and willing. I belonged. I wanted this new peace, this serenity to last forever.

Then I understood why I saw Sponsor Ship, while Pig and Muley didn't. Not because they had saltwater in their eyes. They saw, but didn't comprehend, because they lacked spiritual discernment.

I'd been blind to that dimension until my epiphany. Alcoholism dragged me to the edge of death, and until that day, I didn't care. Stark reality stole my breath. Nothing in life is more intense than staring death in the face.

I rejoined Legless and Oily at step one. We pushed the long oar out and quickly fell in rhythm with the others.

I asked, "We're making good time without the sail, but why aren't we headed to Sobriety Island? It seems we're on a parallel course. Are we searching for more abandoned alkies?"

"You found it didn't you?" Oily asked.

"It? Not sure I understand."

His face beamed confidence. "Inner peace and new understanding."

He's been there too. "Yes—exactly that. Peace and understanding and a new willingness."

"You look happy."

"Yeah, I feel different, better. The sense of dread I'd carried so long it became part of me—it's gone. The other shoe, the one that always dropped, is gone. I didn't know how burdened I was until the load lifted. Now I can just be. And maybe, just maybe, stop arguing and fighting about anything and everything."

Legless gave me a friendly elbow in the ribs. "That, me brudder, is a spiritual experience; freedom from self."

The woman sitting in the step-two row in front of me stood and gave me a long hug. Compassion.

"I am so proud of you," she whispered. "You are going to go far in Ordonne."

Our fellow rowers pushed their oar handles down to lift the blades above the water, lest we get slapped about.

"Hi, my name's Ima Stewed, alcoholic. Folks call me Stuey."

"Vonn Thrasher, alky from Baser."

We pulled apart and held hands. "Isn't Baser over Saddle Pass from Ism Harbor?"

Warm hands, strong and calloused from the oars. "Yes, about twenty miles with too many twists and turns." Her red hair was pulled up and covered by a fisherman's hat. A sprinkling of freckles accented her piercing green eyes that locked with mine.

"We always look for wet alkies. That's what we do when we can't reach the island."

Can't reach the island. I heard that on Treatment Ship.

"Hey, you two." Oily interrupted. "Pilot is staring, get over here."

"When the divine winds find us, they'll destroy the fog and fill our sail." Stuey sat down and grabbed the oar. "Then we'll retrieve our oars, and I'll tell you how Sponsor Ship works."

As she predicted, before the midday watch bell, a strong wind came and billowed the sails. Within minutes we picked up speed and ceased rowing. "Pull and secure all oars and bring out the food and drink," the old timers shouted. "Fellowship time."

"Vonn, these are my row-two mates Tanked and Knocked. We're all from Hard Times City," she said as we stood and stretched.

"Easier to just call me Tank. He goes by Knock."

"Sounds good. I'm Vonn Thrasher, Vonn for short, from Baser. You know Legless and Well-Oiled?"

Stuey nodded. "We've been shipmates for a while. Let's find a place on the foredeck where we can talk, and the five of us will tell you how we work around here."

We sat in a circle watching the quartermaster make his way to us with a water bag, generous amounts of baked goods, and hot coffee.

"There's a never-ending supply of wayward alkies trying to

reach Sobriety Island on their own," Stuey said. "Some are from treatment ships. Others fashion homemade dry rafts."

Tank crossed his legs and cracked his knuckles. "Yessir, sometimes one will try to go solo all the way."

"Tank, that's bad for arthritis. Make yer knuckles swell," Legless complained.

"I'll still out row you any day."

"Ahem." Stuey gave both of them an exaggerated grimace. "We try to rescue every wayward alky we come across out here, because nobody has ever reached Sobriety Island without help."

Legless pointed toward the Island. "Aye, the shortest way to Sobriety Island be a death trap."

"An evil fix," Oily said. "Look yonder, even from way out here, you can see the big white shoreline rocks called Relapse Bluff. They're high and slick and home to the baffling serpent hordes. One bite from those cold-blooded beasts leaves even the most sober alky bewildered and senseless."

"You don't want to go there," Knock said. "A while back Captain Bill had the ship a mile out from Sobriety Island looking for wet alkies. One of the crew jumped ship and swam to shore. I guess he had enough of us and sobriety."

"He actually went over the side?" I asked.

"Yip, when no one was looking. He was a great swimmer. Got to the base of the Bluff and up a ways before the baffling serpents attacked him. We anchored and watched him with the ship's binoculars until dark. He wandered in little circles among the rocks. The next morning, he was gone. Something, probably the slippery eels, got him."

"I remember him," Tank said. "Four times a DUI driver. Called him Jumpy John. Nice guy, but he didn't want to be here. We'd talk sometimes. He told me that the courts made him come. Convinced himself that all he needed to do was reach Sobriety Island, that he didn't need us to get there. He planned to jump ship from the start. Yes, sir, he was a good swimmer, I'll give him that. But the baffling serpents got him."

"That's why Sponsor Ship navigates up the coast line," Stuey said. "Past Relapse Bluff and Detox Point, and cuts a wide wake around the poor Abstract State, ruled by King Alcohol and the Four Horsemen." She shuddered and growled, "Bewilderment and Despair, Frustration and Terror."

I mocked her shudder and growl. "King Alcohol and the Four Horsemen? Right—now you're pulling my leg. That's just mumbo-jumbo."

"Funny boy. The Horsemen are real all right, and part of Sobriety Island. King Alcohol reigns supreme in the Abstract State. We avoid that place like the plague because sobriety and the Four Horsemen don't mix."

"We were there a while back. The Four Horsemen stood at the water's edge staring at our good ship." Knock had a wild look in his eye, like he'd just eaten a sour raspberry. "I'm a telling you, Vonn, they're larger than life, black as night and towering like giraffes mounted on horses. And they all carry long swords, tall as you, streaked with dried blood, held high for all to see—"

"The horses. Tell us about the horses," Stuey said.

"Each steed was a different color. Old-timers claim each color represents their curse. Terror rode a dark bay. A blue roan carried Bewilderment. Frustration had a perlino, and Despair rode a leopard appaloosa."

Stuey cupped her hands on each side of her face, like blinders. "Tell Vonn about their faces."

"Faces? They all wore hooded chainmail. You couldn't see their faces. Nothing but blackness, not even eyes. But they saw us and rode those accursed chargers around boulders, beneath cliffs, through tangling thickets and angry surf to scrutinize every Ordonne move until we sailed out of sight."

Legless swallowed his last bite of fried bread and belched. "Aye, King Alcohol and his ghouls eat alkies. They abduct children and attack unwary pilgrims too. Yessir, they know who we be. They're patient and sure of their prize—you and you, and me." He pointed with both hands.

"Surely we won't anchor there," I said.

"Nope. Our port o' call be east o' Abstract and past the Four Horsemen. On the far end o' Sobriety Island be the twelve protected harbors we call da Pop."

I asked, "What, pray tell, is a Pop?"

"Ports of Promise," Legless said. "The Big Book Mountain range blocks the Four Horsemen from campaigning on da Pop. Don't know which of the twelve we'll see this voyage. Captain B keeps da enemy a guessing. Last time we docked at New Freedom. Before that, New Happiness."

Oily pulled out his deck knife and cut a bagel in half. "We put into the Pops to replenish stocks and stretch our legs on solid ground. If a port feels right, usually one or two of us stay on to find our chosen path. Old-timers call them Pious Trails, and there are lots to choose from—most uphill."

"We all have a mountain to climb on the Pious Trail," Tank added. "That's why I'm staying onboard until I know I'm ready."

Stuey leaned over, bumped shoulders with me, and smiled. "I think the Pop is the best part of our voyage. We do a gratitude gathering around a bonfire."

"Gratitude?" I asked.

"We get a huge fire going to let everyone know we're back." She held her hands up. "Food, drink, fellowship. Old friends drop in from all over to share their experiences. Some rejoin us on the next leg of our voyage. Ask around. There are several alkies onboard that have left and returned. They might share their story with you if asked."

"Wait just a cotton-picking minute." I slapped my thigh. "A beach party is fine, but that isn't what Ism Harbor folks said Sobriety Island is about. I'm supposed to attend a retreat center, a sanctuary where hard drinkers are cured. All I'm supposed to do is get there, get sober, and get home. Now you're telling me all sorts of back and forth stories about King Alcohol and his Four Horsemen."

"Well, yes—"

"Baffling serpents? Climbing mountains? Nice, real nice. Sounds like the island could be tough as the Sea of Booze."

Tank walked over and poured his cold coffee overboard. "People believe what they want about Sobriety Island—some good and some bad. I guarantee you this." He put his hand over his heart. "Where we go holds a lot of promise. My worst day on Sponsor Ship is way better than any of my drunken days in Hard Times City."

I managed a smile. "So, Sobriety Island isn't nirvana? Sobriety isn't served on a platter? The treatment staff implied that I could reach this Cloud Nine in three weeks."

"Wishful thinking." They laughed, and I did too—but out of embarrassment.

How could Demimonde and Ordonne and Sobriety Island exist, and nobody back home have a clue?

The conversation moved from me to their lost friends and places I'd never heard of. With my short attention span, I drifted back to Baser. My job, drinking buddies, and Minnie Codependent. She wore a little black dress like a movie star and drank the old Bloody Bucket dry. We were dogs and loved every minute of debauchery and sex.

Demimonde—thirteen turns in a hangman's knot—was I really that bad? Could I save some of my old life?

Oily snapped his fingers next to my ear. "Hello, hello, earth to Vonn. Are we lost in space, romancing a drink? Stay with us."

I lied. "I'm listening."

"You were talking about Cloud Nine. I haven't seen any of those, but we do see plenty of *them*." He pointed to billowing shapes in the sky. "Pilot calls them cumulonimbus. Sponge divers call them Chara, which is Greek for joy. Ordonnes call them pink clouds."

Their vast, majestic anvil-shaped plumes towered for miles. Stunning colors—a kaleidoscope of white, pinks, and reds, with dark blue capillaries—ran along the base. They bloomed and propagated until they hid the midday sun and commanded the heavens from east to west and north to south.

They dwarfed Sponsor Ship into an insignificant speck.

I am a microscopic nothing.

Oily whispered, "The divine winds bring them, and they liberate the mind."

"Yes—humbling."

The five of us moved to the railing and faced the wind. Air currents ruffled our hair and shirts and rattled our pant legs. The delicious tropical breeze carried a host of intoxicating fragrances—coconut, lavender, and jasmine. But something more made me light-headed and giddy.

I inhaled every scintilla. The pink clouds whispered without words, *Hush my child, all is well with you, be, trust, let go.*

Was this paradise? I wept with joy.

Tank arched his back and took a deep breath, closed his eyes, and exhaled for a half-minute. "Always an interesting panorama, gives a fella a righteous perspective."

"What's that aroma?" I said.

"Island flowers, but I think what's puzzling you are the frankincense trees."

Stuey danced a waltz with herself. "They smell of baby Jesus. And God's lovely aroma. And good fortune. Pink clouds make us safe and merry and grateful. When divine winds blow our way, shipwreck and dangers never find us." She twirled and sang, "I am Stuey full of grace. I am elegant and lovely. I am happy to beeeee."

"Yes, yes, you beeeee," Tank and Knock agreed in tune with her.

"Stuey, Stuey, you are pretty and wise," Oily sang. "'Tis true, tis true. We are given grace when the pink clouds come through."

Legless doubled over, laughing harder than I'd thought possible for the old salt.

"I love you," she laughed. "I love Sponsor Ship," she caroled and spun. "Dear Vonn will you love me forever?"

I should have been embarrassed. In the past, Stuey's little impromptu musical would have been mortifying. But I wasn't. In fact, I wanted more. I wanted to laugh like Legless. I wanted to love Stuey. I wanted what they had more than anything.

Call what happened magic or a psychic change, even a baptism of the spirit. Believe whatever you want. In that timeless moment, the curse, the burden that drove me to drink and plagued me for decades vanished. Contempt, my constant companion and master, created by a failed past and a hundred fears real and perceived, fled.

Sweet exhilaration replaced the never-ending threat assessments that drove my alcohol cravings with a sense of wellbeing, a spiritual vision. This supernatural, unexplainable gift was all mine.

I drank from a divine cup and drained every drop. My senses quickened. I saw beyond the flesh, beyond the ship's wood and canvas; I saw sobriety. My five friends glowed with lovely serenity. I was lovely too, sober and worthy of a new life, christened with new peace, and willingness to throw caution to the wind. In my deepest heart, I knew Demimonde and I were done. I would be an Ordonne.

Legless's words broke through my euphoria. "Aye, under da pink clouds be when we find most of da wet and wayward alkies."

I looked to see if my feet were touching the deck.

The ship's bell rang in the new watch.

Everyone sang and applauded.

"Me friends, let's be joinin' the others amidships. Be a good time fer all to listen and learn. They're about to start the evening stories."

Sponsor Ship was a carved long-ship, powered by sails, oars, and the sweat of our brows. Like the decorated Roman galleys and Viking vessels, the impressive figurehead on the prow looked like a dragon. Later, Stuey explained the image represented our great enemy, the slippery eel. Tall as three men and built of varnished oak, two hooded eyes peered over a gaping mouth full of dagger teeth and a serpent's tongue that hung low and curled into a roll on its chest.

Legless and Oily alleged the figurehead frightened slippery eels. Superstition or not, shipbuilders believed figureheads would ward off evil spirits and sea monsters, and mounted them for all to see.

Having met the eels up close I considered that view wishful thinking. What a nightmare we'd had when abandoned by Treatment Ship to float without direction or hope on the Sea of Booze. All their recovery clichés and pithy chestnuts did nothing for us during the night of the slippery eels.

We faced the ultimate terror—an eel feeding frenzy. They scoured our flesh with huge raspy tongues. They whetted their appetites on our toes and fingers, bleeding the water red. They screeched and growled and knocked us around like bathtub toys. And when they were ready, they fed, pulling five under to their death.

"Question," Watcher said. "Why weren't you eaten?" I'd learned she was always with me, listening to my thoughts and words, detailing my every waking hour.

I walked away from the others to an empty spot along the railing and pretended to watch the waves. "You know, I like how you keep an eye on me and all, but do we have to do instant messaging? I'm trying to build a good reputation here. My friends will hear me and think I have wet-brain."

"You have a reputation now? Perhaps a bad one is better than none at all."

"Ha, ha, very funny." I glanced over my shoulder. Nobody was looking. "Could we start scheduling these meetings? In the real world it's called time management."

"When I ask you a simple question, trust me, the answer will never be another question."

"All I have is questions and so far, very few answers. Why didn't I ask the street woman her name? Why didn't the slippery eels eat me instead of Betty Stoned and the others? Why didn't the storm drag me over the side?" I raised my voice. "Dear Watcher, please tell me which question you ask and maybe, share an answer or two."

"I won't tell you what you already know."

"Ditto." I held up my hands and did two finger air quotes. "I won't tell you what you already know."

"Poor little parrot. One day we'll open your birdcage and let the rattling thoughts in your head fly away."

The click-clack of casters rolling across the oak deck made me pause. Mini-Megan drew near pulling a sudsy mop and bucket. Holding a mop stick longer than she was tall, she smiled and said in a girlish voice, "Vonn, we're on an adventure. We're sober today. Ain't life grand?"

Oh please. Now? "Matter of fact, yes."

We smiled at each other for a moment. She said, "Okay," and began to mop.

I perched on the railing with my feet up while she swabbed the deck clean and stepped back to admire her work. She winked, waved goodbye, and tottered away, towing a bucket that nearly matched her weight.

"Watcher, have you noticed what the pink clouds did to me, how friendly I've become? How serene and willing I am to try this sobriety thing?"

"You almost offered to help Mini-Megan. I'm impressed."

That hurt. Why I didn't think to ask?

I leaned back and looked up the billowing sail to the top of the mast. The person on watch in the crow's nest appeared to be at the edge of the pink clouds, wedged in a wooden basket on top of the world. What could he see?

"Answer the question."

"Names. I know your name and most of my shipmate's names. I'll probably know the rest soon enough. But you're really questioning my treatment of others, not forgetfulness. People irritate me to the point of embarrassment. The Street Woman and the Street Sweeper, and just now, Mini-Megan—I don't know what to do or say, so I do stupid stuff. That's who I am."

"True. Tell me more."

"Mr. Conscience and Mr. Consequence stab unexpectedly like festering thorns I can't remove. They torment me day and night, and never let me forget anything. No wonder I drink to oblivion."

Mini's unique laugh drew my attention to the far end of the ship. She'd worked her way up to the quarterdeck and stood beside Pilot. Their upbeat conversation wreathed their faces in smiles.

Captain Bob took Mini's mop, rinsed and squeezed the water out, then handed it to Captain Bill. My heart skipped a beat when he began to mop.

I am so lost.

The mop and bucket were for me and the scullers, skippers, and navigators to use—not her. I was supposed to clean my part of the deck. Knowing who I was, Mini did the chore without a frown or complaint.

I took a deep breath and stared at my blistered hands. "Watcher, my ego is as sore as my hands. I didn't ask for their names because when I'm me, I don't care. I don't want to know. I want them to go away. But, starting today, I'm going to change."

"For thou shalt eat the labor of thine hands: happy shalt thou be, and it shall be well with thee."

"Scripture? Psalms?"

"Good things reside in your sodden mind, dear Vonn Thrasher. Forgive yourself, for your shipmates have already forgiven you." She paused for a moment. "When you boarded the Treatment Ship, the only thing you worried about was your gut. Today you have grown. Tomorrow we'll explore more whats and whys. We might even wander through an answer or two."

"Don't go. You have to tell me more—why me, why not Granny or Betty Stoned?"

No answer—Watcher was quick to start and quick to end a conversation.

She'd be back, and now, I looked forward to more.

I closed my eyes, cleared my mind with a deep breath, slowly exhaled, and then counted one, two, three—all the way to twelve. When I opened my eyes, for the first time I saw that everything about the ship was there for a reason—including me. Beyond her length and breadth, beyond the strength of every rope and yard of sail, I saw that she was so much more than a wooden ship. She vibrated with life and grace.

Sponsor Ship was created to survive raging storms and sea monsters, to find and save the lost and the doomed—the suffering alcoholic adrift on the Sea of Booze. As long as I stayed on board, a willing and growing sober seaman, I had nothing to fear from the slippery eels lurking in the depths.

We stowed the oars and arranged our sea chests into a rough circle of sitting and standing shipmates. Apart from a few alkies who manned the helm and sails, the rest of us, over seventy, fit in the middle section we called the spar deck.

Captain Bill stood with the sun at his back, casting a long shadow across the gathering. He cleared his throat. "Welcome one and all. Welcome to the sixth bell meeting of Ordonne."

A mix of acknowledgments overwhelmed our small talk. He waited until we quieted.

"Fellow Ordonnes please join me in a moment of silence to be used as you see fit. Remember the many that died trying to reach this very moment. Then we'll begin with the Serenity Prayer. For those who don't know the words, just follow along as best you can."

I closed my eyes and refocused my mind. Waves splashed. The sail popped. The main mast groaned. Two seagulls complained from the sky above.

"Prayer," Captain Bill called out.

We joined in.

"Grant me the serenity to accept the things I cannot change,
The courage to change the things I can,
And the wisdom to know the difference.
Amen."

"Amen," I echoed.

Praying my first conventional prayer felt awkward, but I was happy to join in.

Bill sat on the quarterdeck stairs while Bob walked to the middle of the group. "Thanks to our Higher Power, God, we weathered a terrible storm."

He removed his seaman's cap, knocked it against his thigh, and then replaced it, tugging the brim tight to keep the stiff wind from stealing it. "I'm Bob, alcoholic and co-captain of ship and crew."

A mix of hellos, accolades, and other greetings echoed around the deck.

"Storm was a bad one all right, the worst I ever seen. Except for Juice and Granny everyone survived. They were swept overboard." He paused for a few seconds. "Why them? Why not you?"

I just wondered that very thing.

Bob removed his glasses, cleaned them with his shirttail, and put them back on. A long quiet minute ticked by.

Finally, "Grace of God," one said.

"They were new to Sponsor Ship, didn't know our ways," another said.

"Plain and simple suicide—they just quit—let the white cappers take them over the side," said a third.

"Probably. Maybe." Captain Bob shrugged. "Like most alkies, they met a violent end. Friends and shipmates, the sea swept them overboard and buried their future. But are they really gone? Consider this riddle—a secret truth. If you listen, if you incline your ear to the spiritual realm, you can hear them testifying from their watery grave."

People murmured and cried. They cast fearful looks over their shoulders. They mumbled prayers. But nobody laughed or walked out.

Bob waited for us to settle down. "They tell a timeless story without words. Even in death they testify to the truth. If we open our minds, Juice's memory will tell us a great truth—nobody is immune—nobody is immortal."

"What about Granny?" Ordinary Joe yelled from the port side and waved his hand.

"Good question. What do you think she might tell us?"

"That as long as there's life, there's a chance. As long as we wake up without a hangover, we can be a bell-ringing success."

"Well said. Even an immortal teenager, too young to die, or an over-eighty great-grandparent, too old to matter—will find Ordonne works and works well. Let's learn from them and avoid their mistakes. Make their deaths be our locum so that sobriety will be our life."

He did an about-face and said, "Fact—a stormy Sea of Booze belongs to Demimonde, a cunning and powerful foe with a taste for the young and old."

He quickened his step and walked around the circle to catch every eye. "And together, they prey on the spiritual young and the proud. They prey on the spiritual old and the weak. They feast on incurables. My friends, the truth—Juice and Granny didn't want to be here, and the storm granted their wish."

The circle grumbled and whispered misgivings.

"Enough about the storm. Let's welcome the alkies who do want to be here, the fifteen survivors hailing from the Treatment Ship's aftercare flotilla. Will each of you please stand and give your name so we can get to know you better?"

Phil Blitzed stood and lifted his hand. "Blitzed, alcoholic, glad to be here."

"Smokey Sarah, alky too," she said with a timid wave.

"I'm Relapse Ralph, and this is Blaming Birdie." They were still together, a matched pair.

The Eeyores stood next to the Johns.

"Moaning Marta here. Alcoholic or, or, whatever."

"Everybody, I'm Gloomy Gums," he sighed.

"Round John, alcoholic."

"Tall John, glad to be here."

"And I'm Little John, sober a month, give or take."

The three Kathys joined in, Crazy, Crying, and Coughing.

I raised my hand. "Hi, name's Vonn Thrasher, alcoholic from Baser."

Gabby Gay and Slow Dog chimed in, to make fifteen. Only three weeks ago we numbered twenty-six. Moneymaker went back with the ship, plus our fifteen, meant we lost ten in the Sea of Booze.

The other fifty plus quickly introduced themselves. Some by name, and others with fascinating tags. I'd never imagined so many quirky labels. There were alcoholic codependents and enablers, recovering Baptists and Catholics, addicted atheists and Wiccans, agnostics, and a lawyer or two. Two writers refused to say they were alcoholics, telling us how many books they'd written and sold instead. One alky called himself, "Father" and another, "Pastor." Regardless, we were literally, all in the same boat.

Alcoholism respected no one.

"All—all are welcome. Again, I'm Bob, garden variety alcoholic and uh—ship captain." A couple of us caught the irony and chuckled. "Folks, we are not a glum lot. Laughter is healing, forgiving, good for the soul. So if you want to laugh—laugh."

"Aye, aye, Captain," the group hooted.

"We're going to have what we call a brilliant meeting today. Our topic is a hard one—change. Here's the rub–suffering alcoholics change their lives to make their drinking work, while the rest of the world change their drinking to make their lives work."

The bell rang for the half-hour.

"Who wants to start?"

Not me.

"I'll go first." A man with a fully-bearded face and tattooed arms waved his hand. "I'm Al Cinder, alcoholic-addict, and Iraqi-Afghan Vet. Don't have much to say other than rowing makes me strong, and I'm a changin'. Feeling better every day. Don't know why. Might not ever know why, but I'm grateful. And that's as brilliant as I get."

"Brilliant, thanks for sharing, Al," many voices said.

A tall man near the starboard side raised his hand. "They call me Scotch for a good reason. Whiskey was my drug of choice.

I'm a sure enough alcoholic and a Vet too." He nodded to Al Cinder. His shaved head gleamed above a red beard.

"Tell us your story," Pilot said.

"Got a DUI a few years back. I spent a lot of money, got the charges reduced to reckless driving, and wrote the whole thing off as bad luck and unfortunate circumstances. I figured, who doesn't have a scrape with the law every now and then—no big deal. I still had my car and career. My Shantytown friends said, 'Scotch, that was roadside entrapment. There's nothing wrong with you or your drinking. Get a taxi next time.'"

He looked down, then up and took a deep breath. "But I couldn't leave well enough alone. Later that year they stopped me going home. Cop said I was driving erratically."

"The same year?" I asked.

"Almost nine months to the day. The judge wasn't happy to see me. Said I'd never change and gave me thirty days in jail. Cell six, right bunk, eating fried baloney and eggs every day with three other innocent men."

"Innocent?" someone asked.

"Jail rule number one: everyone is innocent. Cops and lawyers are the crooks."

"I thought that was my rule," Gabby Gay catcalled. Everyone laughed.

"Rule number two: next time will be different. I'm going to get out, get a job and work hard, go to church. I'll love Jesus, my momma, my wife, my cousin, and anybody else—long enough to get law off my back."

He stepped to the rail and spit out a plug of tobacco. "Yessir, thirty days. Lots of time to think. I knew I had to change. I knew I had to fix the problem—so I sold the car."

Everyone laughed.

"The DUI was obviously the car's fault. Sold the darned thing and never got another DUI. Then I had plenty of money to party—brilliant."

"Brilliant," we responded with glee.

A young woman raised her hand to go next. "Hi, I'm Merry Mam, wife and new mother. I married mah best friend and drinking partner a few years back. Everything was great until I turned up pregnant. You talk about change. When I found out, I had eight months to go. Eight long miserable months I went without a cigarette or a beer, let alone the other stuff. I'm a tellin' ya being dry was hard, real hard. But I wanted mah baby to be born right, so I white-knuckled through every hour."

She lit a cigarette, threw the match over the side and pulled on the Camel so hard her cheeks nearly collapsed. "I had a beautiful baby girl without a hitch. So, you know—after the hospital and the baby shower, I figure the booze and cigarette fasting is up, right? Life wuz good again—the comfort of a stiff drink, and an after-dinner smoke was just what this mother ordered." She leaned on a friend's shoulder with a smile from ear-to-ear. "Everything was fine until mah frigging sister stops by."

Two seagulls circled the sails and landed on the rigging above Merry, crying out, "Me, me, me." She slapped at them. They took wing and disappeared.

"Stupid seagulls. What do they know about me? Anyway, she's an RN and thinks she knows everything. Just because she's raised three kids and works at a hospital doesn't mean she can tell me what to do. Long story short—she saw me breastfeeding and drinking a beer and freaked out."

She laughed. Nobody else did.

"So, she tells me, 'That's sooo wrong. If I catch you ever doing that again I'll report you to the authorities.'"

"What a bummer. Yessir, I's in a fix until the next day when I went down to the dollar store. I had an epiphany on aisle three: quit breastfeeding."

She paused to look left and right, but got no affirmation.

"Of course, things changed—got worse. I lost mah husband and mah girl—and here I am."

She raised her hands up high, drew a deep breath, and sobbed, "Brilliant."

"Brilliant," the group replied in a subdued voice.

The sharing continued in no particular order. Some stories like Merry Mam were sad, others funny, but all rang a familiar note. Each tale, groan, and laugh, strengthened me in the Ordonne brotherhood.

A bride invited her alcoholic brother to her wedding, warning him, "You'd better be straight—don't show up drunk and make an ass out of me and you." Instead of weaning off for the day, he brought a girlfriend even drunker than he was as a diversion. Of course, the ceremony was a mess—but not his mess—brilliant.

"Brilliant," we agreed.

Another hard drinker told a story about flying home for Christmas. His mom bought the first ticket for December 22. He went to a Christmas party the night before his trip. "Too drunk and hungover, I missed the flight. So, I called, apologized and bought another one for the twenty-fourth. But guess what."

The group shouted. "There was another Christmas party—"

"That I just couldn't miss. Another terrible hangover. I missed that flight too. I apologized, swallowed my pride, and bought a third ticket for the twenty-fifth. Every ticket almost doubled in price, but three times wasn't a charm. I made it to the airport lounge, but was drunk and missed that flight too."

The group howled with laughter. He raised his right hand like he was swearing in a courtroom. "Of course, my family was angry. I knew when the phone rang on the twenty-sixth, there'd be plenty of heckling. To fend them off and quiet my conscience I did what we're famous for."

The group chanted, "You played the victim's card."

"Yes, I did. When asked how I could ruin Christmas, I countered, "How dare you. I wasn't even there? You are what is wrong with this family, not me. You are abusive and dysfunctional. This is on you not me, not me, not me. Victimhood works so well—brilliant."

"Brilliant," we echoed.

A woman relayed her October promise. "I made a solemn oath.

I promised myself and God, that before my fiftieth birthday on January 4, that I'd change, quit—sober up—even if that meant going to Treatment Ship, or boarding Sponsor Ship, or joining Ordonne. Demimonde had other ideas. By Christmas my vow had resulted in me being shot once, choked down, and left for dead. I'm still on the lam from drug dealers I cheated."

Despite her dark brown complexion, she looked gray and bruised red.

"I'm too old and injured to hook or do anything else. I don't know if I'll see another Christmas. Besides trouble, what you see today is all that I have. This, my friends," she pointed to the Ordonne circle and ship's helm, "has to work."

Pilot stood on the quarterdeck studying every face. "If Ordonne worked for me, it'll work for you."

"Brilliant," we shouted.

Turning points and Christmas woes continued.

A father of two chose to stop by his favorite watering hole for one drink before late Christmas Eve shopping. His kids waited anxiously at home. The next morning, he woke up, sick, broke, and without any presents. Demimonde gave him a Christmas epiphany. No presents. This whole holiday thing is a fake. "Kids, Santa Claus is all about money—commercial. We're above trinkets and Christmas trees, in fact, I've been a bad parent for giving presents all these years—brilliant!"

The group responded as one. "Brilliant."

"Who's next?" Captain Bob said. "How have we changed our lives to make our drinking work?"

For several minutes we listened to the sea's ambience; the gulls' cry, the wind and waves' cadence. The ship ticked and groaned under restless sails, popping and worrying their riggings. A deep voice hummed "Amazing Grace."

Captain Bob cleared his throat, "Burning desire—who wants to finish us up? How about one of the fifteen new alkies?"

During the uncomfortably long silence, I studied every seam and stitch in my deck shoes.

"Share your story." A familiar voice resonated from within. "This is your moment."

"Watcher," I said under my breath. "Be a shame to tilt the ship's mood with my words."

"Remember your mantra, *God grant me the courage to change the things I can.*"

"Who ya talking to over there?" Captain Bob asked. "Please, we want to hear too."

Damn.

"Vonn from Baser here, alcoholic," I blurted out, surprising even myself.

"Hi, Vonn," the group replied.

"Good to be here, off the sauce, and free from Demimonde."

"We're glad you're here too."

"I've been an alky since I was a teenager. From the start, every drink was a roll of the dice. Drunk? Of course, but where would I end up this time? Consequences started with blackouts and terrible hangovers, and ended in jails, courtrooms, and hospitals. Nothing changed except my life got worse every year."

"You're telling my story—say on," someone called.

"Quitting was impossible because I didn't want to, so I tried controlled drinking."

Everyone laughed.

"Yeah, that's a joke, a pipe dream. I believed I'd been cursed to live in the bottom of a nightmarish canyon, because everywhere I went was uphill. Forget hopes and dreams—I had despair and delusion."

The group chuckled. My life was funny now that I was sober.

"I kept telling myself the next time would be different. Better. Then one day, it hit me." I leaned out and nodded at Merry Mam. "Cigarettes and jalapeño pizzas were the problem. Cancer sticks and Italian food gave me hellish hangovers, not booze."

They erupted with laughter.

"Everybody knows that bourbon is medicinal, an age-old pain remedy. Why, I obviously wasn't drinking enough to overcome all the trash food and secondhand smoke. I needed more, not less—"

They laughed even harder. Two or three started hacking and coughing.

"How could I be so stupid? I swore off cigarettes and jalapeño pizzas forever—and continued on my merry snookered way. Believe it or not, I quit smoking. Still smoke-free. Of course, my hangovers got worse. I learned something very important that day—the blame game. Always have a scapegoat or a strawman ready. When I no-showed at work or family gatherings, a bad potato or food truck hotdog got me. Brown bottle flu turned into car trouble—never my drinking. Brilliant!"

"Brilliant," howled the group in a joyous voice.

I discovered two basic laws of time:

First, time stops for no one; days roll into weeks and weeks into years. Friendship and charity are irrelevant. In fact, hardship comes before wellbeing.

Second, the longer you live, the faster time goes. At the beginning, each year is a large part of your lifespan; time moves more slowly. Compare an adult's forty years to a child's five, an eight to one proportion while each adult year equals a much smaller portion of life.

Conversely, a year is a fifth of a five-year-old's life—a much larger portion—and takes more time to experience. Spring break, summer vacation, and Christmas seem to last forever. And before the world strips away innocence, children see magic and wonder in every day, an adventure in every treetop, and treasure in every trip to the grocery store.

I lived like a teenager forever, taking three decades to reach twenty-one, then, a fortnight later I hit thirty-five. Hadn't I just graduated from high school?

Sponsor Ship reset my clock. Time slowed, my days normalized, and once again, I saw wonder in each rising sun, adventure, and treasure in every day. I rediscovered some of the magic from my youth. But our voyage tested me. The ship became my school and my mates, my proctor. They pushed me through the challenges of early recovery and made me fight through fear and fatigue to discover a new way of life.

Dr. Changelove would be proud.

Acceptance, like a key, unlocked the door, or should I say—The Wicket.

And The Way? Well, there were no easier, softer ways.

I didn't know yet. But, honesty, open-mindedness, and willingness had everything to do with The Light and The Truth.

The alkies we called Long Timers had earned the distinction from years of sobriety. Like Mister Way, they wore the honored red shirt. They set our pace and established the rhythm of the ship under oar, the silent rowing.

They'd escaped Demimonde decades earlier, leaving behind the daily cravings and temptation to binge. Nevertheless, Long Timers remained vigilant, never resting on their laurels. "Vigilance, young man, vigilance is our watchword."

Their scars from their former hard life remained, giving them a reason to both hate and respect Demimonde. Their best strategy against our common enemy came from equipping newcomers with inner steel to stay away from the infamous first drink. They loved to say, "The first drink is the killer. Opens the door and invites Demimonde in to fill our house with madness. Aye, one's too many because a hundred is never enough."

Ordinary Joe appeared nondescript except for his riveting blue eyes. He was an Ordonne and my favorite Long Timer—carrying almost forty years of sobriety with quiet dignity. We first met on the Gravel Beach weeks before I boarded my first vessel to cross the Sea of Booze.

Many evenings we'd sit in a circle, every ear inclined to hear his insights. He started every conversation with, "Vigilance is the price we pay for freedom from Demimonde."

Then he would wait for us to ask, "Vigilance? How can vigilance pay for our freedom?"

"Newcomers listen and heed. Demimonde's cunning trap seldom loses the sodden souls ensnared in its dark realm. But some do escape. Each of us in this circle, aye, every blessed soul on this ship has escaped."

Joe would look over his shoulder, lean forward, and glance left and right for emphasis. "Demimonde knows every one of you by name and never forgets a runaway. This very hour, the Four Horsemen stand at the water's edge waiting for us."

"But we're safe here," someone said.

"Safe and stalked."

"Stalked?"

"Demimonde's insidious whispers lull us into delusion. We become lotus-eaters, spiritual butterflies that flit and flutter from place to place, dopey, and asleep on our feet. Today cooing to Stuey and Oily, 'all is well.' Tomorrow tickling Gabby's ear, 'you're special, different from the others. Forget all those Ordonne fanatics and go home.'"

He slapped his knee. "Eeyores—stop complaining!"

We flinched.

Someone brayed, "Eeyores," and laughter followed.

Joe continued. "Voices be telling Mora every morning that she's okay, healed—don't pay attention to a brainwashed old drunk like Joe."

"Well I—"

"Gloomy Gums, you're a young and healthy man. Jump ship and go home—be better and different next time—promise."

"I thought guilt was talking," Gums said.

"Like an old lover kissing my ear," Mora said.

"Sings to me every day," I said.

Joe tapped the side of his head. "My friends, our thinkers be broken. Our alcoholic brains are wired with a short. We spark and hear strange things. That's why we must be vigilant at any cost."

Dr. Changelove's words came to mind. *Demimonde lives in every crack and crevice of society and will be waiting for you when you return. Twisting every alky's mind until he's arrogant and proud, and the party becomes his occupation and favorite watering hole—his church. After all, it tells them, better to be touched by the back of God's hand than never at all.*

"But how can this thing reach us?" I asked. "Demimonde is on land, far off in Shantytown and Baser and Hard Times City."

"Nay, nay, fledglings. Demimonde is everywhere. Demimonde owns Shantytown, lives in a hundred Basers—swims in the Sea of Booze, waits in ancient forests and bright cities. Our great enemy is everywhere. Here's the clincher, my friends. A sliver of Demimonde lives in every alky's soul forever, sober or not."

"How then does anyone escape Demimonde's half-world?"

"On our own—we can't. With a Higher Power, with God, everyone can. Shipmates, here's the rub. We have to find a higher power, a power greater than Demimonde—"

"All hail Ordinary Joe. One day we be strong like you," Slow Dog held a wiggly-finger salute over a big grin. The nineties were really hard on him. He didn't have a whole lot left upstairs so we couldn't tell if he was being sarcastic or kind.

We held our collective breath.

Joe patted his heart. "What are we going to do with Slow Dog? Ha, we'll love him. Everyone has a place at our table. And believe me, sobriety does get easier one day at a time."

Dog raised both arms and wriggled a sitting victory dance. "Easy, easy—easy does it." His broken innocence brought smiles all around.

Joe said, "Easier, yes, and scarier with each passing year."

"Scarier, why?" Mora said.

"Every passing year makes my sobriety more unbelievable, more supernatural. That any alcoholic could stay sane and sober for a year, let alone four decades doesn't happen out in the world."

"But don't you get stronger every year?"

"Spiritually, yes, in most ways. Physically, no. Time is no man's friend. I'm speaking of borrowed time."

Joe saw our glazed expressions; he'd lost us. He pulled out

his pocket watch, untied the fob, wound the stem a few times, and then handed it to me.

The old railroad watch was smooth and warm to the touch.

Interesting. Most of the gold had worn off. How long had he carried the old timepiece?

"Vonn, tell us what my watch is doing."

I held it to my ear, and then studied its face. "It's ticking, but the hands are stuck at 11:00 o'clock."

"That's right. Eleven—it stopped there the morning I boarded Sponsor Ship."

"You still carry it like a working watch?" Mora said.

"More than that. It's my one true treasure—it measures borrowed time."

A strong presence washed over me. I could barely breathe. Watcher was back.

As usual, only I could hear her voice. "My dear Vonn Thrasher, do you remember when we met?"

"Yes," I whispered. "But, please, not now."

"Never forget you must turn before you cannot—for you too are living in the eleventh hour."

Joe held his hand out for the watch and nodded. "Go ahead and talk to her. Watcher and I are old friends."

"You know—you hear her too?"

"Aye, from the beginning."

"Not again." The group muttered and moaned and waved me off.

I found a lonely spot on the railing. "Thanks for another awkward moment. This couldn't wait?"

"Tell me about the twelfth and final hour."

"Fine. The twelfth is the hour of judgment, when the ledgers and the books are opened."

"And why must all things be reconciled in the twelfth hour?"

"Because the thirteenth hour doesn't exist. Not for me or for any creature. The thirteenth is too many, too late.

"You remember well, Vonn Thrasher. Unfortunately, so does Demimonde. Lately, your name has become a topic of unpleasant discussion in the half-world. It knows you are growing strong and has no intention of letting you become a Redshirt, let alone another pilot or a captain. You've been given the number thirteen—the number of months until you ascend the thirteen steps of a gallows deck—and the number of twists in a hangman's knot. It's a terrible path that you and I cannot change."

"There must be something I can do. What if I stay onboard, stay sober?"

"Wise choice. But if you relapse, you'll fall in Demimonde's path."

The Wicket, The Way, The Light, The Truth. "I remember."

"Vigilance must be your watchword. Live your borrowed time grounded in the light and the truth, or in thirteen months you will be taken."

Then she was gone.

When I rejoined the group, Ordinary Joe said, "As long as I hear my Goldie tick, I know that payment isn't due. The old Grim Reaper will have to look elsewhere."

He leaned forward with a boyish grin and looked left and right. "Enough dark penance. Let me share a funny story and a secret fear."

"A parable?" Pilot appeared at the back of the circle. "I won't miss this little ode to woe."

"Ha. I thought I sensed your bright and cheery presence."

We laughed and made space for Pilot to sit with us.

Joe took a deep breath. "Now, where was I? Oh, yeah—a funny story and a secret fear, or a funny fear and a secret story—take your pick."

"Story first," I said.

"Once upon a time, when the earth was green—uniforms actually—I was a soldier. And like thousands of others, after a war in a faraway land I came home and became a civilian. I was a hero in my own mind, yet for the next two years, I did my best to drink myself to death."

"You had PTSD," Gabby said.

"No, I had alcoholism."

The group laughed while Joe swallowed more coffee.

"I was a duck out of water, a self-appointed victim. I hated the Army and civilian life equally, but after wandering in nasty bamboozles for a couple of months, I found my solution—cable TV and copious amounts of bourbon. Demimonde told me that I didn't need to work, so I scheduled myself for early retirement. Yes, sir, I burned off two years doing absolutely nothing of value."

We laughed.

"Secrets were my disorder because I had to lie—daily hangovers, bad phone calls, empty wallets, along with skimming and hiding. If I lived another day, I drank another day. Here's the funny part—I thought everybody drank a fifth a day."

The ship's bell sounded for the evening watch change. Supper time.

"Then one Sunday afternoon a man knocked on my door. Don't remember his name right now, but I'll never forget his face. Kind of happy and serious all at the same time. He wanted to talk about football and life and drinking—mostly about my drinking. He got my sodden brain to thinking, and I kind of realized how bad things really were. One thing led to another, and I ended up in a hospital. They got tired of me after a week. So, off to Sponsor Ship I went, wide-eyed and bottle green. But I was ready. Had the bug—wanted what Ordonne had—and been here ever since. Forty years this coming Christmas, sober and still grateful for my forecastle hammock."

He stretched his back left then right, and then touched his toes. His neck crackled and popped.

"I don't know what hurts worse, arthritis or the stretch. Ladies and gentlemen, and you too Pilot, here's the scary part. Four days—forty years."

Nobody wanted to venture a guess.

"The best that I could do was four days dry. Today I'm in my fortieth year of sobriety."

We listened and waited.

"I couldn't stay off the sauce for four days. Never could, never would, and today I have almost four decades. How can that happen?"

"I'll answer that," Oily said. "We are powerless over alcohol. All sobriety and abundant life comes from a Higher Power called God."

"Aye, and from that heavenly station shines a great truth—and my secret fear—I'm a walking dead man. I should have died in the bottom of a young man's bottle a long time ago. I was hopeless, hell bent, and didn't care. That's my truth."

"And your secret fear?" Pilot said.

"Today, I live on borrowed time. Apart from God I'm nothing, gone, a bad memory. Only by his pleasure do I draw each breath. If I jump ship and go back to Shantytown, how long would I last—hours, days, a week, perhaps a month at best? I'm one swallow, just one swallow of bourbon away from eternity—and that literally scares the hell out of me."

Blaming Birdie spoke for the first time. "You'd never do that."

"That's what you and I think, but history proves us wrong. Pilot, do you remember old Fallen Phil?"

"Sure do. Old Fallen, he was the mate that ran the Gravel Beach fireside meeting for years. I think he was a retired doctor or surgeon, had almost twenty years sober in Ordonne. One day he got a letter, bad news from somebody, and over the side he went. I heard that he fell in with Moneymaker and died the same year. Real shame."

"Drinking and drugging are as natural to the alcoholic as breathing," Joe said. "Slipping and sliding around—trying different things is what we do. But Birdie, relapse isn't our worst danger."

"Not the worst?" Birdie asked.

"We quit. Young lady, we quit and run right to prison, asylums, and the grave. Insanity, yes, but that's what happened to Fallen. At a certain point in time he decided that he'd had enough—enough God, enough Ordonne, enough Sponsor Ship, and yes—enough sobriety. And he quit, for keeps, and never came back."

"Oh Lord, keep us far from Demimonde's temptation," Birdie said.

"Amen," someone said.

"Everyone has flashes of insanity from time to time. I had one this morning. And for one unholy moment, Demimonde had me—I wanted out. He waved his arm right to left and slapped the deck. "Done I tell you, with you and you and this ship. Why not jump ship and find a raunchy corner in Shantytown?"

"I don't know. Because wanting Shantytown is insane," Gabby said.

"Nay, nay, wrong and crazy never stops an alky. Fear makes us thirsty. What stopped me was the voice of an angel."

"Angel?"

"I heard Mini-Megan's girlish voice, all happy and aglow, 'Are you feeling alright, Joe? Can I bring you something, a sandwich or a cup of coffee?'"

"How'd she know? Did you look sick?"

"Soul sick maybe. Mini cares enough to look and see a need. She knows how to help. She brought me right out of that rat-race scratching around in my head. 'Yes, you may,' I said, 'and thank you for noticing.' She prayed a little prayer for me. After a bite of bread, I got right back into my duties and haven't thought about a drink until this hour."

Joe rubbed his hands together and studied our faces. "This is my point. Even after all my sober years, that old dark sliver of Demimonde twisted my thoughts. I needed help. And like a voice from heaven, Mini wiped away my stinking thinking."

He stood and reached out for Dog and Gabby's hands. "Healing hands." We responded and completed the circle. "We can't see ourselves. We can see each other; you can see me, and I can see you. So, watch out for one another. Our strength lies in each other, not in time or funny traditions or platitudes. If you slip and fall over the side, don't be afraid to come back, to ask for help. If you remember nothing else, remember this: if we quit, we neither win nor lose, we drown in a Sea of Booze, or die alone in a Shantytown shack."

"On Thirteenth Street," I said.

Pilot and Joe looked at me and smiled. "On Thirteenth Street."

Chapter Seven

Member Ship

Sponsor Ship was much more than a carved long-ship.

She was a spiritual entity. Open to all seekers, yet denied by many finders.

She was the wise Captains and Long Timers who shared their experience, strength, and hope.

She was the sober men and women who spent hundreds, even thousands of hours together in the spirit of unity, service, and recovery.

They climbed the center mast every day.

They trimmed the sail and prayed that God would fill it with goodwill and fair winds.

They manned the twenty-four oars, growing stronger, preparing for life.

We taught each other how to care, to laugh, and to love.

We came to believe that God loved us.

We came to believe that we were worthy and had a purpose.

Those were the best days of my life.

Not every newcomer had this experience. Being cast out of a Treatment Ship to fend for myself wasn't a unique occurrence. Every week we found more lost souls bobbing in aftercare preservers, on homemade rafts, and Ism Harbor dinghies. Hopeful, and like Muley and Pig, stubborn to a fault. They intended to get there on their own.

For every person rescued, another refused to board. That sliver of insanity—Demimonde—twisted their minds with misguided ideas about Sobriety Island. They booed and beat their breasts and called the alkies that boarded brainwashed fools. Then they gave us a one-finger salute and vanished into the Delirium Fog—the same fog that protected the slippery eels from the sun—and provided a daytime hunting ground.

A clear mind, and hindsight, and an awareness of my surroundings allowed me to see that all newcomers and castaways woefully underestimated the slippery eels. No encounter with them was random chance or bad luck. Those intelligent, methodical creatures hunted in schools. Like the hunter and prey relationship of polar bears and seals, we were their primary food source.

Slipperies were never impressed with our medications, prescribed or not. "Pills make us taste better, like salted pork," Captain Bob said. True or not, they followed every ship and castaway flotilla, biding their time, and grew fat on the lost and naïve floaters.

Not every rescue involved wayward and wet newcomers. One of our more remarkable rescues was one of our own, the Member Ship. We had anchored on of the lee side the Coast of Frustration to weather a nasty squall. Legless and I were on watch and had just returned to the quarterdeck after lighting the port and starboard anchor lanterns. We were happy to see a canopy of heavenly stars replace the storm clouds, testifying that we were in for some fair weather. Gentle waves rocked the ship and crew, now peacefully swinging in their hammocks.

A voice rose from the deep. "Hush, little baby, don't say a word, papa's gonna buy you a mockingbird. And if that mockingbird won't sing, papa's gonna buy you a diamond ring."

"What?" I leaned over the starboard rail. "Legless—do you hear singing?"

He pointed into the night. "Aye, be voices out there."

I cupped my hands around my mouth. "Hello, hello."

Legless rang the ship's bell a dozen times.

"Hello out there—identify yourself," I yelled.

"And if that diamond ring turns brass, papa's gonna buy you a looking glass. And if that looking glass gets broke, papa's gonna buy you a billy goat."

Captain Bill was on the stairs. "Who rang the bell? What's going on?"

"I did," Legless said. "Listen—there's someone out there."

"And if that billy goat won't pull, papa's gonna buy you a cart and bull." The singing was stronger, closer, more than one voice.

Lullabies? More likely a trap—pirates or—the Four Horsemen?

"Whoever is singing, identify yourself."

"There, I see movement." Captain Bill pointed to the outline of a lifeboat that emerged from the shadows. "Ship's Captain here, you're welcome to board. Quiet down and come on in."

"Can't," a woman shouted over a man singing, "and if that dog named Rover won't bark, papa's gonna buy you a horse and cart."

A woman screamed. There was mumbled shushing, then, "We have to sing to keep the slippery eels away. Put down the rope ladder. We're coming in."

Sponsor Ship came to life. There were voices in the hold and footsteps in the galley. More lamps were brought to the side.

The beat-up lifeboat sat low in the water. Two women rowed and two men bailed with their hats. The lamplight reflected off several large eyes—circling—the slipperies hadn't yet given up on their prize.

"Skipper Sharon here," said the first person to board. She was a scrappy little blue-eyed blonde barely five feet tall, with a voice that tried to end everything she said with a laugh. "I used to be a liar. Ha, still am but now I've stopped drinking, cheating on cards, and men, I'm the best damned ship's captain to sail the Sea of Booze!"

We looked over the side at the sinking lifeboat.

She grinned, "Well, maybe not anymore. This is Blotto Don my first mate."

"Call me Blot." A ruddy faced man said as two more climbed over the railing. "This is Barfly Bruce and Reeling Rachel, able bodied sailors. We're all that's left of Member Ship."

Member Ship was Sponsor Ship's sister, a fine seaworthy vessel launched in the same year. She had a smaller sail and a few less oars, but had rescued countless unfortunates from every part of the Sea of Booze. Mini and several others had served on her in the past.

"Call them Barfly and Rach. I go by Skipper—we're among friends—right?"

"Bruised, exhausted, and starved," Captain Bill said, and then paused to study them. "And wanted, just like the rest of us. My friends, welcome to Sponsor Ship."

I led them below deck to towel off and change into dry clothes. We returned with Captain Bob and a dozen other sober sailors, freshly bandaged, food and drink in hand.

My shipmates were milling on the main deck, murmuring, suspicious about the situation. Oily spoke for the group. "So, tell us how you lost an Ordonne ship of the line."

Skipper paused between bites of biscuit and sat down. "No booze."

"Yeah, then how?"

"Stormy weather. We were off the coast of Abstract State trying to reach a bunch of aftercare castaways before they passed beyond the rocky Point-of-No-Return. The craving currents and white cappers tossed them violently further and further toward the Four Horsemen."

"Four Horsemen?" someone asked.

"Oh yeah, they were there all right, waiting for the slaughter, horses blowing green rot and bellowing terror. I knew we were in dangerous waters, but I thought I had enough sail to reach the castaways."

"Risky, but we had the time," Blot said.

Captain Bill pulled a three-legged stool up and sat down so close to Skipper that their noses almost touched. "A hard decision indeed. When is the ship more important than the newcomer?"

Fear washed the color from her face. She leaned back, tucked in her chin, and took a deep breath. "The ship. Without the ship there are no more rescues."

"What happened next?"

"Despite the currents, we got close enough to start throwing lifelines. The Horsemen were pacing and howling from the shore—way closer than I ever wanted to be. But we rowed Member Ship hard and held our course. We had time to save them and get away."

"Then we hit a resentment rock and lost the rudder," Blot said. "The helm spun like a fan."

Skipper hid her face in a towel and trembled.

Mini rolled her eyes and hummed, "Hush Little Baby" while refilling our coffee cups.

Barfly had a bloody white bandage wrapped around his head. He stood tall behind her with his hands on his hips, chin up, and walleyed. "We could smell them."

"Smell the Four Horsemen?" I asked.

"Aye, do you know what Bewilderment, Despair, Frustration, and Terror does to us?"

"Nah," Legless said. "Nery was that close."

"They turn the air green, and your skin crawls. They're rancid, worse than a bloated dead cow. I swear there were blow-flies and maggots crawling all over me. Everything I could do not to flip out and jump with the others."

"Jump ship?" Captain Bill said.

Skipper tossed the towel away and stood. "The Horsemen's curse got the crew. They panicked and jumped overboard. Sea of Booze, eels, anything was better than the terror and bewilderment lodged in their minds. With a dead helm the ship busted up in minutes."

Most of the crew stood around us listening like a jury, grimacing, clearly unhappy.

She studied their faces. "I know what you're thinking. Why are you here? Why didn't I go down with the ship?"

"We're listening."

"As God is my witness, I was the last one to leave the ship. I yelled and yelled and ran stern to bow looking for anyone—they were gone. All of them were with the eels except for the three in the lifeboat, begging me to come on.

"The green stench—I retched—maggots and flies were all over me. The ship was breaking in half. There was nothing left to save. Blot, Barfly, and Rach wouldn't leave without me, so I jumped and swam hard to catch the lifeboat."

"Skipper speaks the truth," Barfly said. "If we'd a got into another set of waves, the lifeboat would have gone into the rocks. The last thing I saw before we rowed into the night was Member Ship busted into a hundred pieces—"

"And what was left of the crew and castaways bobbing like chum in the bloody water," Blot said.

We bandaged Rach's blistered, bleeding hands. A blow to the face had given her a black eye.

She hid behind her bandaged fists. "And, and poor Sally Boot."

"Sally Boot—"

"Was a good friend a mine." Her brown eyes were wet. "She screamed over the gale winds. Terror—one of the Four Horsemen on a dark bay steed held her like a rag doll, pulling her apart, limb by limb. Meanwhile the other three paced at the water's edge, waiting for the next half-drowned unfortunate to wash up."

"What a nightmare," Skipper said. "Four out of over twenty sober seamen and castaways survived. Demimonde is a world-class killer."

Captain Bill turned. The full crew assembled around us. "World. Class. Killer. Never forget that our enemy lurks near, because Demimonde will never forget you."

"I'll hate the Horsemen forever," Blot said.

"But the nightmare didn't end there. The slippery eels kept

after us all the way here." Rach stepped to the railing and leaned over the side. "Lifeboat's gone, torn up and sunk."

"Good. And I hope all our shipwreck memories too." Barfly held both arms out wide. "I was this close to jagged teeth when the eel bit off a chunk of the gunwale. I swear the scaly bastard winked at me before sliding back into the water."

Skipper said. "Screaming and beating them with oars didn't help. Fight one off and two more appeared. They were in a feeding frenzy."

"So we figure, let's stop bellowing," Barfly said.

"We're dead anyway." Rach said.

"Using my lowest baritone, I sang my kiddo's bedtime song, *Hush Little Baby*," Blot said. "My voice carries you know, and just like the old poet said: music hath charms to soothe the savage breast."

"Then we all joined in. Probably the only reason we aren't in the belly of an eel right now," Skipper said.

"Unbelievable how fast the Sea of Booze turned on us," Blot said. "At sunrise we were a fine ship and crew. At sunset all were lost, save four hands in a life boat. Some to the Horsemen, some to slippery eels, the rest drowned and lying at the bottom of the sea."

Skipper said, "They were a good bunch. I loved them. I really did."

"How'd any of us survive Demimonde's grip?" Barfly said.

"But, some of us did survive. I see four survivors standing among us tonight," Captain Bob said. "And you, like all the rest of us here, have a purpose, a reason to rejoice and serve. Ordonnes, welcome home."

Chapter Eight

Serenity Harbor

The fourth of twelve ports of promise beckoned to us. The sun traveled the clear, blue sky farther south, telling us that autumn waxed strong, bringing brisk morning air and early sunsets. September? Maybe October? Didn't matter; one day was as good as another on the high seas. Days were impossible to count.

Far from rush-hour traffic and blasting sirens, from calendars and clocks—we measured time with a different ruler.

We made time for each other.

We did the next right thing as opportunities arose.

We changed, grew strong.

We created a new history.

Let tomorrow take care of tomorrow. We were ready to be tested today.

Today—let me love—let me be my brother's keeper.

One day Captain Bill stepped forward at the six bells meeting. "The ship's manifest is full and our cupboards empty. Today we sail for Serenity Harbor, the fourth of twelve ports of promise, to replenish supplies and take shore leave. Some of you will stay there to begin your spiritual journey back to your homes and families in the real world."

Few cheered. "Change? Move on? No thanks, I like a sailor's life."

"I bet the happy ones are staying on board," I said.

"Have faith," Watcher whispered. "You'll never be alone."

"Bittersweet, yes, we'll miss you," the Captain said. "But family reconciliation and reunion is our way, our design. Now, Hazy, will you tell us about Serenity Harbor?"

Despite his stooped posture, Hazy Hap was still tall. A Redshirt's Redshirt and a man of few words. When he spoke, everyone listened.

He walked to the middle of the gathering and stood next to the captain. Fisherman's hat in hand, his long gray beard waved in the wind. "I've been to the twelve ports of promise many times and Serenity Harbor twice. Fledglings, don't you worry. The Big Book Mountain range blocks the Four Horsemen from campaigning on the ports of promise. All twelve ports are safe."

"What's good to eat and drink?" Birdie said. "Tired of ship's grub."

"You're lucky Birdie, Serenity Harbor be the pick of the litter, a tropical paradise smack dab in the middle of Ordonne country. Has a sweet water brook loaded with perch and catfish running into the harbor. A sand and gravel beach bordered by hundreds of trees loaded with spiritual fruit. Better than hard candy I tell you. And anyone open-minded enough to walk a bit, will enjoy many different virtuous vegetables growing wild all over. I swear a stay there will cure the common cold."

"Open-minded?" I raised my hand. "Why would anyone not eat?"

"Be surprised," Hazy said. "Some folks won't try anything different."

I spent the last three days at sea on the twelfth step row, sitting between Bar Rag Brian, one of the youngest men aboard, and Dodgy Sandra, a southern belle trying to dry out from too many mint juleps.

Our ongoing discussion centered on carrying the message, the good news. Dodgy sat holding her knees to her chest, salt and pepper hair and rosy high cheeks shining in the sunshine, sharing her favorite axioms in a delightful Georgia drawl. "When there's an alcoholic in the house, the whole house is alcoholic.

Only takes an alcoholic one year to sicken any home. First with resentment—then comes the blame game."

"Blame game?" I asked.

"Oh yes." She slapped her knee and pointed. "Shuddup, you're the reason I drink."

She grabbed my collar and tapped my chest. "You make me sick. You're ugly and worthless. You can't do anything right."

Dad's screaming tantrums. "Mom and I walked on eggshells for years. Still do, but since I left home, I don't hear him anymore."

"You still hear his voice up here." Bar Rag tapped his forehead. "His voice will never leave you until there's an amends."

Dodgy straightened my collar and patted my chest. "Unlike other games, there are no winners—only losers. Of course, all players have to hide this, and steal that, and lie about everything to make life work. We had to make the house look good, you know. The children reverse roles with the parents, abuse abounds, and violence is sure to follow. By then Demimonde owns the family, title and deed. Lord have mercy, the chaos and never ending lies they tell."

Three pelicans flew inline by the ship's mast studying our twenty-four oars moving in unison. We weren't stirring up fish in our wake so they kept going. Dodgy stood to watch them vanish into the low-lying clouds. "Like those pelicans, they want to fly away. They want to escape, but how?"

"Parents divorce and leave town," I said.

"That hope surfaces too late. Demimonde's half-world has been firmly planted in their minds. The lawless party culture, violence, alcohol and drug abuse infests their thought processes. Good times or bad, no matter what situation they encounter, a needle, a drink, or a snort seems a viable option. Many children are alcoholic long before they take their first drink as this disease passes from one generation to another consuming whole families."

"I saw the abuse too many times with my own eyes," Bar Rag said, a remarkable example of Ordonne. Sun-bleached hair, tanned, happy blue eyes, and full of energy, he was wise beyond his years—only twenty-seven with nine years of sobriety—how could anyone quit that young?

"That was me growing up. But someone carried the message, reached out. You should've seen my family after we got help. The alkies, Mom and Dad and I, now sober members of Ordonne. Everything changed—including the rest of the family. A refrigerator full of food, children's laughter filled every room, fresh paint, and friendly neighbors. No longer was our house sick, but a home of recovery, hope, and good possibilities."

"We did okay, didn't we Son." Dodgy rubbed Bar's shoulder and winked.

"Yes, we did, Mom."

"You're a mother and son—who would've thought?" I said.

"What about your mom and dad?" Bar asked.

"Our last evening together wasn't so good."

"How so?"

"We had dozens of Thrasher house rules, starting with how we breathed and finishing with how we folded clothes. But the number one rule was shoes must be left at the front door. And number two, he who speaks first loses."

Dodgy said, "Control issues."

"They drove me out a long time ago. Anyway, they were tight-lipped and embarrassed about the treatment ship. I sat quietly on a plastic covered club chair, looking at the picture of a blue-eyed Jesus hanging on the living room wall. They grimaced, staring at the holes in my dingy white socks.

"Dad's quivering voice broke our fragile peace. 'Oh, Vonn, when will you grow up? Stop all this drinking and bar hopping bulloni. Sobriety isn't that hard. Just stop drinking. I did.'"

"Recovery rules too? How'd you respond?" Dodgy asked.

"How do you respond to a dry drunk? I left. Actually, I was shown the door. Parents and pain—aren't they the same?"

"Hmm, I know that family. They live on the corner of Dark Street and Depression. Leave them, and come back when you're better equipped."

I said, "Ugh, and I went back for another ass chewing month after month expecting—no hoping—things would be different. What's wrong with my thinking?"

"An alcoholic mind is a broken mind, and no amount of sobriety will fix it. We have to be careful about what we think. Thoughts are the beginning of everything good and evil."

"Tell us about your last day on Treatment Ship," Bar said.

"Do you know an alky named Hoopy?" I asked.

"Ha, oh yeah, I know that old sot," she replied.

"Hoopy was a stowaway. Never knew he was there until the day we started aftercare."

"Aftercare?" Bar asked.

"Actually, aftercare life preservers, in other words, sink or swim time. Program over, money spent, someone else needs your bed. We didn't get a group hug or a chorus of Kum Ba Yah. But we did get the gangplank—"

"Get outta town. You're joking, right?"

"Nope, castaways, complete with delirium fog and slippery eels."

Dodgy laughed and pulled a sugar cookie from her pocket, broke it in thirds, and handed me a piece. "What's the truth about our drinking?"

"Progressively worse, never better," Bar said.

"Likewise, sober alkies get better but never get healed. We're terminal. Nothing we buy or rent will grow our sobriety for the rest of our life."

"Nothing?" I asked.

"Three weeks or a year, therapies and prescriptions have an end—they work until they don't, and that's the problem. Meanwhile Demimonde patiently waits to welcome everyone home."

Bar said, "We're all about finding a higher power—"

"Yeah, Hoopy was hiding out." I raised my voice to change the subject. "But he still yelled, 'Wait for Sponsor Ship. Don't try to reach Sobriety Island on your own.'"

Bar chuckled. "Hoopy and his brother Barnacle have been living on one treatment ship or another for years. Sometimes they're serious and work a program. Other times they just want a place to crash. It's the only life they know. We call that being institutionalized."

"Why would anyone spend their lives stealing around a treatment ship? Crazy, they need to get going and join Ordonne," I said.

"Vonn, don't be so quick to judge," Dodgy said. "Hoopy and Barnacle are good eggs. They've found a way to get by. Recovery means different things to different people. There's a wide spectrum of possible solutions. Some alcoholics work a spiritual program like we do here. Others find their answers in churches and temples, treatment centers and hospitals—even jails."

"A temporary solution is better than none at all," Bar said. "Booze has damaged them. They're doing the best they can with what they have, just like you and me."

"For the Hoopys and Barnacles of this world, their high-water marks come from staying sober most of the time. Sometimes they stow away on the New Life Treatment Ship, sometimes a hospital." Dodgy leaned over and hugged both of us and kissed me on the cheek. "But you, young man, have no right to criticize unless you have a better solution."

"True dat," Bar said. "If they ask us for help, we'll be there. But we, this ship, have a better solution, not you."

Skip, Blot, and several other alkies spent their last three mornings at sea standing on the bow. They were almost giddy about searching the horizon, hoping to be the first to see the sun highlight Sobriety Island's mountaintops.

I, on the other hand, didn't want to see the island. Because when we anchored in Serenity Harbor, I was expected to make a decision. Begin my spiritual journey back to Baser, my hometown, or stay onboard with the captains, Redshirts, and shipmates that I loved.

The Pious Trail was fraught with challenges that would test me. What kind of Ordonne was I? Was I institutionalized like

Hoopy and Barnacle? The Redshirts told me that I was ready. But on my own, would I fail and disappear? I wasn't sure I was ready to rejoin society.

Even after we sailed into port and dropped anchor, I was torn with indecision.

While everyone else hit the beach and scattered, I volunteered to stay on board; working with the quartermaster, going back and forth with barrels of fresh water and various fresh foods that the ground crew had gathered. One morning, Pilot and the Redshirt Mister Way boarded the rowboat with full rucksacks. They were serious business. "Take your time," was all they said while studying the mountain trails with their spyglasses. Then with a wink and a nod, they offloaded and vanished into the forest.

On the fourth day, an evening bonfire celebration marked the end of Sponsor Ship anchorage. We finished refitting the ship, and she would sail with the morning tide. I waited for my turn to go ashore. Skip stood next to me. "Where's your rucksack?"

"Just going to the celebration. I won't need one."

"Wrong answer. You're one of the five that won't be returning tonight."

"That's not my choice. I've decided to stay on board."

"The Four Horsemen smashed my ship on the rocks. You were a castaway on the Sea of Booze. Unfortunate? Yes, but we were rescued, and here we are. Today's the day to move on. My crew and I are staying on in Serenity to find a new place in Ordonne and put down some roots. Pack a good ruck and shove off—"

"No, I'm good here. Not ready for another big change."

"Listen, we've been shipmates long enough for me to see that you're a good seaman. You're sober, learned to follow Ordonne's simple rules, and care about your mates. Now it's time to move up the Pious Trail and share your sobriety with others. Trust God with this: there's something out there much larger than this boat waiting for you."

My first island sunset was beautiful—and foreboding. The sharp autumn air pushed Rach and me under a blanket by a crackling fire. But blankets and campfires couldn't touch the strange chill that gripped me that night. Dread and sorrow, relentless cold spirits that scoffed at strength and station in life, were breaking my heart. The magic of early recovery and life on Sponsor Ship was slipping away. I didn't want to be left behind.

We leaned against our over-packed rucksacks at the edge of the light and watched the Ordonne celebration. Blot and Oily grabbed each end of a big log and with a running start threw it on the blaze. Sparks and firebrands swirled and vanished into the night sky. The salty smell of burning driftwood added mystique to the air.

Pilot and Mister Way returned from their overnight incursion with empty rucks and slipped into the crowd near Captains Bill and Bob. Several long looks told me that they were talking about me and the Member Ship crew.

Two Redshirts, Big Bill and Hazy Hap, played guitar and worked a squeeze box's bellows through one happy sing-a-long after another. Stuey and Mini played ringing tambourines and led a conga line that circled the camp and wandered through the edge of the surf. Everyone celebrated sobriety and the next voyage into the deep blue Sea of Booze.

"You're quiet tonight. Whatcha thinking about?" Rach asked.

"Oh, nothing. Just taking it all in—"

Barfly joined us under the blanket. "Back on the corner of Dark Street and Depression?"

"Ha, no, well maybe. I got mixed emotions—I'm sad and grateful. My life, sober and all, is better than ever." The wind shifted and we held our breath while smoke passed over us. "Even though I'm sitting with a shipload of friends, I still feel cold and lonely. I'm really down about Sponsor Ship leaving tomorrow without me—"

"Without us. The Member Ship crew and you, the last I heard."

"Scary all right," Barfly said. "Never been here or on a spiritual journey before."

"A toast," I said. "Back home to friends and family." We held our guava glasses high and clacked them together. Bright red nectar splashed on our hands.

"Salute—to a world complete with Ordonne and Demimonde," Rach said.

"To the ones that never made it, Juice and Granny," Barfly said.

I sucked the salty-sweet liquid off my fingers. "To the ones who vanished—dead or alive—who knows. To Moneymaker and all the gray-faced Shantytowners—"

Pilot waved me over from the other side of the fire. "Vonn Thrasher—a word please."

I whispered to my friends, "Watch my stuff. I hope I'll be right back."

We stood next to each other warming our hands by the fire. Pilot's eyes looked glazed from obvious contemplation. A gust of wind fanned the flames. Stinging embers and smoke swirled, burning our eyes, and driving everyone back.

"Blot, would you leave the damned fired alone?" Skipper yelled over the singing. "You're killing me with smoke."

Blot moaned and rubbed his watering eyes. "Not me. I only threw a log on the fire. The wind can't make up its mind tonight."

Was there a message hidden in the tiny particles rising around us? Yes, I could taste it—bitter humility mixed with patience and respect.

I held my peace.

Pilot asked, "Mister Vonn, have you ever heard of the Magic Twenty?"

"No. What is it?"

He pulled a money clip out of his pocket and handed it to me. I saw Andrew Jackson's wavy hair pictured on a folded green bill. Spendable currency. I didn't have a dime to my name.

"For me? Traveling money? Thank you, sir."

"A long time ago when Sponsor Ship still smelled of new wood and canvas, there was a Redshirt called Deadpan. He was one of the original Ordonnes that led me and a hundred other newcomers through the step stations. He gave me that clip and magic twenty-dollar bill when I began my journey. More powerful than paper and coin, it helped me become Pilot. I hope it will help restore you as well."

I rubbed the smooth silver clip, feeling better about my journey already. "Thanks. Deadpan? That's a serious name. Where's he today?"

"He lived to be ninety before he died in his own bed, sober and loved by many. But back in the day we were all out here together."

Pilot pointed to the end of a log someone had pulled up to sit on, with enough room for both of us.

"Do you understand spiritual tools?"

"You mean churchy things, like prophecy and speaking in tongues?"

Pilot pulled out a plug of tobacco and bit the corner off, wallowed it around against his cheek, and spit a stream as black as coal. "No, those are spiritual *gifts*. In Ordonne we receive spiritual *tools* to benefit ourselves and Ordonne as a whole. All spiritual tools have a blessing, an enabling. And some, like that Magic Twenty carry a curse—"

"Naturally, nothing is free and easy in Ordonne."

"Vonn, do yourself a favor and quit looking for free and easy."

We stared at each other for a minute. I grinned.

"Now listen. Every time you need money for the offering basket, food or clothing, the Magic Twenty will be there. Money for the kids or to help a friend, even a beggar on the street. If you spend your twenty in the morning and need more in the afternoon, the clip will magically refill in your pocket or bag."

"I'm with you."

"Good." He walked to the edge of the fire and spit. The flames hissed a reply. "If we do what's right it comes back in kind. I just gave you mine, but the Magic Twenty will be back next time I have a need, in my pocket, clip and all."

"Wow, what a great gift."

"True. But blessed money comes with a curse—if we ever blow money like we used to, the Magic Twenty will know that you broke the promise and vanish. So, no more drugs and alcohol, no cathouses and casinos, not even a pirated movie."

"Gone forever."

"But not the curse—oh no—that stays with you for life."

"The curse being that I lose the twenty forever?"

"Aye, and much more." Pilot plucked the clip out of my hand in the blink of an eye. "And just like that, the twenty will take every dime and dollar you have." He opened both hands and waved. "Gone."

I studied his bare hands, arms, and the sand beneath our feet, then looked in his eyes. "Gone?"

"You'll be forever poor, cursed with poverty that you never thought possible. Because you can't make money fast enough that the curse won't spend every dollar before you get to the bank."

"That's how Shantytown—"

"Yes, the sorry truth of too many Shantytowners."

"Hmm—I don't know. Having a perpetual twenty-dollar bill is great. But a curse? I don't trust myself. Make a mistake and blow it on booze and junk and I'm Shantytown poor forever—too risky for me. Have you given this to other Ordonnes?"

"A handful. And two refused to accept."

"Have you heard how they did?"

"Now and then. I think they do well somewhere back in the world. But the other two—"

"Yes?"

"One's dead and the other's been stuck in Shantytown for a long time. You see, neither one intended to stay sober. Sobriety Island was just another bump in the road. Vonn, the Magic Twenty doesn't give you a better heart. It makes you a better servant."

"Well, I—"

"You'd be wise to pass if it wasn't for the Moral Compass."

"Moral Compass? That a navigation instrument, magnetic north and all that?"

"Better than a chunk of glass and metal with a needle that points north. Moral Compass is Ordonne's good spirit, a unique consciousness that dwells in your heart and mind. It knows your emotions and motives, and always points toward truth and wisdom and honesty."

"Wow, so this thing will show me the way out of trouble and fiascos—"

"If you accept your compass and the twenty, cherish them, listen and heed what they say, then the three of you will survive. Oh, Demimonde will still try to kill or capture you, but you'll go far in Ordonne."

Pilot opened his hand. The Magic Twenty lay pretty on his palm.

I put it in my pocket. "That's all I need to know? No other perks or pitfalls?"

"There'll be other things to learn along the way, but if you keep your nose clean and love Ordonne, everything will work out."

Sponsor Ship pulled anchor and headed out to sea with a full sail shining in the morning sun. The Skipper and the other three had wasted no time, found their path, and left me alone on the shore. I walked to the end of a sandbank and waved, but the ship was too far away for any on board to see me.

Me—an insignificant speck. Someone else would take my place and talk to my friends. No one was irreplaceable—life would go on until it didn't.

A shiver rolled up my back. A dark spirit of loneliness.

"Watcher, am I doomed?"

No answer. An ugly thought taunted me. *I'm going to die in the middle of nowhere and go straight to hell.* "Demimonde, thanks for that reassuring thought." The ugly beast always whispered at the edge of my mind.

I checked my pocket. The silver-plated money clip still held the magic twenty-dollar bill neatly folded in half. Pilot had etched *Ordonne* by hand on one side, but what good was money out here?

"Poor woe begotten man. Vonn, I am Watcher, guardian of reason and hope. I am with you always."

"Yes." I spun, hoping to see her, but Watcher was never seen, only heard. Unlike Mr. Conscience and Mr. Consequence, however, once or twice I felt her presence. A pleasant touch, like the wind ruffling my hair. "I'm so glad you're here—please, stay. We can walk and talk together."

"You've come far my fledgling. Remember when my presence embarrassed you? You pleaded to be left alone."

"I was a klutz, afraid of my own shadow. Forgive me."

"We learn from our errors, forgive, and move on. Let's talk about today."

"Let's."

"Today you're sober and equipped with spiritual tools which will enable you to climb every mountain on your journey to the real world, with all its Basers and Vilers and Sordids."

"And best of all I have you, Watcher, all the way from Doc Changelove's office."

"Yes, we met there. But I'm from the fourth dimension—beyond the constraints of time."

I put on my ruck and hat and jumped forward two steps to test the weight. "Touch heavier, but the shoulder straps feel good. Did you see that my shipmates gave me a new hatchet last night? Shall we take the first hill? You can tell me about the fourth dimension."

"We? I'm not ruled by gravity or time, so *we* won't be climbing anything—you will—I'll watch. And by the way, you should already know that I don't take orders. I remind and exhort."

"Okay, I'll be grateful for whatever we discuss."

"Vonn, remember the smell of Doc's office?"

"Yes, camphor and witch hazel."

"Do you remember the wrinkled old placard fastened to the door?"

"Four simple lines: The Wicket, The Way, The Light, The Truth."

"You've opened and passed through the Wicket, and you're well along the Way. Look for the Light and you will find the Truth."

She was gone. Watcher came and went on her own terms.

Serenity Harbor reminded me of a gigantic cream pitcher with the lip being the entrance. The beach rose up to a line of hills and ridgelines that ran along each side of the inlet to the base of a mountain. I counted a dozen footpaths that meandered up in different directions before disappearing into the forest. One trail stood out—the eighth was clear and well-used.

"I wonder." I held the Magic Twenty up to my ear. "I'm told that eight is the spiritual number for a new beginning. What say you?"

Nothing.

"I hope you can listen and talk because out here, all we have is each other and, may I say, God."

The polished silver money clip flashed and reflected a sunbeam on a pile of sticks. A flame flickered, then disappeared when I blocked the sun with my hat. On the third try I got a steady flame. "This will be very handy for lighting campfires."

On a whim, I held the Magic Twenty against my chest. A warm and reassuring wellness encompassed me. It spoke the language of the heart without words. I understood that God didn't bring me all the way from Baser to Serenity Harbor to let me die in a forgotten patch of woods.

And so I began my spiritual journey.

The punishing sun dominated the blue sky, driving all wise mountain creatures into the forest's deep shade—except for me. I pushed on, up and down ridges and draws and across meadows until my body screamed. The thin, high-country atmosphere taxed me more than the humid air covering the sea far below, but the inspiring panoramas offset the trail's demands. The wind and sun created glittering green and gold decorations. I could see forever, horizon to horizon, and all the virgin conifer and broadleaf forests in between.

The island, unscarred by houses, roads, or plowed fields, was alive with music. An orchestra of whispering trees sang with sweet water springs and brooks, sparkling and cascading down rocky beds to the harbor far below. Voices of birds and animals singing completed the chorus.

Drawn by fresh energy and newcomer's zeal, I continued until the trail led me to a massive elm at the edge of a meadow. Its ancient green crown ruled the skyline and shaded the forest floor, deeply layered with colorful leaves. Feeder roots as thick as my waist stretched out from the trunk to form a chair, a mile-high living throne overlooking Serenity Harbor. I dropped my ruck, took off my boots, and reclined.

The compass and twenty spoke to my heart and warmed my chest pocket. Communicating without words. *Welcome Vonn Thrasher, you are safe.*

My stomach growled, reminding me that I had a good supply of pemmican. Dried meat, fruit, and berries pressed into small loaves—not bad as long as I had a full canteen of water.

"Keep your eyes and ears open," Pilot had told me before I left. "You're not carrying enough food for the entire journey, so look for native fruit and berries. Trails to nowhere will crisscross all the way. You'll know the good ones by their direction—they go up. The bad go down—easy at first, but with a pitfall at the end."

"Always go up," I said.

Fortunately, my senses were sharp—remembering to use them was another issue.

The number eight trail climbed through heavy oak brush and pine trees before crossing the imposing ridgeline high above me. I recalled Pilot's final words. "Sooner or later you'll reach the plateaus. Do yourself a favor and check in with Wilson."

"Wilson? Who is he?"

"Wilson Cabotage, an old friend of mine. You might say he's a mountain man."

"So, the five of us won't be the only people on that part of the island?"

"Ha, no sir, trail life can get quite busy on occasion."

Before the sun hid behind the western trees, the magic money clip caught its last ray and started a fire. I'd walked and talked to myself until my shoulders and legs were numb and my feet hurt all the way up to the back of my knees. My first night was balmy, but I needed the flames' reassuring light. I ate mountain rose apples I'd gathered, a little bland, but safe, and with salt, palatable.

I watched the glowing embers rise and disappear into the Milky Way. Was Eden like this? Could Sobriety Island be part of heaven? "God, thank you for spiritual tools, for rose apples, for a good trail day, and this bedroll next to a popping, bright fire."

I had a kernel of faith, but I was growing and believed that Ordonne was my Way. Somehow, I would come back to Baser a better man, sober, and ready to reunite with family and friends.

My mind drifted to a familiar place at the edge of sleep where memories wrestle with reality, where ego, Ordonne, and Demimonde meet on equal ground.

Redshirts called that stinking thinking, a sick distraction. They taught me how to say no. Back in Baser, alcohol twisted my mind until I could actually think long enough to hurt my own feelings. The problem wasn't an overactive imagination or obsession with deep thoughts. I fabricated scenarios because I needed them to become a hero, a martyr, or an innocent victim with every right to smoke and drink it all away.

"Not tonight—tomorrow I will look for the Light and find the Truth. Tomorrow I will meet Wilson."

The morning sun peeked over the eastern horizon. Long shadows—remnants of the night—reached and then retreated into the early light. Forest creatures stirred and created enough commotion to rouse me from a stiff and sore slumber. I opened one eye. Two mockingbirds stood beside my dead fire studying me, squawking, and crying.

"Really? Feathered hecklers? Watcher, come on—feathered stand-ins for Mr. Conscience and Mr. Consequence?"

I rolled out of the bedroll and waved my arms. "Shuddup."

The aptly-named mockingbirds flew to the top of a tree and continued their racket.

I laid down and covered my head with a blanket. "So, what if I stay here all day and do nothing? I don't have to punch a timeclock. I'm on my own. My feet are blistered and my shoulders raw. I'll climb the mountain tomorrow."

A murder of crows landed in the elm and joined the avian racket of coos, caws, rattles, and clicks—destroying all my peace and quiet. So, after a bite of pemmican, I refilled my canteen, shouldered my gear, and waved goodbye to the winged critics.

By midday, the footpath reached the crest of a ridgeline and forked before leveling off on the other side. Someone had made a bench out of several large flagstones and scratched, *Enjoy the view *JC* 1992*, on the seat. "Sounds good, JC. I'll stop for a breather."

The distant Serenity Harbor lay below on the left, about to disappear behind the ridgeline. I'd meet Wilson at the plateaus on my right.

I climbed the first plateau with ease, but the others ascended until they and the distant Mountain vanished in the clouds. This island wasn't a resort cay a few miles across. Sobriety Island was enormous.

Beyond a half mile of canyon, dozens of tall objects dotted the Pious Trail. Were the light-colored things dead trees, signs, or crosses? Too distant to see clearly, they exuded an ominous air.

More choices came with the proverbial fork in the road. "Watcher, a little help here, left or right or go back?"

No answer.

"Which trail leads to the light and truth—or darkness and death?"

Oily's voice came to mind. "Easy does it. Be patient. Do what you can when you can."

"Okay, Oily." I pulled out my hatchet and ran the carbon steel edge across my cheek. Sharp enough to shave. I easily lopped off a straight branch from a young tree, whittled the bark off, and fashioned a knob on one end.

Still no Watcher. I stretched out in the shade and napped.

A familiar sweet smell roused me. A spice shrub or nearby flower? No, more medicinal. Like the Doc's office. I sniffed my hands and realized I'd cut a camphor tree staff. My Moral Compass warmed. Somehow, this staff would strengthen my walk, be a balm for my hands, and incense for my soul. Thank you. Higher Power, Lord, God, wherever you are.

I pointed my staff across the canyon and shouted. "Left." My voice echoed three times.

I stepped forward and pointed again. "Right?" The canyon parroted *right, right, right.*

How much fun is this? Even louder, "Vonn!" *Vonn, Vonn, Vonn* bounced to and fro.

I pointed left and—

"Stop right there. Cease and desist."

"Watcher! There you are. Good afternoon. This spot yields the best echoes. Want to try?"

"Did you think for a minute about who might be listening? You might wake the dead."

"I—"

"Lesson One: someone, somewhere, is always watching and listening. Around here that someone usually isn't good. My mockingbirds and crows frantically tried to warn you about an enemy on your track. But you stayed under your blanket until it was almost too late."

"Late? But I—"

"Lesson Two: silence is an answer. I may choose not to reply. You must learn to think and decide for yourself. Now, don't let your mouth confirm that your eyes and ears made a fool of you."

"Who's tracking me? What are those things standing along the trail?"

Silence. I looked and listened—nothing but the wind, trees, and me.

So, left, or right? On Sponsor Ship, we sailed by the Abstract State and the Four Horsemen to the south, but this path on the right made me uneasy.

"Moral Compass, what say ye?"

Left stuck in my mind.

"All right."

CHAPTER NINE

Wilson Cabotage

ozens of hand-hewn crosses guarded the Pious Trail as it ascended the first two plateaus. A few were whitewashed. Mountain weather had cost the rest their bark. Seasoned gray timbers leaned in every direction. Without exception all faced down the trail toward Serenity Harbor.

Their silent language indicated guards, a ghoulish audience with a hidden warning.

Wake the dead? Were they memorials or tombstones?

There were no graves.

Wake the living? Who built them and why?

On the third plateau the mountain fellowshipped with the clouds and filled the thin high-country air with fog. Only my heartbeat and heavy breathing broke the dense silence. The haze concealed the sun, obscuring my sense of time and true north. I would've lost my way in the fog, but the face of each cross kept me on the Pious Trail.

A sudden lightning bolt flash momentarily blinded me. The ground shook under heaven's thunder. Static electricity set my hair on end, snapping and jumping across my hands.

Was I at the edge of eternity, or the center of an angry tempest?

Watcher and my Moral Compass were silent.

No shelter. No place to run and hide.

Trees shuddered and bowed under howling winds. They tried

to throw off sheets of driving rain, but the merciless storm ripped, pummeled, and carried away their limbs.

Freezing sleet stung my face. I huddled, shivered, and rocked under my poncho, teeth chattering. I labored for every breath. Cold rainwater trickled down my back and pooled in my pockets. My boots felt like boat anchors.

Fear linked with unbounded misery.

Pain froze my soul.

I hoped lightning would finish me quickly.

Then awareness, an intuitive understanding filled me, and I heard a great truth.

There'll come a time when the only hope, the only defense, the only solution is God.

"God," I bawled through clenched teeth. "Whoever you are, please help me."

Otherworldly warm air encompassed and caressed me, sheltering me from the storm. The forest reappeared with a bright gold and emerald coat, as the trees waved and whistled a weird and wonderful harmony.

Had I reached the fourth dimension? Was I dead?

To the contrary—I was never more alive. I was at peace. God plucked something old, heavy, and ugly out of my heart. Twenty years of pride tangled in thousands of dirty lies and secrets that I'd borne like a millstone vanished.

The morning sun pierced the clouds and painted my face with warmth. I opened one eye, then the other, and ran my fingers through my dirty mop of hair. A couple of twigs and a dead beetle fell out. I'd survived the storm.

Everything after my prayer was a blank. Whether a mental breakdown, a seizure, or a near-death experience—something amazingly good had happened.

Ravens squawked and chattered complaints from the tree above me. "No wonder you're called an unkindness. Would you stop—"

I remembered Watchers admonishment, "Okay. I'm moving."

Human words lacked relevance to ravens, but my voice certainly wasn't in God's kingdom. I was relevant. Transformation followed my simple prayer—because he heard me. Inside, I had changed.

The secret place where my obsessions began, where my ego fanned the flames of fear and rage and created unquenchable thirsts—remained quiet. He had lifted my burden and set me free.

I had more than cheated death—I'd been liberated. On a nameless mountain, surrounded by an unkindness of noisy ravens, God rescued me from two decades of emptiness and filled me with faith. Elated, I laid in the sticks and mud and laughed until my belly hurt and tears washed my face. I had a baptism of the Spirit.

A meal of pemmican and a pair of dry socks revived me. I faced the washed-out trail covered with deadfalls, using my Moral Compass for guidance. By midday, I reached the south side of the mountain beyond the storm's fury.

When the clouds and fog returned, I shrugged off fear. After surviving the tempest and losing most of my pride, I felt energized. The urge to smoke or drink seemed a million miles away.

The trail leveled and crossed the edge of several large meadows on the fourth plateau. I was certain that Wilson Cabotage lived nearby, because the crosses stood straight, their hewn wooden beams and nails almost new.

I was about to take a midday break when I came upon two whitewashed crosses on opposite sides of the trail. Over ten feet tall, one was secured with new rope. The other had a single spike driven through the crooked crossbeam. Wilson's work? Both sides of the skewed beam had symbols or unreadable words. I turned the wood until the crossbeam rested on the other side. What I'd thought were archaic pictograms were actually upside-down English.

SAVE ME was burned into the surface.

A twig snapped signaling nearby movement in the foggy forest edge.

"Who's there?" I growled.

An old man with long white hair and stubble beard stepped from behind a tree. His slight frame was clad in denim and buckskin leather giving him a frontiersman look. He stared at me with one good eye. "Who are you?"

My strength failed. I grabbed the cross to steady myself. Surreal wreaths of clouds swirled and danced across the small meadow covered with low ivy. We stared at each other until a chill ran down my spine.

I wiped cold sweat from my face. "Vonn Thrasher. Might you be Wilson Cabotage?"

"That'd be me." His black complexion highlighted his right eye, solid white, like marble. His bass voice revealed a deep south upbringing. "Thrasher, you done wandered way off up here and into a fix. Don't move. You're standing in mountain laurel. Get a snoot full of that and you'll stop breathing."

"Yes, sir. Right. Where do I go?"

"Use your footprints to return to the trail. Go up that way, or Pious Trail as you pilgrims call it, a couple hundred yards. You'll see my lodge. I'll meet you there." In three steps he vanished.

The sun had burned off the fog, and the wind chased away the clouds by the time I reached his place. His log cabin perched at the edge of a hillside meadow. A rock chimney rose over a wood shingle roof, but the pots and pans around the front yard fire pit indicated he cooked outside. Wilson sat in a homemade rocking chair on the porch. His good eye closed; the marble one wide open. There were books stacked in the doorway, floor to ceiling.

I walked up and leaned against the porch upright. "Hell of a storm last night."

"Over on the north side of the mountain. I's spared here."

"I see that." I drummed my fingers on the beam. "Pilot told me to check in with you and send his regards."

"Pilot, huh?" Wilson stood and moved close, studying my face like he was reading a book. "Maybe the witch be talking for you." His breath smelled of smoked fish and sweet berries.

"Witch? Not me, Pilot. Not—let me restart." I took a deep breath. "Pilot told me that you and he were old friends, and for me to do him a favor and check in with you."

"That old longhair. Is he still stumping around on a wooden peg leg?"

"Pilot? No, he shaves his head every morning and all his parts are working."

"Hmm—that was you yelling yesterday?"

"Left, right, Vonn. That's me."

"Damned fool. Is she following you?"

"Watcher, yes she's always—"

"No. The witch."

"You keep talking about a witch but—"

"Maybe Watcher fended her off. You're lucky you got to the plateaus."

"Okay, now I understand. The Witch is the enemy that Watcher was talking about. She said someone was tracking me. Is the witch part of Demimonde?"

"That's why you're here. Drop your ruck. I reckon I gotta teach you how to survive the island. You can stretch your bedroll out on the porch." He turned his head and waved the air like he was swatting a fly, and tossed me a bar of soap and towel. "You smell like a goat. Did you roll in every mud puddle on the mountain?"

"Maybe, I—"

"Be a chest deep pool in the creek back of the cabin. Water's cold but you'll get used to it. Now get those filthy clothes off. Scrub them and yourself until you're clean and hang them on tree limbs to dry. Time you get back supper'll be ready. Got fried trout with wild mountain rice and onions, and a sweet berry mix that makes your mouth water. You're the dishwasher."

Wilson kept refilling my plate, and I kept eating until I

couldn't breathe. After supper we reclined across the fire from each other, watching the flames slowly ebb into glowing red and orange coals. The smell of burning pine took me back to early boyhood when Mom and Dad and I were happy and clean in more ways than one. Reminded me of the beach bonfire and Pilot's parting words. I'd made it to Wilson's camp for a reason. He was a key part of Sobriety Island and I needed him.

"Feels good to be clean."

"Does."

I pointed at the pots and pans. "That was the best campfire fixings I ever ate. Thank you."

"I enjoy cooking what the mountain gives me." He hid a smile behind the stem of orchard grass he used to pick his teeth.

"Mister Wilson, can I ask you about the crosses?"

"Wilson will do. Ask away."

"Who built them? What are all those hundreds of markers for?"

An owl hooted an eerie call across the top of the dark eastern forest. Another one answered from the west side. We listened for a third, but they'd flown away. I threw another chunk of wood on the fire.

Wilson cleared his throat. "Crosses go back to the witch. Everything around here seems to revolve around her."

"You built them to fend her off?"

"That was my theory, but the truth is wooden crosses don't trouble her much. Nah, I put a new cross out every full moon to guide you and the other pilgrims on their way back home. Unless I lost count, there's way over twelve hundred along the Pious Trail."

But that would mean you've been here a hundred years. Not going there. "So, as long as I keep seeing crosses, I'm okay, still on the trail. How'd you come to live way up here? We must be over a mile up."

"Near as I can tell, about six thousand feet above the Sea of Booze." When he threw a rock into the darkness, it hit and rattled off something. "Enough distance to keep us out a harm's way when the witch comes hunting. You see, there are easier marks down in the lowlands where traveling be easier."

"Like the old saying, I don't have to outrun the bear. I just have to outrun you. Smart."

I woke to the fragrance of coffee brewing. Wilson was busy cooking pheasant eggs and Dutch oven biscuits. I stretched and sat up on the edge of the front porch. "Smells great. You should've gotten me up to help."

"Naw, I got this. Breakfast is my favorite meal."

"I got cleanup."

"That you do."

I washed the pans and dishes in the stream and came back. The fire was dead, and Wilson sat in his rocking chair, moving slowly back and forth with his good eye closed. "Set them on the fire pit rocks to dry in the sun."

"Yes, sir."

"Tell me pilgrim, where you from?"

"Over the pass a good way north of Ism Harbor, there's a one-horse mill town called Baser. Twenty bars, twenty churches, a post office, and a cop shop. I've worked for Honesty Manufacturing making aluminum doors and windows since I was eighteen. You?"

"Baser—that's funny. I hail from a little port town called Duelo."

"Say what?"

"Dwell-oh. Spanish for duel. I used to pilot a ferry around there. My wife, Joy, and I raised two kids and lived a great life together. I drank a little back then, but I kept my hard liquor under control. Yessir, everything was pretty good until our twenty-sixth Halloween."

"Halloween? That's when I hit bottom."

"Holidays damn near killed me before I got to Sobriety Island. The hard times between Halloween and the New Year got longer every year. Back then, Joy and I went all out with lights and ghoulish music. We served candy to the kids and hot toddies and schnapps to the grownups. But that year, death came trick-or-treating. Slipped in the backdoor and waited like an assassin. Joy went to the kitchen to refill the candy bowl and never came back. Took her while I was talking with friends at the front door."

"Oh man, that's tough—out of nowhere."

"Went to check on her," he wiped his eyes with a sleeve, "and there she was lying on the floor, her lifeless eyes staring at the ceiling. I tried to hold on, I really did, but Thanksgiving, Christmas, and another new year. Zilch, nada—nothing worked. Best I could do was bourbon and beer, reruns and football games. I slid over the edge little by little."

"Depression and grief."

"Emotions swung back and forth like a playground swing. I'd prop myself up with a sip of wine, a bite of food, a friend's conversation. But loneliness never let me alone. I'd look at Joy's empty chair, at her good china that'd never be used again, and waves of grief flattened me. Good memories turned bad. I's mad sick. Couldn't get away from the ghosts unless I hit the hard stuff."

"Gin and tonic."

"Damned little tonic."

"A glass of whiskey and a splash of coke."

"Oh yeah, one about this tall." He held his hands a foot apart. "Then I'd turn Pharisee. And believe me, with a belly full of booze and a head full of rage, I can hate with a religious passion."

He pointed at me. "This's your fault."

He pointed down the trail. "And their fault."

He pointed to the stars. "And God's fault. He hates me. That's why Joy died."

"Was there an intervention? How'd you get to Sobriety Island?"

"Misery got me here. Booze quit working, but I was hooked." Wilson reached up and waved his hand in the air. "But the good buzz was long gone. In the end, all the booze, painkillers, mood pills, shrinks, and drunk tanks could only give me a pathetic numbness."

"You're telling my story. I couldn't live with it and couldn't leave it alone."

"Demimonde is an insidious disease—gets worse, never better." He took a swallow of coffee, swished around in his mouth and spit. "Liquid Alzheimer's—a progressive illness of more. I want more, I need more, and I take more."

"I've had the same danged nightmare for decades. I come out of a blackout laying naked in a ditch. There's a body next to me and—"

"You flip him over, and he is you."

"Here's the sick part, as soon as I figure out that I'm dead, I take off looking for a drink."

Wilson said, "Gotta wonder if you're having nightmares or prophecy."

I tossed a stick in the fire pit. "Or both."

"Likely both. Anyway, I heard about Ordonne and ended up in Ism Harbor. They got me on the Sponsor Ship and after a season or two, I began my spiritual journey up the Pious Trail. Found this meadow one day—well actually, the witch helped me find my place." He laughed and shook his head. "Decided to stay and built a log cabin. People from Sponsor Ship keep me resupplied well enough. I like being up here in the clouds with God, peaceful, and a long way from the witch's hunting grounds."

"Hunting grounds?"

"Oh yeah, the lowlands be where the witch hunts Ordonnes like deer. But she doesn't come up here on the plateaus much. I's convinced that God keeps her at bay because he wants me right where I am." Wilson pointed to the ground. "Helping Ordonnes. You might say that my humble camp is a roadhouse, a sanctuary for pilgrims like you."

Thunder boomed in the distance, and the refreshing scent of coming rain drifted through the camp. We listened to the lowlands getting pounded. "The witch is never far away. I expect she knows you're here. Sometimes on a full moon she screams my name and beats on the crosses. She caught me twice in the

Island's lower reaches and damn near killed me. Yessir, I know the deal. On my own—without the good Lord—I's a dead duck."

Wilson took a break, then returned to his chair. "She's not afraid of my crosses or any other manmade charm or trapping. The good Lord be all she respects. I build the crosses to mark my time and keep folks on the trail. Otherwise, they might stumble in the mountain fog and walk right off a cliff."

"They work. The face of each cross told me that I was on track."

"Most pilgrims tell me that." Wilson closed his eyes, took a deep breath, and relaxed.

I folded my clothes and repacked my backpack, then quietly poked around in the woods near the camp. I found a large garden protected by a lodgepole fence that resembled an old western fort. Wilson had already harvested half the crop, allowing rows of squash, pumpkin, and potatoes to spread out in tangled green mats. By the gate, he'd built a pallet inside an open-sided lean-to. No doubt he rested there while guarding his crop.

Wilson was still napping when I returned. I rolled a tree trunk round into the shade by the cabin and sat down.

He cleared his throat. "Lord, may you guide and protect and provide all our needs. Amen." He opened his eyes. "Yes, sir, life is good."

"Amen. Life is good." Did I just say amen?

"Aye, up here with the Lord."

"Quite a homestead you have." I pointed toward the well-worn path. "Heck of a garden. I'm impressed."

"Ain't all me. Sponsor Ship people give me the seed. I plant and till the ground. The Lord provides the sun and rain." He smiled and leaned forward in his rocker. "Then the game begins. All manner of four-legged critters, crows, and magpies watch and wait. Probing, hoping to steal some and ruin the rest. But I stop 'em."

"How do you keep them out? You got a shotgun?"

"I do, but haven't shot a shell in years. Done killing over a stupid ear o' corn. Sleeping out there and a good fence keeps most varmints out. Now and then I trap and relocate a hard-headed coon."

"No wonder your garden looks like a small fortress."

"If you tend your garden, it'll feed and teach you things."

Doc Changelove told me my garden was full of weeds. "Teach?"

"Fer instance about the Lord's ways. The Good Book says to cut your wheat and barley high and round the corners of your field, so you leave some for the stranger and the animals, that all may eat. If I's generous—he's generous—there's always enough somehow or the other. Besides, I's all over this mountain foraging for bark and wild berries. I take more from them than they steal from me. That's the game."

"Up here in God's country. But aren't you lonely? Would you—if you could—leave and get your old life back?"

The sunlight painted Wilson's weathered ebony face with a mystical aura. His marble eye, toothy grin, and white whiskers conveyed experience and wisdom. "Naw, I'm supposed to be right where I am. You and I are here for a reason."

"I don't know if I could ever be a mountain man."

"Ha, with that beard and head a hair, you already have the look. Tell me, have you read this poem?

All that glitters is not gold
Often have you heard that told.
Many a man his life hath sold
Gilded tombs do worms enfold.
Had he been as wise as bold,
Young in limbs, in judgment old,
Fare ye well. Thy suit is cold—"

"Shakespeare?"

"Yes. *The Merchant of Venice* with a change or two. Meaning?"

"Well," I replied. "Money, property, and prestige aren't everything."

"They can be a curse. That's why I'm here today. I like the status quo. I don't want what's over yonder or the real world's trinkets and trophies. Here, I have a purpose, a life high in the clouds—"

"High on God. I like that. But how does the witch figure in?"

"Ever read any of Percy B. Shelley's works?"

"Frankenstein?"

"That was Mary. Percy was her husband."

"Never heard of him."

"Back in the day, he wrote, 'No more let life divide, what death can join together.'"

"Meaning?"

"Hope was gone, youth was dead, all things dear to him were withering away. Percy's estranged first wife drowned while heavy with child. Years later, tuberculosis took his best friend and fellow poet, John Keats. Then before his thirtieth birthday, Shelley drowned with two other men during a shipwreck. Was he suicidal? Was the Don Juan an unseaworthy sailboat? Or did bad navigation cause this tragedy? Nobody knows."

"Now I understand."

"Start using your mind. Read and read well—the classics, poetry, and scripture. There's a reason why hundred-year-old books are still valid today."

I glanced at the books stacked throughout the cabin. "Gosh, besides work manuals, I haven't read prose or poetry in years. Back in school, I read *Old Yeller*, and *The Yearling*. That's how I escaped my parents' yelling matches—under the covers with a flashlight and *Treasure Island*."

"I bet you lost interest in books after your first drunk. Hello— where's this been my whole life? Why read when a bottle will really do the trick?"

"That's the hook."

"That's insidious. Demimonde will break your thinker and trap you in a half-world."

"Yes. But during the big storm last night, I had a spiritual experience, a soul baptism that renewed me. I'm different today. The old dark thoughts are gone."

He stood, yawned, and scratched his head. "Maybe, time will tell if they're still there."

"No doubt."

"Back to Percy. He mourned a lost one, but I think he was also writing about how you conquer old dark thoughts. Ego has to be smashed before we can connect with God and live on a spiritual plane."

I tucked my knees under my chin and stared at a couple of clouds. Highlighted in the morning sun, they looked like jack o' lanterns. Were they smiling or smirking? "No more let life divide what death can join together. Ego, hmm, that's hard."

"A spiritual way of life is filled with service. More action, less talk. Thinking of others before self is hard, because self naturally demands first place and constant attention." He handed me a pair of work gloves. "Here. Let's get spiritual and work a little of that piss and vinegar out of you. Grab the rope, a double jack, and a splitting wedge. I'll bring my axe and bucksaw. I want to split and stack a few cords of wood today. Winter will be here before you know it."

"Cords?"

"Three steps long, one step wide and shoulder high. Stacked tight enough to let in a rat and keep out the cat."

At a quarter-mile or so up the mountain, Wilson selected two dead standing trees that went down easily. Then the real work began. We roped the trunks, and like a pair of mules pulled them down the hill to the edge of camp. Despite their size, gravity and a clear route made moving them doable for us.

If his stories were accurate, he'd long passed 100, maybe even 130, yet his stamina challenged me to keep up. His idea of splitting and stacking a few cords and mine were miles apart. In two days of bone-aching labor, we put up enough firewood to last all winter. My back and arms went from pain to throbbing numbness, but we laid in an impressive supply of firewood. We were proud of our work.

After supper, we cleaned up and sat beside the fire pit, listening to the crickets and other nocturnal creatures serenade us from their safe havens. Wilson stared into the flames, barely keeping his eye open. I examined my stinging assortment of nicks, bug bites, and blisters on my hands and arms. Even after washing I smelled like pine.

The spirit of a thousand trees whistled through our camp like a dust eddy. The fire joyfully hissed and popped, filling our camp with reassuring light. Watcher's familiar voice waxed poetic. "Stay close little man. Learn. Only a higher power can save you from the creatures of the night."

She was gone.

As I stared into the tree line, the firelight caught movement. Creepy. What lurked in the shadows? Not far away, something cried out in distress. Wildlife? Or the witch?

"Creatures of the night?" I murmured.

Wilson clapped his hands.

"What?" I jumped and spun around. "Don't do that."

He busted out laughing. "Boy, lookee here, nature can be a little scary. But let me tell you about power. The witch kicked my tail all over the side of this mountain, not once, but twice before I wised up. Witch be sayin', 'Come on over boy. Let me show you how I work.'"

"How I work?"

"Called me by name: 'Wilson, be a man. Everyone drinks and drugs. Come on out and play in the dark.'" He laughed. "Sometimes we're stupid and sometimes we're funny. That day I was both. I saw places on this plateau that nobody ever saw before—face down in the dirt."

"What could be wrong with organic beer and gluten-free bourbon?"

He slapped his knee. "Approved by Shantytown vegetarians and alcoholic vegans everywhere."

He put on his buckskin coat and handed me mine. The dirty old pea jacket smelled like canvas and seawater, but the blue wool blocked the chill. I hadn't worn it since the day I found the Ordonnes on the Gravel Beach. I'd jumped into another dimension since I shared their campfire.

"Nice of Watcher to stop by. Always a good omen."

"And *poof*, she's gone. Been that way since day one."

Wilson cleared his throat and pointed at the top of a tree, illuminated by firelight and stars. "Orion is bright tonight. Do you know that his belt is the birthplace of stars?"

I guessed we were done talking about Watcher. "No sir."

"Nebula. Tell me, Mister Vonn, what do heavens declare when Orion stands bright in that massive mountain sky?"

"Hmm—no clouds?"

"Cold weather's coming. He's a winter constellation." Wilson sat, rubbed his hands together, and held them near the fire. "What does Orion say about the witch?"

"Well, you told me that the witch hunts her prey in the moonlight, when she can see. Tonight's dark, a new moon. So, we're probably safe."

"Yes." He nodded and gave me a thumbs up. "Vonn Thrasher, remember my words—know your enemies—never underestimate their power and tenacity. Too many alkies hide their eyes and stumble into their grave. Their souls belonging to Demimonde forever."

"There are more foes than Demimonde and the witch?"

"Many. There are three clans on Sobriety Island called the Lings."

"What are Lings?"

"Centuries ago, Demimonde dragged some of the lost from the edge of hell and enslaved them. They came back strong in the flesh, monsters that were never supposed to be. Now they live to hunt the Pious Trail and devour Ordonnes."

"More island monsters? Like the slipperies and the witch weren't enough."

"I like your wit. Pilot says that Lings were politicians in their former lives. Anyway, around here anything that has a name ending in -ling is a changeling, a shape shifter. They can transform into anything they want to be, man, woman, beast, or fowl."

"Amazing place. You know, a few months ago I went to see the doc about my drinking. Had concerns, anxiety about my cravings and shakes. And, today, I'm in the middle of the Sea of Booze on an island that gets larger and more dangerous by the day."

"Only a few months? Think about it."

"Well, Treatment Ship lasted three weeks. We were rescued by Sponsor Ship and sailed by the Abstract State. I'll never forget the Four Horsemen. Then we rescued Member Ship, and here I am. Seems like a few months, but then again maybe it's closer to a year."

"Out here, life's challenges set the pace, and time isn't a constant. Hours can drag on and on. A day can last a month. But when we finally change and grow up—we flash into a new life and future."

"I worked the same job, drank the same beer, woke up with the same hangover, and puked in the same commode every day for ten years," I said.

"Let's stay on topic. We call most Lings Darklings or Wretchlings. They're pretty harmless. Ugly little vandals that hoot and howl at night. Sometimes they sneak into camps to steal."

I pointed into the darkness. "Those weird noises might be Darklings?"

"They change into ghastly little beasts. But the worst of the worst are Mudlings. I think the witch is one of them. These deadly creatures barely resemble the humans they once were. They can look like anything from an innocent girl to a hideous reptile. Demimonde has warped them into wanderers driven by hunger and hate. They have the unique ability to hear, or sense tremors—a kind of music from the fourth dimension. Using dark powers, they take every man and woman captive through trickery and seduction, to feed on in Ling camps. Then they harvest more and more."

"Hellish."

Wilson said, "Don't try to figure them out. Lings boast about their twisted Demimonde existence. Ruled by their cravings for violence, and flesh and blood, they live a toxic life."

"Reminds me of alcoholism. I defended my drinking at all costs—while booze slowly killed me."

"The Mudling witch almost killed me the first time the ship returned to Serenity Harbor. I went down to see about reboarding, and she met me halfway. The second time I went up the Pious Trail into Big Book Mountains. She met me before I got out of the plateaus and tried to tear me limb from limb. I almost popped a gut running back here with her right on my heels."

I looked behind me and leaned forward. "What'd she look like? I mean—like a monster or ghoul?"

"Ha, that's what you'd think. Her name's Lily, and she's a pretty little freckle-faced woman about this high," he put the blade of his hand across his chest. "'Mister Wilson,' she said with the sweetest voice. 'I am headed down to the harbor. If you walk with me and keep me safe, I'll tell you my island secrets. I might even show you my treasure map.'"

"'Treasure? Here on the Island?' I was dumb as a sucker fish. Might as well had a hook in my mouth. 'Oh yeah,' she said. 'My map shows where a tribe of erotic womenfolk live. Beauties they are with lots of gold and jewels.'"

I sat up straighter. "Gold and jewels? Who wouldn't be taken in by a pretty little woman telling that story?"

"My conscience was singing, telling me this was too good to be true. A trap. But foolish man that I am, we marched off arm-in-arm, cooing and pecking all the way to Serenity Harbor. Yessir, I was smitten—until she hit me so hard I rolled halfway to the next plateau. When I pulled myself out of the dirt, I saw that Lily wasn't vulnerable. Little creature's true nature came out—Mudling—ugly and strong as a bull."

"What happened next?"

"She knocked me down again and again and stood over me, laughing, breath smelling like piss, stale beer, and rotting flesh. 'Who do you think you are? Leave? You want to leave me? Pitiful old drunk, you belong to me, forever. Now crawl back to your hole and pray your stupid prayers because that's the only thing that'll save your sorry hide.' Then she kicked me until I crawled under a thick bush."

"Terrifying—"

"Longest damned mile I ever—"

"All the way up the mountain?"

"So beat up and sore I couldn't breathe. Her voice boomed like a bullhorn across ridge and draw. Ever' time I stood up, Lily laughed like a devil and mocked, 'Down. Get down and crawl like a real drunk, or I'll put you down.' I'd drop all right, on my bloody hands and knees all the way here."

"How'd you lose her? Did she stop at the crosses?"

"There weren't any crosses back then. But the closer I got to this place, the less of Lily I heard. Wasn't hard to figure out where I needed to go. Now this meadow is my home."

"Here to stay."

"But foolish man that I am, a season or two later I tried again. Thought I had it aaaall figured out. When the ship's out to sea the Lings watch me like a hawk. I am the only game in town." He tapped his finger against his temple. "I needed a diversion."

"Ah, ha. What kind?"

"Safety in numbers. I waited until Sponsor Ship came back and the Ordonnes scattered all over the place. Figured there'd be too many alkies for one witch to watch."

"A logical plan."

"My first mistake was leaving God out of the decision-making process. He'd a told me, 'No, Wilson, that's a bad idea.' But I didn't listen and took off in the opposite direction for the next mountain."

"Lily caught you again?"

He nodded. "Topped the pass and had a good start coming down the other side when I saw her. She pulled a pine tree out by its roots and threw it across the trail."

"A tree? Oh, come on."

"Aye, and sat on its trunk naked as a jaybird, singing, 'She'll be coming 'round the mountain when she comes.' She smiled and waved. 'Hi babe—oh, we'll all go out to meet her when she comes.'"

"That is beyond—"

"Wicked, yes, singing like a loon in the bright mountain sun, her long red pigtails lay across bare freckled breasts."

"What'd you do?"

Wilson shook his head. "Again, foolish man that I am, I stepped into the open, eager to see—big mistake—I'll never forget what she did."

"What?"

"Roaming eyes be a curse—saw way more'n I needed. She leaned way back exposing her whole upper body, then laughed like a banshee, looked me dead in the eyes, and held up a bloody head in each hand. Had 'em by the hair on the top of their heads danglin' like puppets on a string."

"Damn! You knew them?"

"The heads of my shipmates from the ferry, Old Fallen and Jaywalker Don. Somehow they's alive, tormented and openin' and closin' their bloody mouths like fish out of water."

"What happened next?"

"'Well lookee here,' Lily taunted. 'Wilson's out on another walkabout. Come join us, we're about to begin an Ordonne meeting. Your old friends were about to share how they got drunk and lost their wallets—and heads.' She howled her terrible laugh and my knees gave out."

"You passed out?"

"Paralyzed like a deer stuck in the headlights—under a spell. But a minute later the Lord, always faithful, broke the curse and gave me an idea—run—you gotta flee from sin just like the Good Book says. Otherwise, Demimonde will pull you into one trap after another."

"But what'd Lily do?"

"Hell's bells, that witch wasn't happy. Screamin' and bellowin', she kicked at my heels all the way back to the fourth plateau."

"You've been here ever since."

"And happy to stay. This is my home, a sanctuary guarded by a hundred crosses. Got no more delusions about running away. No, sir, I work for the Lord, and my work is good. Lily will always hunt me and without his protection, she'll roast me on a Demimonde fire. That Mudling is a power greater than Wilson Cabotage, every day and twice on Sunday, not that I care about days anymore."

"What about joining up with someone like me going back to the real world?"

"Oh, here we go. I've heard that little plan more than once. Vonn Thrasher, who did Pilot tell you to find?"

"You."

"Wilson Cabotage, that's who. Here I'm somebody. Where you're going I'm nobody."

"True. You are important here, but what about your family in the real world?"

"Shush." He waved his hands like he was swatting mosquitoes. "My wife and best friend are dead. My kids are grown and gone. Did I tell you that I passed out one night with a lit cigarette and burned my house down? That's how I ruined this eye." He pointed to his face. "If that weren't bad enough, the fire spread and burned the neighbor's house too. Terrible—their two kids hospitalized. My insurance paid out okay, and court restitution took the rest of my money. But nobody there wants to see my face. Nothing back there that hasn't been ruined by me, the bottle, and Demimonde."

"We can't control how people react," I said. "We're supposed to forgive and forget once we set things right."

"Uh-huh, I heard that before. Sounds good doesn't it? My friend, amends work like this. When a carpenter drives a nail in the wrong place, he sees the mistake, pulls out the nail, taps it straight, and reuses it. But what about the ugly hole, the scar that was never supposed to be?"

"Well—"

"That hole will be there forever. One day the house will be finished with nicely painted walls that cover the nail hole. Nobody knows it's there except the carpenter and God. This plateau, my cabin and crosses are my wall. My past sins are forgiven and hidden by God's house. And I praise him every day for it."

We sat, listening to the flames pop and crackle. The two owls announced their return.

"Booze ruined my past and stole my future. Most years I don't remember my birthday. I never think about Halloween or Christmas. All I have is today and this patch of dirt. But I've got no complaints." Wilson cupped his hands around his mouth and hooted back at the owls. They ignored his call. "Vonn, this mountain is my friend. Silence and solitude are my companions. Every day can be Thanksgiving Day up here with God. I've never been closer to him."

"This plateau is your friend?" Anxiety stole my breath. When did I lose the real world? Is a lonely plateau on some Big Book mountain my new life? No, no that hurts too much. "That's so damned sad I can't stand it." I muttered, "Got smoke in my eyes."

Blinded by tears and remorse, I stumbled into the forest, fell on all fours, and wept my soul empty. My ruined future spelled Demimonde or Ordonne—the choice crushed me. Was this another soul purging?

"There'll come a time when your only hope, only defense— only solution is God. Time to sweep your house clean," Wilson called. "Let the past go."

I rolled onto my back. "My only hope, only defense, only solution is—oh God, whoever you are, help me."

Something old, heavy, and ugly—my sick faithless ego—rolled away with my tears and soaked into the forest floor. I realized I'd never loved anyone because I didn't understand love. Not since lust for Pearl consumed me.

But I loved Wilson Cabotage. He was real—a mountain man who lived in the clouds with his higher power—among enemies. He served others, teaching them to walk the Pious Trail. I wanted that gift, but knew I was too weak.

I yelled, "I love you man."

"I love you like a son," he responded.

Truth is, we did. But, *this plateau, my cabin and crosses are my walls*, scared me, told me to leave. Because the Fourth Plateau was a purgatory for us, and anyone who chose to stay. I'd miss him, but the thought of living the rest of my life on a mountain repulsed me. I didn't know how or when, but I intended to return to the world, to a life in Baser.

Lacking the power of midsummer, the autumn sun crossed the sky on an ever-diminishing path. How many minutes does a sunbeam and its shadow companion need to reach us? Wilson's old encyclopedia told that a particle of light takes eight minutes to travel to the earth. If what we see is already eight minutes old, without the sun's light, would time cease? Would all creatures vanish like a lamp's light without oil? When asked, Wilson winked and said, "Your thinker is racing a little fast for almanacs and encyclopedias."

With the wood stacked, we spent almost two days digging his garden, sorting and sacking potatoes, and carting them to the root cellar. Wilson was ready for the Island's winter. The Lings left us alone, and we enjoyed our time together during those easygoing days.

A cool breeze pushed through the cabin's open door. Sunbeams reflected off shrubs and trees wet with morning dew, and reached around the curtains to create shadowy marks on the floor. They moved steadily, deliberately, marking the day's length. Morning and evening shadows, once understood, tell forest secrets, reveal hidden things, and highlight the truth and the unseen.

The long shadows revealed their message.

Time to leave.

Chapter Ten

Demimonde

The sun burned off the gold-rimmed morning clouds, allowing the trees to cast a kaleidoscope of red, orange, green, and yellow colors across the mountain. A stream rushed out of the upper forest, plummeted over boulders, and roared around deadfalls until liberated to flow as crystal-clear water. The watercourse slowed and snaked across a grassy meadow, then pooled, forming picture-perfect places to cast my fishing line.

My third cast was spot-on. The red and white bobber nodded and dipped down the bubbling current, dragging my line and baited hook along the rocky streambed. Coded messages pulsed as my thumb pushed against the monofilament.

… Be ready Vonn Thrasher

… any second

… a fish will strike

… and run downstream.

But the bobber paused in calmer water.

Wait—wait.

Trout fishing tested patience and prudence. Spoken words forewarned failure. Concentration brought stealth, a deep seclusion. The smooth water became a mirror.

I saw myself.

Blue eyes, no longer bloodshot, gazed back at me. Streaks of gray lightened my temples and beard, framing the high cheekbones of my angular face. I leaned forward for a closer look. Squared shoulders topped a lean body; no longer bloated or young. I waved, and the image waved back.

The Magic Twenty warmed in my pocket. The smell of Changelove's office—camphor and witch hazel—alerted me to Watcher's presence.

"Hello, Watcher."

"Not a good spot for trout fishing. Not to worry, you're about to catch something much more important."

I reeled in my line and leaned the pole against a tree. "I saw my reflection just now."

"You're different, lanky, older with long hair. Believe me, Vonn, sobriety becomes you. You're a handsome man."

"I haven't used a mirror since Treatment Ship. At first, I didn't recognize myself. How could I change that much in a few months?"

"The man in your bathroom mirror was a lie—a composite of painkillers, hair dye, booze, and bloated ego."

"You really think I'm handsome?"

"I only speak the truth."

I looked at my reflection again, then downstream a quarter-mile away where Wilson worked his fly-fishing pole. "All is well?"

"All is well. Sit down and breathe deeply. Open your mind and I will take you to another time and place."

Time-travel or the mysterious fourth dimension? In a dream-like state, my spirit fused with her voice; her words transported me from Sobriety Island. I couldn't see Watcher, and to this day, have yet to see her, but we linked in boundless connection, unity, and compassion.

"Welcome to the Italian city-state of Ferrara, a place of high society lords and ladies."

"Wow. Traveling with you—that's intimacy."

"Christopher Columbus lives today." Watcher moved the vague semblances into three-dimensional images. Three exquisitely dressed ladies lay on a palace great room floor beside a fireplace.

With every hair in place, they looked like expensive china dolls with odd, exaggerated smiles and powdered white faces. Their lifeless dilated pupils stared at the candelabra.

"Why am I here?"

"Showing is better than telling." We moved closer without walking. I could have touched the bodies. "Behold, three of a multitude—victims of a cunning and powerful predator."

"Demimonde?"

"Has been trapping mankind since the days of Noah. Relax, dear boy, we're completely safe. No one can see or hear us."

"Who are they?"

"Quarry, foolish moths who flew too close to the flame."

"How?"

"They refused to grow old. Renaissance-era women put a belladonna cocktail in their eyes. That tiny drop of poison produced an erotic excitement—a return to youth for a few hours. Like all addictions, they needed increasing amounts to reach the desired effect until the cocktail killed them. Smell the incense, their perfume. Observe their wigs and powder, cognac and sweet delights. Such are the things men and women do for beauty and youth—a lovely, yet dreadful price to pay."

"Different day—different drug."

"If you lack peace with God, you'll never experience peace with your age, your neighbor, or the miracle that happens next to you. True then and true today."

I said, "The Demimonde way says I'm a victim of society. If there is a God, he hates me. Life is random chance, bad luck, and circumstance. Therefore, I take what I need to live another miserable day."

"You've come far, Vonn."

A mahogany wall panel opened. A well-dressed man and woman with an adolescent girl entered from a secret passage and stood over the dead women. They beamed like wild boar hunters claiming their prize; they laughed, poured a drink, and toasted with a mantra.

"Antediluvian language," Watcher said. "To die. To never grow old."

"Cold blooded killers."

"Meet Gobin and Clarisse Fabbro and their adopted daughter, Amia. Forty-seven foolish dreamers and would-be aristocrats have perished at their hands. Rich and well connected, they play a game called sting and poison—the last heartbeat—murder. The Fabbros love their victims' final quivers and convulsions; they crave the sight and sound of writhing agony with as much pleasure as sex."

"Is there no end to depravity?"

"Not in Demimonde. And the Fabbros were great Demimonde subjects."

Unlike her parents' multicolored finery, Amia wore a black dress which set off her platinum curls. Her nimble hands quickly stripped the dead women of their money and jewelry, which she stashed in a purse. Then she played a gilded harp while Gobin and Clarisse waltzed around the dead women. The intriguing melody soon had me swaying to its rhythm.

Watcher hissed, "Stop. Have you learned nothing? Temptations of the eye and ear lead to broken thinking."

"Sorry. Strange—I didn't realize I was dancing."

"The devil's dance catches prey unaware."

"I remember. Wave goodbye if you dance with the devil because you won't be coming back."

She continued, "Though suspected, they escaped arrest. Their game ended when they killed a powerful Mafioso's son. They were taken to the same lake where they discarded their victims, beaten, and shot without mercy on the beach."

"One Demimonde met a bigger Demimonde."

"Likewise, in your day, many monsters set traps for you. You must face them before making your way back to the world."

"I'm stronger. The Pious Trail and great storm changed me. The Fourth Plateau, Wilson's stories and wisdom—the Sea of Booze, Treatment and Sponsor Ships—they're part of me. I'm ready for the challenge."

"Hm. You know the wrong way, but need to learn the right way. You're not ready for the trial."

"Trial?"

"A sore test. You're a popular man in Demimonde these days. One might say all the rage."

"With the Lings? I'm not worried about little pests poking around in the shadows."

"With their master, Demimonde. Your enemies have no intention of letting you leave the island. They've planned ambushes to kill or capture you in the wilderness beyond the plateaus."

"I can defend myself."

"Oh really. Now you're a surefooted soldier marching across the spiritual realm, fighting shadowy monsters real or imagined."

"Well, if you put—"

"Beware of Demimonde's darkest secret and greatest tactic—today."

"How could today—" I launched into a coughing and hacking fit. "Something's stuck in my throat." I fought with every breath. Burning lungs and chest pain—my old nemeses, emphysema and bronchitis.

A high-pitched elderly voice said, "Steady, young man." Mr. Conscience was back. "Another little keepsake from your smoky barroom days."

"Sea of Booze," I wheezed. "Salt air fixed me. First spasm I've had in—"

A slow rumbling voice said, "Salt air?" His brother, the walking obituary Mr. Consequence, joined us. "You're nothing more than a simpleton whistling in the dark. I'm thinking past emphysema to lung cancer."

I swatted at the voice and gasped. "You're worse than a pair of houseflies. Didn't I leave you back in Ism Harbor?"

Watcher intervened. "Gentlemen, leave him be. Vonn is at least leaning in the right direction."

I held my hand up. "My lungs—on fire."

Watcher touched my chest, and my airway immediately

cleared. Panic over, I inhaled air like a track star, blinked and straightened. "So much better—thanks. What brought that on?"

The Con brothers answered. "You did—a long time ago."

Watcher said, "A reminder that the wreckage from your past waits to thwart you."

Images of a smoke-filled Bloody Bucket Bar came to mind. Johnny Denial and Minnie Codependent pounded shots with Shotglass Sam and laughed at Nappy Norm's crude jokes. Across the small dance floor, a cue ball scattered a new rack of fifteen balls all over a pool table. The Boilermaker boys and the High-flyer girls cheered and booed over a dart game. A funky couple pawing each other in a highbacked booth brought to mind the comment, "Get a room!" All the while jukebox rock 'n' roll permeated the place.

"Waiting? Yes, but I say no."

"Ordonne has given you the power to choose today. And tomorrow. And the next day. But be assured—temptation is relentless. Demimonde will make you choose until your spiritual strength silences its voice, or you fail."

"I'm done with my old life."

"Demimonde beckons the lost to join old friends and lovers in a half-world, where the sick and lonely are made carefree and popular."

I panted in agreement. "Everything is just one hit away. A shot and a beer make every day Christmas morning. One big happy family."

Watcher said, "There's a steep price to pay. Demimonde takes the second half of their life as payment. 'Give me your distant tomorrows when your soul is old and worn out, and today I'll make every mirror your friend. You'll be popular; leader of the gang, happy, wealthy, and loved.'"

"Like the three dead women," I said.

"Yes. The foolish takers think, 'So what? I hate my life. If I can have what I want today, let Demimonde have the second half—the old useless years that I may never see anyway.'"

"The invitation to dance," I said.

"The hook. Early on the takers actually experience a pleasurable high."

"Nirvana. Where has this been my whole life?"

"Once the wedding dance is consummated by addiction and insanity, it controls their thoughts, and they find themselves in gray Shantytowns."

"Wondering what happened."

"Demimonde never intended to wait. In a few short years, it takes half of today—their nights."

The Fabbro's mantle clock chimed twice.

In a flash we stood in Changelove's office. The smell of camphor and witch hazel morphed into unbelievable pain. Haunting nightmares about lying dead along a deserted road, or running naked from personal demons down alleys and across fields surrounded me. "Madness. No, please not again."

Watcher growled, "Remember the eleventh hour of the eleventh day? Only a dead man's clock has a thirteenth hour. Remember your Demimonde fate—thirteen steps ascending a gallows deck—thirteen twists in a hangman's knot."

Real or imagined, I looked down. I stood on the top of thirteen large and long steps. I couldn't move. My legs mutated into tree roots growing out of the steps. I heard Moneymaker taunt from the shadows. "Nobody cares about you, or me—or this ship of fools."

Thirst, dry mouth. I groaned, "Water, I want—"

"Demimonde takes the night and controls your days. You'll die before you're forty."

I couldn't cringe or hide my face. Rigor Mortis?

Suddenly I stood near the three dead women again.

Amia grabbed their hands and dragged them out of the room one at a time. Their lifeless heads bobbed, squeaking, crying, pleading.

"Am I dead or alive?"

Watcher was silent.

Gobin and Clarisse smiled, sipped their wine, and looked right through me.

Watcher said, "The Wicket, The Way, The Light, The Truth."

Freezing cold—wooden legs, terrible pain—the image of the wrinkled yellow placard fastened to Changelove's door.

I swiveled my head. "Get me outta here."

I stood in the bright morning sun by the mountain stream. Exploding with rage, I wanted to kill someone, anyone—Watcher, Wilson, even myself. A wind gust knocked me to the ground. I buried my face in the grass to escape the fierce attack of whirling dust and leaves. Then the overpowering aroma of fresh rain and rich black earth lifted my fear and hatred.

Watcher's voice silenced the wind. "Focus, Vonn. Count your heartbeats."

My racing heart slowed to a perfect rhythm. I timed each breath, four beats in, and four beats out until I relaxed. "No more time trips."

"I thought you liked pretty women and afterhours parties."

"The Fabbros are right out of Poe's *The Tell-Tale Heart*. Madness and murder."

Watcher said, "Demimonde traps aren't black or white decisions. They're always gray. They look good on the surface, but cravings capture victims with unquenchable obsessions. You'll dance until you're given a belladonna cocktail."

"That's an ugly thought."

"Yes, but your Moral Compass will alert you to hidden danger."

Wilson moved upstream to another spot and rolled out a short cast with his fly rod. A classic scene of serenity from a magazine cover. No wonder he'd never leave. He was whole, but I remained fractured. Part of me still belonged to Demimonde.

My recent history had good memories and a new faith. None were more powerful than my first night on the plateaus, when God saved me from the terrible thunder, lightning, and driving rain. "Freedom and power, the Creator lives, and loves, and delivers the poor in spirit."

That had been a turning point, but Demimonde still owned my nights. The struggle came and went—lurking in idle thoughts and twisted daydreams, breeding resentment and cravings—I was one drink away from Shantytown.

There weren't any trout hanging on Wilson's stringer. "How long—"

"Island time, a few minutes. He knows I'm here and will be along later."

I pointed at Wilson. He saw me and waved. "Watcher, I'm a beginner. And I don't know how or when, but I want what Wilson has."

"You want sanity, serenity, and sobriety to have the strength to stand on solid ground. You can't have Wilson's. You must find your own."

I grabbed a rag out of my fishing creel and walked down to the stream. I took a big breath and splashed water on my face. No coughing. I tried to scrub the memory of the wicked Fabbros away in the cold mountain water.

Watcher said, "You think too much. Strengthen your resolve young man, we have one more meeting to make."

"No more time travel. Not again."

"No more time travel. We're going to eavesdrop on the neighbor's fireside chat. Demimonde knows you by name, and you might say they want you over for dinner. Fear not—"

My spirit merged with her voice, and her words carried me away in a blur—a suspension of my senses.

Long shadows draped the scene.

The sun peeked over the island's western mountains, coloring the clouds red, orange, and yellow. We stood in the middle of a trashy camp, dark and foggy and smelling of swamp mud, sewage, and wood smoke.

"Like the Fabbro outing, they can't hear or see us."

"As if I had a choice."

Changelings abounded. Dozens of misshapen filthy creatures gathered around an expansive fire pit in the middle of camp. Most of them were waist high and littered with scars and open sores. Many were naked. The rest wore tattered rags, an assortment of what they'd pinched from unwary Ordonnes walking the Pious Trail. They spoke in loud guttural voices and shrieked like wild animals.

One, however, stood out. A beautiful woman sat in a large chair at the edge of the firelight. Clouded by a misty green aura, she had an otherworldly appeal. Her woven wood chair was alive, writhing and slithering like a mass of vipers.

I whispered, "A throne of serpents?"

"Look again. What do you smell?" Watcher replied.

Wine—the unmistakable smell of fermenting grapes. "Wine—her clothes and throne are grapevines, alive and animated."

The vine's leaves and fleshy fruit made a kaleidoscope of red and blue, black and white, emerald and gold that sparkled and glowed like Christmas tree ornaments.

The woman's long legs rested on a Ling's back like a footstool, while two others massaged her feet. A fourth stood on a stump and combed her flowing hair which changed with every movement. Brunette on one side, blonde on the other, then black and white, red and gray. When she spoke, her flesh shifted from chartreuse to black, then white, brown, yellow, and back to green. A mottling of tiny brown marks and symbols shaded her forehead and cheekbones. Bright red lips and fingernails completed her vivid appearance.

"Watcher, is she—"

"Demimonde? Yes, and this Ling camp stands between you and the world."

Despite the clear danger, her beauty and filth were magnetic. Enthralled, I shouldered my way through the Lings to the front of the throne to touch her. Confused Lings snarled and slapped each other when I bumped them out of the way.

She morphed from feminine to masculine and then something

in between. Raw lust consumed my thoughts. I couldn't take my eyes off of her face. Relapse be damned—I inhaled her decadence, and pushed forward intending to climb her throne and bury my face in her breasts.

My Moral Compass burned hot.

I entered into visions of drunken orgies, riots, and sacks of gold, gorging on bloody red beasts, wolfing down every loaf and cake within reach, and washing everything down with liquid oblivion.

Almost there—to touch her could cost me everything. I didn't care.

Gut wrenching cravings made my mouth water.

Every cell in my body screamed for wine. I tasted bourbon and smelled beer.

My chest ached to feel opium's sweet glow.

I heard Moneymaker's taunt. "Thrasher, this Watcher's a hoax, and you're a fool. Nobody cares about you—or me—Ordonne is a ship of fools. Run, Vonn, run to the throne, before you lose what's yours. Before it's too late."

I shut my eyes and covered my ears. Run—hide—deny everything.

In a moment of clarity, I stopped. "Nooo—" I backpedaled and turned to flee, stumbled, and fell on my face in the slimy mud. A confused Ling tripped over me. Another one stepped on my hand, shrieked, and kicked me in the ribs.

Could they see me?

Wood smoke and green vapors stung my eyes. I couldn't get up.

"On your feet, young man." Watcher's unseen hands lifted me. "Steady now."

The Lings swarmed like angry bees, yelling and shoving each other. Their numbers grew by the second. Several giant ones waded into the fight, cursing and swinging clubs. Every blow sent another sprawling.

Chaos exploded.

"Riot," Watcher shouted over the din. "Move to the edge of camp."

"Over there?" I pointed upwind from the fire to a cluster of dead trees.

"Escape," she said.

I ducked and dodged through the confusion to the trees then threw up until I had dry heaves. Finally, I caught my breath. Bruised and shaky, but momentarily safe. I slapped my head and moaned, "I'm an idiot."

The din grew louder. Bouncers couldn't quash the bloody brawl.

Demimonde grinned over the angry mob, relishing the violence. She didn't look at, as much as through, the teeming mob.

"Does she know we're here?" I asked.

"Probably," Watcher said.

"So much for stealth."

"You can't be a good spy with intoxicated flesh." Watcher's invisible touch relieved my nausea. "Welcome to Demimonde's lair. With me, you will survive. But alone, all men and women die here. Tell me, young man, what you see?"

"Main gate to hell must be here." I bent forward and put my hands on my knees. "And that creature, Demimonde, is beyond exotic—whether a witch or a demon. I felt a powerful hunger and thirst, lust and greed, fear and anger all mixed together. But I didn't care. I wanted every scintilla and her green vapor too."

"Demimonde has been called many things, including the devil. This queen-like creature can be a naïve young man or a clever old woman, be handsome or hideous, a giant or too small to see. It's a gale force wind that beats 10,000 Shantytowners into submission. So, yes, the word it is closer to the truth than he or she. Regardless of form or fashion, this evil entity has successfully exploited mankind's weaknesses since the days of Noah."

A giant Ling roared like a grizzly and backhanded two Lings in a short arc to the foot of the throne. Demimonde's consorts fell upon them with clubs, beating them until they stopped writhing.

"Wow."

Watcher said, "Now you see the real Demimonde. Open, unabashed, brutal hatred."

"I was there," I said.

"Upside-down."

"For a moment I hated you and everything Ordonne." I turned and spit something brown and bitter on the ground, and then wiped my mouth with my sleeve. "What I wouldn't give for a glass of clean plateau water."

"Vonn Thrasher, tell me the truth. What sword or rifle would you use to attack Demimonde?"

"Neither."

"Is there a shield or kind of armor that you might wear to defend yourself?"

"No."

"Agreed. This is a battle of the senses. Demimonde uses your eyesight and hearing, your smell and taste, even your feelings against you. It twists natural instincts and needs—for friendship and sex, for food and shelter, even God's gifts like compassion—into insanity. That's how it breaks humanity."

The riot tapered off. A Ling wearing a deer antler miter walked through the crowd, beating a tin bucket like a drum and yelling, "Quiet. Shuddup you miserable sots." The creatures gave way and began to pull each other up from the slippery sewer that was the courtyard.

"Listen up," Watcher said. "That's Petri the Darkling, and it's about to ask Mondi a question that you'll find very interesting."

"Mondi?"

"Mudlings, Darklings, and Wretchlings call the enthroned one Mondi. Their twisted, wet brains cannot pronounce anything more complicated."

Mondi stood tall in front of her throne; her raised arms were illuminated by the fire against the dark. The crowd stilled. She stared into the mass of Lings with concern, turning left and right, and sniffing the air with feral intensity. With every breath, her flesh rippled from chartreuse to charcoal, then gold and red, and the tiny symbols on her face strobed like rhinestones. She forced a smile, shrugged her shoulders, and sat.

The creatures, now over 200 strong, crowded near her, bustling and buzzing like a beehive.

The Antlered Darkling stood on a pile of rocks at the edge of the crowd shouting abuse. His oversized mouth opened ear to ear, giving him a tall bullfrog appearance with a croaky voice to match. "Silence—all you filthy low-life drunken toads. Silence— look to the throne."

The Lings whistled, farted, and blew raspberries. The giant ones ambled through the crowd with the clubs on their shoulders, shushing the catcallers.

Every twisted face had a smile. Real or delusional—they adored Mondi.

"Amazing. How can they live in all this squalor and still love her?"

Watcher replied, "Remember Doctor Changelove's forewarning? History is the Lings' common enemy. If they live long enough, time twists their minds. They become arrogant and proud of the difference between themselves and earth people. *After all,* they boast, *it's better to be touched by the backhand of God, than never at all.*"

Petri dropped his alarm bucket and stood with both arms raised, waiting for quiet. "Listen up, guttersnipes." His voice, deep enough for a creature twice his size, echoed across the camp. "Darklings, Mudlings, and hideous little Wretchlings—all rise and face the throne."

He cleared his throat. "You know what to do. On three. One … two …"

"Oh, great and mighty Mondi,

"Give us flesh and beer,

"Make us nasty,

"Give us fear,

"So that we can live another year."

The mixed mass howled, backslapped, and cheered.

A dozen giant Lings stood at the edge of the firelight behind several massive hollow logs, arranged to point left and right of the throne. I could have walked upright inside the length of the tree trunks, yet they barely hid the giant's legs. They held their clubs ready, waiting for a cue.

Mondi nodded, and the hideous drummers beat the old dented wood, producing a rhythmic thump. Rousing and primal sonic waves pulsed through the camp, rattling their clothes like a stiff breeze, tearing leaves off trees, and setting twigs flying. Many covered their ears and ran, but the hollow log drums were magnetic to me. Without thinking, I began to move to the beat.

"Remember the Fabbros' waltz," Watcher said. "Temptation of the eye and ear leads to broken thinking."

"I do—sorry." I straightened and crossed my arms. "Loud. Why didn't I hear this racket up on the plateaus?"

Mondi's consorts grabbed two dead Lings from in front of the throne and tossed them on the fire. The hungry flames flared tall as a tree, lighting up all of Mondi's courtyard.

As the crowd wailed, the giants picked up the thumping tempo.

"They must have been soaked with gasoline."

Watcher said, "Their blood runs cold with alcohol, so they burn like Molotov cocktails. All that's left of their humanity is just enough blood to color their flesh red."

I turned away from the blistering light. "But there's nothing to drink on this island."

"The Changeling condition got them here. It's permanent now—they don't need to drink to be the way they are."

Other Lings broke out of the crowd running in pairs, carrying tree trunks and limbs, braving the hellish flames long enough to throw them into the inferno and dash away. One got too close and caught its stringy hair on fire. It screamed for help and rolled in a mud puddle to douse the flames. The others laughed and stepped back. Several hoisted smaller Wretchlings on their shoulders for a better view.

Seared hairless and charred, the burned Ling staggered to its feet and disappeared into the darkness.

"Enough fun and games." Petri cupped his hands around his mouth and shouted from his rock pile. He only had three fat fingers on each hand. "Ling clan, listen up."

The giants abruptly stopped beating the logs.

"I have good news. The moon is waxing strong. Another Ordonne ship is sailing into the harbor. Tomorrow night will be good hunting."

The crowd erupted into happy howls and dancing.

Petri yelled, "Before we sink our teeth in their flesh, I have a point-of-order."

Mondi held her left hand up to Petri. The assembly fell quiet.

She motioned the fire down with her right hand, quelling the flames by half, and sat back on her throne. The writhing grapevines slithered around her, glistening with multicolored lights. She interlaced her fingers and smiled with evil delight. "What mayhem do you bring me?"

Petri stumbled to the foot of the throne and kneeled. "Great and mighty Mondi, may we kill the man tonight?"

"How fun you are. The man is a survivor. He's too valuable to destroy right now."

"The man?" I asked, "Who—"

"Hush, we're here to listen and learn," Watcher replied.

"But man is made for killing," shouted a feminine voice from the dark.

Heads turned. Without hesitation, the Lings parted and made a way to the fire pit.

"What manner of creature this must be," I said.

A Mudling woman with red hair and a freckled face approached the throne. Unlike the others, she was clean and pretty and dressed in bright clothes. She might have been a school girl walking to class. "Yes. Cruelty and conquest are delicious dishes to eat."

"Lily, you are a wicked little terror," Mondi said. Her throne's shimmering vines lit up and undulated. "Why, I'd love you if I were capable of that kind of weakness."

Oohs and ahhs rippled through her throng of hideous shills.

"Lily," I said. "She's—"

"Wilson's old enemy," Watcher replied.

"Nay, nay, my little Lings, everything in good time." Mondi's voice boomed across the camp. Her subjects moaned and cowered, anticipating the wave of pain that usually came with a no. But this time she was kind and jovial. The seizures and agony never came. "Let him live, aware of his past and what he will create for me—a community of suffering and apostasy."

"Wicked leader, I ask once more," Lily partitioned. "Let me have the young man. Let me show him how much he must suffer for the great and powerful Mondi. Cabotage has grown old and careful and boring. I need a fresh soul to break. Reward me with his fear and anger. Let me consume his madness."

Two throne vines shot up tall as a tree, and lashed out like massive bullwhips at anyone close. The crowd dived and rolled out of their range. "Test me not with another demand, lest I strip you to a Wretchling, sucking blood from salamanders in the black bog."

The Lings looked down and held their breath. In the silence, only the fire crackled.

Mondi continued, "Vonn Thrasher must become a useful vessel, and return to Baser a broken man—drunk, mean, and full of rage."

My heart skipped a beat.

"Dear Lily, don't worry. If that damned Watcher and Ordonne prevail—we will kill him. He will not leave Sobriety Island a free man."

"Freedom. What a disgusting thought," Petri said.

"Brainwashing future subjects using Ordonne lies," Lily said. "A true enemy."

"Just thinking about Ordonne makes me want to destroy someone," Mondi growled. The crowd gasped and turned away. "Thrasher is too important. That's why I'm assigning him to the Night Terror. He'll be dead or delivered to me a shivering, broken man. Either way, I win. Ordonne loses."

"Night Terror? Watcher, what—"

"Even to me, an unknown. Few have survived the Night Terror to tell their story."

A bug-eyed Ling covered with bloody ulcers staggered out of the crowd and hobbled toward me.

"What the—" I recognized the ragged El Dorado Carnival shirt. It belonged to Pighead Tom, the carnie I sailed with on Treatment Ship. He had changed for the worse, smaller and more grotesque, but remained the same bully—the thin-skinned gym rat. "Pighead, I thought the eels got you back in the Sea of Booze."

My eyes narrowed—payback time. "Watcher, I know that one. Hey, Pig, where'd your muscles go?"

"Vonn, slow down. They cannot see or hear us but sometimes they—"

"This one will know I'm here."

Pig was two steps out when I launched and double stiff-armed him, sending him sliding on his heels into the crowd, knocking three or four other others flying like bowling pins.

"They smell us—that wasn't a good idea," Watcher said.

"Intruders," Mondi bellowed.

Petri beat an alarm on the old bucket.

Lings screeched and barked. They ran in every direction.

Mondi rushed from the throne to Pighead and the other fallen Lings. "I thought I smelled a human."

"Oh, no," I whispered.

"Spies," Lily shouted.

"Cowards," Mondi screamed and raised her fists. "It's Watcher. Thrasher too—they're here—spread out. You can grab them even if you can't see them."

"Follow your nose," Lily shouted over the clamor. "They reek of soap and coffee."

Petri waved a club over his head, "They taste like fear."

"Good with taters," thundered a giant.

Mondi yelled, "Drag them to me, and I'll give you Thrasher's right arm."

They closed the distance between us, swinging and grabbing at the air. I glanced left and right. No escape. Dozens marched my way to the beat of the hollow logs. All chanting, "Mondi, Mondi, mine, mine, mine."

I retreated until I stumbled backward against a wall of smooth sandstone. A cliff—I was trapped.

The giants pulled down a tree and beat the ground with the branches.

"I smell his delicious terror," Mondi bellowed. "Chop-chop, Thrasher has trapped himself."

Watcher roared, "Halt!"

Her voice rolled the Lings like a blast from a firehose.

Before they could untangle themselves, she yelled, "Out!"

Mondi's throne twisted into a knot. The fire flashed, swelled, and then blew apart, destroying Mondi's throne and sending hundreds of rocks, vines, Changelings, and glowing embers up in a billowing cloud of ash leaving a pitch-black camp.

I couldn't see my own hands. Scary, but good because Lings were completely night-blind.

"Dark," a Ling yelled.

"Hurt," another moaned. Others cried out for Mondi.

Silence.

The minutes lasted forever. "Watcher, did you stop time?"

Like scared children hiding in the dark, no one moved. Then trade winds pushed the clouds away from a bright waxing moon.

"Damn you," Mondi berated from across the moonlit camp. "Regroup."

The big Lings growled and stomped the mud. "Grab 'em. Rip 'em limb from limb."

The wind parted the last of the ash cloud, revealing a teeming mass of arms and legs coming our way.

"Watcher, give us another yell."

"To the cliff—attack—pull down the dead trees," Mondi and Lily commanded. "Destroy everything and we'll get them too."

A rock in one hand and a hefty stick in the other, I braced

for the fight of my life. I yelled, "Watcher. Nice knowing you."

In a flash, I was swept out of the camp by an invisible current, tumbling above the trees until my spirit levitated to a dimension beyond the clouds. A place deep as an ocean, immeasurable, muffled, weightless, and safe from Mondi and her followers.

Gravity pulled me back toward the world, resetting my internal stability. I smelled pine, heard rushing water, and watched ravens soar above me. A breeze carried the scent memory of a million forest leaves, blades of grass combed by an unseen hand. A long-stemmed foxtail tickled my face.

Watcher said, "That wasn't good scouting."

"On the other hand—great fighting," I snorted. "Impressive. One more shout out, and you'd have blown away the whole durned camp."

She sighed. "The things you find funny. We were supposed to watch and learn, not fight. Now Mondi's agitated hordes are seeking revenge."

"Let them. I'll never see that village again."

"True, you won't. Next time they'll be waiting for you along the Pious Trail."

"Seriously?"

No answer—Watcher's standard dismissal.

"Think positive. Sometimes we have to look past our disagreements and celebrate the win. Gloom and doom aside, we put a hurting on them."

Silence.

"Lings are worse than lepers, but—"

She interrupted. "Not so. Unlike you and Lings, lepers tend to be innocent. I thought you'd grown up, but you're still impulsive—one drink away from Ling citizenship—no different than Pig."

"Pig. No way. You're wrong."

"Hey," Wilson called. He stood downstream a couple hundred yards with his hands on his hips. "What are you yelling about?"

I sat up and shouted over the rushing water, "I'm okay." He waved and picked up his fly pole. I looked out of the corner of my eye, hoping to catch a flicker of Watcher. People claim we can see ghosts and apparitions with peripheral vision, but there was nothing—not a shadow or footprint.

"We've been together since Changelove's office. I wish I could see you just once."

Silence.

"There's always a first time."

Only the wind and birds answered. Her silence was unbearable.

"I'm sorry about the Ling camp. But I'm telling you, I will be free."

"Free?" Watcher hissed in Mondi's voice, "To create a community of suffering and apostasy?"

"Ha, Mondi—yeah, she said that. But that doesn't mean it's true."

"Then vigilance must be your watchword. The price of freedom. If you continue to live on impulse and ignore your Moral Compass, you'll fall into Mondi's hooks and traps."

"I can be vigilant."

"Vigilance requires surrender. As long as you fight Demimonde by struggling and plotting, hoping that next time will be different, you'll lose. You'll trap yourself before you leave your house in the morning."

"Surrender?" I pulled my knees to my chest. "That doesn't make sense."

"Hitting Pig almost got you killed. One shove—remember that. You must quit fighting anyone or anything, period."

"Fight?" I remembered Pig's dazed expression as he slid and rolled into the other Lings. I picked up a fist-sized rock and grinned. "Yeah, I knocked Pig down. But before that, I can't remember the last time I fought anyone. Come to think of it, I haven't even shouted at anybody since boarding Sponsor Ship."

She raised her voice. "You're trying to use a rifle to get sober."

"They're waiting for me. I have a right to defend myself."

"Insidious."

As a hard wind bent the trees, autumn leaves swirled and vanished. The flattened shrubs and grass revealed an enormous snake with charcoal-black scales. Raising up waist high, it inched forward and flicked the air with its forked tongue.

I jumped up and hustled behind a tree. "Snake! Oh no, I—I can't."

The snake slithered into a strike position a dozen steps away, elevated its scaly head to eye level, and flared a golden hood—broad as my shoulders and marked with two false eyes.

I stared across twenty feet into round unblinking eyes of glaring death, and heard a bone-chilling growl not unlike an angry mastiff's warning. A tear rolled down my cheek.

Watcher cautioned me. "Don't stare back. That's a challenge."

I looked away. "Watcher," I squeaked. "Giant cobra—please—do—something."

"Saul, meet Vonn Thrasher. The pigeon who thinks he's a falcon. Vonn, meet Saul, king cobra and island regulator. He is neither good nor bad, but prevents Mondi and her subjects from doing every evil they intend."

"Saul. I, I—"

"Something about Saul that every islander should know—he demands peace and quiet."

"Quiet?"

"He loves to sleep for days on end, sunning on grassy hillsides. The wind whistling through the forest and the waves breaking on the island's rocky beaches calm Saul's aggressive nature."

He uttered something guttural, looked left and right, then slithered forward ten feet. He opened his mouth wide to brandish two fangs longer than my index finger.

"Guess who woke him today?"

"We—"

"You did. You disturbed his blessed tranquility. He's quite the restless spirit when irritated, and he's here to settle the matter."

"Settle?" I peeked around the tree trunk. Saul moved forward.

"In more ways than one. He sleeps for a month after feeding because Lings take a long time to digest. You've probably guessed by now that the uproar at the camp unsettled his stomach, and, well, he lost his supper, and he's here to fix the problem."

"Me?"

"Fortunately for me-ee-e," Watcher stretched *me* into three syllables. "He knows me-ee-e as a peacemaker, an endearing trait for the king cobra. He also knows that the enemy of my enemy is my friend."

"Demimonde?"

"Saul and Demimonde hate each other in equal measure. Mondi tries to kill him and steal his dominion. He in turn, feeds on the Lings. As you might guess, they hate being eaten. He has little use for Ordonnes either. But, because I intercede and resolve confrontations, he tolerates the occasional pilgrim that wanders off the Pious Trail."

Saul hissed in my face. His tongue tickled and tasted the sweat on my forehead. His breath smelled worse than a dead rat. I pushed my head back against the tree bark, closed my eyes, and held my breath. Bile rolled up and down my throat.

"Matter-of-fact," Watcher said, "Thrasher is clean and sober. And yes, I'll owe you another one large if you let him go."

"Please," I whispered.

A clicking hiss led to a fading slither. I opened my eyes as the last twelve or thirteen feet of Saul vanished in the denuded tree line. I fell to my knees and began to breathe again. "Thank you."

"If Saul tasted booze in your sweat, he'd have eaten you like a fat Ling."

"Sobriety saved me."

She sighed. "Someone much higher than that."

"God did. And you, and Pilot, and Wilson, and a hundred other Ordonnes."

"Yes." She plucked the rock from my hand, elevated it head high and crushed it into dust. A gust of wind carried the fragments away.

"I didn't realize I was still holding it."

"More like brandishing it. Trust me, your fight is beyond this three-dimensional world. Your willful days must end, or you'll never stop wrestling Ordonne for your soul. Be vigilant. Be abstinent. Be humble and kind and you'll be shielded in Ordonne. Walk the Pious Trail—"

"Like a ghost and leave this island like I was never here."

"Yes. Paul, a very wise man, wrote about our struggle many centuries ago. 'For we wrestle not against flesh and blood, but against principalities, against powers, against the rulers of the darkness of this world, against spiritual wickedness in high places.'"

"You must learn how to survive—"

"Or I won't. But how can I stop fighting when I don't know I'm fighting?"

"All fights start with a no."

Watcher lectured me.

I said nothing.

"No, pride sings it's beneath me.

"No, greed snarls it's mine.

"No, lust mocks with a kiss,

"Even your sons and daughters are mine.

"No starts a war.

"No loses the farm.

"No brings famine and want in time."

"No," I said. I got the lesson.

"No is a half-brother of ism. And ism is the nasty beast that pulls self through no's open door. And self brings I will, *I want*, and *I quit* into the house. Drunkenness and abuse are sure to follow. Then *I'll kill*, often myself, takes the master bedroom and joins every conversation. Violence has a powerful draw on the unbalanced mind."

I slapped the ground and jumped up. "That's what happened—I want pulled me to Mondi's throne. Then—I'll kill got me to attack Pig."

"Demimonde whispers when you're high, and shouts when you're low.

'Step into the twilight.

'Give me your spirit.

'Be free, of pain and suffering.

'Be free, to live neither here nor there,
'Be free, join the sad poet, the brave explorer,
'Chase your darkest dream,
'Make the sun set in the north.
'And embrace me and die.'"

I said, "The Shantytown way is a bottle, a needle, a pipe, or a rope from a rafter."

"Thirteen turns in a hangman's knot," she said.

"I understand—"

"More and better, but you still have some growing to do. Our roust at the Ling camp busted them up pretty well, so there won't be any patrolling the plateaus for Ordonnes anytime soon."

"Hadn't thought of that," I said. "We might've saved an alky or two."

"Less fortunate than you," she said. "If you ever hope to see Baser again, others must come first. Caring for someone small and defenseless will allow you to survive the Pious Trail."

"Caring for someone?"

"Be safe."

"Small? What are you talking about?" She left, as usual, without a goodbye.

I stretched out in the grass and watched the clouds float across the clear blue sky. No and Step into the Twilight. Poetry or song, words put to rhyme stay with a fellow. What about Mondi? A walking obsession. Intoxicating beauty and ugly terror all in one green body.

I ran my fingers through my hair and tugged my beard. It almost touched my chest. When was the last time I had a shave and a haircut? The Treatment Ship? Yes. The day before Captain Know tossed us overboard.

"We were so done. Slippery eel chum." I laughed, hoping Watcher was listening. "You knew that day was the beginning of my recovery, not the end. Now, I know too."

My days had rolled into seasons. Abandoned on the Sea of Booze, then rescued. Good days on the oars, pink clouds, the unstoppable Skipper Sharon, and other new friends. We made it together, we really did. The beach bonfire was bon voyage. Then we left in five different directions. Mine was the high plateaus. I hadn't seen a shipmate since.

"Un-frigging believable. Rach—Barfly—where are you today?" The forest echoed my words.

A rattling tackle box told me Wilson was coming up the trail. "Did you come to fish or talk to yourself? They're not going to jump on the stringer if you're just lying there."

I stood. "You know better than that. I've been with Watcher."

"The Ling camp? I thought as much."

"King Saul too."

"I thought I saw him slithering up country." He handed me his catch. "Ten. I caught 'em, you clean 'em."

"I'll tell you all about Mondi on the way back."

CHAPTER ELEVEN

Broken Hills Wilderness.

We sat together on the cabin porch, enjoying an Indian summer day that rendered human speech useless and unwanted. Wilson hummed and whistled an old sailor's ballad while sewing the last few stitches on a new pair of buckskin moccasins, and I enjoyed an old copy of *The Great Divorce* in the discreet afternoon sun.

When I inclined my ear just right, I heard the wind whispering a lonely song, a mournful poem of a love lost forever. The day was a gift, a rare magical moment, a slice of heaven that I never wanted to end. But it followed the pattern of other magical days that faded away like feathery clouds traveling across the blue sky. Sometimes they joined other clouds and rained their hearts out. Other times they quietly vanished over the horizon. Loaned for an hour or two, and taken in a second. Such moments can never be planned, for time cares nothing of man's longing to hold on to transient beauty.

Listening to understand is the sincerest form of love. And love was relevant on Sobriety Island—not time. Wilson didn't wear a watch. I'd lost mine in the sea. Without timeclocks to punch or calendars to plan, minutes and hours were figures of speech. I'd grown to love Wilson Cabotage. Regardless of our differences in age, race, and background, I trusted him more than any other man, even my father. He listened to me, and I listened to every word of his counsel and stories. Days blended into weeks, then seasons. I treasured the recovery time I had with him, but it was time to leave. Memories of family and friends called my name. I had to find my way back home. Goodbye would be hard.

Wilson beaded a turquoise eagle on each side of the knee-high leggings. The buckskin moccasins were well-made works of art. Packing a rucksack well was also a craft, because every ounce carried mattered. Each item had to be useful or left behind. In two days, all the planning and packing would become life on the trail.

I hoped that he'd give me the moccasins, but wouldn't ask. Wilson was a man of few words, and I knew better than to ask before he was ready to answer—about anything. He held his creation up in the sunlight, turning them to inspect every stitch and seam with his one working eye. "I did a good job." He grinned, "Put these on and see if you like them."

I slipped into them and laced them to the top. "Beautiful." I looked at him with the biggest cow eyes I could make. "They're perfect. Could I—"

"Here." He chuckled and handed me a tin of mink oil. "You already knew they were yours. Rub a little of that on them every spring and fall and they'll last a long time."

"Wow, thank you. They'll make walking the Pious Trail easier."

"Aye, they'll save you a blister or two." He pointed to the open cabin door. "Look under my rack and get my sea chest. Got something else that'll help you."

I brought out his old weathered sea chest and set it next to his chair.

He winked, popped the latch, and opened the lid. "Been a while since anyone got as far as you have."

"I had a lotta help."

I couldn't see past the lid, but smelled something unfamiliar, unique and pleasant, almost like Doc Changelove's office. He handed me a bundle of new socks wrapped around a pair of tin salt and pepper shakers with screw on caps, small enough to hold with one hand.

"Can't have too many socks. Thanks."

"Shakers will add flavor and keep your food from molding. Best yet, when shaken together over toxic foods like poison berries and hemlock, and wounds like beestings, snakebites, and burns, they neutralize their effect."

I smelled and tasted each one, then promptly sneezed. "Nice. Not much different than Mom's kitchen shakers. What's in them?"

"Call them quash. A salt and pepper base, with a little mountain secret of this and that, and of course, Cabotage love and magic."

"Magic?"

"Like your Magic Twenty, if you use quash like you're supposed to it'll outlast you."

"No vice and ill-gotten gain."

"Or you won't be able to salt a tomato." He held his hand up. "Watcher's here."

She said, "Wilson, good to see you again."

"Ha, wished I could say the same. Good to hear you though."

"Vonn," she said. "I see you received a little gift."

"Wilson just gave me these." I stood and hopped from one foot to another, pointing to the buckskin moccasins. "And these." I held out the quash shakers.

"Aren't we the happy camper? What have you given dear Wilson?"

"Well, I—"

"Don't have anything that hasn't been given to you? Not so, how about spoken love and gratitude, or a promise to pray for him? Think on what you have, not on what you don't have, and you'll always have something to give."

"Give Vonn a break," Wilson said. "We're doing fine."

"Fine?" she answered. "Fine won't keep him out of Mondi's claws or keep him sober the rest of his life."

Watcher was prickly.

"He's as ready as any of us were."

"Find out soon enough, won't we?" She groaned, "How are you? I'm fine—Freefalling, Insecure, Neurotic, and Emotional. I'll be a Mudling next week—but I'm fine."

"I hear the Fines are Mondi's fire tenders," Wilson said.

"Fines?" I said.

"A family of four that tried the Pious Trail many seasons ago," Wilson said. "Strange bunch. They refused to admit they were in danger or needed help. They talked and talked until they drove everyone away."

Watcher said, "The only thing they wanted was the fastest way back to where they came from. I looked for them when we were in the Ling camp. I saw Neurotic. The others were gone."

"How do alkies fall into her clutches?" I asked. "How could I go from a bar in Baser or a party in Sordid, to being a Ling in Mondi's camp?"

"Friends and family think they die. Transformed is more accurate." Wilson closed his sea chest. "Or they mysteriously vanish one day when nobody is looking."

Watcher said, "The lowest point on the island is a swamp below the Ling camp called Mondi's bog. A polluted portal where Demimonde twists lost souls into Mondi's foot soldiers."

Wilson said, "They leave Mondi's bog as three-fingered Lings. Some become Darklings, or Wretchlings, or Mudlings. Booze be their blood on Sobriety Island."

"Mondi's slaves forever," I said.

Wilson said, "Everyone stops drinking on Sobriety Island. Unfortunately, most become Lings."

I cleared my throat and stood. "But some of us listen and learn and walk the Pious Trail."

Wilson stood and put his hand on my shoulder. "The wilderness will finish what Sponsor Ship started. You'll leave Sobriety Island with a mission and powerful voice—to carry the good news to people suffering in Demimonde's domain."

Watcher said, "Mondi is desperate to capture and turn you into a Ling—"

"Or kill you to keep alkies enslaved to drugs and alcohol."

We sat quietly for a time. The gravity of what was expected of me was gratifying and scary.

Watcher broke the silence. "Vonn, I also brought you gifts today. Look in your rucksack."

A long-sleeved khaki shirt with pockets and epaulets, a boonie hat, and a new pair of cargo pants were neatly folded on the top. "When did you do that?"

"Go try them on," Wilson said.

"Thanks." I stepped inside the cabin for a quick change. "Wow, they're perfect. New clothes head to toe."

"Check your left pocket," Watcher said.

I unbuttoned the flap and looked inside. A gray mouse looked back and blinked twice. "Mouse—a pocket mouse?"

"Say hello to your new traveling companion," Watcher said.

The mouse climbed out and onto the back of my hand, twitched, and wiggled its nose and whiskers. I took a deep breath. "Why?"

"To be your friend," she replied. "To ride on your rucksack or shoulder, eat what you eat, and tell you mouse stories and trail secrets."

"Ha, okay, I get it. A goodbye joke. Funny, now can I—"

"Get rid of it? Best not," she said. "The only way you'll leave Sobriety Island alive is to take that mouse with you, every step of the way, alive and well. Your life depends on your tiny new friend."

"Oh, I see. The mouse is punishment for the fight at Ling camp."

"No, proud man." Watcher sighed. "This mouse has talents and skills you need. Work together and you'll probably see Baser by Christmas. Desert the mouse or let it die, and that's exactly what will happen to you."

"You want me to make friends with a mouse?"

Wilson nodded.

I looked at the mouse sitting patiently on my hand. "Hello, there. You seem to be a happy little rodent."

Silence. Ask the mouse its name?

"My name is Vonn Thrasher. What's yours?"

The mouse squeaked and scampered up my sleeve onto my collar and tickled my ear with its whiskers. "Cotton."

"You have a big voice for a mouse."

"Watcher gave me human speech so I can tell you things that men never know. Like all mice, I can smell danger and vanish before it arrives. My presence means you'll be safe."

"Early warning. I understand. Are you a boy or girl mouse, and how did you get here?"

"Males are bucks and females are does. Are you listening?"

"Yes," I said.

Wilson nodded.

"I'm a doe. But I'm not about having a mess of pinkies running around underfoot. I'm a seafaring adventurer, a stowaway from Member Ship, lost on the Resentment Rocks over by the Four Horsemen."

I said, "My ship got there after Member Ship broke up and we rescued four Ordonnes from a sinking lifeboat. They're somewhere on Sobriety Island today. How'd you survive?"

"Almost drowned before I climbed on a chunk of the ship's hull and rode a wave to the beach. Horsemen don't care about mice when they have alkies to eat, so I slipped away. Wandered here and there, doing much of nothing until Watcher came by. Said she had a mission for me. High adventure."

"Across the Broken Hills Wilderness," Watcher said.

"My name's Cotton, and you're my human."

Two days later Cotton and I left; packed and ready for the challenges. By midday, we'd passed most of Wilson's crosses guarding the Pious Trail and stood at the top of a sharp ridgeline, looking down into the Broken Hills Wilderness.

My old friend's parting words were firm. "Every step o' the Pious Trail runs right through the wilderness. Be a different walk for every Ordonne, but all trails end in Farland. And there, dear Vonn, be where you'll find the way back home.

"Far what?"

"Far land. Farland. You gotta get there or stay on the island forever."

"You must know by now that humans don't survive Sobriety Island forever," Watcher said. "They reach Farland or…"

Wilson and I stared at each other. He shook his head. "There's only one mountain man."

I groaned. "Or I'll become a Ling."

He nodded. "Remember everything in the wilderness revolves around the witch."

"Witch? You mean Mondi or Lily?"

"All Demimonde. Demimonde be a freckled-faced Lily girl one day and a green-skinned Mondi the next." He waved his arms wide. "And a lotta Lings foraging all over the Broken Hills."

Watcher said, "There aren't any crosses after you drop off the edge of the plateaus. You and Cotton must depend on each other to stay on the trail. Wherever you go, whatever you do, remember the three Ts: Time, Treasure, and Talent. Use them wisely. Listen to your compass and twenty. Walk the Pious Trail wisely and finish what you started in Doc Changelove's office. Become an Ordonne, sober—"

"Or become a Ling. I hope you'll be with us," I said.

"I will always be with you," Watcher said and vanished.

The last cross was a live pine with a horizontal bar fixed higher than every rock and tree around the edge of the plateau. Wilson had built a small deck, a crow's nest, in the crown of the tree, and lopped off enough limbs to fasten rungs all the way to the top.

"Looks like a green ship's mast to me," Cotton said.

I dropped the ruck and grabbed my spyglass. "I'd expect as much from an old salt. You ready?"

The view was breathtaking. The island seemed to enlarge every time I looked through my spyglass. Distant hills and valleys extended until the wilderness faded into a blue-green haze.

"Little buddy, we gotta lot of forest to walk, but it's all downhill from here."

"I was a stowaway," she said. "Now I'm a backpacker."

"Farland is somewhere between us and the horizon. By chance, have you been down this trail before?"

"Never. You know more about Lings and trails than I do." Cotton gripped my ear lobe and tugged. "Smoke."

Several miles to our left, smoke drifted out of the forest, and cut a thin white ribbon across the blue sky. I recognized the sandstone cliff surrounded by dead forest. "Smoke's from the Ling camp."

"Foreknowledge is fair warning," she said. "Let's go straight down the trail and leave them behind."

Fortunately, the Pious Trail looped far enough around the Ling Camp that we never encountered Mondi's minions. But coming off the plateaus with a full ruck was hard. By midafternoon, I'd lost count of my slips and falls. The last one was the worst. I stumbled on a patch of slide rock, fell, bounced, and rolled to the bottom of a dry gulch. Cotton emerged from a cloud of dust, and nimbly hopped from rock to rock down the slope to where I was lying.

"I thought you were supposed to warn me when danger was near," I moaned.

"You're safe when I'm present, not when I vanish. I bailed when you went over the edge."

I winced and pulled a thorn out of my cheek. "Nice. Thanks for asking if I'm okay."

She twitched her whiskers and watched me stand and dust myself off.

"Got lucky, just scrapes and bruises, but nothing's broken or missing—"

"And kicked up enough dust to mobilize a battalion of Lings."

I studied the long steep slope for another way up. "Slide rock makes climbing tough."

Something very loud roared from above the trail. Bloodcurdling screams bounced off the canyon walls and surrounded us.

"Someone just got eaten," Cotton squeaked.

"There's our sign." I threw on my ruck. "Pious Trail or not, I'm not climbing back up there." Cotton scampered up my arm, and we limped along the bottom.

She tapped my chest with her tail. "Apparently rockslides make for unhappy carnivores. Let's follow this streambed outta here before the monster does a looksee. Sooner or later we'll pick up the Pious Trail. Besides, all the commotion will rouse the giant cobra."

"Saul. Yeah, he'll be slithering this way."

The dry creek bed contained downed trees and big rocks. Tough traveling, but eventually we lost sight of the distant plateaus behind us and wandered into rolling hill country. Walking was painful. I needed to find a good place to lay up. Tonight and tomorrow would be long and excruciating.

The streambed ran through a large stand of oaks and elms. Their canopies interlocked, shutting out the sun and prying eyes looking from the surrounding ridgelines. A freshwater spring bubbled up and pooled in the streambed, then continued as a small creek. Wild apple, pear, and apricot trees greedily crowded the bank, their limbs bent with fruit.

I plucked a blushing yellow apple and took a bite. "Hmm, tastes great. Bite?"

She nibbled a groove in the side, and then we shared bites down to the core.

"Little buddy, this's better than a city park. We'll rest here for a day or two."

"Shouldn't we ask somebody first?"

"Who?" I threw the apple core over my shoulder. "Squatters' rights."

Cotton shifted to my other shoulder. "What's over yonder?"

An old trellis lay against a rock face. Camouflage or an old decoration? Broken vines and denuded gray bamboo uprights told me that nobody had tended it in years. I pulled on one side and the whole thing fell apart. "Hello, what do we have here?"

A cave.

My compass and twenty warmed. "Someone tried to hide the opening."

"Careful, Vonn, all sorts of mouse eaters like snakes and bobcats live in caves."

"Oh, let's explore a little." I chuckled. "Consider the cave an extra-large mouse hole. Hey, maybe your relatives are guarding a treasure chest." I lit my camp lantern. "Ready?"

We entered the hole which appeared to be an old mine. I couldn't tell what minerals or ore the miners were after, or why they quit, but their rusted tools, timbers and chains, and 10,000 shovel marks told a story of hard labor. A hundred feet in, someone had chiseled three lines on the sandstone wall.

"What's it say?" Cotton asked.

Trespasser Beware
Greed Brings Ye In
Insanity Finds Ye Out.

"Good enough for me," she said. "Turn around and head back to the light."

"Relax. We haven't seen anyone since leaving the plateaus." I pointed down the dark drift. "I think there's something worth finding here."

"Vonn, this place belongs to someone." She clutched my earlobe hard enough to hurt. "They could be waiting for us."

"Ha, I thought you were a swashbuckling adventurer."

"I'm vigilant," she sighed, "and claustrophobic."

"You're afraid of small spaces? Don't mice live under floors, and inside barrels and walls?"

"Yeah, well, we all have a thing, don't we? How can anyone be hooked on beer?"

"Point taken. If we weren't broken, we wouldn't be here."

The mine continued downward and to the right until the adit vanished in a black void. The air was sticky and warm and the lamp gave everything a dull green glow. Several drifts went left and right. But all stopped before reaching the end of the light.

"Cotton, nothing's precious here but us."

I was wrong.

A sudden roar turned the mine into a deafening echo chamber.

My compass and twenty burned against my chest. Cotton vanished.

A roaring creature was outside. We were trapped.

"Who dares eat from my tree and trespass in my mine?" I cringed against the rock wall and held my breath.

Watcher whispered, "The truth brings freedom."

"I know you're in there. Answer me," the voice demanded.

I inched along the mine far enough to see a huge shadow cast across the entrance. I wiped the sweat out of my eyes. Every thorn, cut, and scrape screamed.

I sat down. "Name's Vonn Thrasher."

"Come out in the light of day and answer for your sins."

"Please, I mean no harm."

Silence.

Half-steps. "Honest, I'm a puny worthless human, flavorless, toxic actually." My stomach rolled. I tasted apple a second time.

I shuffled closer and listened. Heavy breathing—the monster's or mine? "Traveling with a mouse of all things. Going to Far-land. Had an accident and fell off the Pious Trail. And—and—I stopped here for a minute, only to bandage my wounds and rest."

A throaty growl.

"Cotton," I whispered through gritted teeth. "Where are you? You're supposed to know what to do."

"Now," the shadow barked.

"I'm coming—coming with my hands up."

My eyes adjusted to the bright sunlight, and I saw a man riding a saddled bear about thirty feet from the entrance. "Name's Teller and this is Law. I do the talking for both of us."

Law was a silvertip grizzly, walking five feet high at his shoul-ders and weighing over a half-ton. He wore no halter or bit in a mouth full of teeth—large enough to swallow my head in one gulp. Teller could've been Moneymaker's scary twin, with a shaved head and 400 pounds of belly and muscle. Sitting in a tooled leather saddle, he looked like a tattooed Buddha. I felt like a boy in front of a Mack truck.

The apple core rolled up between my feet.

"This is all a mistake," I stammered.

"Law, why's the mistake always in their favor? Look at this puny man a'standing there with your fruit stuck in his teeth and spewing lies."

Law growled.

"Law says all men are liars. You stole his apple, destroyed his gate, and searched his mine looking for gold." Teller brandished his meaty fist at me and growled. "And now you have the nerve to say you made an honest mistake."

"I only—"

"You have no idea what fresh fruit and human flesh does to a grizzly's appetite."

"Can I—"

"Shush." He hoisted a double-bladed axe and pointed the blade at me. "Nobody eats Law's fruit without permission, not even me. Now, I can usually calm the bear; you might say intercede. Question is—why should I? Why would I deny my best friend justice? Puny man, what can you do to set things right?"

I loosened my shoulder straps and glanced left and right for possible escape routes.

Law looked down his huge black nose at me and growled a warning.

"Easy with the eyes, pilgrim," Teller said.

"Trust me," Watcher said. "Be brave. Stand and atone."

Law and Teller didn't break their hard stare. Obviously, they couldn't hear Watcher.

"I took without asking and trespassed in your mine. Sorry—"

Law slapped a paw full of rock dust and leaves at me and roared. I cringed and covered my face.

"Sorry is another lie." Teller leaned forward in the saddle and scowled. "No good."

I coughed and pulled a twig out of my hair. "Law made that very clear. What can I do?"

"Amends. We know about you and the Ling Camp. A powerful gift gave you victory. I want this power. Give me your magic or fight to the death."

"Vonn, beware," Watcher whispered. "Teller and Law are powerful and unyielding—you have to give them a way out."

The Magic Twenty warmed in my pocket. "I'll give you the gift called Magic Twenty. But you should know; Watcher destroyed the Ling camp, not me."

"Watcher?" he roared. "Another lie. On your knees, toxic man."

I dropped to both knees and pulled the silver money clip from my chest pocket, glanced at the magic twenty-dollar bill and held it out with my eyes fixed on the ground. "Here. I've carried this since my first day on the island."

"No tricks." They walked closer. "Don't even breathe."

I didn't want to. The grizzly smelled like a wet dog that had rolled in a hog wallow. His dinner-platter paws sported black claws as long as butcher knives. Bile rolled into the back of my throat. *Watcher, please, please save me.*

Teller plucked Magic Twenty, slapped my hand down, and they shuffled away. I dared to look up. He held up the silver clip and turned it in the sun. It flashed and sparkled.

Law woofed an agreement.

"Acceptable."

"Can I—"

"You got three days to build Law a new gate. Everything you need is around here. The Lings are terrified of me and this place, so you can work and rest in peace." He glanced at my torn bloody khakis and paused long enough for a hint of sympathy to show. "The water is sweet and good for healing. Eat whatever you find in Law's orchard."

"Agreed. The gate will be strong and beautiful."

"We don't care if you agree or not. Need I tell you the penalty for failure?"

Teller and Law sauntered away. "There's something weird about you, Vonn Thrasher." Before they disappeared in the forest, he yelled over his shoulder, "Wasn't for somebody looking out for you, you'd be a dead man. Don't you worry, I'll be around."

That someone was Watcher. And—dare I think, God?

Cotton reappeared on my shoulder. "Of all the things you never want to break, Law's gate has to be number one."

Chapter Twelve

Solitary

All the needed hardware and tools were in the mine. I finished cutting limbs and oak vines from the valley on the second day, and admired my finished work on the third. The heavy strong gate, anchored, would take two men or a bear to move.

Teller's parting words were true. The garden spring water had healing and renewal qualities. Fountain of youth? Myth or not, all my cuts, blisters, and bruises were gone. Hard to describe, but it was like trying on a favorite old pair of jeans from the back of the closet, from high school—and they fit. Cotton and I had the immortality of youth.

Rest assured, we were good stewards. Not a twig or a leaf fell from Law's fruit trees. I would've defended them unto death before facing that grizzly again. Unfortunately, we couldn't take much with us. Law's garden was in the bottom of a deep valley with steep sides that ran for miles before cresting near the clouds. Hard, thirsty climbing. I would drain both canteens in two days.

By midday we were halfway up the ridge. Far below, a murder of crows squawked and circled above Law's garden.

"They're baaack," Cotton said.

Law roared and emerged from the garden, standing tall and lashing the air with his huge paws. Teller rode him like a broncobuster, yelling and waving a big axe—not curses and threats—but echoes of joy and laughter. They saw us and jumped into a full gallop across a meadow, then disappeared into the mountainside forest.

Snapping tree limbs and a column of dust told us they were closing in. I sat down and sighed. "Does it ever end?" No use running. Law could outrun a horse even carrying Teller.

Cotton nervously rubbed the back of my ear.

"You haven't vanished yet?" I scoffed.

"I know we'll be okay. Be encouraged. He's not here to kill."

Law charged out of the trees and slid to a stop. Their heavy breathing filled the air with reek of carrion. Teller leaned forward in the saddle and grinned. "Here, puny man," Teller tossed the magic twenty to me. "You think you can outsmart an old bear, but you can't. Give me the real treasure."

"I have no idea what you're talking about."

Cotton crawled inside my collar.

"Law, Vonn's playing coy." Teller hung his axe on the saddle horn, slid off the bear and lumbered toward me. His stiff knees and bowed legs drove his red cuffed riding boots deep into the soft trail dirt. He smiled a devilish grin and wiggled his Kielbasa sized fingers. "Come on, I gave you back the magic twenty. Now you give me what I want—power."

"Careful," Cotton whispered. "I smell danger."

"Power? Good grief, you and Law are three quarters of a ton standing there. How can I give you any power?" I held up the Magic Twenty and clip. "Sir, I assure you that I am powerless and this's the only treasure I have."

"Trade. I give you back the twenty and clip, and throw in Pious Trail protection. You give me power."

We stared, waiting for someone to break the silence.

"What about Law's gate?" I said. "Doesn't that matter?"

Teller waved me off, walked over, and sat on a fallen log. We were still the same height. He looked straight in my eyes. "Give me the power to throw off my yoke and leave Solitary."

"I don't understand."

"This country is called Solitary for good reason." He swept his arm across the vista below. "Forbidden to leave. We're cursed to guard what imprisons us—the garden and spring water."

"Cursed? You mean blessed with healing and renewal. After a good drink or two, I almost watched my wounds heal. I haven't felt this good since I was a boy."

"That's what you think. But afta' ninety summers in Solitary Valley, I'm done with guarding fruit trees and water. Year afta' year watching the world go by without kinfolk or cubs kinda bends a soul. Makes ya crazy mean."

Law ambled over and put his head down in the giant's lap. Teller stretched his legs out and scratched behind the bear's ears. Law leaned forward. "No sir, Law's spring water won't heal ma' knees or fix what's really wrong. We're stuck in Mondi's curse—Purgatory."

"Purgatory is just an old Catholic fable—not real."

"Then why have Law and I been stuck," he pointed down the trail and raised his voice, "in that valley for over ninety years and haven't aged a month?"

"The orchard and spring water," Cotton said.

"Who said that?"

Cotton moved from behind my neck. "Hello, I'm Cotton."

"Well, I'll be—a talking mouse? I've seen everything."

"Law talks to you," she said.

"Yeah—" Teller paused mid-thought. "Weirdos one and all, aren't we? Anyway, the garden's just the mechanics of it." He tapped the side of his shaved head. "The question is how to break out of this fractured mind."

"Come again?" I said.

"Every week I wake up and swear today's the day, pack a saddlebag and head up one of the many trails outta Solitary Valley. Yessiree Bob, we get right on up the way. Most of the time we clear the last ridgeline and almost make our way to the Pious Trail before all hell breaks loose. The sun falls behind the Broken Hills, and the whole damned country starts moving with shadowy monsters. I snap—turn into a bawling, babbling idiot."

"Is there a real threat out there?" I said.

"Boogie men. Mind monsters—the what could and would horrors."

"I can identify," Cotton said.

"No doubt," Teller said. "In the light of day, Law and I aren't afraid of anything on this island, not even Mondi or death come knocking. But full moon or not, if we're out of the valley at night—my brain snaps. We turn 'round, charge back down the hill lookin' over our shoulders, back to the same camp, doing the same cursed thing—shiver by the fire and wait for sunrise."

"That sounds like fear of the dark—Nyctophobia."

"You can call it naca-whatever-phobia, but I call it Purgatory."

"But what can I do?" I asked.

"Unlock this invisible prison door so Law and I can get outta here."

"But, how?"

"Change things. Fix me."

"I can't do that. When's the last time you talked with another man?"

"Nine, maybe ten years." He pulled out a leather covered jug, took a pull and offered me a drink. "Sweet cider—good for what ails ya."

I smelled the top.

"No booze. Haven't made hooch or had a drink in over ninety years."

"Thanks." I tasted the sweet blend of fruits. "Haven't had cider in years."

He corked the bottle and slid it in a pocket. "Wilson Cabotage taught me about the Pious Trail many moons ago. Did all right until I heard about Solitary and jumped off the trail. Gonna get rich, weren't we, Law?"

Law snapped his jaws.

"That's right. Greed, gluttony, and sloth, even a bear knows the fix they'll get you in. Now we're stuck in Solitary Valley playing the same damned game every miserable day."

"Game?"

"Called creepers," he said. "The Ling game." Law flopped down and put his massive head between his front paws. "Far as you can see in every direction belongs to Mondi and her creepy Lings. They sneak around sabotaging and killing. Steal your head if they get a chance. Law and I find most of them before they can do any real damage. Used to be fun, a game, but now it's brutal—eye for eye, tooth for tooth. Love? Ha, don't know what that means after ninety years in the hole. Mercy? Yeah, that's what Lings scream before Law crushes their heads."

The familiar smell of camphor and witch hazel told me that Watcher was present. A power to be reckoned with, she'd been with me from the beginning. I trusted, dare I say loved and needed her. "So." I ran my hand through my beard. "Teller, you're hoping there's another way out of Solitary. I think the magic twenty gave you an epiphany."

"Epiff-what?"

"Epiphany is an awakening, a moment of clarity or new aware-ness. Mine happened on the top of a mountain. Out of nowhere, a terrible storm struck, with thunder and lightning and driving rain. Trees crashed all around me—I was a dead man shivering under a poncho. But instead of death by lightning, I was given a powerful insight." I patted my chest. "God was with me. I was going to live, and since then I've carried an unwavering sense of right and wrong, a gift that can't be ignored. Today I have a purpose far above the bottle or bags of gold."

"A higher calling," Cotton said.

I walked over to Teller, and handed him the Magic Twenty. "What makes Christmas wonderful?"

His frown gave way to a slow smile. "Christmas? That's—well, I haven't thought about Christmas in ninety years." His eyes grew misty. "Celebration, maybe gifts?"

"Discovery, a leap of understanding, being closer to God."

Teller slapped his knee. "Something told me you had a way out."

"Not I. Open your mind. Listen to your heart, and the Moral Compass will give you the best way."

"Best? We want *a* way, somewhere up the trail wherever you're going."

"Like Solitary Valley, there are many ways. You must choose the way of life," I said.

Cotton added, "The honest way was the watchword on Member Ship."

Law grumbled. Teller nodded and said, "Tell us more."

Serenity Harbor came to mind. On my last night as a sailor, the bonfire's smoke and cinders gave the air a mysterious taste— bitter like milk thistle, yet sweet as licorice root. "This must be overwhelming. Let's walk a while. I'll tell you my story and what I've learned."

"You askin' us to travel with you?" Teller stared at me. Law held his breath.

Cotton pulled my ear and whispered, "They're thinking years, not an afternoon stroll."

I cleared my throat. "Well, I don't know. I'm headed to Farland to find a way off this island." Not wander around with you.

Watcher roared, "Stinking thinking!"

Teller fell off the log. Cotton vanished, and Law bolted down the trail farting and kicking. I would've run too, but nobody can outrun Watcher.

Teller peeked out from behind the log. "Who was that, a giant mouse?"

"I didn't expect you'd hear her. Teller, let me introduce you to Watcher, invisible guardian of reason. She creates second chances and is a great Ling fighter. Watcher, I'm sure you already know Teller and Law."

"Don't forget us," said Mr. Conscience.

"Oh, there's no chance of that, my brother," added Mr. Consequence.

Law poked his head out of the tree line and sniffed the air.

"Last but not least, say hello to Mr. Conscience and Mr. Consequence," I said. "Hi, ho, the gang's all here."

"Hello to invisible people?" Teller groaned. "Not the kind a company I had in mind. Maybe Solitary wasn't so bad after—"

"Everybody has an opinion," Watcher thundered. "Nobody has an answer. Vonn, why do you have a Moral Compass and Magic Twenty?"

"Well, I—" Something familiar warmed my pocket—another Magic Twenty.

"You've walked so long with clenched fists you don't know any other way. Open your heart and your hands. Stop taking and start giving. Be the one who helps Teller leave Solitary. Trust me, you want him by your side."

I said, "Teller, welcome to the Pious Trail. Be assured, you aren't here by mistake."

Watcher said, "Both of you, use what you have and step out on faith."

We held out our Magic Twenties. We both had a magic twenty-dollar bill, folded and secure in a silver clip etched with *Ordonne* in Pilot's own hand.

"They come with a Moral Compass that speaks the language of the heart," she said. "So that you may hear without ears, see without eyes, and find a new life in Ordonne."

Law quietly joined the three of us, and we huddled together shoulder to shoulder.

"My friends, open your mind. Accept my counsel and you will walk the Pious Trail to a righteous end. Now, close your eyes and hold your gift high."

Flash. Something with large talons plucked both Magic Twenties out of our hands. Cotton vanished. She knew that these were no ordinary birds of prey. They were majestic golden eagles with pale flight feathers and burnished-brown nape shining like polished brass in the sun. They ascended and joined a dozen other eagles soaring in the clouds above us.

"Have I got your attention?" Watcher said.

"Yes," we said.

Such power and authority. Are there no island creatures she doesn't command?

"Listen carefully. You must give as it was freely given to you. Share your time, treasure, and talents with each other. If you covet, you lose and die. If you give, you gain and live."

All of us agreed. Teller craned his neck trying to see Watcher. "But what about Law's garden? Mondi and the Lings will take over the valley."

"I have provided another Ordonne on Sobriety Island who will fall into Solitary. She'll defend the garden and grow strong there."

Two eagles dived out of the clouds and flew towards us at tree-top level. I almost lost my nerve and stepped behind a tree before they spread their broad wings and stalled above us, dropped both Magic Twenties in our hands, and then disappeared over the next ridgeline.

Mr. Conscience whispered, "Step out on faith."

I cleared my throat. "Teller and Law, you're welcome to travel with us all the way back to Baser if you want."

"Pintsize, come here." Teller laughed and hugged me. I hoped he wouldn't crack my ribs. "Little man. You broke mah curse. Law, we're free, free indeed."

Law slapped the ground and kicked his heels. Cotton raced back and forth across my shoulders, squeaking, "Ho ho ho, ha ha ha."

Teller held out his compass and twenty and thundered, "Been a waitin' ninety long summers for a way out. You showed me the door and Watcher kicked it open. Ninety and no more Solitary—Watcher, I owe you one large."

No answer.

"Watcher?" I said.

She was gone again.

Teller mounted Law. "Pintsize, grab your mouse and let's get outta here."

"Mister Teller, my name is Cotton, not *grab your mouse.* And by the way, I'm the seafaring adventurer who survived a shipwreck and a season with the Four Horsemen. Would you please address me by name and accept that I'm a contributing member of this group? I have knowledge and skills that you'll need."

"Survivor, huh." Teller grinned. "You're right. We need every survivor skill we can muster to get past Mondi. Now, let's see if we can find a good campsite before dark."

"Right behind you," I said.

The trail zigzagged up the ridgeline and over several cliffs before entering the thick high-country forest. I hoped a well-marked Pious Trail awaited us, not another ghoulish ordeal. Law walked easily in the thin mountain air, but even after eating and drinking from Law's garden, I didn't. Years of cigarettes and smoky bars had taken a toll. "Must be nice having wheelbarrow-size lungs. Little break?"

Law laughed like a grizzly, by popping his chops and by giving a peculiar whine.

I sat against a tree and slid out of my backpack suspenders. "I swear this ruck gets heavier by the minute."

Teller sat on the other side of the tree, took out a knife, and whittled on a stick. Law relaxed in the shade.

I took a deep pull on my canteen, easing the raspy pain in my chest. "There are other things about that twenty you must know."

"Do tell," Teller said.

"The twenty spent wisely gives blessings. Spent foolishly it creates a curse."

He nudged me with an elbow. "Not another curse."

"When I was given my Magic Twenty, Pilot explained that when you need money for an offering or gift, food or clothing, even a homeless drunk panhandler lying on the street, it's there. Spend twenty dollars in the morning, it'll reappear in your pocket in the afternoon—"

"Like magic."

"Good deeds bring a good return. But things like ultimatums and robbery break the Magic Twenty's chain."

"Ultimatum? You broke the law when you trespassed my cave." He tapped his chest. "You gave me an amend when you rebuilt the door."

I threw a rock as far as I could down the hillside. "Always looking out for number one."

It sailed out of sight, then cracked and popped down through the trees.

"I swear that you and Cotton make more noise than a platoon of sodden Lings. Stop kickin' and throwin' things around. You never know who's a' huntin'."

Cotton reappeared on a limb above us. "Oh, no, that's not me. First day on the trail, clumsy Vonn fell and pulled a rockslide down around him."

"Accidents happen," I said.

The others moaned a complaint.

"Okay, I'll be more careful. Let me finish what I was saying about the compass and twenty. Watcher came because our motives were wrong. I was inside your mine looking to steal. You demanded power to leave Solitary. You needed help, and I wasn't very forthcoming. But when we exchanged our gifts, the Magic Twenty was restored to both, clip and all."

"Aye, now we both have one. A true blessing."

"Yes, but there's a curse—if we screw up and relapse, the Magic Twenty will know and vanish. No more firewater and blow, get rich schemes and dirty dealing, not even a cathouse or casino."

"No more gold mines," he said. "One snort, drink, or pocket picked and it's gone."

"But not the curse. That stays with you for life."

"Curse be I lose the twenty forever?"

"And much more," I said. "The twenty curses your time, treasure, and talent. You can't make money fast enough that the curse won't spend it before you ever get to the bank.

"Gone?"

"Forever poor, cursed with poverty you would never believe possible."

Teller climbed in the saddle and nodded toward the trail. "Jus' got out a one curse, don't need another."

I donned my ruck and stood next to Law. My legs were good

for a long walk, but my aching shoulders told me three hours tops. "So, this curse or whatever. How'd that happen?"

"Let's save our breath for the campfire tonight. Climb up behind me. We'll ride double until we hit the Pious Trail. After ninety summers, I'm not spending another night around here."

We rode into the bottom of a towering wall of gray clouds, splattered with rose and violet colors and a churning charcoal base that swallowed the top of the island. The trail became an elusive shadow, wandering close to sheer drop-offs. Tree limbs snagged our clothes, almost pulling us off the saddle. And this time, Wilson's crosses didn't guard the trail.

"Certainly not a merry pink cloud day," Cotton said.

"Quiet," Teller said. The four of us continued up the trail.

The western sun burned off enough cloudbank to reveal a Broken Hills Wilderness that stretched forever. From our camp high along the Pious Trail we saw distant heat lightning racing through obstinate clouds holding to the north and west. The air was heavy; the heavens dynamic and restless. However, we were spared all but muted faraway grumblings. An otherworldly land? Yes, a deliberate message—was this where God lived?

Later Teller caught the fading sun with his money clip, and soon we shared a cozy blaze under a starlit night.

I paused between bites of pear. "Feeling okay, you know with that phobia-Purgatory thing?"

Teller stopped picking pemmican from his teeth with a penknife. "Little nervous, but the freak-out's gone, like I wish this sliver of red berry was."

"Nice fire," Cotton said. "Most mice are terrified of flames, but I like the light and warmth. I see that Law doesn't mind either."

The grizzly was sleeping at the edge of the firelight, his deep breathing almost a snore, lending a relaxing white noise to the camp.

"He carried us through some tough high-country miles today,"

I said. "But we're on top now. Wilson said that every mile of Pious Trail runs through the wilderness. We'll end up in Farland. That's where we'll find the way back home."

Teller spit into the fire. It hissed a complaint. "Far what?"

"Far-land. We gotta make Farland or stay on the island forever. Do you think you'll go back to the real world or stay—?"

"Don't know," he said. "Been here so long all mah friends and family gotta be dead. I'll decide by the time we get where we're going."

I picked up a stick and jabbed the fire. Sparks swirled, danced, and vanished. "So, tell us about your previous life. How'd you get to Sobriety Island?"

Teller walked over and rubbed Law's neck, and then sat down against his shoulder. The grizzly opened one eye, exhaled, leaned into Teller, and began to snore.

"That bear really loves you," I said.

"Mutual." He lifted his riding boot in the air. "Little help?"

With a moan and cussword or two we pulled his knee highs off. His socks were full of holes. "I know," he said. "After ninety years I only wear what I make or take from camp robbers."

"Lings?" Cotton said.

Teller stretched his leg and wiggled his toes. "Aye, and damned few of 'em have anything that fits me."

A painful memory from my drunken Baser days surfaced. "Oh, I understand—Mom and Dad's place before shipping out for Sobriety Island. You see, they've hated me and my friends for years. We're nothing but embarrassments—"

"Socks?"

"I'm getting there. I stopped by their house hoping to garner a little support. And well, things went south. You see, their house is like a museum. Nothing can be out of place. Appearance is everything." I pointed at his feet. "And the number one house rule is leave shoes at the front door."

"How many rules are there?"

"Depends on who you are," I snickered. "If you're the mayor or church cardinal, there aren't any. You can track mud and kick a hole in the wall. But for me, their only begotten son, there's a hundred. Number two's the ringer. Stop. Turn around and hit the road, Jack."

"And number three, don't you come back no mo, no mo," Cotton squeaked.

We laughed like braying mules.

"Now, where was I?" I wheezed, "Oh yeah, holey socks. Dear Mom and Dad stared at my bare wiggling toes and snarled, 'You're a filthy disgusting drunk, when will you grow up and quit running around blaming everyone else for your problems.'"

"Nice," Teller said.

"Well, to say that I wasn't invited to stay for supper is an understatement."

"Tossed?"

"And never went back."

Teller waved his arm. "Cold. You're drinking yourself to death, and they's worried 'bout socks? Shoes weren't all they left at the front door."

"We have a long and rich history. Truth is, they haven't loved me since high school. Most of the damage is on me, but there's no reconciling with that pair. All they worry about is their image and standing among Baser's upper crust. They're terrified that I'll tell our dirty little family secrets in a barroom or Treatment Ship therapy."

I pulled two pairs of socks from my ruck. "Give as it was freely given. I think they'll stretch."

"That's about the nicest thing anyone has done for me—"

"In a hundred years," I said. "Your turn. Tell us a good drunk-a-log."

"Yeah, well," he coughed. "Been a long time since I thought about how I got to Sobriety Island."

Cotton jumped off my shoulder, scurried around the fire, and up Teller's arm. "Oh please. I love a good swashbuckling adventure."

"Ha, I'm more the villain than hero."

"Even better," she squeaked.

Teller's Story

"Once upon a time, I lived in the great city of Funfair, in a faraway land called Spent." Law rolled on his side and yawned. "He's heard this before." Law grumbled, and we laughed. "Anyway, I was an up and coming pro wrestler, the 'Terror of the Center Ring' known as the Teller, because I rang up mah opponents. Yessir, when I had two good knees, I could moonsault, drop kick, pile drive, and Boston crab with the best of them."

"And the name stuck," Cotton said. "What's your real name?"

"Not sayin'. Better left forgotten. Anyway, size, strength, and skill made me unbeatable. For near three seasons I wore a champion's belt. But two bad knees ended mah career, and Father Time stole my title. Love of card tables, fast women, and booze took everything else."

"Alky in the end?" I said.

"Aye, invincible and loaded with pipedreams. Always gonna get mah knees fixed. Always gonna make a comeback. Three years later I was living on the street. Dark days they were. Told wrestling stories for drinks, panhandled and stole everything I could get mah hands on. Horrible, everything you can think of and some you can't."

"Every day like a hundred yesterdays," I said. "Chug enough booze and it'll go away—"

"Till tomorrow. You know the alky way."

A night flyer called out from the heavens, no doubt hoping to flush out an evening meal. Cotton crawled under the giant man's ear and whispered, "Monster."

Teller didn't flinch. "Probably a great horned owl. You're safe with me. Now, where was I? Oh, yeah, a cruel little runt named Sting was the sheriff of Spent. Hated honkytonks, especially the Akasen, a red-light dive I bounced. But, he sure 'nough loved floodlights and firehoses—especially at five in the morning. 'Wake up Teller, shower time. Let's loosen up some of that lard and peel off a layer of dirt.'"

"That's police brutality," I said. "Didn't you file a complaint?"

"Naw, believe me. Sting was the least of mah problems. When you fall in with mobs and street gangs, every day ends with a question mark. Anyway, I's in jail the thirteenth time when a preacher—Smiling Jack Grabber—stopped by to talk. Had a storefront church called, Magnetic House of Love. They focused on the three "Ss," Sobriety, Salvation, and Service. Said he'd save my soul and bring me into his ministry."

"Sounds good," I said. "Did they help you get to Sobriety Island?"

"Nah, that came much later, but he did spring me out of jail. I drank his Kool-Aid and lived in the back of his church, cooking and cleaning and worshipping with all the other newbies. A team of us went out in the streets most days, carrying the three Ss to suffering sinners and lost drunks."

"Then what happened?"

"Did well for a year. I's a new age John the Baptist a' cryin' in the red-light wilderness. Walked every shantytown street and back alley bar, filled the pews every night, twice on Sunday. But there were problems."

"What?"

"Jealousy. Our moral hootin' and howlin' weren't good for late-night business. City Hall put the squeeze on the House of Love, and the jealous old-timers freaked out. You see, they were already bitter about all the new faces. We came and went without permission. Talked to whoever would listen and worst yet, brought them home—not good. You don't challenge the old guard's rules without collecting enemies. In the end, Smiling Jack and the elders cut me loose."

"No different than my dad," I said. "All about money and power."

"I yelled across the pews on my way out the door. 'Throw me out? Ha, losers, I'm doing God's will.' As you might guess by me being here, that wasn't entirely correct."

"Demimonde plays hardball—" Cotton said.

"And hits everything we throw out of the park. Over the next several months I did okay, preaching a little here and there around truck stops, late night strip clubs, even my old hangout, the Akasen. Most Funfairies hated to see me coming—but I gathered a few friends and followers." He shook his head. "Truth is, we weren't long for the world. Some relapsed, and the others— who knows. One day they were there, the next day they weren't. Demimonde thinned our ranks like a gardener pulling weeds."

I leaned back and threw a stick on the fire. "The street is tough."

The wind provoked the fire to whistle and snap and brighten our camp. Teller pulled out a whetstone and began to sharpen his knife with deliberate circular motions. Deep in thought, Teller stopped every so often and touched the keen edge with his thumb. Finally, he looked up and cleared his throat. His face was wet with tears. "That was when I lost the only person who ever loved me. Peach."

"Oh, man. Sorry, was she part of your street ministry?" I said.

"From the beginning." He nodded and wiped his face. "You see, Peach was mah first and likely last love. A tall woman with the purdiest big brown eyes and braided hair, outspoken, yet she always had something good and kind to say. Told ourselves that we got it," he fist pumped and smiled. "This time would be different. Yessir, we were joined at the hip and going to live happily ever after in a cozy little apartment on the back side of Funfair."

"Lofty. You used each other to escape the past," I said.

"One day, she—" Teller glared and looked away. "Oh, what's the right word—warped. A fuse popped in her head, and all of a sudden we weren't good enough. She wanted something, and it wasn't a man."

"They say relapse comes days before the first drink or drug," I said.

"Truth is, I was nothing to her in the end." He sighed. "Nobody jonesed harder for cocaine and scotch than Peach. She robbed a liquor store and vanished. Two weeks later I found her lying in her own puke in a meth house over by the shooting gallery. Sheriff Sting said she was dead two days. Not a day goes by that I don't see her cold and twisted body lying on that filthy floor. Smiling Jack's storefront church, our ministry, plans for a life together? Nada. Pipedreams. Things to do until someone relapses and dies."

I wondered about my ex, Minnie Codependent, and our drinking buddies down at the Bloody Bucket. Were they alive or dead? "My old love, Minnie, and your Peach were different but the same. When I told Minnie that I quit drinking and booked passage on Treatment Ship, she blew up and stuck her finger in my face. 'I turn down better men than you every night,' and stomped out the room, yelling, 'Just go—go and pretend with someone else.'"

"Jealous like you'd picked up a new lover." Teller leaned over and nodded. "That'd be Demimonde talking, not Minnie or Peach. Hard not to take it personal, but we gotta try to hang on to the good memories and love we had." He cried out into the starlit night. "Peach, wherever you are, I still love and miss you."

We watched the fire and listened to the island's nocturnal voice. A faint beat of giant Lings drumming massive hollow logs reverberated across miles of forest. "A tall man can walk upright inside the length of those tree trunk drums," I said.

Cotton peered into the dark trees. "They've rebuilt and are up to something."

Shifting winds drove me and the smoke to opposite sides of the fire. "Likely looking at an anchored ship."

"Aye, but we're safe here," Teller said. "Now, where was I?"

Cotton said, "You were grieving over Peach."

"Back in Spent. After Peach's death, my life was a rollercoaster. One day I'd call myself a fool and start packing a bag. The next day I'd put on my crusader's helmet and pound the sidewalk. Somehow, carrying the good news to any miserable Funfairie that'd listen made her death matter and eased mah pain."

Cotton sang out. "Back in the saddle again."

"Yessir, they called me the Holy Hulk. The big preacher a standin' outside their haunts and covens yellin' the brutal truth.

'You're nothing but slaves living at Death's door. Drugs and alcohol have twisted your natural instincts until you're damn near a changeling. Today's the day to stop—follow me—I found a way out.'"

"Did they listen?" Cotton asked.

"Oh yeah, a lotta folks were looking for a way out. Unfortunately, Demimonde was listening too."

I added, "And turned up the heat—"

"Somethin' powerful." Teller coughed and rubbed his eyes. "Like this smoke that somehow follows me."

"Like the Four Horsemen," Cotton said.

Law rumbled.

Teller interpreted. "Right you are. Mondi and her Lings. Yeah, before Peach overdosed, life was kinda simple. Just another pair of street idiots wandering around saying whatever came to mind. Demimonde ignored us. But the Holy Hulk's preachin' brought out another side of the beast."

Cotton ran up my arm and settled on my shoulder. "Now we're getting to the good part."

"Peach's death taught me what's real and what's a smoke screen. Preaching about Demimonde became a calling. Mah story grew from a drunk-a-log, to a warning that cut to the quick. I called people by name and challenged 'em to follow me."

Teller pointed left and shouted, "Alky Ann, Jake's Clown Room will wait ten minutes. Turn out the lights and bring Down Danny over here."

Then he pointed right. "Blister Bill and Nappy Nan, as I live and breathe, I can't believe you're still alive. Y'all remember me. I bounced Akasen a while back. We drank and sang and danced all night."

"Big Katie," he waved. "We painted every Boozeville door red. And lookee here, there's my favorite Funfairie, Mister Johnny Gotta Cigarette. That rotgut will wait. Come on over and let's talk about taking the edge off."

"They came?" asked Cotton.

"Staggering and babbling. 'Ain't that bad, everyone does it.' So, I'd ask them, if it isn't that bad why are there pickle jars half full of cash on every bar? Cards and flowers for someone in the hospital or jail or dead. Half of the regulars never return. Funfairies, listen to me. You're living in hell's gate asking for a warmer room. There's a better way. Turn and walk with me."

I said, "Back in the day, Shotglass Sam kept a card and flower jar for the Bloody Bucket. Every week they wanted five dollars for somebody."

He said, "In the end, all we're worth is a five-dollar bill and a round of drinks."

"Real or delusion, every morning I saw a dead man in the mirror."

Teller looked at me out of the corner of his eye. "Yessir, in our cups we're all part dead."

Cotton said, "You guys make me grateful to only have mouse problems."

"Yes, ma'am, someone always has it worse." Teller leaned forward. "Hope was my hammer. Hope beat a hole in their wall of ignorance. 'Friends,' I'd say, 'I bring you good news. I know you're sick and tired of being sick and tired. Well, I found the way out. Stop thinking and pointing and follow me. If it works for me it will work for you.'"

Cotton stood on my collar and said, "What's the wall of ignorance?"

"Good question," Teller said, "Every time we play a victim card, we build another wall. Over time, the walls grow heavy enough to crush churches and businesses; so strong they drive away family and friends. Everyone in Shantytown and Funfair has a fistful of victim cards. Boys, belly up to the bar, and ante up. We're playing five card innocence, three card your fault, and everyone's favorite, seven card I'm not hurting anyone. Denial is always the wildcard. Bar Rag Brian, shuffle and deal—everybody plays—everybody loses."

"Hey, I remember that name," I said. "Bar Rag was my shipmate on Sponsor Ship. Did you help him get there?"

"Not unless he's a hundred years old," Teller said. "There's a familiar face and name in every Demimonde crowd."

"True," I said. "Demimonde doesn't care if someone leaves the game for a week or two, because it plays the long game. Patient? More like relentless, cunning, and baffling. But let one go? Never."

"Can't save a mouse from a great mousetrap," Cotton said. "The mouse got away today, but sooner or later, it'll take the bait."

Teller pointed at Cotton and winked. "I shook the tree hard. Alkies started to fall out and get away. I had to be silenced—not killed. Demimonde fears a martyr. No doubt it regretted taking Peach because her overdose sent me on a crusade. Nope, I had to relapse. So, a trap was set. And like Samson, I lost my moral platform, and the Funfairies ran me out of town."

I threw a log on and watched the fire pop and spark. "Teller, you're not getting away with that. No shortcuts. Finish your story."

"Shortcut? Ha, it's the longest way between any two points." He chuckled. "Well, inside a year my ministry grew into 630 men and women. I know because I took a headcount every week. Alkies and addicts climbed on the Teller wagon, and their families followed with open pocketbooks. Wallowing in high number glory, growth became mah new drug. I craved more and more, until mah ministry unraveled. Demimonde had me perched on the edge of a cliff. Bright lights on top, gloomy and—"

"Dark at the bottom," I said.

"Pride twisted mah primary purpose. You and he and she, became me, myself, and I. Pride goeth before the fall—"

"Proverbs 16. Even a mouse knows that one."

"Demimonde pumped me until my head wouldn't fit through a church door. I was the man. Political endorsements, money and fame, stadium rallies, flashing cameras, newspaper and television interviews. And like a good alcoholic, I even started writing a book."

"About Demimonde?" Cotton said.

"About me." He laughed and slapped his thigh. "The Saint of Funfair—legend in my own mind."

"You didn't," I said.

"Oh man, I's sick. Above the law—my way or the highway."

"Bet that didn't sit well with every Funfairie," Cotton said.

"Nope, I sure 'nough collected plenty of enemies. But I blew off their complaints. After all, doesn't the end always justify the means? Eventually, I crossed every line. A first-class hypocrite preaching on the evils of alcohol and popping speed on the way to the podium. Skimmed and scammed until my ministry became a racket."

Teller shook his head and moaned. "One morning, Sheriff Sting and two smiling deputies showed up at my condo. Guilty as charged. They seized mah books and run me outta Funfair. Charges pending, hated and unemployable, I tossed mah real name, and I've been Teller ever since. After wandering around Spent a few months, I heard about Ism Harbor. Booked passage on an asylum trading ship, and been on Sobriety Island ever since."

"You put into Serenity Harbor?"

"Naw, I started at the sixth Port of Promise, Easy Harbor. But like you, I found the Pious Trail and spent a season or two up on the plateaus with Wilson. One day, we found an orphan bear cub." He pointed at Law. "Three of us had a good summer. Best time of my life."

"And many adventures since," I added. "How long has Wilson lived up there?"

"Hard to say. The way time stretches and contracts on the plateaus, 100, maybe 200 years."

I said, "One day can last a minute or a whole week. But when it's time to go—"

"You're gone. Yessir, went back and forth up one mountain and down another. Saw all twelve Ports of Promise. Coulda left a few times on one ship or another, but I got sidetracked."

"Lost?" I said.

"Ha, more ways than one. One day Law and I came across a Ling squalling like a hyena in the bottom of a tiger pit."

"Mudling, Darkling, or Wretchling?" I said.

Teller drank the last swallow from his canteen. "Law, what was that Darkling's name?"

The bear rattled off a wordy sound.

"That's right, Beerbell. Ugly little moss crawler was terrified that Saul would eat him. 'Please pull me up,' he howled, 'and I'll tell you about secret riches.'"

"You pulled him up?" Cotton hopped to my other shoulder.

"Aye, and he told us about a magic garden hidden deep in the bottom of a valley. Miracle water bubbled up out of the ground like Ponce De Leon's Fountain of Youth. Pan for gold and silver, mine for rubies and diamonds. We didn't want to believe him, but his story had a ring of truth. You see, Lings are headhunters. The only treasures they crave are the Ordonne heads they lay at Mondi's feet to gain her hellish merit. Got no use for gold and jewels. That's why Beerbell wasn't prospecting."

"Jackpot." Cotton waved her little arm. "A pot of gold at the end of your rainbow."

"Ha," Teller howled and slapped his knee. "Cotton, you're a funny mouse. Yes, ma'am, we pulled him out and headed to Solitary Valley. Didn't know it then, but the whole darned thing was a trap. Treasure was the bait. I's the fat tiger in the bottom of the pit."

"Mondi saw you coming a week out."

"Can't outsmart that ol' green skin. Beerbell vanished the second night, and we couldn't find the valley. But lo and behold, couple days later Mondi and crew crossed our path over on Twisted Mesa."

I clicked my tongue. "Amazing coincidence."

Teller stared at several large hornets flying around. "Yessir, Mondi's a tall glass of bourbon—long flowing hair is the only thing a coverin' her changeable green skin. All the while, those tiny marks on her face sparkled like rhinestones."

A hornet buzzed me. I swatted and scooted to the other side of the fire. "Good grief, that thing's big as a coffee cup." They hovered for a second or two and then flew off. "Good riddance. Anyway, is Mondi male or female?"

Teller pointed at me. "Doesn't matter after a few thousand years."

"Gentlemen," Cotton interrupted. "Let's leave gender assignment alone for a moment and talk about these hornets. Are they spying for Mondi?"

Law groaned and rattled an answer.

"Yes, ma'am," Teller nodded. "Law calls them sparrow bees and they be bad news. She'll know we're here afore long. Just like on Twisted Mesa."

I sat and scratched a mosquito bite. "Do tell."

"Mondi was waitin' by the trail with a wink and a smile. 'I'm so glad we found you. I heard about Beerbell's travesty and came to set things right.' She snapped her fingers and a giant Ling smashed Beerbell flat right in front of me. 'Regrettably, he was a runaway. His death will serve me better.'"

"Giant Lings and their tree trunk clubs," Cotton said.

"Was I next? I raised mah battle axe and three giants stepped forward. 'Relax, my dears.' She smiled and raised both arms. 'Teller, I bring good news. You and Law are about to become fabulously rich.' She waved the Lings back. 'Beerbell wasn't lying about the valley. There's more treasure there than you'll ever spend. All yours, provided we shake hands on a simple business arrangement. A partnership if you will—good for as long as you live and work my lands.'"

"Wilson had told me that Mondi was a fierce enemy, never to be trusted. I pretended indifference. But wasn't I looking to leave the island a wealthy man? 'Not so fast,' I said. 'Why don't you order your Lings to mine the valley?'"

"'They have other pressing matters to attend to, like the never-ending run of sponsor ships dumping Ordonnes on my island. And that damned cobra,' she growled. Her face morphed into Saul's scaly head and flared golden hood for a second, and then returned to her previous beauty. 'My offer's a fifty-fifty cut. Sacked, bottled, or buried. Carry your treasure out anyway you want. We'll settle up when you board a ship.'"

"No meant war. And, well, I wasn't up for a life and death

fight." Teller scratched his head and cleared his throat. "After all, wasn't I on a treasure hunt? She smiled like a movie star when we shook hands. 'Congratulations partner, you're on your way to a very long and wealthy life.'"

"You actually took Mondi's hand?"

"Fiddy-fiddy as they say in the hood. And you could write a book about everything that went wrong."

"All that glitters is not gold," Cotton said. "But greed will make a pine knot shine like doubloons."

"I was a thinkin' how I could transport all mah gold, silver, and jewels to a ship. Meanwhile, Mondi was a playin' me like a Hawaiian guitar. She knew there'd be no leaving Solitary Valley, not today, not next year, not in a hundred years. I sold mah freedom for something absolutely worthless. That magic spring water, gold, and jewels might as well be pond water and sacks of gravel."

Cotton ran down my arm, threw a twig in the fire, and jumped on Law's back. "How so?"

"Let me tell you about that ol' green skin's trickery. Two days later we found Solitary Valley. All the stories were true. The place was loaded." He raised his right hand and laughed. "I found three nuggets the size of mah thumb the first morning. And the magic water, or ponce as I call it today, gave me all the time in the world to mine, pan, and sack."

"Not so bad," I said.

"The first season or two, we mostly liked Solitary. Law never had a better coat. Every time I shaved, mah hairline lowered and beard thickened. And healing? My nearsighted vision's gone." He tapped the side of his head and grinned. "Shortsighted thinking's still there—but I'm hoping. Vonn, you'd never believe how well these ol' wrestlers' knees got to working. We panned dawn to dusk, found gold nuggets large as your fist, and mined a bread sack full of diamonds—"

"Let me guess. You found the motherlode. But nobody cared, least of all Mondi," Cotton said.

"Screwed from the jump." Teller wagged his head. "You see, Mondi already got what she wanted—mah freedom. Trinkets and gold? Ha, they's just bait. Worthless except for boat anchors and bragging rights."

"Mondi never stopped by for Christmas tea?" Cotton said.

"Funny mouse. Solitary Valley was mah very own prison labor camp. Countin' gold and silver we couldn't spend. Then came the worst part—mind and body started fighting each other. Every time I sucked down that spring water part of me sank to the bottom and never came back. Racing thoughts twisted everything into—well, I'll just say that birds and squirrels became giant Lings moving in the shadows."

Cotton said, "Paranoia?"

"More like terror." He tipped up his cider jug so Cotton could drink, then took a swig and handed the jug to me. I dribbled some on Law's tongue, took a swallow and handed it back.

"A wee bit be good for what ails ye, but a whole bunch? Not so much." He corked the bottle and winked. "Within a year we's hooked on ponce. Couldn't gorge enough to stop eating. Then things got really weird." He spread his arms twelve feet wide. "We started growing—a head taller and doubled our weight. Every bone in mah body screamed. Sometimes I'd sleep for days." He studied his massive forearms and grinned. "Reckon I lost mah heart. Nothin' left but a little boy whistling in the dark. Had more bad thoughts than blood running through mah veins."

I said, "Now I get the chiseled lines on the mine's wall. Trespasser Beware – Greed Brings Ye In – Insanity Finds Ye Out."

Teller nodded. "I hoped I'd be long gone, time someone read that."

"Trapped and nobody to help," Cotton said.

"Nobody but this old bear." He rubbed Law's back. "Even after all the crazy, today's-the-day escape runs, you never ran off and left me, did ya?"

Law popped his jaws and rumbled a response.

"That's right, we never cleared the last ridgeline. Always ran out of sun and sanity. I woke up every morning for ninety damned years in the bottom of Solitary Valley. Oh, once in a blue moon someone would wander by. But when they saw us," Teller patted his chest, "they ran. Until you two showed up. And that, mah friends, is how Law and I lived in Solitary Valley for over ninety years."

"Three quarters of a ton of man and bear." I pointed at both of them. "Tonight, you're free."

Cotton scurried over to a big rock by the fire. "Let's give ourselves a name, something that will bond the four of us."

"Got something in mind?" I said.

"Well, we've lost our families. We're four orphans stuck on the Pious Trail."

"Orphan isn't much of a name."

"Urchins." Teller stomped his feet and pointed with both hands. "A spiny little brat, a rascal, and a pair of rogues. I like it."

Cotton jumped and shouted. "Urchins, it is."

"Urchins," we shouted, "on a journey to Farland."

Law roared and Teller translated. "We start a new life together."

Contemplation

Thoughts of sparrow bees and giant Lings pushed me out of a deep sleep. Before moving a muscle or eyelid, I listened to my three friends' rhythmic breathing. We'd live another day.

I stoked the fire, made a pot of mint and milk thistle tea, and waited for sunrise. Camp tea wasn't Earl Grey, but wasn't too bad. Many edible plants and berries grew wild along the Pious Trail, and Law knew every one of them. He and Cotton ate them whole, but brews and soups were best for Teller and me.

Red, orange, and yellow colors began to push the dark from the eastern skyline. A hint of blue silhouetted the wilderness mountaintops, retiring the stars one by one. I edged closer to the fire, and for one never-ending moment, drifted into forevermore.

Infinity. Limitless time and space stretched to distances without end.

Eternity. A certainty existed beyond death, an ultimate reality for every man and woman—never-ending life.

The High Seas. The world's life blood came from a fusion of sun, wind, rain, dissolved salts, and countless minerals from snow-packed mountains and sand hills. Purified by cascading falls and fed by thousands of rivers in countless green valleys, only God could fathom the never-ending cycle.

I stood at the edge of something far greater than ships and sea monsters, majestic pink clouds and violent tempests—the spiritual war for the souls of man. And there, I saw a selfless love in every harrowing rescue. There, I heard a distinctive voice in a hundred Ordonne conversations. The voice was God. He unlocked the Wicket, the pedestrian passage built on the towering gates of hell, and freed me from Demimonde.

My sobriety was his. My life was his.

The Sea of Booze. Saltwater spray had stung my chapped lips. My old friend, Dodgy, had shouted a warning from the crow's nest. She'd spotted an angry gale headed our way accompanied by a school of slippery eels eager to find us. Hunting port and starboard, they'd sorely tested the ship and crew.

The ship's bell rang the air full of fear. Sailors scurried to their stations. Captain Bill commanded Pilot to bring her into the wind. Captain Bob shouted from the quarterdeck. "Bosun, pull the halyard and secure the sail. Scullers, get to your long oars—quickly now—time your rowing and pull—pull like your life depends on every stroke."

The Sponsor Ship. More than a carved long-ship with sails and twelve long oars, it embodied unity, service, and recovery. We sailed where others turned back or sank—through treacherous gales, delirium fog, and shallow waters to throw a lifeline to castaways and rudderless ships. The ship's crew was the genesis of countless recoveries, and together we were fearless. We drank danger's bitter bile. We gorged on fair weather desserts and inhaled enough magic to paint every cloud pink.

New love. Adorable Stuey had red hair tucked under a fisherman's hat and cocked over just enough to show a sprinkling of freckles and piercing green eyes.

We loved and danced to "Divine Winds and Pink Clouds Bless our Voyage."

We loved and sang to "May Shipwreck and Danger Never Find Us."

Of all the faces and voices I encountered, aside from Teller, Moneymaker was the most remarkable. We called the big man the mad Buddha—but never to his face. He never climbed on the wagon. The last time I saw him, he threw an empty bourbon bottle at me, but I bet he's still alive fighting his weight and whiskey, planning his nineteenth voyage on the Sea of Booze. Why not? He owned Treatment Ship and half of Shantytown.

For a season we'd sailed at the edge of paradise, then anchored at Serenity Harbor. The Island promised a good ending to a challenging voyage with an overblown retreat center and twenty miles of marked trails across the mountains. Alkies expected to find their new me on a wind-swept promontory or a sunny beach. Pipedreams I tell you—premeditated resentments. Instead they got blisters, cold rain, Lings, and plenty of time to worry. I still don't know where heaven went, but it sure wasn't in the Broken Hills Wilderness.

I began the Pious Trail with a rucksack full of provisions, Magic Twenty in my pocket, and a heart full of Moral Compass. After final goodbyes the night before, the other wayfarers quickly found their paths and never looked back. I stood alone, waving at Sponsor Ship's sails disappearing over the horizon—too far away to see me—an insignificant speck.

Aloneness. To lack help happens at times in life. But for the alcoholic-addict, the best meaning of aloneness is terminal uniqueness. Cursed to a solitary wandering in a wilderness full of people. We're perpetual window shoppers looking for what we never got—inside. Fear locked us out of every door. Misery drove us to escape the gray wilderness. Our best ideas led us to Shantytown, to find the elusive Mister Good Time and his sack of magic pills.

Growing up in one Shantytown or another, my shipmates knew isolation and despair. Most hated the old ways and loved the new life they found under the ship's canvas sails. They wouldn't leave because they feared the unknown or were prudent. So, they sailed away on another high seas adventure.

Sobriety Island, a land mass on the scale of Iceland or Cuba, occupied the center of the Sea of Booze. King Alcohol and his Four Horsemen ruled Abstract, the largest state. Mondi claimed most of the Wilderness, but to the east, beyond the Big Book Mountain range, lay the twelve Ports of Promise where my journey began.

I had enough scars to know that the island ate the proud and foolish. Wilson and Watcher's words haunted me. "Humans don't survive Sobriety Island very long. They reach Farland or— well, you get my drift. All trails end in Farland, and there, dear Vonn, be where you'll find yer way back home." Wilson might live on Sobriety Island for hundreds of years, maybe forever, but my destiny beckoned from Baser. Staying would be worse than death—I'd become a Ling.

Vonn, be careful what you think about.

Our journey extended from weeks and seasons, to an undefined end. Fatigue and doubt changed Farland into a myth. The spring water was long gone, and my chronic pain returned with a vengeance. I didn't complain, but something was wrong, really wrong with my raspy lungs. Asthma or emphysema, or heaven forbid, cancer.

Vonn, stop awfulizing. Focus. You have today, each other—and hope.

As the Urchins, Cotton, Teller, and Law were in their second or third lives. Even without magic water, they were better pilgrims than I was.

Cotton had a seventh sense beyond intuition that few four-legged and no two-legged creatures ever knew. The lay of the land spoke to her. She heard the native grass sing about rock-slides and windfalls, overheard the trees whisper secrets about ambushes and tropical storms.

Typical of the mysterious creatures that dwelled on Sobriety Island, Law was a magnificent beast, a throwback to the pre-historic bear called the Missouri Monster. Measuring almost six feet on all fours, he could outrun a race horse. But the only time he ran was for game—or toward the enemy. Intelligent, he understood every word we said. And with Teller interpreting, I began to understand how well suited he was to thrive on Sobriety Island. Law was arguably the uncontested master of his domain.

The Urchins were more than a mouse and a bear, more than a couple of men fleeing a common enemy. We became a family that shared every rag, morsel, and story that nourished and comforted us. Hardship gave us an edge, a level of trust and loyalty that only survivors know.

Cotton scurried up my arm, studied the sunrise for a second, and then tugged my hair. "Watcher is here."

Watcher never came without a purpose. As a minimum, she jinned up memories I'd sooner forget. One in particular, at Doc Changelove's office, was especially painful. Thirteen steps ascending a gallows and thirteen twists in a hangman's knot. Did each knot stand for a season of life or decade? Regardless, the thirteenth was my alcoholic fate—Demimonde's sordid realm–no hometown or Wicket Gate, no compass and magic twenty, only a protracted death.

A wind gust brushed the firebrands to life, twisting the smoke and flames into a dancing column that reached into the sky, brightening, covering our camp with the earthy sweet scent of cut grass and bosky sandalwood. The air was too hot to breathe. Every muscle complained. I stood, wiped the sweat off my face, and tossed my pea jacket. Was this another brain overload, or was Watcher making another point?

I paced. Why was Watcher flexing her muscle? I'd seen enough to know she was a powerful mix of the natural, supernatural, and maternal love—and I never wanted to be on her bad side; no one would want that.

I knew things were coming to a head. The faint rhythmic thump that had followed us for weeks grew from a distant tick to a booming heartbeat, echoing over miles of Broken Wilderness to our camp. The Lings were gaining ground and declaring their evil intent. *We're coming for you.*

Teller and Law stood at the edge of camp. And Cotton? Gone wherever she went during risky times.

"Urchins, greetings and salutations." Her voice might've been in my ear or from the other side of the camp, echoing slightly. "You do well to travel so far on the Pious Trail."

Cotton peeked out from some tree fronds. "Welcome to our camp."

"I bring news of Darklings, Mudlings, and Wretchlings," she said. "The giants' drums tell us that Mondi's grapevine throne is dead, and the Lings have deserted their camp."

"Lovely," Teller said.

"Mondi's mutated into a giant Ling, tall enough to look Law in the eyes. Half of her hair is burned off and her green hands are scarred crimson."

"Giant? So much for Mondi's striking beauty," I said. "Guess Lings don't heal?"

"You may be pain free when alcohol fills your veins—but there's no healing," Watcher said. "Mondi is mad dog insane, kicking her stunted attendants around and laughing like a hyena. Lily threw ten Lings into the bonfire and beat a hundred more, because you escaped from Solitary Valley. Vonn, everything they say is a curse or threat ending with your name."

My Moral Compass warmed. "I hope they wipe each other out."

"Not likely," Teller said from the shadows. "For every Ling

that dies, one or two more crawl out of the bog fresh from the real world."

A blast of cold air brought a cloud of leaves, blanketing us with a thousand red, yellow, and orange flora hands, touching and rattling in a language I would never know. Then as quick as they came, they vanished.

Watcher raised her voice. "The island trees tell a dreadful story. Last night Mondi screamed until her eyes flashed red, 'Who's the Queen of the Broken Hills?' Every time the Lings chanted, 'You are. You're the greatest queen to ever live.' Any slight or insincerity brought double pain and suffering."

I shivered. Memories of the Ling camp battle or the chilly morning air? "Glad I'm here."

The column of fire died, allowing the morning shadows to retake the edge of camp. My three friends quietly returned, Teller riding Law and Cotton high on his shoulder.

Watcher continued. "Mondi screamed, 'Losers! I'm surrounded by losers. You let the fat man and his bear escape Solitary. They united with Vonn and his damned mouse, and now they have a name—the Urchins. Does anyone know what that means?' Lily screamed the answer, 'Ordonne.'"

"What?" I was horrified. "They know our new name?"

"Sparrow bees. We haven't exactly traveled in stealth mode," Cotton replied.

"In Mondi's sodden mind, the Urchins are the Lings' fault." Watcher mimicked Mondi's voice. "'Useless fools, now there's an Ordonne clan in the middle of my kingdom. Who thinks that's funny? Who wants to run and be an Urchin?' Then she pointed across the teeming mass and growled, 'What about you, or you?'"

Teller said, "Nice to be important people."

"A hundred yowling nos arose from the filthy horde. She turned bright green and towered higher than all but the largest Ling giants. 'Changelings—do not underestimate me. We will campaign against the Ordonne. We will hunt down every Urchin. We will exterminate them or—you will be exterminated.'"

My heart began to race. "Why am I so important?"

"I'll let Mondi answer in her own words. 'If Vonn reaches the real world, he could destroy Demimonde's harvest of souls. Generations of disease will be lost.'"

Terror and disappointment tightened my chest. "Harvest of souls? First I've heard of that. And, you say I'm in the middle of this?"

I found breathing difficult. My fears raced. I stared across the vast wilderness straining to see the plateaus beyond the horizon. I wanted to run and hide behind the biggest cross I could find. "Oh, no, that's too much. Nope, time to go back to the plateaus. Life was good—"

"Never," Teller slapped the flat of his battle axe and snarled, "You. Will. Not. Run! We aren't going anywhere, 'cept right up that trail."

Cotton vanished.

Law growled. His breath carried the awful stench of blood— or was it death?

The Con Brothers warned. "Leave your friends on this trail, and Mondi will tear you apart before you ever reach the plateaus."

My ears rang. "Harvest of souls? That's eternal. How can I possibly—?"

"Trust the one who saved your life and carried you from Baser to here?" Watcher's voice was sad. "Running is betraying."

I mumbled, "Is there no other way?"

Cotton reappeared on my shoulder and clasped my earlobe with her bony little paw. "I give you what I hold most dear, my life. I will die by your side so you can reach your appointed hour."

My Moral Compass burned like a branding iron.

Law roared a long, mournful cry that reverberated across the valley, echoed off the mountaintop, and returned through the wilderness like a chorus. Teller came over and put his hand on my shoulder. "We," he pointed at Law, "give you all we have, our lives. We will die that you may reach your appointed hour."

Mr. Conscience's high elderly voice pierced my stubborn heart. "There's no greater love than to give your life for your friends."

I didn't have a home, nor a bed to call my own, not even a safe place to escape the voices that demanded the impossible. But I did have an appointed hour along an endless journey that grew harder by the day—the Pious Trail.

In that secret place where thoughts and emotions form inside every man and woman, God liberated me from the ogre ego that had ruled me since I crawled out of the crib. My soul opened and he gave me the power to deny self.

I took a deep breath and considered my three friends. What I would've given to read a good book on Wilson's front porch again, but there was no other way. "My problem is thinking that conniving leads to winning, but I'm a walking dead man. We must go forward together. Should we fall, we fall together."

Teller whispered in my ear, "Don't ever make us doubt you again."

"This is the way, the only way for you," Watcher said.

Cotton sat on top of Law's head holding an ear. "We win or die together."

We listened to the giants' distant drumming. They were two, maybe three days out. Watcher spoke. "Brace yourselves. The cloud of leaves said the Lings will intercept you on the Pious Trail before you reach the High Mesa. She'll lay an ambush to kill all of you on sight."

"Not while I'm a riding a grizzly and swinging this," Teller winked and ran his thumb down the cutting edge of his war axe. "I've lost count of how many Lings we've sent to the burn barrel."

Watcher said, "Like all bullies, Mondi is driven by fear. She dreads Law, Saul, and me. Teller, you'll be number four."

"King Saul?" I looked over my shoulder.

"Now he's a king?" Watcher almost laughed. "The cobra's timing and tactics are a mystery, but he'll repay me an old debt. Urchins, this battle will either end or define your lives. Live, and you'll find Farland on the coast below."

"Why can't we time-travel to Farland?" I said, "Like the Italian Ferrara Fabbro trip?"

Silence.

"So," I mumbled. "Not a good idea."

"Watcher, if I may?" Cotton said. "I sense an edge from you. A battle plan, perhaps?"

"Yes, but I don't fight battles you can win yourself."

"So, we can win. Will you use your special powers against our enemies?"

"You're shrewd." Watcher said. "What do you propose?"

Cotton spoke with confidence. "You tipped your hand when you said, 'When alcohol fills your veins, you may be pain free, but there's no healing.' Like all coldblooded beasts, Lings don't do well in the cold. They tire, get discouraged, and are quick to run. Perhaps our encounter will come with a fierce sleet and snow storm."

"Done. And look for a quick way to end Mondi's ambush."

CHAPTER THIRTEEN

The Battle of Cold Meadow

We stood in the dark watching the sun peep over the horizon. Every point on the compass was downhill from the tree line where we stood, straining to hear the Lings. They waited for us in the tangled forest across a broad high country meadow, blocking our path to Farland, my only way back home.

We'd slept little since meeting with Watcher. Our cautious pace for the last two days had unraveled our nerves. Fatigue changed a hawk's cry or a snapping twig into a column of Lings. Every spinning tree leaf mimicked a giant moving through the forest. Mondi was out there; my Moral Compass burned hot. What was she waiting for?

A billowing mountain squall dropped the temperature twenty degrees and flung a wall of sleet across our backs. I squelched my normal complaint—this was Watcher's storm, delivered as promised. The cold would give us the edge we needed to survive.

Law bared his teeth and growled an ugly warning; his hackles rose. Cotton scurried through my filthy hair, tweaked my ear, and whispered, "We smell hundreds of Lings in the woods."

Mondi had outmarched us and laid her ambush; she knew we had to come to her to reach Farland.

Teller stepped near me and shouldered his axe. "They're watching us; waiting for us to make a move."

"I'm here," Mr. Conscience said. "I will cripple your enemy's will."

"I'm here," Mr. Consequence said. "They will see every monster that ever lived in their minds."

Then they chorused, "They'll learn what fear of fear means."

The far wood line erupted with howls and curses. Mondi and hundreds of Lings emerged, milling and looking over their shoulders. Jacked up by the Con Brothers, they'd ruined their own ambush.

With driving sleet and chaos falling all around us, Teller turned to me, and we locked eyes. The morning sun highlighted every whisker on his grimaced face. "Aye, we be walking dead men. Let's take Mondi with us." Then he winked, broke into a toothy grin, and howled a sarcastic, slightly insane laugh void of fear or regret—he was created for this hour. Today was his day.

He mounted his saddle like a young man, kicked Law's ribs, and yelled, "Urchins, the day is ours! We got 'em right where we want 'em." He charged, riding back and forth, bellowing insults and swinging his battle axe, hacking down small trees with single blows.

The enraged Lings set the woods on fire. They beat their log drum. The flames competed with hundreds of screaming voices to fill the meadow with burning madness.

I followed Law into the open with Cotton on my shoulder.

A wind shift brought a wall of smoke across the meadow.

"The battlefield is ready," Watcher called over the chaos. "Cover your eyes."

The sun broke over the horizon and struck the meadow with a blistering beam. But the sleet and billowing smoke blocked the light, obscuring all but the tallest trees behind a toxic gray wall. Smoke blind and woozy, I fell in the cold mud crying out for air. My old enemy, Asthma, was suffocating me.

I swayed on my hands and knees, too weak to move, retching. *I'll never make it outta here.*

My arms felt wooden, my legs like stone. The forest floor seemed as cold as a new grave.

Cotton shouted and danced on my back. She nibbled my ear.

The giant's drum persisted—or was it my heartbeat? Beyond caring, detached, I was as they say in the islands, gone travelin'.

Watcher's voice pierced my death cloud. "Vonn Thrasher."

I whispered. "Sorry, I have to go."

"This is not your hour."

"There are no hours. Take my last breath and let me go."

"All life and death belong to the Father, not man. You'll live to finish your race."

The drum stopped.

In a flash, I stood, gripping my staff with both hands. My heavy breathing broke the cold silence. My pain was gone.

"For now, your malignancy has been set aside. Go, quickly, and rejoin the battle."

I marched downhill and stood in the swirling foggy smoke. Cotton, my tiny sentry, ran from shoulder to shoulder. "There—footsteps."

"Yes." Faint and sporadic at first, then there were many.

"Vonn," Teller shouted from the shadows ahead. "Steady boy-o —steady—they be a comin' yer way."

"Courage, Vonn Thrasher, you died once," Mr. Conscience said. "Make the best of this go-round."

Cotton tugged my ear. "Listen for my voice. I am the eyes in the back of your head."

My fists ached from white-knuckling my staff.

Something fast and charcoal slipped through the thin layer of gray snow on my right. The huge cobra slithered into view and circled me once, flicking his forked tongue. He lifted his scaly head to eye level and flared his golden hood—broad as my shoulders and marked with two false eyes. He nodded and disappeared. A snake in a snow storm? Yes. Saul, king cobra and archenemy of every Ling, had joined the fray. And together, we'd answer blow for blow.

Teller cursed and Law roared. A big Ling stumbled near, howling and swinging a club like a blind boxer. Law had ripped most of his face off. He dropped his club, spun on his heels, and fell twitching to the ground.

Cotton dug her claws in my ear. "On the left, two headed our way."

Two Lings staggered out of the white blindness. They might've been teenage girls before Demimonde. Blood-spattered and one missing a hand, they'd obviously encountered Law.

One stepped forward and spoke through busted yellow teeth, "Vonn. There you are." Her voice cracked into a sob. "Remember us?"

"Amoré twins?" I gagged up something bitter. "How? You disappeared years ago in a state mental hospital."

They sashayed shoulder to shoulder toward me, arms open for a hug. "My, my, look how handsome you are today. Dear old lover boy, come—be with us—it'll be just like the old times."

"Oh, no. You're Demimonde." I shoved the wounded one down with the point of my staff and then bounced the other end off of her sister's head.

They rolled and bucked in the mud, barking and snapping their teeth like mad dogs. "Vonn, Vonn, Vonn."

"Do I leave or finish them?" No answer, but then I knew there wasn't one.

I started to edge away when they jumped up and laughed, "No white wedding for you," and coughed a column of brown smoke at me laden with the strong vinegar-like smell of brown heroin. I sidestepped and took a haymaker swing at them. They ducked, laughed, and went howling back into the fog and smoke.

"I'm glad I'm not a human," Cotton hissed.

"I'd trade places with you today."

"They know where we are." She climbed on top of my head. "Get ready for more."

Cold Meadow erupted with shouting and cursing, ringing metal on metal, and splintering wood. Loudest of all, Law roared like a thunderstorm. A hard wind drove the smoke and sleet away; intense eastern sun spotlighted every combatant. Cotton and I manned high ground on the near side. Mondi and a couple dozen Lings clustered in the middle. Teller and Law held the long area in between with Saul fending off Lings trying to advance toward me past stacks of bodies.

"There." Mondi pointed at me. "I'll roast his soul for supper."

Drunk with power and the souls of ten thousand alcoholics, Mondi's burned and haggard green body pulsed with every curse and command. "Attack formation. Hurry up, quickly, and bring every weapon you have—we finally got 'em."

A giant concealed in the forest beat a quick attack tempo. Over a hundred Lings of every size and color swarmed, stomping and wailing, crossing the field to stand three and four deep with Mondi. They stunk of old whiskey and rotting flesh.

We stared at each other across a hundred yards of no-man's-land. Save a giant's nervous cough, the battlefield was mute.

Teller leaned forward in the saddle and bellowed, "Green skin, I's here to settle up. Got naw gold for ya, not even a single jewel." Then his deep, crazy laugh erupted. "Instead, I brought my freedom—and this." He swung his axe over his head twice and leveled the blade at her. "And today, one of us will die to keep 'em."

"Death to all Ordonnes," Mondi thundered. "Give me the victory I crave—half my kingdom for any man's head—the other half for Saul's hood."

Cotton stood on my shoulder, hiding inside a mop of my hair. "Start praying."

They charged. The unholy horde closed the gap. Rocks, javelins, and arrows fell around us.

Teller and Law plunged through their middle, disappearing in a swarming line of Ling clubs and spears.

"Cotton," I yelled. "Can you see them? Did they fall?"

She raced to the top of my head. "There."

Our friends dropped Lings left and right. Law had a spear in his shoulder and another hanging off his hip. Tellers face and chest were covered with blood. But they fought on, standing back to back, battle axe and grizzly claws tearing limb from limb.

Law slapped three Lings rolling, giving Teller time to pull the spears out, turn, and throw them with such force that one pierced two Lings. He remounted and they galloped through a gap onto high ground.

Saul flanked Mondi's formation and attacked the back of their line. Red with Ling blood, his deadly venom dropped them left and right with lightning speed and efficiency.

A dozen or so Lings on the right pulled away, regrouped, and rushed at me.

I pelted them with rocks. Two fell, but the others kept coming. "Cotton, it's been real."

I planted my feet and started swinging.

Seconds stretched to minutes. The air filled with mad faces. Bloody hands reached and clawed. Bloody hands clubbed and cut. My busted staff and hatchet grew slippery with gore.

Mondi shouted over the din, "Get him while he's alone."

A giant Ling stomped through the melee swinging a tree trunk club. I was three steps from being bludgeoned when Saul slithered between us. Lightning fast, he encircled the giant and sank his poisonous fangs in his neck three times and rode him to the ground. Then he slithered off the convulsing giant, flared his golden hood and rose up ten feet, looked Mondi in the eyes, and rumbled a ravenous savage growl.

What a magnificent creature.

Teller and Law drove through the Ling's faltering line to rejoin Saul, standing between me and Mondi. Both sides paused long enough to steal a breath or two and look for better footing.

The Con Brothers made their move. They twisted and filled every Ling head with the worst monster—fear of fear—a panic attack. Deadlier than Teller's axe or Saul's venom, their intense fear outweighed anything Mondi could say or do. A dozen bug-eyed giants dropped their weapons and stampeded right over the top of Mondi.

My great enemy went down in a cloud of dirty red snow, trampled by her own soldiers.

"Mondi's dead!" echoed across the battlefield. Flustered Lings ran to and fro, brandishing their weapons at each other as much as us.

"Tell them the battle is over," Watcher said. "Tell them if they leave, they live."

I climbed on top of a boulder. "Leave and live. Go back to your wilderness—now!" My voice echoed across Cold Meadow, but few turned their heads. "Go. Never raid the Pious Trail again."

Law slapped the ground, sprang forward, and roared. Some Lings dropped their weapons and ran. Others limped away looking over their shoulders. All melted into the rain-soaked wilderness.

From that day forward, the Lings lived in their natural state—wet-brained camp thieves and hecklers, never again a military threat.

Wounded several times, Saul left a bloody trail to the edge of the trees. He paused long enough to catch our eyes, and then vanished.

"Will he live?" Cotton said. "Watcher, what can we do?"

"Nothing. Saul will seek a quiet sunny place in the lowlands to rest and heal. Save a scar or two, when he resurfaces, he'll be the same old cranky snake."

My ringing ears, bruises, bloody knuckles, and knots on my head were nothing compared to my friends' wounds. Dazed, I struggled to calm myself as I slumped away from the others and hid behind a tree. To this day, I have no idea where I got the ornate goad I carried in my quivering hands. A Mudling had clearly spent a lot of time knurling and polishing its hickory staff and steel point. The blood-soaked grooves told me that the owner was dead.

I took off my soiled shirt and walked into the field. The midday sun burned off the sleet and snow, warming my battered mind and body. Cotton reappeared and climbed onto my shoulder. We slowly surveyed the ghastly panorama. "Thanks be to God and friends, we survived the Battle of Cold Meadow."

"Yes," Cotton said, "The battle that changed Sobriety Island forever."

At a nearby stream we found Teller and Law soaking their wounds in a deep pool. Cotton and I waded in and submerged in the bracing water. I held my breath and stayed under as long as I could, watching Cotton kick around on the surface. Then I let the water take me up and funnel me downstream to another pool.

Cleansed from blood, the solitude enabled me to study each unique passing cloud. The weight of the battle disappeared. Nothing could touch me.

Was I numb from trauma or the cold water?

My teeth began to chatter. How long could I stay in before dying?

Law's heavy breathing made me look up. My three friends stared at me from a big fallen log.

Teller cleared his throat. "Boy-o, ya need some serious groceries. I can count every one a your ribs from here." He tossed my rucksack onto the bank. "Bet there's a towel in there."

I got out and dried. "No wonder my clothes are falling off." I pointed. "Teller, look at your wounds. They—they're almost healed. Law's spear wounds and mine too."

Teller laughed. "Watcher be the healer. Told us, 'Great sacrifice demands great rewards.' Figured we'd let you find out on your own."

"Watcher," I called, scanning the sky. "You're awesome."

We ate a bite of pemmican before leaving. I grabbed Teller's arm as we walked. "I gotta make sure she's gone."

"Mondi?"

"Yeah."

A short time later we stood by Mondi's lifeless form. Her smashed body sprawled in the mud.

"Hard to believe," Cotton said. "The queen of Lings is actually dead."

I nudged her green foot with my toe. No response. "Yep."

Somehow Mondi will resurrect and come at me again.

"Have faith, there's nothing left to fear, dear boy," the Con Brothers said. "Mondi's realm is no more."

Watcher said, "For a long season, there'll be peace and serenity on the Pious Trail, and in your soul, provided you quit tilting at windmills."

I rubbed my temples. "What does that mean?"

"Attacking imaginary enemies. A relapse is your last monster to fight. Pick up what you haven't lost and follow the western sun to the ridgeline above Peace Harbor. Wait for me there."

Teller stepped forward. "I wanted to—"

"Not now," Watcher said. "The scavengers are coming."

"Scavengers?"

"Yes. They're large, aggressive, and not particular what they feed on."

Cotton raced down my arm and jumped on Law's shoulder. "Good enough for this mouse. We need to be long gone before they arrive."

An hour later, the four of us looked back.

I said, "Hell of a fight. But together we won."

Teller pointed. "There's movement in the eastern sky."

Hundreds of ravens, vultures, and condors descended on Cold Meadow. Some were small, others had wingspans broad as a house. They swiftly stripped the flesh from the carcasses.

"Vonnie boy, let's go. Nothing we need to see a goin' on back there."

We left the high country before dark and made camp on a ridgeline near Peace Harbor. We walked quietly thinking about the battle and what tomorrow might bring. Teller dropped an armload of firewood and sat. "I could eat a whole hog and a peck a fried taters."

"Best we can do tonight is boiled wild spuds and onions," I said. "Tea's brewing."

"Law and Cotton still digging around for their own supper?"

"Yeah, somewhere down the hill. They already brought this by and went back out." I held up a blue porcelain camp plate I'd heaped with the honeycomb.

Teller stuck his finger in for a taste. "That be the sweetest golden-brown honey I 'er had."

After I stoked the fire, I stirred some wild herbs and spices into the pot. I tasted it, and added quash. Its unique aroma brought back a Wilson memory. "A salt and pepper base with a little of this and that and, of course, Cabotage love and magic."

"Smellin' mighty fine, mighty fine. Yessir, can't wait to dig in. Hey, I hung mah nose o'er the last ridge long enough tah see Farland ain't much. Lookin' like a ghost town to me."

"Why not? Matches everything else on this island."

We sat back and watched the pot come to a boil.

"What about Watcher? At first I's thinkin' she's a figment of mah broken mind."

"Too many blackouts and blows to the head."

"Then I figured she's yer guardian angel."

"Who knows?" I poured two mugs of tea and handed him one. "Never told me one way or the other."

"Aye, well, this much is for sure, she's damned powerful and master of—well, everything."

"Saved me from dying drunk in a Baser ditch. Then today, I was two heartbeats from dying in the frozen woods when she pulled me back."

"In the fog?"

"Smoke and fog and fear—lungs failed me and I don't know— might have died, might've had some kind of resurrection."

"Then ya fought hard, held yer own."

"Thanks, but Law, Saul, and you saved me from a giant's club. And Cotton? She had my back every minute. But you know what? The Con Brothers carried the day."

"Had the whole durned bunch a them bug-eyed and beatin' on each other."

"Yessir, he who controls the mind controls the battlefield."

We watched Law amble up the hill. I knew Cotton would be riding along holding one of his ears.

"Teller, I don't know how long I've been gone. The last calendar I saw was on Treatment Ship, so I don't know for sure. But I'm thinking three years since I drove into Ism Harbor and sailed the Sea of Booze."

"Hard to say," he replied. "But don't hurry to leave. Hookin' up with you be the best darned thing that's happened to me since bein' with Peach. Don't ya see? Together, we beat aloneness. We carried our friendship to the top of the mountain and back."

Watching the sun disappear behind the mountains was like turning the last page of a beloved epic novel, melancholy. When Watcher returned, she'd send us in different directions to write the next chapter in our book of life. The Urchins as a group would cease. We lamented the end of our time together.

Grief pervaded the fireside gathering.

I wiped my eyes and looked up. Teller faced the woods to hide his tears. Law and Cotton cried as animals do, with jagged breathing. We mourned each other, the day, and innumerable forgotten days demanding to be remembered.

"Why do you spend your last night together grieving?" Watcher's voice echoed across treetop and trail. "Your heavy hearts prove you're new creatures, worthy and beloved. Dry your eyes and stand shoulder to shoulder one more time—united not in hardship or heartache, but in victory and love—rejoice!"

Teller leaned hard on a rock outcropping. "Easy for you to say. I's a losing mah best friends."

"My friends, I've shepherded a host of alcoholics from a dozen different Basers and Shantytowns. Most crossed the Sea of Booze. Some started the Pious Trail, but few walked far enough to find a new life. You, my Urchins, have skirted every cliff, ascended every mountain, and fought every fight with courage and distinction. Well done. You've earned a seat at the Ordonne fire."

"Truthfully," I said. "All I've done is trust you and put one foot in front of the other."

Law ambled up behind me, bumped me with his soggy black nose, and grumbled. Teller chuckled and patted my back. "He said, 'Remember back at the mine when we rolled the apple core between yer feet?'"

I sat on an old log by the dying fire and dried my face again. "Thought I was a goner."

Teller sat next to me. "We's all goners. Gone from Solitary, from Mondi, from the drink and madness that ruled our lives. Gone is good."

"Not bad for a pocket mouse," Cotton chirped.

"Not bad? Ha, you're the eyes in the back of my head, my life-saver and friend forever." I shouted at the sky. "Hey, Con Brothers, nothing from the conscience and consequence department today?"

"Urchins, well done. All we see tonight is good," they said.

Lightning flashed and thunder boomed over the wilderness we'd left behind.

Teller said, "What's the verdict? Where are we going next?"

Watcher said, "Cotton, you'll return to the Plateaus. Stay with Wilson and wait for the next overconfident Ordonne, like Vonn, to walk the Pious Trail."

"And he or she will be fortunate to have you," I said.

"Hear, hear. How can an old drunk love a wee mouse?" Teller blotted his face and grinned. "With you dear Cotton, it be very easy."

"Teller and Law," Watcher said affectionately. "You are bona fide living heroes. But I tell you this with all love. There's no place for you in today's Funfair."

"Figgered as much."

"The faraway lands have dramatically changed over the last ninety years. All the people you knew are either dead or have become Lings. New drugs and stronger booze, power trips, the sex trade, and big money continue to turn people into Demi-monde's minions and fill its realm."

Teller slapped his knees and stood. "Funfair was like that back in mah day."

"Today's depravity is worse. You'll be judged a threat, a violent freak of nature. Without money and friends, the Funfairies will throw you in a circus cage and make you do tricks for booze until you die a wretched death."

Cotton climbed on top of my head. "That is not acceptable."

Teller and Law looked at each other. The bear gave a mournful moan and Teller said, "Yeah, they'd come after us all right. But I'm a telling you that there'll ne'er be a cage for Law, nor jail for me. No ma'am, a whole bunch a folks will die afore they roll us in a grave."

I jumped up. "And I'd burn the town down the next day—"

"Easy boys," Watcher said. "The war is over. No more Cold Meadows. No more killing and burning. No more drinking your life away. We're moving in a new direction toward a better life in Ordonne."

Thunder clapped and the wind picked up a notch. We smelled rain.

"Destinies can be changed. One good decision today makes everything right. Teller and Law, listen carefully. I offer you the best of both worlds."

"Say on."

"You like the high country between Solitary and Farland and have earned the right to call Cold Meadow yours. I offer you a life with mission. Stay and hold the high ground. Build a cabin from the best trees, next to the cleanest water. Be my Guardians of the Pious Trail and live your lives protected by me and an island that loves you. And like Wilson, you'll become a living part of Sobriety Island. Legends about the high-country giant and his grizzly will be told around campfires forever."

"Guardians, huh. Of what? Lings ain't much a threat nah more—"

"To you and Law. But each Ordonne will present a different set of needs and challenges."

Teller said, "So we're to patrol all the trails looking for sick and lost Ordonnes, and be free to go anywhere on the island?"

"Coast to coast. Not even Solitary Valley will have power over you."

He leaned over and elbowed Law. "We could visit ol' Wilson, and drop into Solitary for a little ponce when the knees get ta' hurtin'."

"You'll always have the power of choice. Even if you want to leave Sobriety Island and age out."

Law grumbled and smacked his lips. Teller interpreted. "He said, 'Or stay and live indefinitely.' Yes, we'll take another ninety summers."

A couple of lightning bolts flashed. Cotton said, "Too close for comfort. There's a large rock overhang a little way down the trail. Let's hurry."

We found a dry place inside and dropped our gear before the wind delivered a cold drizzle.

"Urchins," Watcher said. "Listen to the story of Farland and what awaits Vonn in Peace Harbor."

I put on my pea jacket and leaned back against Law. He sloshed the side of my head with his big wet towel-tongue.

"Over a hundred years ago, a group of wealthy tycoons and bankers claimed Peace Harbor," Watcher said. "They brought in construction and supply ships and built a power plant. A saw mill and rock quarry provided raw materials for a new drug and alcohol treatment center called New Life Treatment. Early results were promising. They mixed new and traditional medication and therapies, advertising that they were the best recovery known to man.

I snorted. "How many times have we heard that?"

"Soon, Peace Harbor bustled with every kind of hopeful alcoholic and addict. A little arts and crafts community grew around the facility, and together they became known as Farland."

"Lemme guess," Teller hooted. "Demimonde came a knocking."

"Thus, your lesson of the day. See your opponent without prejudice or assumption."

Thunder troubled the sky, and lightning illuminated our cave. Watcher waited for a quiet moment. "Sun Tzu states in *The Art of War*, 'He who exercises no forethought but makes light of his opponents is sure to be captured by them.' Not only did Farland underestimate their enemy, they wrote off valid stories about Mondi and her Lings as patient gossip and old island fables."

I shook my head. "Ignoring Demimonde gave the Lings an advantage."

"Demimonde whispered in the director's ear, 'Recovery is a science. Forget all the spiritual mumbo-jumbo.' Then Demimonde began picking off patients before they left the campus. Tabloids called Peace Harbor *Agony Island* and *Crash Cove*, and ran stories about waterboarding, frontal lobotomies, straightjackets, and padded rooms. Eventually, New Life ran out of patients and money and tried to sell. First as a medical facility, then as a resort, but even at ten cents on the dollar, Peace Harbor's remote location and ghoulish reputation scared off every buyer. In the end, they abandoned Farland and went back to the mainland."

Cotton ran across my shoulders and pulled my hair. "Didn't you start out on a paddle wheeler called New Life Treatment Ship?"

"Same company a hundred years later," Watcher answered. "As Vonn knows, nowadays they run three-week excursions back and forth from Ism Harbor. Never touching Sobriety Island, but never going bankrupt either."

"That's why they tossed us overboard," I said. "After three weeks at sea, they ordered us to move to the front deck and jump. Captain said that the waters around Sobriety Island were too shallow and treacherous. 'You can make it on your own—the island isn't far away.'"

"And you did," Cotton said.

"Not everybody did. Twenty-five went in the drink, fifteen were rescued by Sponsor Ship, and the slippery eels got the rest. The drunken owner, Moneymaker, catcalled from the upper deck."

Watcher interrupted. "Let's focus on Farland for now."

Teller said, "Yeah, I wanna know what's goin' on down there."

"After New Life was abandoned, things ratcheted up. Ordonne declared the grand hall and grounds were theirs by default and moved in. Demimonde pushed back and set Mondi up in Peace Harbor. Obviously, Ordonnes and Lings can't live together and the hotly contested ground became a warzone. Over the next ten years much of Farland was destroyed by neglect and skirmishes. The conflict ended in a draw. Neither side had enough power to gain the advantage."

"So Cold Meadow wasn't the first battle?" I said.

"Or the largest. Believing there was nothing left for their enemy, both sides licked their wounds and withdrew—Mondi, into the Wilderness Mountains. Ordonne, out to sea, but not before establishing Wilson's roadhouse on the plateaus. Common enemies like Saul—"

"And now me and Law be keepin' the Lings honest."

"Wilson!" I said, "That one-eyed mountain man never said anything about ten years in Farland—"

"Nary a hint ta me either."

I walked over to the mouth of the cave. "After all these years, why does the Pious Trail still end in Farland?"

Watcher said, "Everyone has a winding path, a valley to cross, and a mountain to climb. One man's trail ends here, another over there. Some take a few months, others, like you, need years. The ultimate goal is about the traveler more than the destination. Pious Trail shaped you through people and events. Your goal was always to reach Farland's gateway."

"Gateway—like Changelove's office?"

"Yes, but with a different challenge."

Heavy wind and rain pushed us back to a drier spot. Everyone was content to listen to the storm's bluesy melody, until Cotton pulled my ear. "Pay attention to my seventh sense, my instinctive awareness. Heed my words. Farland is dangerous. A no-man's-land doesn't mean nobody is there—believe nothing you hear and half of what you see."

Watcher said. "A Changeling called Night Terror waits for

you in Farland. With Mondi dead, she's the deadliest Ling on the island."

"Do you mind?" I moved Cotton's sharp little claw off my ear. "You're about to draw blood."

"Sorry."

I said, "Mondi bragged about Night Terror at the Ling Camp."

"Yes," Watcher said. "This one works through cunning and stealth. Unlike other Changelings, Night Terror remains ghostly and weak until she captures and pulls the life out of an Ordonne."

"A vampire?"

"Not quite. Night Terror craves human emotions—rage and lust, grief and utter despair, even insanity draw her like a magnet to iron. Once fed, she's nearly invincible. But unless she feeds before every new moon, she becomes cold, stiff, and pale, and can't warm up even at a fierce campfire."

Muffled voices and a bright cloudless sky woke me. Teller had saddled Law, and Cotton perched on his shoulder as they stowed the last of their gear.

Fear of Night Terror tumbled over and over in my mind. I dreaded Farland like a skydiver does a faulty parachute, but dreaded leaving my companions even more. "Guess Watcher is long gone."

"Aye, sometime after we nodded off." Teller patted Law's back and forced a grin. "Vonn, we gotta lot of travelin' to do. Be a week to the plateaus and the three of us wanna put twenty high country miles behind us today."

I pretended to be stoic. "Yeah, thin air makes for hard miles." I got up and stretched. "No use hanging around."

They ambled close, and I scratched Law's ears. "Man, oh man, we hiked many a good mile since Solitary Valley."

I put my hand on Teller's shoulder and smiled. He sighed and turned away.

Cotton appeared on my shoulder for the last time. I held her in my palm and looked into her dark eyes. "Loyal friend and warrior, may you enjoy a long and successful life with Wilson."

"Vonn Thrasher, there'll never be another band of swashbucklers like the Urchins."

"No, there won't."

She nodded toward Peace Harbor. "You must face your appointed hour when you can't trust your eyes and ears. Trust Watcher. Listen to the Con Brothers. Use your Moral Compass, and you'll live."

Teller climbed in the saddle and Cotton scurried up to his shoulder. We held our magic twenties out and touched the silver in a goodbye salute. Minutes later, the three of them looked back and waved before rounding the bend on the trail that led into the trees.

My life has never been the same.

Chapter Fourteen

Peace Harbor

The western sun painted the hogback ridge above Farland a tawny red and gold, stretching my shadow down its steep incline toward the small meadow far below. A lazy mountain stream wandered through the grass and shrubs to the end of the meadow, then plunged a hundred feet down the side of an abandoned quarry, exploding, churning the lake below like a roiling pot of hot water.

The stream reappeared on the lake's far side, escaped the quarry's chiseled walls near a collapsed bridge, then meandered before disappearing into the saltwater cove.

Bamboo, golden pothos, and creeper vines competed with wild mango and banana trees to hide the old asylum's ruins. Windows and doors were broken, and several roofs had caved in. Sobriety Island was erasing man's failed attempt to claim Peace Harbor. Farland was a ghost town.

"Hello?" I shouted three times. Nothing. Not even an echo surpassed the waterfall's roar.

Tonight would feature a new moon. Would the fresh lunar cycle provide a welcome chapter in my life story? Time would tell.

Sobriety Island time was a mystery, unmeasured by watches and calendars. Days started and stopped, turned, and accelerated any way they wanted. Three weeks on Treatment Ship had become three years and counting. Wilson and Teller and

Cotton had extraordinary lifespans, and what bear ever lived over ninety years? We had unlimited time. Yet, the next Ordonne that donned a ruck and headed upcountry could vanish before the first plateau.

Sobriety Island demanded that every man and woman grow up. Demimonde's schemes and traps, the always uphill Pious Trail, my heavy rucksack, and every scrape and blister had made me into a better, stronger Vonn Thrasher.

The world saw a down-and-out scraggly vagrant with a three-year beard. I owned nothing others wanted. But in Ordonne, I'd gained what the world would never value—Watcher, the Magic Twenty, and a Moral Compass that would never fail.

I donned my rucksack for what I hoped was the last time, picked up my steel-pointed goad, and descended the last four hundred yards of Pious Trail.

I was going home.

I sat cross-legged on my sleeping roll watching the waterfall from across the lake; feeding my campfire one twig at a time. I didn't need the heat in the tropical lowlands. A measure of anxiety had set in, and I hoped a cheer-up fire would help.

Someone destroyed the bridge and the road on the far side during the fight over Farland. Were the four charred abutments a standing warning to go back?

A hornet buzzed me. I ducked and ran back to the fire. Then another attacked, and another, until a dozen or more buzzed around my camp. Mondi's sparrow bees, the Lings' reconnaissance flyers were back—big as coffee mugs and angry. Their stingers made golf ball sized boils.

I swatted at them and threw green fronds on the fire. Billowing smoke eventually drove them away. "Damn. Whoever's running the Lings will find out where I am."

I studied a wall of dark clouds building over the distant mountains. The approaching storm would punish anyone navigating the Broken Hills Wilderness. "Lord—Watcher, thank you for bringing me out of the wilderness and saving my life on Cold Meadow. Please deliver Cotton, Teller, and Law. And while I'm talking and praying, could you send a little help my way? I think the fight over Farland just ratcheted up a notch or two."

Several peacocks called with sharp, repetitive cries. Their voices, easily the loneliest sound in nature, cast a foreboding aura on forsaken and overgrown Farland. Were they mocking my prayer? I missed Teller and Law's fearless presence more than ever.

"This place is creepy. Until I know what's going on, I'm staying near the bridge."

No answer.

"Watcher, you can find me here the next time you drop in," I mumbled, "hopefully soon."

I walked to a stand of palms, hoping to see an Urchin or hear a familiar voice. Nothing.

"Anytime," I yelled over the waterfall and pointed. "I'll be right over there."

A day turned into a week without a word from anyone—not even the Con Brothers. And let me tell you that peacocks are poor companions. I lost interest in everything and spent whole days sleeping in the shadow of the waterfall that seemed to grow louder every day—numbing, pushing my thoughts and dreams back to my old life.

Idiot. How can you catch Sponsor Ship when nobody knows you're here?

Fool. Farland is purgatory—another Solitary Valley.

Loser. Your old shipmates are on a grand adventure, meanwhile...

Chump. Johnny Denial and Minnie Codependent are sleeping in your bed together.

I flung my clothes off and dove into the lake to quiet the

voices, but the water was beyond cold—like yesterday's glacier ice. I hurried out and tiptoed to a sunny spot, shivering, and lay in the sun to dry and warm.

The voices. Were they from the dreaded Night Terror?

Hasty. Was a game of 8-ball and listening to the jukebox so wrong?

Bored. Wouldn't you love to laugh at one more of Nappy Norm's crude jokes? Right now, Shotglass Sam and the Boiler-maker gang are toasting you at the Bloody Bucket.

Quit. Join your highlife friends and lovers forever. Dive in the lake and never come up.

My Moral Compass energized, warming my chest.

"Stop right there," Mr. Conscience barked.

I yelled and slapped and kicked the ground where I lay. "At last, somebody finally answered the damned phone."

He growled, "Babbling again?"

"Well, I—"

"Overthink and obsess until you hurt your own feelings. I told you a hundred times that you gotta be careful what you think about. But do you listen? Oh, no. Instead, you choose to lay naked in the dirt and romance a drink like an old fool. Don't you remember the language of the heart? Take action to help yourself or another person before someone far worse than an angry cop knocks on your door?"

"Where'd everyone go?"

Another voice answered. "Probably went on vacation waiting for you to do something."

I recognized Consequence's slow rumbling tone. "Hi, ho—hi, ho, both my brain barkers are back." I stood, knocked the sand off, and put on my ragged clothes. "Hey, after Cold Meadow I thought we were tight. How about a little Vonn love?"

"Instead of wasting your days hoping for a better past, get up and start walking." Their voices harmonized like a barbershop duet. "Find what you're here for and you'll find your way home."

"Heckling in harmony. Nice. Well, finding is easier said than done. I'm already here seven or eight days. How about a little fourth dimension encouragement and direction? How about you tell me when Sponsor Ship is coming, so I can get off this island?"

"Shall we spoon feed the boy again?" Mr. Conscience said.

"One last time," they chorused. "There'll be no ship for you. Get off your butt and look for a red door."

"No ship?" I kicked the sand. "What the—red door—where?" No answer. They were gone.

I stood on the rickety steps of an old gazebo thinking about home and listening to the myriad of nocturnal sounds that filled Peace Harbor. Man may have abandoned Farland. The island wildlife had not.

The morning sun reached over the horizon and struck the Grand Hall's round superstructure, dampening the nighttime voices, pushing them back to their hidden nests and lairs. A cloud of bats flew in and funneled through gaping holes in the hall's roof to access their roosts. A committee of vultures guarded the largest thoroughfare, screeching complaints about every feathered cousin that came and went.

Some doors hung open. Others were sealed by creeper vines and banyan trees. Many windows were cracked or gone. But enough glass remained to create a monstrous face, like an ogre crawling from an enormous grave.

An excellent place for murderers and monsters.

Watcher's warning came to mind. "There's an unknown, a mysterious enemy called the Night Terror lurking in Farland. We didn't see this one at Cold Meadow. Be wary, fools never live to tell about this creature."

I reached down and tapped the hatchet hanging off my belt. "Nope," I whistled and kept on walking. "Not today, not by myself, and not ever at night. No red doors around here."

On the harbor side of Farland, I was drawn to an odd repetitive noise, squeaking like a loose bearing or children's swing set.

A one-story quarried building stood on an overgrown side street facing the rocky beach. **House of Friends** was chiseled in the wall above the portico. The front door was weathered—and red. A wooden sign dangled by one corner from a rusty chain above the steps, twisting and turning in the sea breeze. From the top step, I reached up and steadied it, stopping the noise. It read,

Nightly Readings.

"Please let this be easy for once." I looked left and right and knocked. Nothing. The door only opened a few inches. I shouldered it and pushed through.

The nearly overpowering smell of birds, mice nests, and mildewed books engulfed me. Yet a hint of something else, flowers, perhaps honeysuckle, graced the air.

My eyes adjusted to the dark interior.

Layers of cobwebs covered everything. Stacks of books and magazines, busted furniture and mounds of suitcases full of rotten clothes covered the floor. Thousands of puzzle pieces and dozens of paint-by-number kits carpeted the fractured tile. Rows of sagging and collapsed bookshelves still boasted alphabetic listings on their endcaps.

"Nobody's read them in decades." Or had they?

The library was a loss—except for a massive tome resting on a podium in the middle of the room. I picked up an old straw broom to knock the cobwebs down and sent several books flying off a reading table.

The room jumped to life.

Mice and bugs scuttled everywhere. Bats and barn swallows fluttered and screeched their way out of a broken bay window. I stepped back outside, coughed, and slapped a couple spiders off my arm. "Well, at least there are no vultures."

After the last bird cleared the building, I braced myself and stepped back inside, swinging the broom like a broadsword, cutting my way to the lectern.

I ran my hand along the book's tooled leather covers, admiring the artistry. Considering the years and where it sat, it was in great condition. Nearly a yard tall, the book was embossed with a pattern of ship's mast nets, clockwork gears, and sea snakes. Dozens of brass rivets and two heavy straps with golden locks held it all in place. Old English lettering on a solid silver plate read, *Lectures Nocturnes.*

"Night readings," I whispered. "Now how'd I know—okay, Watcher, I can take a hint."

Foraging for valuables and looking for the key, I followed a narrow path winding through the clutter to a hallway and stairs. Next to the banister, I spied a silver dollar on the floor—drilled with holes like Changelove's clock pendulum and tie clasp. "Three holes for three Sobriety Island years." I slipped it into my chest pocket, right next to my silver-plated money clip. "One man's loss is another's—no—nobody lost this. Thank you, God."

An old windup alarm clock sat on a stack of books, its white face yellowed with age and covered with years of dust. I moved it ever so slightly, and it rang and rang, loud and raucous.

I found the off switch.

How could it still be wound up? Had it alerted every ghoul in Peace Harbor?

I held my breath and listened. No voices or footsteps.

Outside, the clouds parted, and the sun pushed through the windows, illuminating the library. "Ah, ha, there you are." Shining like a new penny was a small key sitting in the clock's dust shadow.

"Okay, Watcher. I can see a little stage management going on this morning. Thanks."

I brushed the dust off the book and tried the key. The lock's stiff tumblers gave way. The calligraphy and flourishes were beautifully done with fountain pen or possibly a quill. Page after page held words in languages I didn't know, possibly Latin or Greek. On page twelve, I found a poem in English.

Wayfarin' Man
The light cannot penetrate your darkness,
The angels stopped singing your name.

You're your own shadow, living only at night.
Riddling what's good, destroying what's right,
Wayfarin' Man
You lost the words of the grasses,
You ignored the songs of the trees,
Sparrows and hawks've left, even the crows have flown away,
To live in the sun and redeem their day,
Wayfarin' Man
Ordonne knows your darkness; understands the contrast of souls,
For they've lived the nightshade, and know its bewildering hoax.
And today they stand in a doorway, lighted by candor and truth,
A living poem with a servant's voice,
offering understanding, love, and hope.
Wayfarin' Man
Listen to wise counsel,
Leave the darkness and stand.
Walk through Ordonne's doorway and into the light.
And serve your fellow man.

I stopped reading. "I declare that I am, and will continue to be Ordonne."

Static electricity charged the air, snapping and popping across the hair on my arms and hands. The poetic words blinked twice and arose from their pages, spinning and bright, like a floating cluster of tiny Christmas lights. They ascended to the dark rafters and vanished, leaving page twelve blank.

Outside, someone hawked up a wad of phlegm and spit. Then a raspy sarcastic voice ripped through the quiet library, laughing and wheezing and coughing. My Moral Compass flashed hot, almost burning my chest.

"What manner of hell, Lings? No, not today." Pulling my hatchet, I ran out and stood ready to fight on the portico.

Nobody. Nothing there but the dangling wood sign and my racing mind.

"The voice wasn't my imagination." Lying in front of the door was a gob of yellow snot; a peculiar smell hung in the air.

Different, yet similar to what I'd sensed when I first walked into the library. A waft of cheap perfume? Hard to tell, but I thought the voice belonged to a woman—or what was once a woman. Night Terror? I was sure of one thing—I had an enemy in Farland.

Nothing new. I'd been collecting enemies since my first drunk—the biggest one glared at me every morning in the bathroom mirror. But the thought of losing my way before I could find it and being stuck forever on Sobriety Island outweighed any Demimonde threat.

I took a deep breath and sighed, "Watcher, back inside or somewhere else?"

My Moral Compass warmed, and I knew the last piece of the puzzle was somewhere under the House of Friends arched ceilings. My way off the island was close. I could smell it.

Standing at the top of the stairs, I held up my silver money clip. It flickered and then flared bright, illuminating several flights of stairs beyond me crisscrossing their way down before vanishing in the darkness far below.

A buzzing rattle heralded the unmistakable warning that an intruder had entered a rattlesnake's forbidden domain. Partially veiled by heavy spider webs, a diamondback thick as my arm coiled at the end of the first landing. Beautiful as it was deadly, its triangular head and grey-green eyes followed my every move, declaring, "Thou shall not trespass my realm."

"That must be ten feet long," I whispered.

"Stare at it long enough and it'll be twenty feet," Mr. Consequence said.

"Yeah, okay, I get it. This scene is right out of a horror movie—another Demimonde deception. Gentlemen, my motives are right, and I have nothing to fear. Let's see if this snake bleeds." Holding my hatchet high, I started down the stairs.

"Stop!" Mr. Conscience shouted so loud I winced. "Don't be a fool. A catacomb rattler will nail you three times before your first swing. Take a deep breath and remember our code. In Ordonne, we stop fighting anyone or anything—even a rattlesnake."

Mr. Consequence added, "You'll win the day with wisdom and heart, not with club and hatchet."

"Yeah, right, what about Cold Meadow?" I took two steps down. The snake elevated its head and rattle waist high, showing two fangs as long as my thumb dripping with venom.

"Violence always begets violence," Mr. Consequence growled. "It scars your soul. Oh, you may escape with a scrape or a bruise today, but the dead you leave behind will fester and haunt you like a malignant wound for decades. Gets worse, never better; and rest assured, dear boy, one day I'll be back for my due, payable with unbearable interest."

"Catacomb rattler? Guys, it's a snake, not a man or woman."

Mr. Consequence said, "Have you noticed how much Watcher likes snakes?"

"Yeah." Mr. Conscience cleared his throat. "Saul can do no wrong with her. Hey, Vonn, who lives here, and who's the intruder?"

My mouth was unbelievably dry. I stepped back, holstered my hatchet, and took a long pull off my canteen. "Me."

"Okay, Mister Me, why don't you try singing instead of swinging?" they chorused.

Hands in my pockets and careful not to stare into the snake's eyes, I slipped down the staircase singing what I hoped would calm the rattlesnake's fears.

> *One step at a time, there's nothing to fear.*
> *We're friends, today and all year.*
> *Today we share a lonely stairway.*
> *So please let me pass and go my way."*

I made it to the corner of the landing. The snake stopped rattling, hissed one last time, then slithered away and vanished through a crevice in the stonework. Was it Watcher's power or my horrible voice?

"Even in a dungeon," I sighed, "violence can be avoided."

"Like most creatures, the catacomb rattler only fights when threatened," Mr. Conscience said. "You'll be all right now."

Twelve flights of stairs ended at a corridor at the bottom, lined with twelve doors standing six on a side down a long hallway. "Catacomb? No doubt lots of Ordonnes are entombed here. Or is this another puzzle—eleven wrongs and one right?"

All were locked save one, the last door on the left.

The rusty hinges squawked and groaned. Then the door pulled out of my hand and closed behind me with a heavy click. Typical for Watcher—action over talk. The money clip lit up a large six-sided room, a polygon with an arched ceiling and varnished tongue-and-groove pine walls covered with thousands, perhaps tens of thousands of names carved in the wood.

A set of three wood carving knives sat on an old tobacco table near the wall.

"Hello." My voice echoed. "All the way from Doc Changelove's office to Farland, and here I am, at—"

"Great Ordonne Hall. Cloud of Witnesses domain," Watcher said.

I picked up one of the knives and pointed at the wall. "Cloud of Witnesses, huh? I get it. All these names testify to the power of Ordonne. Obviously, I'm here to sign up, but how can I add my name when there isn't an open spot?"

A slot at the top of the closest wall popped open, and the ancient hardwood wall slid upward like a rolling garage door. For a long minute, thousands of names clattered and flashed by. Then the wall stopped abruptly, leaving a clean blank surface peeking through a cloud of dust.

"The gallery is now open for signatures," Watcher said.

I waved off the dust and coughed. "Good thing you healed my asthma. I'd never get back up those stairs." I ran my hand along the varnished wood. "Vonn Thrasher? Hmm, no, now I'll be something fun and different. Maybe King Vonn the—"

"Ego," Mr. Conscience hissed. "What do you think this is, tagging?"

"Okay, okay—Vonn Thrasher. Ordonne in good standing, sober three years on—I don't know what year, let alone what day."

No response.

"All right, I got it." Vonn Thrasher—Rescued by Ordonne—Summer of 1995.

"Done. Let me get outta here." I tried the door.

Locked.

"You have one last duty before you leave Sobriety Island," Watcher said. "Bring the massive tome from the lectern upstairs and place it on the table behind you."

"The *Lectures Nocturnes*? Yeah, no problem."

"Yeah, big problem, and it's called *Night Terror*."

"The raunchy laugh I heard when the poem blinked and spun into bright lights?"

"Yes. Night Terror hasn't fed this year. She's weak, but desperate. Once nourished, she's nearly invincible. A worthy opponent even for me."

I placed the wood-carving knife on the old tobacco table. "There's an ancient legend about an evil spirit posing as a woman offering food and shelter to lost travelers. After they dropped their guard and slept, they were done."

"Similar," Watcher said. "But Night Terror traps her victims wide-awake and feeds on their emotions. She uses pride, greed, and carnal lust, and then spins a web of insanity around them, feasting on hate and anxiety as quickly as love and compassion."

The door clicked and swung open.

I took a deep breath. "Dinner for one coming up."

The money clip illuminated the stairs all the way to the ambient light at the top. Happy the rattler was gone, I took the stairs two at a time. "Watcher, my plan is to grab the book, haul it downstairs, and secure it in the room before Night Terror can react."

Silence.

"Maybe I'll sleep in my own bed tonight if—"

Somewhere upstairs a sweet island voice, possibly Jamaican

Creole, sang about love and longing, tugging at my heart, calling me to come.

A ragged, gaunt woman danced to her own music around the lectern. Her large green eyes bore dark circles, matching a dozen faded tattoos scattered across her body. A bewitching beauty simmered beneath her hard appearance.

Was she a sixty-year-old island woman or a centuries-old Night Terror?

She stopped mid-note, nodded, and smiled from across the room. "Me name be Velvet, Velvet Shroud." She pushed her sun streaked hair from her face. "But I goes by Vel amongst me friends. And who might you be?"

My Moral Compass warmed. "You're Night Terror."

"Night Terror?" She chuckled and waved like swatting a fly. "Ha. Don't know what you be sayin'. I's just a lonely woman lookin' for a little company. Who be you?"

"Ordonne." I studied her face for a reaction.

She winked and stepped forward. "And?"

"Vonn Thrasher's my name. Came in on Sponsor Ship a while back. Got here on the Pious Trail. I was looking around Farland when the red door caught my eye."

A flowery aroma filled the room. Lilacs and gardenias mixed with something else—possibly a skunk—gave me a sense of ease and comfort. Even the hunger gnawing in my gut vanished. Did I overreact? I had to wonder.

"Honey, every islander hears about big man Vonn. You da hero of Cold Meadow. Welcome to Farland, the place where every-body wanna go somewhere." She stepped toward me, opened her arms wide, and winked. "Come give ol' Vel a hug."

I held my hand up. "Islander? Are you Demimonde or Ordonne?"

"Demi what?" She tucked her chin and shook her head. "I tell you, me name be Velvet. Now ease up with all the huma-huma, who-be-who and give me a chance. You'll see I'm no enemy."

"Why? I'm not here to make friends." I pointed at the *Lectures Nocturnes*. "I'm here to take that book—"

"Why? Because one be a lonely number." She grinned and furniture-walked closer. She looked younger with every step. "Because I be longtime waiting for number two."

If this stove up old woman isn't Night Terror, then who is she?

"Because I be generous." She extended her bony hand adorned with gold and silver rings, grinned wide enough to show several gold teeth, then slipped off an ornate ruby ring and held it out. "Here, for friendship with you. Go ahead. Take it."

Why didn't I notice those rings before? Beyond temptation, the twinkling blood red gemstone filled me with a craving for prestige and power.

She pumped her hand like she wanted to toss it to me. "Enemies don't be giving gifts."

That ring is a covenant with Demimonde. "No thanks. I don't wear rings."

"You'll change your mind." She looked over her shoulder like someone might be listening, leaned forward, and whispered, "There be more. I knows all da island secrets. Mysterious places loaded with gold nuggets and gemstones big as your fist. Treat me nice and I show you da sacred path to the fourth heaven." She winked, and ten years fell from her face, "Be where many a pilgrim get back to da real world."

I wagged my head and mimicked her voice. "Naw. That be da hook that took Teller and Law down for ninety years."

Anger flashed across her countenance before she could hide behind another smile. Dangerous or not, Vel had a powerful draw—an adrenaline rush that was difficult to abandon.

"Vel, been nice talking, but I'm kinda busy. If you'll excuse me, I gotta get to the book sitting behind you."

"Come on baby, you can play librarian tomorrow. Let me give you a taste of paradise today." Her green eyes enlarged and twinkled, the dark circles vanished, and her yellow teeth faded to bright white. Her ragged dress looked brand new. Another twenty years slipped away.

She purred. "Hmm, you like what you see?"

"Well, I—"

"Sea breeze be carrying magic from far across the sea." She unbuttoned the top two buttons of her dress and nodded toward the door. "Let's make some magic together."

Lightheaded, I wondered if she'd infused the room with some mind-bending elixir, as sweet as a candy store's lobby.

Confusion boiled into clinched fists. "Beware, you have an unshielded mind." Mr. Consequence said. "This creature gorges on righteous anger as fast lust and greed."

"Unshielded?" My stomach knotted like I was standing on the edge of a cliff. I forced myself to look away from her spellbinding eyes and stumbled over a pile of books and fallen shelves.

"Careful." She chuckled and blew me a kiss. "Don't be wantin' you hurt."

My Moral Compass blistered my chest. I struggled to my feet and toward the tome.

She licked her lips and drew a long deep breath. "Hmm, what a lovers quarrel do for me."

"We quit fighting anyone or anything." Mr. Conscience's voice was weak, distant. "Use your Shield of Faith."

She stood directly in front of me, slapped her thigh, and howled. "Pushy boy doesn't know what he do without fightin'. I be fallin' in love already. Relax. Let go and live a little. I gotta love nest over in the main hall. We'll worry 'bout that ol' book when we get back."

Mr. Conscience barely whispered. "That's a one-way trip."

She was unimpressed that I was a head taller and had fifty pounds on her. I tried to step past her, and she blocked me, near enough now to shake hands.

"Get away."

"Shh, pretty boy. This be a nothin' from nothin' game."

I shook my fist. "What's your deal with me and the book?"

Her wicked energy loaded the room with another heady scent. She slipped out of her silky dress and tossed it in the air. The spirit-filled gown spun and twirled around me and became invisible. But Vel sure wasn't. She was a tall, stunning woman. Every craving I ever had, and some I never thought of raced across my heart and mind.

"Come here lover boy," she cooed. "Let me hold you tight. Let me feel ya heartbeat, and I'll scratch every itch and nasty anxiety be growin' in ya soul."

Lust and fear wrestled with reason and courage.

"Vonn, be me big man. Help me rule dis island and you'll never want for anything."

"Big man? You mean dead man." The Con Brothers' voices sounded muffled as though they shouted from a distance. "She's feeding on you and stealing our voice."

"I got nowhere to go," I yelled.

She stepped in my face and hissed, "Take my hand."

She lost the island dialect and spoke perfect English. I backed up and shook my head.

She moved forward and stuck her finger in my face. "You owe me. I gave you what you wanted for twenty long years, and now it's my turn. Take my hand."

"Owe? You're crazy, I never met—"

"Well, Mister Thrasher," she wagged her head and snarled, "Aren't—You—Precious. Or should I say, Pearl? Waiting's over. Today I'm taking what's mine—you."

I sidestepped and kicked a stack of books at her. "I belong to no one."

She stepped over them, laughed, and drew a long deep breath. "Hmm, how I love the taste of fear and anger. You are so worth waiting for."

We stared at each other for ten very long seconds.

She crossed her arms in a mock hug. "Big Vonn grew up and forgot his first love. Don't you remember our first warm embrace behind the school gym? How I made you feel ten feet tall? How

I gave you friends and unlocked every teenage social door? You fell in love with me, all right. You named me Pearl—your code for bourbon and blow."

I barely breathed. "Pearl?"

She batted her eyes. "Yes, darling?"

I waved her off. "That was a long time ago. I'm done with drinking and—"

"Liar. You carry a hundred nasty little secrets in your dark heart." She stuck her finger in my face. "I smelled their delicious stench when you walked in the room."

"No, I—"

"You still crave the warm glow that made your pathetic life work."

"No."

"Still dream about the day you drink my burning kisses with impunity."

I cringed and staggered back. "Vel—"

She screamed, "Vel my ass. My name is Queen Alcohol, Mistress Suicide, the Overdose Rider. My Father is Fear. My Mother the Lie. I'm the Master of Obsessions and the definition of Night Terror. Now listen to me, you little punk—you will not walk away from me just because you spent a few months on a stupid Ordonne boat."

"No." I grabbed a busted chair and held it like a shield. "I know your game. One's too many and a thousand is never enough."

She slapped the chair away and gave me a staggering blow to the chest. "Clichés don't work here. Game's over—time to pay up."

I scrambled behind a fallen shelf.

She followed.

"You're not ever leaving Sobriety Island." She lunged, grabbed a double handful of my hair and shirt and pulled me so close our cheeks touched. "Fight, lover boy. Give me all your hatred. Steal everything you find. Hit me in the mouth. Kick the life out of me."

I couldn't break her grip. We grappled like wrestlers until she was as strong as three men. She dug her nails into my neck, pulled, and flipped me on my back. Then crawled on top of me like a lioness on a fresh kill.

She said, "Say goodbye world," and kissed me long and hard.

I couldn't pry her cold hands off or look away. Her eyes revealed the place reserved for the doomed—a netherworld where flashing and swirling lights wrestled with the darkness surrounding a tangled mass of writhing people—Demimonde's domain.

"My little pigeon." Vel's voice reverberated through the madness. "This is how Changelings are born."

The light that was my soul faded into Night Terror's domain.

"Enough." Watcher's voice penetrated the abyss and rescued me from the utter darkness. "Pray to the one who has all power, and you will be heard."

I closed my eyes and groaned a fragment of the only prayer I could remember. "Deliver me from evil, for thine is the kingdom, the power, and the glory forever and ever."

Vel's skin turned as tight and leathery as a mummified corpse. She rolled off kicking, and then screeched and growled like a mad dog. Too weak to stand, we writhed on the floor not six feet apart.

"Lord, save me from this evil Queen. Deliver me from Demimonde."

Her dancing dress reverted to dirty rags and fell back on her.

The room filled with Shantytown stench. Sewage and rotting flesh, stale beer and rancid ashtrays sickened me. I retched until something imbedded inside me ripped loose. Pain? I never understood pain until the moment the last shards of the old man died. Sobriety Island had stripped and sanded off every emotional wart and spiritual blemish. Demimonde would never dominate my life again.

I crawled over and leaned against the podium until my strength, or, more accurately, God's strength, returned.

Night Terror huddled under her rags and kicked at me.

I needed both hands to lift the heavy tome, tuck it against my body, and navigate the clutter. I paused to slide the silver money clip over the lock straps, flare and briefly illuminate the long stairway. Vel crawled over and grabbed my pant leg. "Have mercy on a sick old woman. Vonn, take me with you. Please, don't leave me here."

Without a glance or a word, I pulled away and descended the steps.

Exhausted, I leaned on the handrail and staggered to the first landing.

Vel thundered an insane laugh from the top of the stairs. "Loser. You're nothing but a stinking dry drunk. A pathetic excuse of a man. You couldn't pop a pimple on a good Ordonne's neck."

I groaned and continued down. Behind me the Catacomb Rattler slithered onto the first landing, coiled, and rattled a no trespass warning.

I yelled, "Hag, talk to the snake—"

"You want a rematch." Mr. Conscience's voice was strong again. "We quit fighting anyone or anything."

I walked down twelve flights of stairs listening to Vel threaten and curse me and every relative who ever lived. She would've made an Army drill sergeant blush.

The Great Ordonne Hall door was ajar. I placed the *Lectures Nocturnes* on the table and listened for Vel's footsteps. Satisfied that she didn't get past the rattlesnake, I bolted the door and sat, bruised and exhausted. My breath fogged in the cold air, but I was too jubilant to care. I'd survived Night Terror with faith and prayer.

In the quiet moment, her words came to mind. "My father is Fear and mother the Lie. I am the definition of Night Terror."

"Vel beat me like a stepchild in the perfumed hell of a broken old library."

"You almost lost me forever." Mr. Conscience said.

"Life without a conscience?" I stood and stretched. "Hmm, no thanks. I kind a like having you around."

"For moral support and validation rather than another heckling annoyance."

"Forevermore."

Mr. Consequence said, "Your Shield of Faith and prayer saved you."

Confusion and doubt were gone. I had the foundation to grow my trust in God. "I was lost and then forgiven; a castaway on the Sea of Booze. Rescued by Sponsor Ship, I survived the Pious Trail, the Ling Camp, and Solitary Valley. Discipled under Wilson, I walked with the Urchins and witnessed Ordonne's greatest enemy die on Cold Meadow. Today I stand in the midst of the Cloud of Witnesses to swear that I will carry my Shield of Faith forevermore." A beating heart replied. Then the one became two, and the two became three, and the three became dozens, and hundreds of heartbeats filled the Great Ordonne Hall.

The chiseled names came to life. Boasting vibrant colors, they took flight and whirled together like butterflies in a mating dance.

At first two voices whispered, then more and more joined in until the room was filled with mixed conversations. They called me and the Urchins by name. They spoke of Pilot and Wilson, the Pious Trail, and Cold Meadow. Then they faded into a silence so profound even my breathing sounded loud.

Who had called the Hall to attention?

A chorus of powerful voices broke the peace, speaking in unison like an angelic choir. "You have a gift that grows from trial and suffering. You have the Shield of Faith. You are Ordonne."

I raised my hand. "Your words are now my life."

Watcher's presence warmed the Great Ordonne Hall. "Well done, Vonn Thrasher."

"I say, well done, Watcher. You and God are why I'm alive today."

"You yearn to reconcile with friends and family?"

"I do."

"Remember how shocked you were when you saw your reflection in the mountain stream?"

"A remarkable change for the better. You said I was a hand-some man."

"Still true. Besides your appearance, you have a powerful voice and a confidence and energy that your family will find intimidating."

"Sobriety. The drunken thirty-five-year-old boy is gone."

"Nobody's doormat. And because you've become who you were supposed to be, they'll barely recognize you. You'll be the bewildering stranger that makes many people uncomfortable. So, don't expect a welcome home party."

"Other people will accept and love me."

"Yes, many. However, I offer you a choice. You may stay on Sobriety Island."

"Like Wilson and Teller?"

"Important servants and beloved Ordonnes."

I walked over to one of the varnished wood walls and stud-ied the multitude of names. Here or there, I was Ordonne and Demimonde was Demimonde. The people, places, and things would come and go, but the struggle was eternal. I liked the idea of staying where I was somebody. Perhaps the new guardian of the *Lectures Nocturnes*? But I knew I had to go home. Besides Mom and Dad, my house, and resurrecting my career, a powerful desire to help the sick and suffering alcoholic-addict made up my mind. I knew that I could make a real difference in people's lives.

"Watcher, send me home. I must see who and what part of my old life can be saved."

"You'll leave the Island today, but remember that status quo doesn't exist anywhere in our sober world. You haven't graduated and never will. Demimonde will never stop scheming ways to pull you back into old haunts."

"I am Ordonne. I will carry my Shield of Faith."

"Well said."

A loud thump and a crash sounded upstairs followed by a scream in Creole. Then a door slammed.

"Night Terror?"

"That old barfly is one mad demon today," Watcher said. "Now, let's talk about destiny. Listen carefully for I'll only say this once. Beyond time, there's a sad state called Squanderwood, where destinies play out before becoming reality and later, eternity. Your story ended there on a cold rainy night when a distracted driver and staggering drunk met halfway across the Crosstown Bridge. The accident killed you and destroyed the driver's life."

"Why must I know this tragedy?"

"The driver never recovered from watching you die. Unable to forgive herself, she fell into a deep depression and committed suicide. One of her emotionally scarred children would eventually commit suicide too. Thus, Demimonde's legacy continued on and on, from one generation to the next. I intervened before you crossed that bridge, and then Mr. Conscience, and Mr. Consequence started occupying lots of your head space. Then you," she emphasized, "decided to see Doc Changelove about your drinking. You know the rest."

"But why do I need to know?"

"Because that eventuality still waits for you in the bottom of a bourbon bottle."

I walked to the *Lectures Nocturnes* and ran my hand along its tooled leather covers, admiring the brass rivets and golden locks. "Brutal truth is hard to hear."

"You and this island will soon become a memory. Back home, most people will refuse to believe anything about Sobriety Island. Over time, you too may wonder what part is true and what's imagined. Understand that old memories are just old memories. They won't keep you sober next week, let alone ten years from now—because you live in today—not in yesterday or next year."

"Unless they've walked their own Pious Trail, people will write me off as a lunatic—"

"And drive you away."

"I'll carry my Shield of Faith—"

"And listen to your Moral Compass. Use your Magic Twenty to

prove who you are by helping people. Do this and you will live long and go far—even into Demimonde's stronghold—Shantytown."

The door opened and warm sea air filled the room. A seagull flew in, circled, then landed on my shoulder.

The picture of Jesus on Mom and Dad's wall came to mind.

I ran my hand along the bird's gray and white feathers. "How did you get here?"

Watcher said, "He didn't. You already know that you have to be careful what you think about, for all actions are first conceived in the mind. Listen to what I say about dreams. The hows and whys of visions and dreams aren't for you or me to interpret. What you must understand is what dreams do to men and women—what they've done to you."

I raised my hand. "I've had vivid dreams and nightmares for years."

"And Demimonde uses them to its advantage—even pleasant ones. People romance the good ones like old friends until they're firmly entrenched in their thought processes."

"How so?"

"The Tomorrows. The imaginary treasure ships that never come in. Tomorrow I'll eat better, stop smoking, and quit drinking. Tomorrow I'll be promoted. Tomorrow I'll have a new lover and a big house on the hill. Tomorrow I'll fix me and you. In the meantime, their excuses and prescription prayers fail. Their lives fall down around them, leaving them isolated, bitter agnostics."

"You just described half of my friends."

"Trauma creates powerful dreams. Add sleep deprivation, mix in drugs and alcohol, and mental illness abounds."

"I can't tell you how many times I woke up dead in a ditch."

"Somehow, the sick nightly ritual must end—but the older, more powerful dreams now have a life of their own and refuse to stop. They fight through sedatives and therapy, punishing their host as if he cut off his own ear. Without help, only death can break the cycle."

She's talking about me.

"Let me help you renew your mind."

The seagull flew out and away.

"Recurring nightmares?" I peered out the dark doorway. "Gone just like that?"

"Gone like a seagull riding the ocean wind over the horizon."

"Free of Night Terror? Yes, please cleanse my mind and soul."

I expected a flash of light or new awareness—but felt nothing.

"You've finished the final leg of your journey."

I put my hand over my heart. "I will never quit on God, Ordonne, or myself."

"For by quitting, you neither win, nor lose—you die. Never forget that you were saved to be my witness and carry the good news to the still suffering alcoholic."

"I found a way out of Demimonde. And if I can, they can too."

She elevated her voice. "Love the man who hates you. Love the vulnerable and weak, and the enormous power of unconditional love will keep you from falling into Demimonde's traps."

I nodded and pointed into the dark exterior corridor. "Is Sponsor Ship anchored in Peace Harbor?"

"Follow the seagull. This voyage is by faith."

"Like when we went to Ferrara and the Ling Camp?"

"Similar."

"What about my things? My ruck is stashed down by the quarry."

"Unneeded. What do you have on you?"

"My hatchet." I went through my pockets and pulled out the drilled silver dollar from upstairs and the Magic Twenty folded in the silver money clip.

"Leave the hatchet on the table for the next pilgrim."

I peeked down a corridor so dark I couldn't see the first door. "Leaving with the clothes on my back—"

"Close your eyes and open your mind."

I nodded, took a deep breath, and stepped into total darkness.

Warm sweet air and a wave of jubilation washed over me. My spirit somehow became our spirit, an intimate collective that was bound together. Was I part of the Cloud of Witnesses? Intuition told me that I was standing in more love than anywhere I'd been since I stood in a toddler's crib.

I walked toward the sound of rushing water. A waterfall? Was there a cliff ahead?

Watcher whispered, "Shield of Faith."

I couldn't tell if the floor moved like a treadmill, or if I walked an unknown distance, but the sound pulled me until I stood an arm's length from a thunderous waterfall. I was an insignificant speck watching an enormous column of water without beginning or end. A rainbow of colors and blinking orbs bounced free of the crush of falling water. The smell enticed me. What would the water taste or feel like? I yearned to reach out and hold an orb.

"This is Living Water," Watcher said, "not found in any river or sea on Earth."

I stuck my hand in the flow and then quickly pulled back. A tiny array of lights sparkling like precious gems raced up my shirt sleeve, across my chest, and then faded back into the waterfall. "Watcher, are you—"

A wave of Living Water reached out and washed me in a pleasant and soothing embrace. The Spirit of Humility pushed me to my knees. A euphoric oneness connected me with everything good and eternal. I would never go back—not through the Great Ordonne Hall, not back to the Plateaus, not across the Sea of Booze, and never to my old way life. I'd entered the fourth dimension.

I waved goodbye and crawled into the wall of living water.

CHAPTER FIFTEEN

Lee Lea's Teashop

Distant Christmas music and laughter filled the air. A few snowflakes drifted down and landed on my face. Before boarding Treatment Ship, I'd sat on the same bench outside Lee Lea's Teashop. I was back in Ism.

"Here in a blink of the eye."

Inside, dishes clattered. Mamasan and her girls laughed and talked.

I yelled loud enough to make the pedestrians across the street pause. "What day is it?" They pointed and hurried past.

A young woman's face peeked around the front door for a second, then ducked back inside. Mamasan appeared, grimacing and shaking her finger at me. "Drunken bum. Stop yelling. Bad for business—go unless you have money."

"I got money." I felt the Magic Twenty in my pocket. "Just waiting for you to open for business."

"You drunk," she countered. "You lay there shivering. Filthy, no winter coat, I know you come from Shantytown."

"Not lately. Mamasan, I could eat a table full of your best entrees. Can you help a pilgrim out with a hot shower, a haircut, and a shave?"

She held out her hand and studied my face. "I bet you no have one dollar."

I pulled out a roll of twenties. My Magic Twenty and Clip worked.

Being a good customer and generous tipper has a way of speeding up friendships. I quickly became the long-lost friend they never knew they had. In two hours, I had soaked in a hot tub until I was pink and wrinkled, gotten a great haircut and shave, and was sopping up the last of the bulgogi gravy with a chunk of fresh bread.

Without asking, Mamasan brought her cousins, Handy Tailor and his brother, Dandy Cobbler, to fit me in new clothes and shoes. I certainly needed them. I could wiggle my toes through the holes in my buckskin moccasins, and the beaded eagles on the leggings were long gone. My khaki shirt and cargo pants were rags.

When they learned that I was Ordonne, Mamasan and her daughters, Moon and Cookie, entertained all my questions. Big man Moneymaker constantly came up with his financial and political strongarm tactics to absorb Ism. He loved to say, "I don't want much—only what's next to me."

Handy Tailor said, "If Moneymaker ever takes over Gravel Beach, Ordonne will be out and Ism will soon be another Shantytown.

I was happy to be back and even happier with my new friends, but the longer the day went, the heavier my heart got. I did what I dreaded—borrowed the house phone and called home.

Mom answered. "Who? You said Vonn?"

It was all I could do to keep my voice from cracking. "Yeah, Mom, it's me."

"I don't know who you are but this isn't funny. My son is dead, lost at sea years ago. Treatment Ship said he went overboard and was never seen again—"

"No, Mom, I didn't fall overboard. They tossed us. And no, I didn't drown. I made it to Sobriety Island and back. I'm alive and well, and I'm standing in Lee Lea's Teashop in Ism."

Silence.

"I hope to grab a bus and come home if—" I choked back a sob. "Mom, don't you recognize me?"

Her voice cracked. "No. I don't believe you."

I softened my tone. "It's me. Your prodigal has returned, sober, with a changed heart."

"We haven't seen you since—" She mumbled and blew her nose. "How can you just appear out of nowhere? Everyone thinks you're dead. We even had a memorial for you last winter."

"Mom, I—"

"Sobriety Island? You mean grief and sorrow. Almost killed your father. Your job and your house are long gone. Dad took over the lease, and we got people living there that actually answer the phone and pay rent."

"Mom, I don't care about the job or the house right now. I understand where you're coming from. I owe you and Dad big time. I'd tell you that I'm sorry, but I know that's—"

"What you said every time you called from jail." Her normal voice was back—flat and emotionless. "Or when I caught you taking money from my purse."

"All I can tell you is that by God's grace and Ordonne I'm sober today. A different man than the drunken Vonn you despised. And I'll pay every cent and—"

"Yeah, that's you. The same old you. This story is too much for me to handle. I'll talk it over with your Dad. Call back after five."

Dial tone.

My new friends stared. Moon and Cookie's pained expressions matched my feelings. I hung up and headed for the door. Mamasan met me halfway. "Give you mom some time. She think you dead—now you alive—too much for one day."

"Can I have a moment?"

She put her hands on my shoulders. "We understand Demimonde and Ordonne. You always welcome our house."

Moon said, "Don't go without saying goodbye."

I walked up the street surrounded by chaotic music and barking hawkers echoing off cobbled streets and rows of junkshops. Nothing had changed in three years. Lost souls and all, Ism Harbor was still a vanity fair, a recovery carnival.

"Do you think you could live here?" Watcher said.

"I was hoping you'd stop by. I don't know. Maybe, if I had to."

"Time takes time. Your parents need to process your return. You know that they made a pictorial memorial to you on their wall, right next to your favorite picture."

"The blue-eyed Jesus? Maybe there's hope after all."

"Catch the evening bus and knock on their door. If it goes well, that's great. If it doesn't, be understanding and leave with a smile. Let them have the choice of when and where. In the meantime, your place is here."

I pointed toward Lee Lea's. "With Mamasan and family?"

"Yes, and with the folks across the street."

At the end of the block, a couple was walking my way, knocking on doors and handing out flyers. "That's the Amors, Louie and his wife, Maria."

Mr. Consequence chimed in. "And they're looking for Rosa for the sixth time."

"I wasn't very helpful, was I?"

"You were a sick boy then," Watcher said. "Listen, Lee Lea and the Amors need you as much as you need them. Ignore all the racket. Go. Tell your story. Be their ray of hope. That's how sober life works."

~

"Mr. and Ms. Amor, you may not remember me, but my name is Vonn Thrasher, and we met a few years ago while you were searching for Rosa."

Louie said, "You look familiar."

"Have you seen my Rosa?" Maria held up a flyer with Rosa's name and picture. "When she relapses, she disappears and always runs to Ism. We know she's here somewhere."

"Or, Shantytown. I've got a few hours until my bus leaves. Let's go over to Lee Lea's and get you off your feet. We'll rest a little and talk. I have a couple ideas that might help us find your daughter."

The Mystery of Ordonne

One lord – One faith – One body
Two lives
Drunk or Sober – Jekyll or Hyde – Sober Life or Spiritual
Bankruptcy.

Baser: Vonn Thrasher's hometown, where Mr. Conscience, Mr. Consequence, and a thousand nightmares spoil Vonn's party life and drive him to an alcoholic bottom.

Battle of Cold Meadow: Vonn and his Ordonne allies engage Demimonde in open battle.

Broken Hills Wilderness: A vast mountainous wilderness controlled by Mondi's forces between the Plateaus and Farland. The Pious Trail is the only possible passage.

Castaways: Alcoholic patients who set adrift from the Treatment Ship in the Delirium Fog to swim to Sobriety Island on their own.

Changelings: Shape shifters known as Mudlings, Darklings, Wretchlings, or simply the Lings. They are mortal enemies of Ordonne.

Cotton: Watcher pairs Vonn with Cotton, an adventurous mouse with a sharp tongue and an invaluable sense of impending danger, to become his traveling companion.

Demimonde: A French word, meaning half-world. Pleasure-seeking people unbound by morals, religion, or tradition trapped in a moral and spiritual catchall, an in-between place for those lost in their insanity, alcoholism and drug addiction.

Doctor Changelove: Vonn's family doctor's office is a portal where he meets Watcher, his invisible guardian of reason, and together they begin his journey to sobriety and a new life.

Gravel Beach: An unspoiled rock-strewn shoreline where Ordonnes meet and offer alcoholics a way off the well-worn path to Calamity Ridge and the Bitter End Wilderness on the other side.

Great Storm: Violent wind and waves almost sink the Sponsor Ship.

Ism Harbor: Home port to Treatment Ship and a vanity fair selling recovery from every ailment known to man.

Lectures Nocturnes: Vonn is challenged to carry a priceless tome to the Great Ordonne Hall in the catacombs, but his greatest enemy, Night Terror, has sinister designs on his soul.

Ling Camp: Home to Mondi's throne and hundreds of Lings who harass and ambush the Ordonnes walking the Pious Trail.

Longtimers: The vigilant and faithful Ordonne pace setters who establish the rhythm of Sponsor Ship under oar, the silent rowing.

Sixth Bell Meetings: Evening sharing and prayer time on the spar deck.

Member Ship: Sponsor Ship's sister ship lost at sea off the coast of Abstract State.

Mondi: The brutal and powerful queen of the Lings. Cloaked in a misty green aura, her clothes and throne are living grapevines, animated and intoxicating.

Moneymaker: A wealthy powerful man who is trapped in a cycle of food and alcohol addiction. Owner of Treatment Ship and many businesses of differing reputations in Shantytown.

New Life: Vonn returns to Ism Harbor and is welcomed by Lee Lea and friends, his new family.

Ordonne: A benevolent society of storytellers who reach out to all sobriety seekers, sail the Sponsor Ship, rescue castaways and shipwrecked alkies, and prepare them for Sobriety Island.

Peace Harbor: Vonn's faith and hope are sorely tested at Farland, the abandoned New Life treatment center and former battleground located next to a rock quarry on the harbor shore.

Pious Trail: Vonn's chosen path from Serenity Harbor, across the island to Farland.

Plateaus: Ordonne Territory. Highland mesas safe from Demimonde's creatures.

Sea of Booze: Large saltwater sea, home to sea monsters and mysterious islands.

Serenity Harbor: The fourth of twelve ports of promise where ships replenish supplies. Vonn disembarks to begin his spiritual journey to new life and home in the real world.

Shantytown: A tangled mass of old weather-beaten houses sitting on dirt roads that serve as sewers. A Demimonde stronghold teeming with the lost.

Slippery Eel: Nocturnal snakelike creatures that inhabit the Sea of Booze. They swim deep all day but return every sunset to start their feeding frenzies. Their favorite prey is alkies.

Sobriety Island: A large isle shrouded by Delirium Fog and surrounded by shallow treacherous waters. Sobriety and a new life are found there—along with dangerous creatures.

Solitary Valley: Vonn falls off the Pious Trail and meets new friends. He discovers that healing waters cannot cure pride, greed, and gluttony, but honesty, willingness, and an open heart can.

Spiritual Awakening: New spiritual vision; hearing and understanding about God.

Sponsor Ship: One of two Ordonne ships powered by Higher Power sails, twelve oars called Steps, and twelve oars called Traditions.

Teller and Law: Teller, an ex-professional wrestler and his grizzly bear traveling companion, Law, are trapped in a personal purgatory, languishing in Solitary Valley for over ninety years.

Treatment Ship: A three-deck paddle wheeler that sails on three-week excursions to Sobriety Island.

Urchins: Cotton, Vonn, Teller, and Law become the Urchins, sworn to love and defend each other.

Wilson Cabotage: The mountain man who keeps a roadhouse on the plateaus, providing traveling Ordonnes safe haven and training them to survive the Pious Trail.

The Serenity Prayer

God grant me the serenity to accept the things I cannot change,
Courage to change the things I can,
and Wisdom to know the difference.

The great 20th-century Protestant theologian Reinhold Niebuhr is usually credited with penning the original Serentiy Prayer in the early 1930s. The untitled prayer was widely circulated, often without attribution.

This did not appear to disturb the theologian. Niebuhr refused to have the prayer copyrighted, and instead was intentional about allowing his works which could provide comfort to others to be dispersed widely.

In 1941, the prayer was brought to the attention of Alcoholics Anonymous. AA co-founder William Griffith Wilson noted, "Never had we seen so much A.A. in so few words."

Acknowledgements

I would be remiss if I did not acknowledge the invaluable input of my editor, Jan Powell, and my proofreader, Julia Cressler. Thank you.